The Glory Boys

Also by Douglas Reeman

A Prayer for the Ship
High Water
Send a Gunboat
Dive in the Sun
The Hostile Shore
The Last Raider
With Blood and Iron
H.M.S. 'Saracen'
The Deep Silence
Path of the Storm
The Pride and the Anguish
To Risks Unknown
The Greatest Enemy
Rendezvous – South Atlantic
Go In and Sink!
The Destroyers
Winged Escort
Surface with Daring
Strike from the Sea
A Ship Must Die
Torpedo Run
Badge of Glory
The First to Land
The Volunteers
The Iron Pirate
Against the Sea (non-fiction)
In Danger's Hour
The White Guns
Killing Ground
The Horizon
Sunset
A Dawn Like Thunder
Battlecruiser
Dust on the Sea
For Valour
Twelve Seconds to Live
Knife Edge

The Glory Boys

Douglas Reeman

C

Century · London

Published by Century 2008

2 4 6 8 10 9 7 5 3 1

First published in Great Britain in 2008 by
Century
Random House, 20 Vauxhall Bridge Road,
London SW1V 2SA

www.randomhouse.co.uk

Addresses for companies within The Random House Group Limited can be found
at: www.randomhouse.co.uk

The Random House Group Limited Reg. No. 954009

A CIP catalogue record for this book
is available from the British Library

HB ISBN 9780434013524
TPB ISBN 9780434013869

The Random House Group Limited supports The Forest Stewardship
Council (FSC), the leading international forest certification organisation. All our
titles that are printed on Greenpeace approved FSC certified paper carry the FSC
logo. Our paper procurement policy can be found at www.rbooks.co.uk/environment

Mixed Sources
Product group from well-managed
forests and other controlled sources
www.fsc.org Cert no. TT-COC-2139
© 1996 Forest Stewardship Council
FSC

Typeset by SX Composing DTP, Rayleigh, Essex
Printed and bound in Great Britain by
CPI Mackays, Chatham, ME5 8TD

For you, Kim, with love and thanks.
We shared it.

"So stand by your glasses, steady!
We've all got to go by and by.
Here's a toast to those gone already,
And good luck to the next man to die!"

Coastal Forces song

Next of Kin

The sea was dark grey, metallic in the poor light, with a steep swell unbroken by wind or current. It seemed to merge with the backdrop of cloud, with no margin to reveal either horizon or distance. And the air was like a knife. Common enough for the North Sea in winter, where you could never take the weather's moods for granted. Tomorrow it might change just as swiftly, hard and bright so you could see the land, the shoreline of Suffolk perhaps, and familiar landmarks, and obtain a compass bearing and fix your position. But that was tomorrow.

It was close to noon, but it could have been nightfall, or the start of a new day.

The only sound was the dull, monotonous clang of a wreck-marker buoy, one of the many dotting the swept channel along the east coast. Victims of nearly four years of war.

The new noise seemed like an intrusion: the regular *thrum, thrum, thrum* of engines, powerful but contained.

Then all at once the source was visible, the sturdy shape of an Air-Sea Rescue launch, vivid, almost garish with her stark yellow markings and R.A.F. roundel. There was no chance that she might be mistaken for M.T.B. or E-Boat, no matter which flag they flew. Or fired on by the trigger-happy gunner aboard some luckless convoy straggler, unescorted and vulnerable.

When every sound or movement was a potential killer, it was always *shoot first!*

The launch's commanding officer stood in the forepart of his compact bridge, wedged in a corner, legs astride, as if he had never moved. Despite the seaboot stockings and layers of warm clothing, he was feeling the cold, and watching his own breath like steam against the bridge screen.

He had heard the wreck-marker buoy, saw it in his mind as clearly as if he had been checking the chart. How many times must they have used it to fix their course and position? At low water you could still see a rusting funnel and one remaining mast above the surface: not a victim of bomb or torpedo, but a collision with an overworked escort vessel when a northbound convoy had grid-ironed through its southbound opposite number in pitch darkness to avoid attack. She had been an old paddle-steamer, well known on the routes to Southend or down into the Channel and the Isle of Wight, usually packed with day-trippers and families. The war had changed that, as it had for almost every serviceable vessel: a coat of grey or dazzle-paint, and a White Ensign instead of a house flag, and she was in the navy. She had been armed with concentrated anti-aircraft weapons, and sent to fight.

The bell was fading now. It was time to alter course.

To give up. Was it pride, or conceit? He had been nicknamed The Fisherman by both naval and merchantmen who used this coastline, because of his success in finding and rescuing so many airmen who had gone down in the drink. Some never made it, and perhaps the last thing they had seen was this or another black and yellow hull speeding past, the search abandoned.

And there was the question of fuel. They had been at sea far longer than intended, and the engineer had already thrown out some heavy hints. *They'll have to send a search party for us, if we keep this up!*

He saw the bows dip, and the spray spatter across the deck. Some of it reached the bridge screen, and did not move. It was freezing.

There was no point in dragging it out. Several aircraft had been reported crashed, and an unidentified explosion had also been slotted into a curt signal, but it had not been much help. As one wag had remarked, "What can you expect on New Year's Eve? All too pissed to stand up and transmit!"

He tucked his binoculars into the front of his coat to protect them from the spray, not that it did much good.

New Year's Day. Maybe the realization was only just hitting him. There had been a few grins and mock punches against the layers of clothing they all wore. Another January. Another year of war. How many more?

He said quietly, "I'm going to alter course. Make a signal to Base . . ." It was as far as he got.

"Starboard bow, sir! Flashing light!"

He steadied his glasses, seeing the lookout's face in his mind. The newest member of their little company. He could recall the time they had picked up a downed air crew, Germans, and had heard him swear and exclaim, "Let the bastards swim home!" His mother and father had been killed in one of Southampton's air raids. But he had turned down the chance to transfer to another branch of the R.A.F., and he was still here.

We all have our reasons.

"Starboard twenty! Midships! *Steady!*" He found the button and pressed it.

Then he trained the glasses again, taking his time, holding his breath as the tiny light filled the lenses, awash on the dark water. Not flashing, but dipping repeatedly out of sight. He heard the familiar sounds of feet and equipment as his men responded to the alarm, but it was only routine. Nobody could still be alive in this.

Their searchlight cut through the mist and spray: this was the moment. Two— no, three of them, tied or clinging to one another. One of those small life rafts almost submerged beneath them.

"Shall I switch off, sir?"

He breathed again. *"Hold it.* One of them's alive."

He saw the hand lift, to shade his eyes from the light, or to acknowledge that he had seen them. That the impossible was happening.

Now it was part of a drill: harness and tackle, hands ready to guide and cushion the first impact.

The engines stopped, and the hull rolled heavily on the swell. Voices were shouting orders; someone else called, "'Old on, mate, nice an' steady!"

All three were alive.

The Fisherman felt the engines respond to the telegraph, the sudden surge of life from the screws as the launch began to turn, under command once more.

The raft had already drifted clear, tossing like a leaf on the mounting wash. There was no time to waste: back to their base and alongside before complete darkness made things even more difficult. The drab field ambulances would be waiting. They always were.

The Fisherman peered at the compass repeater and wiped it with his sleeve. Instinct, luck or stubborn pride, but they had done it.

He listened to the powerful engines, saw the spray rising from either bow. The deck was empty now, the tackle stowed out of sight. Until the next time.

He looked at his watch without seeing it. This was the worst part.

"Call me if you need me." Nobody spoke.

Once below it seemed almost warm, with hatches sealed and deadlights tightly screwed across every scuttle, and the light was hard and glaring after the bridge, and the groping moments between. Even the engines' steady beat was muffled; he could hear the quiet chorus of clinks and rattles from the bottles and jars lining one bulkhead. But always the same. Towels and blankets, dressings and bandages, and something hot to sip or swallow, for those who were capable of it.

The senior medic looked up.

"We were just in time." He tossed some rags into a bucket. "Not for one of 'em, though."

The airman in question was lying on a mattress, held and supported by two other medics. There was a lot of blood, or had been, and they had to prevent him from clawing at his torn uniform, although his strength was almost gone. One of his companions was propped on one elbow, watching, leaning nearer as if to hear what he was trying to say.

As the medics allowed the dying man's arms to fall to his sides, one said abruptly, "He's gone, sir." Then he frowned as the other German reached out as if to touch him. "*Kaput*, see?"

The senior medic said, "A miracle he held out this long." Then, surprisingly, his face spread into a broad grin. "This'll even the score, sir." He watched as a blanket was lifted, very carefully. "One of ours for a change!"

The Fisherman leaned down and grasped the hand. Like ice, but responding.

"You're safe now," he said.

The grip tightened slightly, gratifyingly.

"Thanks . . . to you."

Someone called, "You're wanted on deck, sir!"

Even that seemed unimportant. Soon it would all make sense: the naval uniform with its two tarnished stripes on the uncovered shoulder, and something else, something familiar, at odds with the tension and the vague signals following that solitary explosion, which had remained uppermost in the Fisherman's mind. Had made him persist when another might have given up the search.

"We're going in now," he said. "Try to rest."

The senior medic was holding up an identity disk.

"Name's Kearton, sir. Lieutenant."

Even that seemed familiar. He realized that the rescued man's eyes were open, unmoving, coming to terms, accepting the stark truth of his survival. He tried to turn his head as the dead airman was covered with an oilskin, but the effort was too much.

The Fisherman murmured, "Did the other one give you any trouble?"

The lieutenant smiled, or attempted to.

"I'd be dead, but for him."

A steaming mug had appeared. "Try and swallow some of this. It'll help." There was rum in it. Nothing in the medical log about its benefits, but it often did the trick.

More voices; he had to go. But he said, "Kearton, right?"

The lieutenant tried to nod, and some cocoa trickled over his chin.

" 'Bob' will do . . ." Then he fainted.

The Fisherman groped his way up to his small bridge again. It seemed much darker after the bright lights below. *I must be getting past it.* But he kept thinking of the handshake. Like a reward.

Someone reached out to slap his shoulder as he passed. A signal had to be acknowledged, and an outward-bound minesweeper was flashing another: *Happy New Year.* Faces grinning in the shadows as the lamp clattered some witty reply.

He listened to the reassuring power of the engines. For some, it was already over. *But we are going home.*

Lieutenant Robert Kearton turned his back to the solitary window and glanced slowly around. Three days, two nights to be exact, since he had been brought ashore from the Air-Sea Rescue launch. A spartan room, a couple of chairs and a table, and some sort of cupboard which he had never seen opened. And the bed. Different now, with blankets folded and clean sheets lying across one end. Waiting for the next arrival.

Two nights. Was that really all it had been? He could not recall falling asleep. Always the sense of shock, the inability to relive those lost hours, to accept that he was alive and safe. *Nothing.* Once, he must have called out, and a sickberth attendant had appeared with a flashlight.

"Thought you was in trouble." A pause. "Sir." It had sounded more like a rebuke than sympathy. A chief petty officer in rank, so he had probably seen it all.

He took a deep breath and looked at the suitcase beside the bed, the uniform jacket draped across the back of one of the chairs. His best jacket, brought here by a friend from the depot ship in the harbour.

He tried to clear his mind. *It was today*, not part of a dream or nightmare. Today, and he was leaving here. A new beginning, as originally intended. Ordered . . .

He heard someone call out, or cough. The S.B.A.s were waiting to come and prepare the room. A small local hospital, taken over by the navy at the outbreak of war, this had most likely been part of the staff quarters. It felt remote: hard to believe it was less than a mile from Harwich and Felixstowe, the thriving and ever-busy naval base.

He turned and looked out of the window again. A yard, with what he thought was a kitchen on the opposite side, empty bins lined up for food scraps or vegetables for the pigs, wherever they were. Puddles left by an overnight rain, although the sky was clear now. He could see some far-off barrage balloons, like tiny whales beyond the harbour, and a solitary vapour trail.

He bent his arm, feeling the bruise. Like the one on his thigh, it was almost black. But he still had no clear memory of what had happened.

He gazed out at the yard. There was a sign pointing to the

nearest air raid shelter, and some sort of ramp, maybe for wheelchairs. He shivered, and stared at his watch. Still working, despite the . . . His mind hesitated, exploring it. *Despite the explosion.*

He concentrated on the watch. A birthday gift from his father, what seemed like a hundred years ago.

He realized that he had his jacket in his hands and was pulling it over his shoulders. It had hardly been worn, except on rare ceremonial occasions, an admiral's inspection, a few Sundays in harbour, and some burial duty. He flicked down the lapels and saw his reflection in the mirror by the window. The blue and white ribbon on his left breast above the pocket: the Distinguished Service Cross. People still stared at it. Out of curiosity, or perhaps thinking, *why him and not me?*

The jacket seemed looser. He thought of his old seagoing uniform, and the sodden working rig he had been wearing when they had hauled him out of the drink. In another wastebin, no doubt.

He stared into the mirror again, eye to eye for the first time. Like an inspection. His eyes were described in his records as 'blue'. That was wrong: they were grey, in this light at least, like the North Sea.

He touched his hair and knew it needed cutting, and soon. He smiled a little and some of the strain left his face, so that it became younger. He could see the strands of white in the dark hair, above the ears, and remembered how it had upset his mother on that last home leave when the boat was having a refit. Even more upset because she had been unable to hide it.

And the tiny, pale scar above his right eye, no bigger than the head of a match. He no longer felt it. A wood splinter blasted from somewhere during a running battle in the Channel. Nothing now, but an inch lower and he would have been blinded.

And yet, when they were ashore in the mess they could still make light of it. Because they had to.

'Old sweat' and 'over the hill' were just a part of it. Surviving. Bob Kearton was twenty-seven years old.

He had been in the navy since the beginning of the war, even earlier, because of his part-time training with the Volunteer Reserve. The Wavy Navy, they called it: the amateurs who had become the true professionals, through hard-won and often brutal experience.

Youngsters . . . He found he was gripping one of the heavy black-out curtains. His mind was clear and sharp now. Youngsters like the sub-lieutenant who was in charge of the harbour launch sent to collect him from the M.T.B. which had been his own command until the change of orders. Kearton had handed over to an officer he already knew and liked, but it had still been a hard moment. Meaningless jokes, handshakes, grins: dragging it out. He had scarcely noticed the M.L.'s youthful skipper. His first real authority, weeks rather than months. And his last.

But he should have been ready, doubly so on that stretch of water. It had been New Year's Eve, no matter what K.R.s and A.I.s laid down: maybe they had been drinking. It did not take much to blunt the edge, the caution, and then it was too late.

There might have been a shout from one of the lookouts, maybe even a scream. In the vague flashes of memory he could even see the mine, and the leaping bow wave as the helm had gone hard over. Then oblivion. No explosion or sound as the hull had been blasted apart, the crew with it. Nothing.

"I see you're ready, sir? There's a car here for you."

It was the same chief S.B.A., a note pad in one fist. A name to delete; another to replace it.

There was somebody outside the room, a Royal Marine, the badge on his beret gleaming in the overhead lights. The Captain, Coastal Forces, had sent his own driver. That must have caused a stir . . .

He picked up the suitcase and seemed to be waiting, until the

9

chief petty officer said, "That's *all*, Royal." Then, after a pause, "Better luck this time, sir."

Kearton put on his cap, tense, already knowing it was pointless to ask.

"Any chance someone else survived?"

The other man cleared his throat.

"'Fraid not, sir. Next of kin have already been informed."

Like a door slamming.

He walked out of the hospital, and saw the Royal Marine standing beside his car. He quickened his pace, feeling the cold air sting his face and eyes. It was over. The chance was his. *If it's got your number on it . . .*

They all knew that, or should by now.

Two young sailors passed him, throwing up smart salutes as if on parade. Probably on local leave from H.M.S. *Ganges*, the training establishment which was not far away.

He returned the salutes and felt the pain lance through his arm. Such young faces . . . only boys. And instead, he saw the subbie aboard his M.L., laughing at something, sharing it with his little crew.

And then he heard the scream.

It was not over.

The car had barely come to a halt before the white-painted pole across the driveway had been raised smartly, and they were waved through. A few salutes, but no questions or identity checks this time. The sight of the big Humber staff car was enough.

Kearton stared over the driver's shoulder, caught off guard by the sense of unfamiliarity: he had visited Coastal Forces H.Q. often enough in the nearly two years he had been based here. From the driveway it still looked like a hotel, despite the uniforms and sandbags, and the White Ensign that streamed so brightly in the keen air. He forced himself to relax. It would pass. It must.

"I'll take care of your case, sir."

He saw the Royal Marine's eyes in the driving mirror. Probably thinking, *another one who nearly bought it*. But he said, "An' to think people used to *pay* to stay in this place!"

Kearton laughed, for the first time.

Inside, it was exactly as he remembered. Bustling figures, some carrying packs of signals or documents, snatches of conversation fading when a senior officer was close by. Open doors and the clatter of typewriters, and the urgent chorus of teleprinters, in stark contrast to the bunches of tired-looking holly and Christmas ribbon draped above framed photographs of the King and Winston Churchill, and a notice that read, *In the event of an Air Raid* . . .

"Ah, here you are. Nice and early, too!"

A second officer in the W.R.N.S., attractive and smiling; not the face he recalled from his last visit, or the one before that. The Captain C.F. must be a hard taskmaster. He could imagine that.

She said, "I'll take you to him. A short cut," and waited for him to follow. "Bit of a flap on today."

Over her shoulder she added, "But you'd know all about that."

Through another office: more Wrens, looking up from their work as they passed. One called, "Is it all right now if—"

"Later! I told you, Collins!"

But she was smiling again when they reached the passageway beyond. It was empty, and comparatively quiet, with one door at the end.

Kearton thought of the quick exchange between his companion and the troubled-looking Wren.

"Spot of bother back there?"

She pulled up her sleeve with its two blue stripes and peered at her watch.

"Just one of those days." She was smiling directly at him

11

now, but it did not reach her eyes. "Ready? He's waiting." She hesitated. "Good luck. I know I shouldn't say that, but . . .'

He touched her arm.

"I didn't hear you."

"Come in!"

She must have tapped the door.

"Lieutenant Kearton, sir."

"About time, too." But he was grinning. "Good to see you, for more reasons than I can shake a stick at!"

The door closed. *As if it were yesterday . . .*

Captain Ewart Morgan was not a big man, nor was he tall. Kearton had once heard him described as "that nuggety little Welshman". It was fortunate for whoever had said it that the captain had been out of earshot, or the sky would have fallen on him.

But as he stood up and reached across his desk to seize Kearton's hand, Morgan seemed to dominate the room, and his grip was warm and strong.

A straight-ringed regular, Morgan had served under Admiral Jellicoe aboard *Iron Duke*, Jellicoe's flagship at Jutland. It was said that he had been on the beach for a while between the wars, like so many others, but the display of medal ribbons on his jacket told another story.

He gestured to a chair directly opposite the desk.

"Take the weight off your feet. It *is* good to see you." He sat down and touched a file marked TOP SECRET on the desk. "I've read all the reports. They've given you a clean bill of health. Never thought otherwise . . ." He leaned back. "Ready to start again?"

Something Kearton always remembered. Incisive. The opening shot.

A telephone rang suddenly from beneath a pile of signal flimsies. Morgan snatched it up.

"I said I was not to be disturbed!" His free hand was turning over some of the signals, as if his mind were already elsewhere. "Well, *this* is important, so tell him to wait!" The telephone slammed down.

Kearton wondered if it was the same Wren officer on the other end, and recalled her comment about 'good luck'.

Someone must have told her about it. Warned her, perhaps.

Whenever a flotilla or group of M.T.B.s had put to sea from here, usually at dusk, to seek out and destroy the enemy, as their lordships might describe it, Morgan had always made a point of being on the pier to watch them leave. His signal never changed. *Good luck.* Then back to the wardroom and a good night's sleep, or so they used to tell each other. But Morgan was always there, watching them come home, back to base again. Most of them, anyway.

And then one night, as the boats had slipped their moorings and Morgan had made his familiar signal, one of the commanding officers had switched on his loud-hailer and retorted, "Actually, *sir*, we rely on skill!"

The officer had not survived that patrol. But Captain Morgan had never mentioned luck since.

He realized Morgan had leaned forward in his chair, as if nothing had happened to interrupt him.

"You're getting a new command, which is why I had you brought back here in such a bloody rush. But you knew that before you requested to make the handover yourself, at sea." He glanced at the door. "Go well, did it? Your successor has a good record . . . Hammond, isn't it."

Kearton felt his hand pressing his leg. The well-known faces, the jokes, the strength of comradeship under all conditions. The moments of stress, and sometimes fear. They would soon forget, and rally around their new skipper. It was the key to survival.

Morgan was continuing, "She's a different class of boat. Bigger, too— but I'll fill you in when I've explained the reasoning behind it."

Kearton wanted to moisten his lips, ease the strain. Had he been bluffing, even up to the last few seconds? Unfit for duty. Until . . .

Morgan said, "Who would have believed, a year ago today, that we might truly be on the offensive again? You've heard of Dick Garrick."

"Captain Garrick, Combined Operations."

Morgan turned impatiently. "Rear-Admiral Garrick, or soon will be, to all accounts." And, almost to himself, "We were snotties together, and *that's* hard to believe, when I look back."

When he spoke again, his voice was level.

"You're going to the Med. Gibraltar first, for orders to take command. It would require too much time to explain the haste, but I want you ready to ship out in three days— *right*?"

Then he came around the desk, as if coming to a decision.

"It's part of a new group, three boats so far. My guess is Italy, the 'soft underbelly', as Churchill calls it. With Rommel and his Afrika Korps in full retreat at long last, Italy seems the most likely target, don't you think?" As usual, he did not anticipate an answer.

Kearton watched the neat figure move to one of his wall charts, and then back behind his desk.

"Who's the senior officer, sir?"

Morgan faced him once more and allowed himself a smile.

"You are. Or you will be, at Gib." Then he snatched up the telephone, the moment past. Perhaps he saw it as weakness, a crack in his armour.

"My assistant has all the details— she knows what to do." He covered the mouthpiece but did not turn toward him. "You're getting a half-stripe, by the way. Acting, of course. We'll just have to see . . ." He snapped into the receiver, "*Yes*, I got your message! What is all the fuss about this time?"

Kearton felt a hand on his sleeve and realized that the door was open.

14

She said, "This may take some time. Sir."

The same passageway, the noise and bustle, more unreal than ever.

A new command, and promotion. Lieutenant-commander. . . . He could still hear Morgan's words, and the rare show of warmth. *Acting, of course.*

"Is this really happening?"

She held out a fat envelope.

"It's all in here, sir. Someone will take your uniform to the outfitters while you're at the base. Captain Morgan has fixed it— with Gieves, he said."

They walked back through the same office, the Wrens still hammering at their typewriters. He saw a clock: it was less than ten minutes since he had been conducted through this 'short cut'. He stopped abruptly, and saw her turn.

"Can you wangle me a telephone? I'd like to make a private call."

She seemed to consider it, biting the end of the pencil which had never left her hand.

"I think we can manage that."

He said, "I'd like to let my mother know. Some of it, anyway."

He saw two of the Wrens bending over another who was seated at one of the desks. One girl had her arms around her shoulders, and her eyes were red with tears. He heard the second officer say softly, "I couldn't deal with it earlier," then she turned to face him, excluding everybody else. "She was on leave. She only just got the news. Her brother's reported missing, presumed killed. His ship hit a mine."

Kearton walked across the lobby, where hotel guests had once lingered, planning their days, and how best to enjoy their leisure. Another world, which might never come again.

He thought of Morgan. *Ready to ship out in three days.* A lifetime. He glanced at the two portraits on the wall. By then,

15

the remains of the holly and the faded ribbons would have been swept away.

A new beginning. He saw the Royal Marine climbing out of his car to stand beside it. Waiting.

He hesitated, half expecting to hear the shout . . . or had it been a scream?

But he was quite alone.

The duty petty officer in his white belt and gaiters pushed open a door marked *Officers Only* and peered up at the dockyard clock.

"If you'll wait 'ere, sir, a boat'll be along directly." He sighed. "There's a queue of 'em linin' up already!"

Kearton saw his suitcase just inside the little room, the raincoat folded across it. His other gear had already gone ahead, or so he had been assured, but he had long ago discovered that it was better to take no chances in the navy.

The petty officer glanced at a list pinned to a square of plywood.

"H.M.S. *Kinsale*. Came in yesterday. Always in a rush, in destroyers!"

Someone shouted and he looked in that direction. "Call me if . . ." But he did not finish it. "What's the matter? Don't they teach you to bloody read in the trainin' barracks? Officers only!" He strode away, already calling to somebody else.

A young seaman was standing beside his kitbag and lashed hammock where they had been unceremoniously dropped, a regulation suitcase at his feet: as new as he was. His dark blue collar and carefully pressed bell-bottoms said it all.

For some reason it seemed to help, steadied Kearton's mind.

He said, "First ship?"

The boy, and he was no more than that, stared at him, the face and the uniform, and nodded jerkily.

"Y-yes, sir. I was delayed."

"You still 'ere?" The P.O. was back. "Wait by the stairs!" Then he relented slightly. "I'll carry the bag— *you* might lose it." He looked at Kearton and grimaced. "What's the Andrew comin' to these days, sir?"

Kearton stood by the solitary window and imagined he could feel warmth in the sunlight through the glass. But it was two o'clock in the afternoon, and would be dark in a couple of hours. He shivered, trying to recall what it had been like. The first ship . . .

He stared across the harbour. Portsmouth: always crowded, always busy. Speeding motor-boats and scruffy working craft, a backdrop of moored ships in dull grey or dazzle-paint. Some preparing for sea, others enduring the indignities of repair or overhaul. The waiting was almost over. He wanted to yawn, and restrained it.

Captain Morgan's three days had become five. And he was feeling everyone of them.

Going over his orders until he knew them almost by heart, not that they ever gave much away. *Go there. Do that.* An unfamiliar bed, and never free to meet and discuss things with men he knew. He had spoken to his mother twice on the telephone; the first attempt had been cut off. Something one of them must have said. A click on the line, then it had gone dead. *Careless talk costs lives.*

They should have been prepared, after all this time. He had also written to her, not saying much. But she would know. She would tell his father then, in her own way.

There was sudden movement abeam of a moored escort vessel, and, subconsciously, his bruised body responded. An Air-Sea Rescue launch, the colours vivid against the sloop's hard-worked and dented plates. He thought of the Fisherman, the weathered features, the handshake. He would be back at sea again, a fisher of men. If only people knew.

" 'Tenant-Commander Kearton, sir?"

17

He was still not used to it, and he was not the only one. The questioning glances, and even when he had seen his own reflection in a shop window it had been like glimpsing a stranger. Could that little piece of gold make such a difference?

It was a tough-looking seaman, cap chin-stay pulled down, face reddened by the cold air. A leading-hand's killick on one sleeve: probably the boat's coxswain.

"I'm from *Kinsale*, sir." He indicated the case. "Ready if you are, sir."

His collar was pale, dhobied and scrubbed until it was almost colourless: a proper Jack, unlike the young rookie with his bag and hammock.

Another seaman had appeared and was already picking up the case. He, too, had glanced at Kearton's sleeve and the new gold lace. *All right for some.* But he said cheerfully, "My brother's in Coastal Forces, sir."

The leading hand grinned. "Then God help us!"

The same petty officer was waiting at the pier, where an assortment of boats was jockeying for position, offloading personnel, or waiting for others to arrive.

"Can you take another one, sir?" He gestured to the young sailor. "'E'll be adrift otherwise."

Kearton nodded. "He's joining *Kinsale*. I'm only a passenger!"

He climbed down into the boat and felt the engine quiver into life. He was back.

2

Of One Company

He was suddenly wide awake, but for a few moments he could not recall having been asleep. His body reacted more instinctively, identifying the pressure against one arm and then the other, the vibration beneath and around him, even as his mind was still grappling with it.

There was a tiny deckhead light, just enough to see the opposite side of the cabin, and the other bunk, obviously empty. And the outline of the door, the one thing that really mattered if the alarm bells or worse should shatter the silence.

He lay listening to the sounds as the hull leaned over: the clatter of loose gear, boots thudding along the deck overhead. Familiar, yet so different from the thrust and plunge of an M.T.B. in any kind of sea.

His first ship on active service, before he had been accepted for Coastal Forces, had also been a destroyer, one of the old V & W class, built for the Kaiser's war. Compared with those, the new breed of destroyers like *Kinsale* seemed giants, superior in speed, armament and performance. They had been deployed at once, mostly in the Mediterranean, and had been in the thick of it throughout those first, decisive months. Now, as far as he knew, *Kinsale* and one of her sisters were the only survivors of their class. Fine ships, and so often in the news reports: one, the *Kelly*, had even withstood torpedoes, only to be sunk by bombers during the battles for Crete. She was still remembered, not least because of her flamboyant captain, Lord Louis Mountbatten, who had survived both attacks and was in service again.

And now *Kinsale* was going back to the Mediterranean. Rejoining the Fleet, as her commanding officer had remarked almost casually when he and Kearton had been introduced, a few hours before *Kinsale* slipped her moorings and headed out into the Solent.

He lay quite still and listened to her now, waking up, albeit reluctantly. Another day: early morning, and still black on deck, but the morning watch taking comfort from the knowledge that all the other hands were being called, to have their breakfast, work ship, and be ready to take over the forenoon watch *on time*. It never changed: four hours on watch, four hours off. Snatch any sleep you could when you got the chance. He rubbed his chin. He would have a shave . . . His mind was now fully alert, the uncertainty almost gone. Sometime today they would sight Gibraltar. *Kinsale* was making good progress, and the navigating officer, whose cabin he was sharing, seemed confident about their E.T.A.

Throughout the four days he had been aboard he had kept mostly out of the way as the ship's company went through all the usual drills and exercises: action stations, defence against possible air attack, submarine alert. Even abandon-ship instruction, if only for the benefit of new hands like the youth who had shared the motor-boat at Portsmouth.

Out into Western Approaches, then south into the Bay of Biscay. It had seemed *Kinsale* would have the sea to herself. There had been an alarm when an unidentified aircraft had been sighted off the Isles of Scilly, even as they caught a final glimpse of England, but nothing worse. The last sight of home had had far more emotional impact, even if the old Jacks made light of it.

He sometimes wondered what the commanding officer was thinking about it all. *Back to the Med*. After a brief visit to England, new radar equipment fitted, a boiler-clean, and maybe a scrap of leave for the lucky ones. They had rarely met during the passage. He was a commander in rank, and obviously proud of his ship, but he remained aloof, spending most of his time on the bridge either sitting on a tall, rigid chair, which was bolted to the deck and in full view of the other watchkeepers, or snatching a few minutes alone in his hutch-like sea cabin, also on the bridge.

Kearton clambered from the bunk and waited, testing the motion. To give himself more time, delay the inevitable.

In many ways it would have been easier to take up his new appointment directly from the home base. He had read and reread his orders, if only to stop himself finding flaws in the concise wording. He could almost hear Captain Morgan's voice dictating them. There would *be* no flaws.

He could see the three boats in his mind, 'D-Boats', they were termed. Larger and more powerful than all the other motor torpedo boats. He had served very briefly in one as part of a passage crew, while his own command had been undergoing repair.

He saw his new working rig, battledress, some still called it, swaying from a rail on the bulkhead, replacing the gear he had been wearing when they had fished him out of the drink.

He heard a clatter from the wardroom pantry: a mug of tea would soon be arriving to start the day. This day. And somebody was laughing.

After Gibraltar, *Kinsale* was going back to the war.

He had never left it.

The three M.T.B.s were moored well clear of the main anchorage and away from the comings and goings of various harbour craft, isolated, if that were ever possible at Gibraltar. Two lay alongside

21

an elderly supply ship, and the third rested against a battered pontoon, rubber fend-offs squeaking now as a small launch ploughed past. There were plenty of ships at anchor or alongside, but a distinct lack of the usual bustle and activity. It was Sunday, and war or no war, routine took first place.

The biggest warship visible was a cruiser, quiet now after the bugle calls and shouts of command. The church pendant had been hoisted while Divisions and Inspections were carried out, and a commodore's broad pendant at her masthead left nothing in doubt. The M.T.B. settled against the pontoon again as the wake rippled along the cruiser's waterline.

Petty Officer Harry Turnbull turned his back and stared aft, along the full length of his own boat: M.T.B. 992, the numbers bright on either bow, like everything else above and below deck. Or he would soon know why. He was the coxswain, and he could still feel something like pride. She was *his boat.*

He walked a few paces, past the two-pounder pom-pom cannon, neatly flaked mooring lines, and freshly cleaned decks. Nothing left sculling about to offend the eye, or give a bad impression. No matter who was at fault, the coxswain always carried the can.

He looked up and over the low bridge at the clear sky beyond. The locals thought the wind unusually cold, blowing in from the Atlantic. They should be in England right now, in January: that would stop them moaning about the bloody weather . . .

Turnbull was twenty-nine years old, and had been in the Royal Navy for eleven of them. He saw his shadow pass across the machine-gun mounting below the bridge; there was a matching pair on the opposite side. He could not help comparing her with a couple of his previous boats: *one* gun, if you were lucky. Speed and agility had come first. And there was a pair of Oerlikons aft, *'ooligans*, the gun crew nicknamed them. Like an M.T.B. and motor gunboat combined. He glanced at the White Ensign, scarcely moving now, and never used since the day they had steered out of the builder's yard. Brand new, like everything else. He wanted to look at his watch, but knew the gangway sentry would see him. Dressed in his best Number Twos, with a freshly blancoed revolver belt and holster at his waist, he was living proof of the significance of this day. For all of them.

Even that brought it home to Turnbull. 992, like her two sisters, was double the size of those earlier boats: one hundred and fifteen feet on the waterline and over one hundred tons displacement. And four Packard engines to move them. The tanks had been refilled and you could still catch the stench of their 100-octane petrol. Ten fuel tanks, he had checked each one, holding five thousand gallons all told. It was something best not thought about. A burst of tracer and you would go up, not down. It happened to others. Not to you.

He stared at the gangway sentry again. Glover, a Londoner. Nothing much else known, yet. But the faces and the names would become individuals, personalities, some more quickly than others, and there were thirty of them in this company, which he would soon know inside out. It was a coxswain's job, or part of it.

He heard a footstep and the quiet cough that always seemed to precede the man. It was the Chief, who took charge of all those dials and machinery, the very power of the boat. Jock Laidlaw seemed too tall for a cramped, noisy existence between decks. He had a narrow, intelligent face and keen eyes that always watched your mouth when you were speaking. It had become a habit after months of reading his mechanics' or stokers' lips when the competition from the engines was too overwhelming, and Turnbull suspected he was probably a little deaf as well, for the same reason. Not an easy man to know, but if you ever managed it, you found a friend you could trust.

He was looking up at the supply ship, where a head wearing a chef's hat was peering through an open scuttle.

"D' ye think he's been delayed?" He did not need to elaborate.

Turnbull shook his head. "There was a signal about it. Jimmy the One told me to carry out the instructions." He ticked them off on each finger of his strong, square hands. "Coming aboard at three bells. No ceremonial, and no change to harbour routine. Local leave if arranged. That's all I know."

Laidlaw said, "Jimmy th' One's probably still brooding." He might have smiled, but it only made him look sad. "What might have been his, gone for a Burton."

Turnbull had thought much the same. But the first lieutenant had to put up with it, no matter how he felt about the orders.

The Chief came to the point.

"Our new skipper— what d' you know about him?"

Turnbull considered it. Some people never made a mark, unless they were listed as a bad lot, or promoted unexpectedly. Or killed in action.

He said, "Kearton? First ran into him a couple of years back. Same flotilla, but not the same boat." He knew the eyes were watching his mouth, and was surprised that it came out so easily. "Good officer, no bullshit. Ready to listen, not like some."

Laidlaw grimaced. "Like a *lot*!"

"No slouch, either. D.S.C. and mentioned in despatches. Twice, I think. In several big dust-ups in the Channel and off the Hook of Holland." He grinned and punched his arm. "Christ, I sound like the bloody *Daily Crapsheet*!"

Laidlaw said expressionlessly, "Good bloke, then?"

Turnbull did not reply directly, surprised that he could still be caught off-guard, when it was something which had never left him.

"It was about a year ago. We were working our way along the Dutch coast. Winter, and bloody cold."

He knew exactly when it was. The day, even the hour.

The Chief said nothing, waiting. Understanding, perhaps.

"We'd received reports of some German lighters in the area, running supplies close inshore. They hardly drew any water, y' see, and like as not a tin fish would've run cleanly underneath 'em."

He looked up at the old supply ship; the chef's hat had disappeared, and there was the sound of music, a woman's voice. The ship's company taking it easy. Sunday . . . It had been a Sunday then.

"So we closed the range and opened fire." He smiled a little, reminiscently. "The skipper never hung about. A bit of a lad. Still at school when I signed on." He paused, and felt the hull nudge against the pontoon again. Another small craft passing, but he did not turn to look.

The music and the singer's voice continued, undisturbed.

"We'll meet again, don't know where, don't know when/ But I know we'll meet again some sunny day . . ."

He said, "Then the E-Boats came out of nowhere, five or six of 'em. There were just four of our boats, Vospers. We caught a packet right away. That's about all I remember. I was in the drink."

He wanted to stop, but something was driving him. Why? After all this time?

Laidlaw murmured, "But you made it."

He shrugged. "The rest scattered. It was as black as hell and there were flares, tracer . . . I can't really remember." He hesitated, and then went on. "Still a lot of flak flying about, but one of our boats turned back to search for us. Just in case. Took guts to do that." He nodded, seeing it. "Yes, he *is* a good bloke."

Someone had appeared around the bridge. "First lieutenant's come aboard, 'Swain!"

Turnbull waved. "Thanks, I'm on my way!" He stared after him. He had forgotten his name.

Laidlaw tapped one of the engineroom vents with his foot.

"Don't you worry, Harry. Old Growler'll give you all the knots you want. Just ring down *Full Ahead*!"

He watched him stride away. "You're not so bad yourself, laddie."

The music had not stopped, nor had the singer.

Laidlaw came originally from Dundee, although he had not been back there for several years.

He reached for the hatch, to shut out the music and the memories. To feel safe.

Lieutenant Peter Spiers saw the coxswain waiting by the brow from the pontoon, relaxed and apparently unconcerned, as if nothing would ever take him by surprise. A good man; 992 was lucky to have him. He had heard that several times, even today, when he had been in somebody else's wardroom for a quick 'wet'. A Horse's Neck, or two; he imagined he could still taste the brandy on his tongue. Maybe it had been unwise, today of all days.

He returned Turnbull's salute and looked along the deck, checking each item. Take nothing for granted. Spiers was twenty-four, the first lieutenant and, to some, a veteran. He could feel the coxswain watching him, probably gauging their immediate future together in the light of this unexpected development.

"Any signals? Messages?"

"As before, sir. Any minute now, I'd say."

Spiers pointed toward the gangway sentry.

"What about *that*?"

'That' was a smudge of white blanco from the sentry's pistol holster down one side of his jumper.

Turnbull said, "See to it— jump about!"

Spiers cleared his throat. "Not now. Too late. What's his name?"

Turnbull replied patiently, "Glover, sir," and dropped his

voice. "He's a good lad." The first lieutenant had bent his head to hear him, and he could smell the wardroom brandy on his breath. Number One was taking it badly.

"Oh, very well. But next time—" He did not go on. He could still feel it, despite all he had tried to do to control it. Disappointment, resentment, even anger. It had all been just a dream to begin with, and then suddenly it had seemed right there in his hands. A command of his own, even if it would have meant having a senior officer breathing down his neck occasionally when one chose to cadge a lift. Now, a new scheme of things, to suit the bigger boats and those who were chosen to lead.

The boat's other lieutenant, Ainslie, a navigation specialist, had laughed outright at him.

"Take it off your back, Peter. We're in for something big and dangerous, if you ask me. Hit 'em hard, where it hurts most!"

Ainslie never seemed to take anything seriously for long, except his bloody charts, and some girl he was always going on about. A nice enough chap, but he had never been in action, so what did he know?

Turnbull was still observing him, without showing it. *Get today over with, and then* . . . He and the Chief might have a few quiet drinks themselves, down aft in the petty officers' mess, separated from the rest of the hull by the engines, and, of course, those five thousand gallons of fuel.

Able Seaman Glover called, "Comin' now, 'Swain!" and looked down at the offending stain. Bloody officers . . .

He felt the deck move evenly under his feet, another launch passing through the anchorage, and standing well clear of the cruiser with the commodore's flag. Probably full of libertymen going for a run ashore, looking for some fun, if there was such a thing in Gib on a Sunday. He thought of his own home in Bethnal Green, in London's East End. The area had been badly bombed, they said, but he could picture his mum and dad lifting a few jars in the old Salmon and Ball pub, if it was still standing. Always lively, with a knees-up or a fist-fight to round off the evening.

He brought his heels together and straightened his back. They'd be really proud if they could see him now.

"Attention on the upper deck!"

Turnbull saw the new White Ensign lift in the breeze for the first time.

He watched the salutes and the handshakes, and the eyes, which said more than words.

The strain lifting, lightening into a smile. The face he remembered after that night in the Channel, when, as he thought of it, life had been reissued. Bob Kearton had come to visit him in the R.N. hospital. Now he, too, had been through that nightmare.

He heard the first lieutenant saying, "Welcome aboard, sir." He was hiding his feelings remarkably well.

Now Kearton was here. The same smile: no salute but a handshake. Turnbull returned it, looking straight into the grey eyes, too immersed in the memories to grin back. There might have been just the two of them on the deck.

"Welcome *back*, sir!"

Kearton stepped over a coaming and paused as if to get his bearings, although it was not that. He had been on his feet since he had first come aboard, and this was the first time he had been alone. He was surprised that he was not exhausted: it was nearly midnight.

The cabin was neat and unlived in, the bunk and shelves above it uncluttered; even his own suitcase and baggage had vanished. The cabin itself was almost square, the side slightly sloped, with one scuttle, at a guess directly below the starboard torpedo tube. A table, two chairs, and a hanging space of sorts, and that was all.

He tossed his cap on to one of the chairs and closed the door behind him. After the other M.T.B.s he had known, this seemed spacious. And it was his own.

He moved to the scuttle and raised the deadlight. It was very dark, more so because the side of the old supply ship seemed to be towering directly above him.

He closed the scuttle and allowed the sounds and smells around him to excude everything else. The gentle vibration from a generator, an occasional movement of the hull against the moorings, someone coughing, probably on the crew's messdeck in the forward part of the hull. The tiny galley and a W/T office shared the rest of the space with the wardroom, and storage for food and ammunition.

He sat down and looked at the gleaming paintwork, so fresh that it almost hurt the eye in the reflected deckhead lights.

He reached out absently and tapped the sloping side, the diagonal layers of wood. It was something he could never resist. He could see his father doing the same in the boatyard on the Thames that bore the family name. Power-boats and sailing dinghies had been his trade. Nothing vast, but situated just above the big lock at Teddington, it was known and respected by many yachtsmen and other, part-time sailors.

Those old customers would hardly recognize the yard now. His father had been forced to take on more workers to keep pace with the growing demands of war, building motor-boats similar to those carried by warships like *Kinsale* and other, barge-like craft for the army.

The yard had owned a little, outdated tugboat, the *Ruffian*, which his father or the foreman would use for hauling fresh timber from another yard in Kingston, or for collecting boats in need of repair or overhaul, and sometimes, as a boy, Kearton had been allowed to head up or downriver as an eager passenger. Maybe that was when his interest, even love for the sea had begun. He had been invited to join a local sailing club, and in no time had been sailing in regattas and winning prizes.

That had been when he had first met Julie. They had sailed together, danced together, and sometimes imagined a future together. And sometimes she told him he was too serious; she was frivolous and lively, full of fun, and always wanted to share it with him. When he had signed up to join the Supplementary Naval Reserve, she had encouraged him in his part-time studies of seamanship and navigation, and forgiven him his occasional trips to sea with the navy whenever the chance came his way.

And all the time the threat of war had been mounting. Some people had dreaded the possibility, but Kearton had been in uniform before the reality hit him. It was another world. And Julie believed she had no part in it.

He could still recall every word of the letter he had received when he had been in his first ship on active service, the old V & W Class destroyer *Viper*.

Three years ago. It did not seem that long.

You will always be very dear to me, but . . .

But was somebody she had met at a War Savings event. He had escorted her home when an air raid warning had been sounded. They were married the following year.

He reached into an inside pocket and dragged out his old wallet. It was wrapped in a square of oilskin, the pieces stuck together, and he had not opened it since they had hauled him out of the sea.

He prised the wallet open. Three one-pound notes, a theatre ticket, and an old mess bill from H.M.S. *Hornet*, the Coastal Forces base in Gosport.

He turned the photograph of her toward the light. Cracked and badly stained, flaking apart even as he held it. He had never replied to that letter, nor would he. *But suppose . . .* The same smile. He thought of the way she used to poke out the tip of her tongue, to provoke him. Excite him.

She might have read about him when he had been decorated. Or thought of him whenever the B.B.C. newsreader intoned, ". . . and last night our Light Coastal Forces were heavily engaged with the enemy in the North Sea . . ."

The photograph had broken apart in his fingers. He must have fallen asleep against the table.

It was more than that. Someone was rapping on the door. He tried to clear his throat.

"I'm here!"

Sturdy, round-faced: one of those anonymous seamen he had seen or spoken to. They all needed time. *Like me.*

He saw the loose overall jacket, the inevitable oilstain. One of the Chief's motor mechanics.

"Rathbone, isn't it?"

The Chief had accidentally called him 'Basil', after the popular Hollywood villain Basil Rathbone, usually seen crossing swords with Errol Flynn or the like.

He grinned. "S'right, sir!" and gestured vaguely. "I was down aft, workin' on a generator, an' I was told you was still up an' about." He was fumbling inside his jacket. "So I thought . . ." He thrust out something wrapped in a piece of spotless white paper. "You might be needin' a smoke after a day like we've 'ad."

Kearton unfolded the paper and stared at the pipe in his hands. He had last seen it, snapped off at the stem, when they had emptied his pockets at the hospital. Like the stained wallet now lying on the table.

"'Ope you didn't mind, sir."

Kearton shook his head. "I thought it had been ditched. I had no idea . . ." and fell silent, staring at it.

Eventually he said, "What were you before you joined up? A magician?"

The grin was back, wider than ever.

"Worked at Finlay's garage on the Kingston by-pass, not that

31

far from your dad's boatyard when you thinks about it, sir. But once old Finlay took you under 'is wing you learned to tackle anything, Rolls-Royce to cigarette lighter!"

They were both laughing.

He dug into his other pocket and dragged out a tin labelled DUTY FREE. H.M.SHIPS ONLY.

"Me an' the lads thought you might be a bit short, sir." He put it on the table.

The door closed. As if he had dreamed or imagined it.

He walked to the scuttle and opened it again; the air seemed cool, even cold. He could feel the hull moving beneath him, restless, impatient.

People sometimes wanted to know the true difference between the 'little ships' and the bulk of the fleet. He looked at his pipe and the tobacco on the table.

There was no easy answer. But *this* was the difference.

Kearton stood by a broad window overlooking part of the anchorage, alive now with launches, and some quaint local vessels going about their affairs as if untouched by a hundred years of history. Outside, there was a stone balcony, and a telescope mounted on a tripod.

He could see the Rock itself from here, dominating everything around and beneath it, hazed with low cloud which remained motionless despite the wind rippling the flags at various mastheads. And from this building with its old cannon, saluting guns in the vanished days of peace.

He had been deeply asleep, although he could not recall having climbed into the bunk. And then the hand on his shoulder, and the momentary sense of danger. He was to present himself at the Signals Distribution Office without delay. A boat was being sent to save time.

He glanced at his watch. Colours had long since sounded; he had heard the twitter of calls and the lordly blare of a bugle from the cruiser long ago, or so it felt. And he was still waiting. It was the navy's way.

Once he had arrived here, there had been no obvious urgency. A tired-looking yeoman of signals had called for a messenger, but seemed more concerned with a ship which was already under way, heading for the last brightly painted buoy and the sea beyond. Without looking, he had known she was *Kinsale*.

He had gone out to the balcony and uncovered the telescope and focused it. Like being part of it. With them.

Again the shrill of calls, the acknowledgment from the cruiser as she passed abeam, little figures at attention, an officer saluting from the forecastle by the empty jackstaff. Her motor-boat was hoisted, secured by the gripes, until the next time. He had wondered if the young sailor who had joined *Kinsale,* his first ship, had found his feet yet in the contained world of the lower deck.

He stifled a yawn. In a minute, someone would come and tell him that there had been a mistake, there was no urgency. It was only one of those things . . .

He looked around the room. A trestle table, scrubbed, of course; a couple of chairs. He could hear a solitary typewriter, very slow, two fingers at a time, probably someone translating a bunting-tosser's scrawl into something legible.

He remembered the faces as he had climbed down into the motor-boat. Weighing the unexpected change in routine. Some men still chewing on their breakfast, a few moving pieces of gear in readiness for washing down under the watchful eyes of a tough-looking leading seaman, the coxswain's right-hand man. The name had slipped Kearton's mind, but his flattened, broken nose made him easy to recognize. Some were still strangers.

He thought of Spiers, the Number One, always ready to answer any questions, never at a loss. Duties, watches, morale. But nothing personal yet to bridge the gap.

His attention returned to the window: a vibration, rather than a sound, had broken the stillness, an aircraft on the Rock's narrow runway preparing for take-off. He had heard people say the experience was not for the faint-hearted, but from a distance it reminded him of his old motor-bike, a second-hand Triumph, when you twisted the grip and made the revs mount up. When Julie had been on the pillion, arms wrapped around his waist. Laughing whenever they hit a hump in the road, or some unexpected pothole, and when they had taken a short cut along the towpath, anglers squatting by their rods and yelling threats as they had clattered past.

The old bike would be on a scrap heap now, written off. And with petrol rationed so severely, joy-riding was just another memory.

He turned. No voices, but the typewriter had stopped, and chairs were being scraped aside.

The door swung open and closed just as casually behind the newcomer.

He wasted no time. "I know who *you* are." He thrust out his hand. "I'm Garrick. Sorry I'm a bit adrift. It takes a month of Sundays to get things moving around here!"

The ready smile and keen eyes, like the handshake, seemed familiar, although they had never met. Captain Richard Garrick, D.S.O., Royal Navy, 'Dick' Garrick as he was called in the popular press, was known to most people following the war's progress at sea and on land; he seemed ubiquitous. Kearton had seen him in interviews on newsreels at the cinema, or photographed surrounded by armed squaddies after some successful raid into enemy territory. Often wearing battledress or camouflaged combat gear, cigarette in one hand, and usually the smile. 'Our man of action', one journalist had dubbed him.

The smile was the same now, but the rest was different. Maybe it was the formality of the smart uniform and its medal ribbons, the four gold rings on either sleeve, and the oak-leaved cap he had tossed so easily on to the scrubbed table, but he seemed strangely like someone playing a part. Maybe he was related to the great eighteenth-century actor.

Even his movements were deliberately light, unconcerned, and Kearton imagined Captain Morgan in his office, heard the Welsh voice: *"We were snotties together . . ."*

Garrick had a strong face and restless eyes; blue or grey it was hard to tell. Norway, Greece, Crete, rearguard actions, but always hitting back, sustaining hope and pride when others had become resigned, even ready to accept defeat.

"I hear you've already settled in? No time to hang about, the way things are beginning to shape up." He waved toward the bare wall, as if he could see a great map hanging there. "They said Rommel's super Afrika Korps couldn't be beaten. Egypt was next, and then on to the gates of India. They were *wrong*. Like the weepies who said nothing could stop the enemy from crossing the Channel to invade—" He tapped the wall. "— and conquer England! We put a stop to that, too!"

He looked down, and tugged the triangle of handkerchief into position beneath the medal ribbons. Even that was deliberate.

"But there are still too many deadbeats left in authority for my liking." He crossed to the window. "When the first D-Boats were delivered there was one senior officer, who must remain nameless, who looked at one of them and asked, 'Is that the boat, or the crate it arrived in?'" He turned again, outwardly relaxed, but the voice was not. "If they were all like that idiot, the swastika would have been flying over Buckingham Palace after Dunkirk!" He smiled, the point made. "You were there too, I believe?"

He did not wait for a response, a little touch of Morgan. *We were snotties together.* But that was all.

They walked on to the balcony and looked out over the array of shipping. There was even a hospital ship now, red crosses like blood in the misty sunlight.

Garrick said quietly, "It's time to turn the tide. Attack the enemy where it hurts, and pin down as many men and machines as we can. They talk about the soft underbelly of Europe, but that's not what the poor bloody infantry see when the landing craft hits the beach and the ramp goes down." He waved, although Kearton had seen no one else. Perhaps on another balcony or at another window? "We can soften it for them, eh?" Abruptly, he walked back into the room.

"You'll be getting your orders today. Top secret, and you know what *that* means. I had hoped for a fourth boat, but we must be patient, as their lordships will expect of us. I'm flying to Malta. Now."

He picked up his fine cap and turned it over in his sun-browned hands, almost as if he had never seen it before.

"You've got a good command, and probably the best crews we can hope for." He looked at Kearton again, the restless eyes quite still. "We shall be 'of one company', as Our Nel once said." Then, "You're not married, or anything, are you?" and nodded curtly. "Good show. One thing at a time." He pulled on his cap and allowed the moment to hang. "This is going to be very important. Who knows, maybe vital. So let's be about it."

He gripped Kearton's hand.

"Safe passage, Bob Kearton." And smiled the famous smile. "See you in Malta!"

The room was empty, the harbour throwing up reflections on the glass.

Garrick was going to board an aircraft, perhaps that same one. He could recall each gesture, each change of mood, but could barely remember his own comments or responses. Maybe Garrick had that effect on everyone.

He picked up his own cap and brushed the peak with his

sleeve without noticing what he was doing. The door was half-open, the room was needed again.

He walked out into a passage, where someone was hovering to guide him efficiently out of their lives.

No questions, no doubts. *Of one company.* The little admiral would have approved of 'Dick' Garrick.

He brushed against a pillar and the bruise came alive again. He ignored the pain. That, too, was in the past. It had to be.

Tomorrow would not wait.

3

Flotsam

Kearton climbed up into the open bridge and paused to stare at the sea alongside. He had been in the compact chartroom, in darkness but for a carefully shaded light above the table, and the contrast was impressive, as if sunset were reluctant to conform to the rules of black-out. The water beyond the bows was unbroken, shining dully like molten copper, breaking and brightening again in 992's wash and the deep, regular furrows that streamed back from the stem. Darkness would be abrupt and complete.

He moved to the forepart of the bridge, where the faint glow of the compass reflected on the helmsman's duffle coat. Other figures were silhouetted against the sky, unaware of his presence or pretending to be, while they moved their binoculars ahead and abeam. Despite the regular murmur of the engines, individual sounds stood out. The twin machine-guns on either wing of the bridge rattled occasionally despite the waterproof sleeves which protected their mechanisms and ammunition, but were easy to clear away at the slightest hint of trouble. And on the forecastle deck someone was stamping his foot as if to restore the circulation. One of the two-pounder's crew, like a hooded monk in his duffle coat, stretching now, and yawning.

Kearton saw Lieutenant Ainslie turning away from the screen, his face in shadow. Probably wondering what he had been doing down in *his* chartroom.

"All quiet, Pilot?" Kearton had only been off the bridge for an hour, but it seemed far longer. Like a demanding grip, dragging at him the moment he turned away from the 'ifs' and the 'maybes'.

He saw the smile.

"Aye, sir. Steady at fourteen knots. I can't complain, so far!"

It *was* steady enough, but it was time to reduce speed, before they lost the light entirely. Then, the slightest swell would make the motion queasy. He looked astern again. The three boats were keeping in line. Good conditions, but that could change. He had seen it several times. Boats increasing speed in the darkness for fear of losing their leader, or worse, being left alone in enemy waters: a single burst of power, and one boat smashing into another. The watchkeeper's nightmare.

Ainslie was already holding his wristwatch up to his eyes.

"Fifteen minutes, sir."

"Very well." He glanced at the compass: due east. He could visualize the neat lines and crosses pencilled on the chart, the open logbook nearby. Ainslie was a good navigator. Outwardly easygoing and friendly, he had been a trainee teacher in a boarding school before he had volunteered for the navy. It must have been hard to distinguish him from some of his own pupils.

Young though he was, he had a girlfriend; Kearton had seen her photograph when Ainslie had opened his wallet. *Like me . . .*

Feet on the ladder; it was the coxswain. *He* did not need to look at his watch.

Turnbull cleared his throat. "Ready, sir?"

Kearton touched his arm. "You never lose it, do you?"

"Engineroom standing by, sir!"

The Chief would be down there, too, just in case. He was lucky to have such a good crew. They, too, were fortunate in the time they had had together before he had even stepped aboard.

The three boats had sailed in company from Milford Haven, on the south-west tip of Wales, for most of the passage alone and unescorted all the way to Gibraltar: almost the same journey he had taken in *Kinsale*, but far less comfortable.

Fate had been generous. There had been no breakdowns, and none of the foul weather that might be expected in winter. And the only sign of the enemy had been a big Focke-Wulf bomber, when they had been giving the French coast a very wide berth. They had gone to action stations and waited for an attack, or for the German pilot to call up reinforcements, but the bomber must have had a more important target in his orders. Nothing had happened. But it had been their first experience of standing together. There always had to be a first time, no matter how many actions you had seen, or if you were as green as grass.

He peered aft, and saw some vague figures crouching abaft the Oerlikon guns. Their little dinghy had needed securing, and his Number One was down there himself. That, however, was as far as it went. This might be a small, crowded warship, but the skipper and his first lieutenant were still miles apart.

He thought of the chart. A thousand miles, or near enough, from the Rock to beleaguered Malta. They could make up the speed during the hours of daylight, but at night they could too easily become the hunted and not the hunters. He half-listened to the engines, the rattle of a bell near the helmsman as Turnbull took his place.

"Cox'n on the wheel, sir!"

And Ainslie's, "Very good. Steer due east!"

As if they had been together for months. And that was a long time, in this outfit.

They had cast off from their moorings this very morning, even as Reveille was being sounded aboard the smart cruiser. In line ahead, hands fallen in, ensigns flying as they had wended past the other moored and anchored ships, exchanging brief signals while the boom-vessels and patrol boats cleared the way. Kearton had noticed that the cruiser had nets rigged protectively along either side of her hull. So even in Gibraltar there was danger. There had been rumours of attempted underwater attacks, not by submarines but by divers, frogmen, some of whom had been captured, but only after achieving their objectives. Something new: it was all very hush-hush, but it was known that bigger, more important ships had already fallen victim to this daring form of attack here in the Med.

He heard someone swear as the hull dipped steeply into a trough, the motion stronger under the reduced speed. The D-Boats were much heavier and more solid than the smaller M.T.B.s with their sleek lines and high speed, weighted by all the extra fuel and ammunition and, in addition, the piles of tinned rations which every warship ordered to Malta was expected to carry.

He recalled Captain Garrick's optimistic prediction of a change of fortune after El Alamein. Perhaps Malta's suffering would end, and the seige be lifted. But at what cost? The most bombed place in the world, one reporter had called it, and that was not surprising, with the enemy's airfields in Sicily only sixty miles away.

"All secure down aft, sir." It was Spiers, peering astern. "I have an extra lookout there, in case Mostyn's boat puts on some speed."

"Good thinking." He had not seen Spiers arrive on the bridge. Tall and broad-shouldered, he moved with the easy familiarity of someone who had wasted no time in getting to know his own boat.

He watched the next boat astern. Spiers knew all their names, too. 977's skipper, Geoff Mostyn, was a face from the past, encountered briefly at Dover during those early, testing battles with E-Boats and armed lighters: he was short, stocky and tough, a Geordie from Newcastle. Very outspoken, or had been then. Kearton had sensed a certain wariness the last time they had met. Did the new half-stripe really make such a difference?

He recalled that meeting, when they had been given orders to

41

leave the Rock. "Get up and scram," as he had heard the coxswain translate it. The third skipper was a Canadian, like the rest of 986's crew. Mostly from the Canadian flotillas which had already been on active service in the Mediterranean. All volunteers. They must be keen, he thought.

Lieutenant John Stirling R.C.N.V.R. had seemed very relaxed, with an easy, untroubled smile. He had commented little on his own experiences, but was eager to point out that he came from Halifax, Nova Scotia.

"Where all the best sailors are made!"

Mostyn had retorted, "Probably ran aground there in the first place!"

They obviously got on well together. A good team. The only hurdle was here.

"You've been to Malta before, Peter?"

Spiers seemed unprepared, either for the question or the informality.

"A few times, sir. Covered a couple of relief convoys from Alex, when things were getting a bit dicey." He paused. "The going was rough. One convoy had to turn back because they lost too many merchantmen to make it worth pressing on." He seemed to be reliving it. "Bomb Alley, we called it. Another time we gave up because the escorts simply ran out of anti-aircraft ammunition."

The bridge was dark now, but he could see him shake his head. "I don't know how they put up with it. And then . . ."

Kearton said quietly, "Tell me."

"The time we did get through, and got alongside, there were people waving to us. One woman brought some flowers. I'll never forget it."

"It does you credit. Nor would I."

A hooded shape loomed through the gate and announced breezily, "Freshly brewed char, gents!" before he saw Kearton. "Oops, sorry, sir."

42

Kearton felt his limbs relax. "Bang on time. Bell, isn't it?"

The seaman grinned, his teeth almost glowing against the sea's backdrop.

" 'Dinger' to his friends, Skipper!" That was Ainslie, the faint compass light moving across his duffle coat as he turned to share the joke.

Spiers said, "When we alter course—" He got no further.

There had been no sound, no tremor that might have been discerned through the regular beat of engines. It was no more than a sensation. Instinct.

Kearton stood by the screen, his mind and body responding to the hull beneath him.

No flashes to light up the sea, only darkness. Even the horizon had disappeared.

His stomach muscles tightened, as if anticipating a blow. There it was again, faint but persistent. Down in the engineroom, it would have been lost in that confined space of shafts and machinery.

It had been a series of explosions, far away and regular, in a pattern. Not bombs or gunfire. He breathed out slowly. *Or mines* . . . It was still buried in his memory. Waiting.

He said, "Depth-charges. Not in our neck of the woods, but pass the word to all hands."

A submarine, detected and under attack. *Theirs or ours?*

He thought of the destroyer *Kinsale*. Maybe she had got to grips with a U-Boat or an Italian submarine while she was still on passage to Malta.

He heard a voicepipe being snapped shut.

"Nothing from W/T, sir."

Ainslie cleared his throat and said precisely, "Some more tea, I think."

Nobody answered.

Kearton moved back to his original corner. The twin machine-guns on the wing of the bridge were uncovered, pointing at the sky, the ammunition clinking to the shift and sway of the deck. More voices now, murmuring to one another. Another fanny of hot tea on its way.

Kearton closed his eyes tightly and heard someone mutter, "Nice tot of grog would be a bloody sight better!"

He leaned back against a handrail but hardly felt it, reminded of the flask of brandy he had often carried. Now it was on the bottom of the North Sea.

"I'm going down to look at your chart again, Pilot."

"Can I help, Skipper?"

Ainslie's boyish informality did more to ease the tension than he could ever know.

"No, I've got to manage on my own!"

Several of them laughed as he climbed down from the bridge.

He paused, staring at the black water sliding beneath the side.

They had laughed. But he was speaking the truth.

The following day proved calm and sunlit, and even when they were closed up at action stations they could feel a touch of warmth on their faces. The sea, too, was clear and empty. Speed was increased to eighteen knots, and the distance between the boats opened to half a cable again.

Kearton had gone down to his cabin to snatch a few moments to shave and change his shirt, his first commanding officer's words lingering in his mind.

A skipper who looks scruffy, thinks scruffy! It still made him smile, although he could remember very little else about the man.

He had passed the little W/T office, with its incessant stammer of morse and an occasional human voice, until the telegraphist realized he was passing. French or Italian, there had been too much static to be certain, but somehow it sounded strangely sad.

Like the cabin, as neat and unlived in as ever, the bunk still waiting, unused. He returned to retrieve his newly repaired pipe and the tobacco; he had seen Ainslie smoking a pipe in the wardroom. For some reason, it had made him look younger than ever.

He sat for a few minutes, but he knew he would fall asleep if he lingered. It was still strange to be continuously at sea like this, one day after another. Before, he had been used to sighting an enemy-held coastline almost as soon as their own had slipped into the mist.

He took out his pocket notebook.

Two days, and they would reach Malta. New orders? A change of direction . . .

"You're wanted on the bridge, sir!"

The messenger sounded breathless, anxious.

He snatched his cap and hurried on deck. Maybe he had been expecting it. It had happened often enough in the Channel, and in the North Sea. But not usually the work of a U-Boat.

He reached the bridge, and took time to wipe the lenses of his binoculars. Drifting wreckage, seeming scattered for miles on this tideless sea. Decking and pieces of timber, smashed cargo crates. Probably an old freighter, fallen astern of a convoy or risking a run on its own. A drifting lifebuoy bearing a Greek name, which was not listed in any of their intelligence notes.

Perhaps a U-Boat had been investigating this same drifting flotsam, if not the actual cause. Either way, the plan had misfired.

There was still a long, trailing slick of oil, and now a few corpses. At reduced speed, the three M.T.B.s circled the remains.

Kearton moved his glasses slowly. So many times, and yet he had never become accustomed to it.

The U-Boat sailors had most likely been lookouts, or the gun's crew. All wore life-jackets, and two appeared to be clinging to a small raft. Or had been.

The depth-charges, which they had felt, had done their work well.

Kearton let the glasses fall to his chest.

"Signal, resume course and speed."

We must have looked like that, to the Fisherman. He turned away.

"One of 'em's still alive, sir!"

Someone else said, "More's the bloody pity."

Spiers snapped, "Port twenty!"

"Belay that!" Kearton had thrust one hand into his pocket, fist clenched so tightly that the pain steadied him. "Hoist that one aboard. *Dead slow* ahead."

Like a spell breaking. Orders shouted, some seamen already up forward, one over the rail shaking out a rope ladder. Lights flashing and clattering between the boats, somebody standing on the Canadian's searchlight platform, training a camera.

Kearton looked down as the bow's shadow moved slowly across the motionless raft.

It only took a few minutes, but the time seemed endless. Taking the forbidden risk . . .

Then the raft was bobbing along the side, its only occupant still staring at the sky, the remains of a leg trailing in the water. The sea churned into life again beneath the stern, and the bridge shook to the sudden response from the Chief and his crew.

Spiers said, "Have him taken to the wardroom," and as an afterthought, "With a guard."

No unnecessary diversions. No distractions. The orders were clear. Garrick would hit the roof if he heard about it . . . *When* he heard about it.

And for what?

Kearton stared across the littered deck and saw the coxswain looking back at him. Waiting. Then, deliberately, Turnbull gave a blatant thumbs-up.

Further astern now, the other boats resuming their station and distance, and fragments still tossing in their combined wake. That, too, would soon be forgotten.

But a debt had been paid.

The three officers stood together on the small bridge as the helm went over, and 992 settled on her final approach.

It was dawn, or near enough, the sea opening up from either bow and land rising from the shadows, still unreal in haze and smoke.

The engines sounded louder, catching a throwback from the coast, the first time for a thousand miles.

The last hours had been the longest, while they had waited to make the easiest and grimmest landfall most of them had ever experienced. For most of the time a prolonged air raid had been in progress, and the flash and glare of exploding bombs and the angry criss-cross of tracer and ack-ack from the defenders made further chartwork unnecessary.

Air raids or not, a boat had come out to greet them. A luxury motor-yacht in peacetime, but showing her pilot's flag, and two mounts of machine-guns to mark her latest, and perhaps final, incarnation.

Kearton leaned forward to look along the forecastle, where the two-pounder gun's crew stood watching the land reaching out. As if they had never moved.

He lifted his binoculars and saw the pilot boat turning slightly, faces visible now in her wheelhouse. They had already passed two minesweepers, heading out to begin the day's work; there had been warnings on W/T of another bout of enemy minelaying. There was no exchange of friendly or frivolous signals this time.

Malta had endured over two years of seige and bombardment. He could smell the smoke, taste it, feel it in his throat.

He heard the wheel creak. Turnbull needed no unnecessary instructions.

He saw the mooring lines already laid out on deck, and a heavy C.Q.R. anchor propped up like a plough beside them, in case they had to let go in an emergency and no moorings were available after this latest air raid.

Spiers had dealt with that. He was gazing at the nearest land, obviously reliving the experiences shared in that rare moment of candour.

Kearton shifted the glasses again. To starboard, Fort St Elmo, bomb-battered but imposing, even majestic. And beyond, through another drifting bank of mist or smoke, the Grand Harbour itself.

Spiers said, "I'll carry on, then." It was a question.

Ainslie twisted round as well, his chin rasping across his coat. He was attempting to grow a beard, without much success. Kearton had already heard the brief exchange between them when Spiers had suggested a shave was in order before entering harbour. Ainslie had tried to offer some sort of explanation, and there had been a sharp retort.

"Just stay on the bridge, Pilot, and the wind will blow it off!"

"Fall out, guns' crews!"

They were moving to their stations for entering harbour, dwarfed now by the long defences on the opposite beam. Fort Ricasoli, which Ainslie had already checked against his log.

Part of history, but the guns were pointing at the sky today, and there were great gaps among the nearest buildings, like broken teeth.

Leading Seaman Dawson had appeared on deck below the bridge, barking out names and gesturing with his fist. His flattened nose gave a twang to his voice, and Kearton had heard the sailors exchanging crude jokes and comments about it. It would be more than dangerous if Dawson overheard them.

He looked aft, and then astern at their two consorts. Figures already appearing on deck, preparing to do justice to the occasion. He had already seen that their own spotless

48

White Ensign, which had greeted him at Gibraltar, was flying again.

He trained the glasses across the ruined buildings and rubble. Valletta had suffered constant air attacks, and had lost more than half its houses. There was a sloop moored alongside at a pier, White Ensign flapping listlessly in the strengthening light. An officer was watching their approach through binoculars; another was reading something, a letter perhaps. An ordinary start to the day.

Except that most of the sloop's stern had been blown off, and been shored up by dockyard workers to keep her afloat. She would be used as an accommodation vessel until she was towed to the breakers. Or until the next air raid.

The officer with the binoculars had focused on Kearton, and threw up a smart salute. It was one of the saddest and bravest things he had ever seen.

He let the glasses fall to his chest again and cleared his mind. Take on fuel, and check all defects immediately. Signal for dockyard aid if need be.

The dust was settling, and there was a sheen of pale sunlight across the harbour. Not many other ships at anchor, which was no surprise.

"Signal, sir! We're going in!"

The pilot boat was turning, someone waving a flag.

A quick glance astern: the others were following closely, men on deck with heaving lines and rope fenders.

A mooring place had been cleared. The rest looked like a scrapyard.

"Starboard twenty! Midships! *Steady!*"

He licked his lips and felt the grit between his teeth.

There were people on the improvised jetty, a few uniforms. The reception party.

Beyond them there were others, civilians, all sizes and ages. As if they had risen out of the ruins.

49

They must watch every incoming vessel, large or small. Everything came by sea: fuel, food, ammunition. Everything.

"Slow astern!"

A heaving line snaked across the gap but fell short. He heard Turnbull mutter, "Sailors, I've shit 'em!"

Another followed and was seized by one of the onlookers. Somebody gave a cheer as the hull loomed over them, and the fenders creaked against the jetty.

People were waving, cheering, shouting. Men, women, even a few children. They said Valletta was built over a maze of tunnels and shelters. Even the famous catacombs were not immune.

Ainslie turned, faint stubble shining in the frail sunlight.

"We made it!"

There were soldiers now, military police, their red caps making a show of authority. They knew about the U-Boat survivor.

The engines were quiet, the smell of fuel hanging over the bridge. The Chief would be making his report shortly.

Spiers climbed up to join them.

"All secure, sir." He saluted, then his eyes moved to the jetty, perhaps surprised that it was not as he remembered it. "I'll get the prisoner brought up."

Turnbull had stepped away from the wheel and was looking toward the Grand Harbour.

He saw it differently, through the eyes of the young seaman he had been in his first ship, the battlecruiser *Hood*. The nation's pride, and the largest warship in the world. Had he remained serving in big ships, what might he be today?

Like the mighty *Hood*, he thought, lying broken, dead on the sea bed.

"You're wanted, 'Swain!"

He sighed. That said it all . . .

Ainslie pulled himself out of his trance of relief and faced the telegraphist who had just appeared, pad in hand, pencil gripped between his teeth.

"What is it, Weston?"

"Signal, sir." He nodded toward Kearton's back. "Priority."

Kearton took the pad and read the signal. It was very brief.

MEET NOON TOMORROW. WELCOME TO MALTA. GARRICK.

At that moment, the air raid warning sounded.

"Down this way, sir! Not far now!"

Kearton stepped over bricks, scattered the width of the narrow street. There had been two air raid alarms since they had moored alongside. Hit-and-run attacks, a few explosions, and once a column of smoke like a solid pinnacle against the blue sky; the crack of ack-ack, then the all-clear. One moment the streets had been full of people, trying to live their lives, or clearing up bomb damage. The next, it was deserted, as if nothing had survived.

He had been openly stared at, and there had been plenty of smiles as well. They seemed to know he had just arrived in Malta, and all that it signified: his appearance would have told them that.

His guide had halted by another turning, where soldiers were re-erecting a signpost that bore several pointers, naval, military, and emergency aid stations.

Throughout most of the journey he had caught sight of the Grand Harbour, reassuring in some way. But what about the civilians who lived here? They must sometimes ask 'why?'

His guide was grinning.

"This is it, sir."

He wore army battledress and boots, a webbing belt with a holster of some sort at his hip, and his eyebrows were pale with dust or sand, but topped by a naval cap and the familiar H.M.S. tally. It was another link.

51

"I'll be waitin', sir." He grinned again. "Or someone will!"

Kearton looked around at the street, rising slightly, a panorama of tawny buildings, old and new, outwardly unscathed, or patched up, some even overgrown. There was a door, already open, a petty officer studying him across a barrier of sandbags.

"'Tenant-Commander Kearton, sir?" He did not look at his watch. He did not need to. "This way."

He could hear guns in the distance. Another hit-and-run maybe. Or practice? Not that they would need any.

The door slammed shut, and after the sun it was oppressively dark, the air stale, unmoving.

Kearton followed the petty officer along a narrow passageway, occasional electric lamps and trailing wires marking their descent. It must be one of the many tunnels he had heard about, which had been dug through the soft sandstone from Lancaris itself to the moat beneath Valletta.

The petty officer stood by another opening. He was breathing heavily, but said, "Safe from air raids down here, sir."

Kearton stared past him into another space, a cavern. It was well lit, with a huge chart covering one wall. Tables, benches, officers and ratings at telephones or working with signals, coming and going. The air was hot and foul, made worse by the hard lighting, some of which was flickering. There was a bin by the entrance, half filled with candle stubs.

The P.O. shrugged.

"Ready for the worst, sir," and he attempted to smile. "You know what they say in this regiment, sir. 'If you can't take a joke, you shouldn't have joined!'"

The lights blinked, and Kearton felt the ground shiver.

"'Ere we are, sir." His companion did not seem to notice.

A dim, shored-up room, lined with raw planking, cool air coming from somewhere, a fan or vent. A rank of metal filing cabinets, another wall chart. And the smell of coffee.

Captain Richard Garrick was sitting at a broad desk, legs crossed, a cigarette in one hand, a telephone in the other. He nodded toward a canvas-backed chair and continued with his conversation.

"You know the score, Terry— it's important. No foul-ups at this stage, eh?"

He held the mouthpiece against his shoulder. "Won't take long."

Kearton sat in the chair and felt it creak. Another survivor.

Garrick was wearing a lightweight drill jacket, probably khaki, although in this uncertain light it was difficult to distinguish. Surprisingly, there were no marks of rank, only a small strip where medal ribbons might have been stitched, with GARRICK printed on it. His cap, lying on a bench, was the only symbol of authority.

He appeared relaxed, but the eyes were hard and alert.

Kearton looked around the makeshift office. Apart from the map, there was only a notice that read *CARELESS TALK COSTS LIVES.* Beneath it somebody had scribbled, *That should keep them quiet!*

The phone slammed down.

"Sorry about that. Means well, but a bit of an old woman."

He stubbed out the cigarette and pulled a fresh packet from his jacket.

"You don't, of course. A pipe, as I recall."

As usual, he did not wait for a response. "Things are moving at last. I read your report— seems you had a good run." He lit another cigarette. "How long do you need to be ready to move?" Again, he did not wait. "Day after tomorrow. One boat." He blew out some smoke. "Yours."

The floor shivered and grit pattered across the desk. "That'll bring out all the bloody sandflies, as if things aren't foul enough in this dump!" He laughed. "Good to have you on the team." And then, "Heard about your diversion. You took a chance there, just to pick up a Jerry. U-Boat hand, no less." He inhaled and flicked ash from the cigarette, shrugging. "I'd probably have done the same. In the good old days."

More thuds, closer this time. Feet hurrying past the door, a bell tinkling somewhere.

Kearton asked, "Inshore operation, sir?"

Garrick nodded. "Good thinking. Might not come off, but I've got the specialists geared up and ready to go." He tapped a ledger by his elbow, but did not open it. "Very hush-hush, no need to tell you that."

The telephone rang again. Garrick took his time picking it up.

He said, "I *know* that, sir." He stubbed out the cigarette. "I have him with me now." A pause, then, patiently, "I'm *quite* sure, sir."

He replaced it almost gently, and sighed.

"You know . . . sometimes, I really wonder."

Outside the door somebody coughed and scraped his feet. Garrick was up lightly, like a cat.

"No heroics, Bob. In and out. You'll have a few extra bodies to carry this time." He thrust out his hand. "Just wanted to see you again." He picked up his cap. "We're in it together," and the mood changed. "As I was just explaining to the Boss!"

The same petty officer was waiting for him.

"Been another hit-an'-run, sir— just to keep us on th' jump. Brought one of 'em down in flames though, for a change."

They had reached the entrance. There was a mat with WIPE YOUR FEET stamped on it, which he had not noticed before, no doubt liberated from a nearby hotel, or what was left of it.

"Watch your step, sir. One of my lads'll show you a short cut."

He was outside, the sun warm on his face, and the smoke and dust in his throat.

Had he been sent for because there had been some doubt?

He recalled Morgan and the suddenness of his promotion. *Acting*. . . . A clear warning, if he needed it.

There was more smoke now, people running. Some sort of engine coughing into life and cutting out. He quickened his pace, and then, like the others, broke into a run.

A different street, but he thought he recognized a tower or dome above the smoke.

Someone shouted, "It's the cellar!"

Kearton pushed past a startled group, mostly women in black, either leaving shelter or seeking another. There was an overturned wagon, the contents smashed among the rubble. And somebody sobbing.

A child was sitting on a crate, her hair covering her face and hands, blood on her bare arm and smeared across her knee. He knelt down and put his arm round her, and tried to brush the hair from her face. She opened her eyes and stared at him as he dabbed the blood from her arm with his handkerchief. It was not serious. She was still shuddering, but trying to smile at him.

Somebody was saying, "She was in the cellar. She's lucky."

Uniforms had appeared, men carrying stretchers, one unrolling bandages.

"You won't need those!" A woman's voice. "Here, *let me*."

She held the little girl's arm, gently but firmly, until she had her attention, and then she burst into tears.

"I've got her." She looked over the child's head. "They're all dead down there. I'll take over now."

Calm, matter-of-fact. She looked into Kearton's eyes for the first time.

"You'll know *me* again if you see me, won't you?" Like a slap in the face.

Kearton stood, and stooped instinctively to offer his hand.

A young woman, dark hair which had pulled free from a headscarf, her shirt torn and stained. A Red Cross armlet stark against her skin. And her voice was as English as his own.

He said, "Sorry I was staring." He tried again. "I can walk with you, if you like. Until . . ."

She did not reply, but snatched the bloody handkerchief from his fingers and began to dab her eyes.

"Sorry I went for you." She shook her head, and her hair, covered with dust, fell across her shoulder.

More people, peering faces. Questions. The invisible engines roaring into life.

She repeated, "They're all dead down there." She pushed the child away. "Here's your mother, Carmen. You're safe now."

They stood side by side, the crowd melting away, a few remaining to watch the men climbing down into the blackened cellar. Her hand, still dabbing with his bloodstained handkerchief, was sunburned, strong. There was a plain gold ring on her finger.

Someone called, making a joke of it, "The Navy's here!" but fell silent when he saw the cellar.

Kearton said, "I can take you home, if you like."

It was a stupid thing to say, he thought. He did not even know where he was.

She stared at him, and then she looked back toward that door and its sandbags.

"Thank you. But I *am* home."

He saw the same rating in khaki, his guide, hurrying toward him, obviously thinking the worst.

He said, "I'm Kearton," and made another effort. "Bob Kearton."

She faced him, her eyes calm now.

"Thank you, Bob Kearton. I'll not forget."

A voice was calling his name, and when he turned back again, she had gone.

He quickened his pace, and saw the gleam of water between the ruined houses. She had dark brown eyes. She was English. And she was married.

He thought of the petty officer's reminder. *If you can't take a joke . . .*

Garrick would like that.

No heroics.

4

A Close Thing

Lieutenant Peter Spiers wedged himself in one corner of the bridge and braced his legs. There was a steady wind from the south, not strong, but at their reduced speed enough to make itself felt. Plenty of stars, but no moon, so that even the sea alongside was faceless.

He restrained himself from using his binoculars. It was pointless. Only four hours since they had left Malta, but it seemed longer. They had the sea to themselves.

There had been another air raid soon after they had cleared the harbour: high-flying aircraft which had not returned when a few fighters had been scrambled to intercept them. A sign of the times, as someone had remarked. The crude repairs to the island's runways, great craters being refilled with rubble from bomb-damaged buildings and hastily surfaced by sappers and civilians, were proving their worth.

He remembered when there had been only two or three fighters left in Malta to retaliate: only a token defence. So many setbacks and retreats: it was hard to accept that, finally, luck was changing sides.

He heard the coxswain repeat, "North-seventy-West, sir."

Spiers glanced around at the other shadowy shapes on the bridge, staring into the darkness or listening to the regular beat of the engines and the occasional creak of gun-mountings. He guessed that Turnbull had repeated the compass course because he sensed his first lieutenant was on edge.

He heard somebody retching noisily abaft the bridge, the sound stifled suddenly, as if he had thrown up.

He took several deep breaths. He was the only officer on the bridge, and this was how it might have been. His own command . . .

He tried to shut it from his mind, thinking of the six extra faces which had been added to their company. Specialists, as an officer from Operations had described them. They had been put aboard from a harbour launch, which had hardly stopped engines long enough to make the transfer before speeding away again.

One of the seamen had commented loudly, "Long time since they've seen soap an' water!"

Specialists. They looked like a bunch of vagrants. Even the one in charge, an officer of some sort, who had introduced himself only as Jethro, might have passed as a tramp. Unshaven, dressed in a ragged sweater and fisherman's reefer, but the voice of command had been unmistakable when some of his baggage had been hoisted onto 992's side deck.

"*Easy* with that, man! One of those little squibs would blow this boat into toothpicks!"

There were no more warnings.

What sort of mission? What kind of men would volunteer for it?

They had studied the chart together; Kearton and Ainslie were down there now checking the final details for the rendezvous. Jethro was with them. All crammed into that confined space.

The rest of the passengers were in the wardroom, with their odd assortment of weapons, light machine-guns, foreign-looking pistols, and knives. Two of them seemed to be Italian. Collaborators.

Ainslie had said coldly, "Traitors, from another perspective!"

59

and had not waited to be contradicted. "My aunt used to live in the Channel Islands. Jersey. There were a few of them there, too, when Jerry marched in!"

Spiers reached out and stretched, loosening the taut muscles, trying to exercise them. He had always been a keen sportsman, playing cricket and tennis whenever he got the chance. He listened to the hull moving and creaking beneath him. When he had not been trying to sell insurance to people who had more money than sense . . .

Turnbull murmured, "Skipper's comin' up, sir."

No matter what, the ship came first.

Kearton was on the bridge now.

"Another hour, maybe less. We'll reduce to ten knots, so warn all hands. It will be a coaster, a schooner of some kind, if everything goes to plan."

Spiers asked, "And if it doesn't, sir?"

"We get the hell out, and try again later." He must have touched Turnbull's arm. "What d'*you* say?"

"Roll on my twelve!" Turnbull said, and they both laughed.

Spiers groped his way to the ladder. How could they make light of it? Pretend? All he could feel was anger.

Now the motion was much worse, and spray flung aft from the stem clattered across the bridge like hail. Bad enough for the gun crews and lookouts, but in the engineroom it would be impossible to stand. Spiers would go through and along the hull, checking each man, making sure nothing had been displaced by the strain. He could be relied on, no matter what he might be thinking.

Kearton tried to picture the different faces, as individuals and as a unit. Most of them had been in action of one kind or another, a few, like Turnbull and Spiers, many times. But together, at close quarters, never.

Some of them must be thinking the same thing about their commanding officer.

He sensed a movement behind him. Light-footed, untroubled by the swoops and rolls of the hull. He knew it was Jethro, if that was really his name.

Despite the discomfort and the tension he smiled to himself, remembering the sailor's loud remark about 'soap and water'.

"Soon now, Skipper," and it was not a question. A brisk, cultured voice, at odds with his unkempt appearance. And very calm. Dangerously so. What made him, and those like him, volunteer for this type of duty? It was one thing to risk death, even to be killed in action, but to be caught and taken prisoner as a secret agent or saboteur was to invite a fate without mercy.

Kearton felt the spray on his face, as cold as the North Sea.

"We can only feel our way."

Jethro might have shrugged. "They will be there. They have no choice."

Ainslie had joined them, but remained unusually silent. Perhaps because of their passenger, the 'specialist', perhaps remembering his aunt in German-occupied Jersey.

"Light, sir! Port bow!"

A tiny red flash in the sky, then another: two pinpricks. But after the blackness, they seemed like thunderflashes.

"Port ten. Midships."

It might still be a false alarm. Or a trap.

Kearton heard the two-pounder swinging slightly, the machine-guns on the bridge wing already depressed toward the invisible horizon.

He said, "Stand by." He could not see it, but the Chief's warning light would be flashing above the big Packard engines. *Ready for full speed.*

He recalled Laidlaw's calm assurance. "Old Growler can give you thirty knots at the ring of a bell, sir." Then his thin smile. "With a following wind, anyway!"

So different from his last command, forty knots flat out . . .

"Stop engines!"

61

The sudden silence seemed almost painful, the sea subdued as the way fell off the thrust.

"Dead ahead, sir!"

Kearton watched the other vessel, a shape darker than the night reaching out, then angled slightly to avoid impact.

Ainslie murmured, "They saw us."

Jethro pushed past him. "*Heard* us."

There were masts now, loosely brailed sails, and the smell of fuel. Voices too, figures hurrying toward the point of contact.

The machine-guns moved with them, and the Oerlikons. No chances even now. *Especially now.*

Spiers was somewhere below the bridge, by the port torpedo, voice crisp and unhurried.

There was hardly any impact, but for a few long moments the two ill-matched hulls swayed together.

Kearton turned from the side as Jethro called out, "To our next rendezvous!"

Leading Seaman Dawson shouted, "All clear, sir!"

The other vagrants had quit the wardroom with their lethal luggage, or if not, it was too late for them now.

Kearton raised his binoculars, but the other vessel, the spectre, had already disappeared. As if he had imagined it.

"Standing by, sir! When you're ready."

He heard Ainslie stagger against something and the clink of his makeshift satchel, in which he carried dividers and parallel rulers, plus a clip of sharpened pencils. In case someone was tempted to 'borrow' them, as he put it.

Pleased, relieved that his part of the rendezvous had gone without a hitch. Now the return to base, in time for a proper breakfast. Or another air raid.

Kearton lowered the binoculars, but kept them inside his coat.

"Not yet, Pilot. Give them time to get clear."

That would bring a few curses. The motion, if anything, was

getting worse. He was fortunate that he had never yet suffered from seasickness. He heard someone groaning, and tried to close his mind to it. There was always a first time.

He sensed that Spiers had returned to the bridge, the white scarf he usually wore on watch rising and falling against the screen with each roll.

"All quiet?"

Spiers might have been grinning. "Some of them are moaning, sir. Much longer?"

Like Ainslie, he was eager to move, and saw no point in prolonging their discomfort. In the engineroom it would be ten times worse.

Some of them are moaning. He could imagine it. *The Skipper's enjoying himself. Making his part seem important, and never mind the lads!*

Like those other times in the Channel and North Sea. The moments of waiting. Watching and listening for the slightest sign, which could blur the distinction between victor and victim.

He stared at the sky, saw a few tiny stars, but only for a minute. If only . . . He touched the side, running with spray like rain. Back to Malta. Maybe there would be new orders waiting. Anything was better than this.

Or was it Garrick's way of testing him?

"Able Seaman Baldwin requests permission to go below, sir."

Turnbull snapped, "Weak stomach, eh?"

Kearton stared past him, tense, knowing there was no mistake. Turnbull had returned to the wheel, head cocked, sharing it. Nothing you could describe afterwards. There was never time.

"Engineroom stand by! All guns *ready*!"

He was at the compass, but seeing the chart in his mind. Like that last time, with Jethro's body odour at his elbow, but all the while hearing the new sound. Steady, unhurried. Perhaps knowing their victim.

63

Spiers said, "Two of them. Due north of us. Closing."

Not minesweepers or routine enemy patrol vessels, not out here. These were under orders. *Like us.*

Kearton cupped his hands behind his ears, hearing them, feeling them. A different, sharper beat: not E-Boats this time. Like a voice from the past.

"Now!" Mere seconds, then the bridge shook to the sudden burst of power beneath them. "Full ahead!" He groped for the binoculars and steadied them across the screen.

"Starboard fifteen! *Steady!*"

He saw the tiny feathers of spray taking shape in the powerful lenses, like leaping fish: the bow waves of the other vessels. Caught unaware, but not entirely. Some flashes, a machine-gun, but all sound drowned by the Packards as they worked up to full speed.

"Open fire!"

The enemy must still have believed Jethro's schooner was making a last stand. Seconds later a star-shell exploded between the converging craft, and in the searing light all pretence was gone.

"Hard a-port!" Kearton felt the deck lean over, watching the two-pounder shells ripping across the leading craft like hammers of hell. The twin Oerlikons had been brought to bear with their sudden, sweeping turn, and flames were ripping from the low bridge. There was a single, muffled explosion.

He saw the tracer rising and cutting through the smoke, now plunging down and tearing across the water, glaring bright in the last of the drifting flare.

"Shift target!" He felt his fists, clenched like steel as some of the shots thudded against the hull. Another explosion, deep down, then part of the other vessel's bows like a black arrowhead against the glare, and more flames, falling astern as they swung toward the second. The machine-guns on the bridge wing opened fire again, and stopped, and Kearton could hear the gunner yelling like a madman, his fury drowned as the guns responded. Must have jammed . . . Nothing mattered but the flashes on the remaining craft. Hit badly, she was turning away, one gun still firing through the smoke.

"Cease firing!"

One of the men had to be punched in the shoulder to make him understand.

"Half ahead!"

Like a curtain falling, they were suddenly in darkness again. Pieces of wreckage bumped alongside and then vanished astern. No fire, no explosions. Only the stench remained.

Kearton licked his dry lips.

"Course and speed, Pilot." He did not wait for a response. "Report damage and casualties."

"Engineroom, no damage, sir." A pause, recovering. "Chief says it was bloody noisy!"

Someone even laughed.

He stood at Turnbull's shoulder and felt the hull respond to helm and thrust, heard voices calling out to Spiers as he made his way aft, spent ammunition rattling underfoot. But all he could grasp was the nearness of disaster. Instinct, experience, luck? Some things never left you. Like the sound of a particular engine at sea.

His first boat in Coastal Forces had been a small Vosper M.T.B., lively and fast, and like some of the early boats powered by fault-free Isotta-Franschini petrol engines, before Italy had allied itself with Hitler. He had never forgotten the excitement of those sorties, on exercise and then in deadly earnest. Or that same pitch of the engines, heard less than an hour ago.

Ainslie said, "Course to steer, South-seventy-East. Fourteen knots." He faltered and had to clear his throat; his first taste of close action had just hit him.

Turnbull eased the spokes and glanced at the compass.

"Steady she goes, sir." Half to himself. "That made 'em jump!"

Kearton listened to the engines, level and unhurried. No emergency pumps, or even the sound of gear being moved to uncover serious damage. A few bullet scars. Jethro and his men would have heard the gunfire and probably seen the flashes, and known how close it had been. Coincidence or part of a plan, but their old schooner would have stood no chance at all.

Ainslie said, "Here's Number One. He was quick."

Spiers brushed by him and said, "One casualty, I'm afraid. Ordinary Seamen Irwin." He was shaking his head, and the white scarf had come undone across his coat. "Couldn't have felt much. Probably a ricochet."

Kearton said, "Take over. I'll go down."

"There's no need, sir." The movement might have been a shrug. "He's by the Oerlikons." He stood aside for Kearton and added, "No damage we can't handle."

Kearton jumped down to the deck, the words still in his ears. *Not worth a man's life* was nearer the truth.

There were a few shapes by the Oerlikons, others, peering from their stations, melting away as he approached.

Leading Seaman Dawson's voice was gruff and unusually patient.

"You've made yer point, Larry— now stow it, eh? It 'appens and you accepts it in this job, or you goes under yerself."

Another voice, younger. "But we'd done what we came to do— we were clear and out of it! It was the Skipper's idea . . ."

Dawson, alone now, loomed out of the darkness.

"Sorry about that, sir. 'E'll shape up."

Kearton steadied himself against the gunshield. He could feel the heat from the barrels, smell the concentrated firing.

He looked down at the body, flat on its back, face toward the sky. Except that there was no face.

Dawson was dragging some canvas to cover him. "They was mates, y' see, sir— wingers. It don't do to get too close, not in my book."

Kearton walked to the guardrail and stared at the water alongside. Black, like molten glass. Their first death.

He recalled his own first commanding officer. The first time they had been in action together, and its aftermath.

Never try to explain. It's out of your hands. But had he really believed that? He had been killed three weeks later. The question remained.

A hatch clicked open and the heat from the engineroom was like an embrace. Without seeing him, he knew it was Laidlaw.

"Tell your little team, Chief, many thanks. It must have been warm work down there."

"Up top too, I'd say, sir." He stretched his arms and sighed. "I'll pass the word. It goes both ways, ye know."

The hatch closed.

Kearton tugged off his cap and felt the spray on his face and lips. In another hour he would have to make a brief, coded signal. Someone would rouse Garrick from his bed to read it, if he ever slept.

Mission completed.

He heard voices; somebody was bringing a fanny of something hot. Tea, soup, coffee, it didn't matter.

Never try to explain. The signal had to be enough.

After the open bridge the chartroom felt humid and stale, and even here the air tasted of gunsmoke.

Ainslie leaned both elbows on the chart table and tried to focus on the patch of light across his pencilled lines and calculations, although he knew them by heart. Whenever he moved his head to scribble a note or identify some new sound he could feel the stubble of his new beard rasp and catch against his sweater, and remembered Number One's sarcasm. He rubbed his eyes. It seemed so long ago. Everything did, except the brutal intensity of action.

He felt the table press against him and had to shake himself to recover his balance. If he fell into bed, he thought, he could sleep for a week. He stifled a yawn. If only that were true . . .

He could smell the mug of soup where someone had wedged it behind a fire extinguisher.

"This'll warm the cockles, sir!" and he had gone away, humming to himself. The soup would be cold by now.

He took another deep breath. It was over, and he had come through it unscathed. Until now, when he had time to relive it.

He stared at the chart, remembering Kearton's hand on his shoulder as he had reported their estimated time of arrival at Malta. Had it been so easy? And the smile. Genuine. After the recognition of danger, the instant decision. *Could I ever be like that?*

He flinched, the change of air a warning as the light dimmed and a door slid open and shut in a single movement. Just for a second he was reminded of their passenger, Jethro, his confidence and patience as they had discussed the specifics of the rendezvous. But it was a seaman named Glover, one of the two-pounder's crew. His eye had been pressed to the sight, his hands on the firing trigger, when the enemy vessel had exploded.

He said, "Jimmy th— er, first lieutenant's sent me to fetch a flag." He was groping in the shadows. "This one." He straightened up and looked at the chart. "What time we gettin' in, sir?"

"Morning watch. We'll have to take our turn."

Was Spiers really so unmoved? The flag was to cover the dead man when they entered harbour.

Glover said, "Might get a run ashore, sir. Few jars an' a bit of what you fancy'll do wonders, eh?" He went out with the flag over his shoulder.

Ainslie leaned across the chart table again. Strangely, he

wanted to laugh. But it had been a close thing.

On the deck below the chartroom, in the box-like W/T office, Telegraphist Philip Weston heard the clatter of crockery and somebody swearing. He had already felt the pressure of the hard swivel seat against his spine as the helm went over, and the engines' vibration increased once more. Maybe on the final run into Malta.

He glanced at his logbook and the signal pad that were always within easy reach, no matter what was happening above or around this little refuge, even during the brief, recent action. The hull quivering and thudding to the crack and rattle of machine-guns, then the heavier bark of the two-pounder overhead. Bullets hitting the side; above the din of engines it had seemed insignificant. He stared up at a tightly sealed scuttle. But enough to kill a man. A face at the mess table. A voice you could always put a name to. They would get a replacement. They should all be used to it by now.

He ran his fingers through his hair, which was fair like Ainslie's. Some of the sailors were making ribald jokes about his beard; even Number One had been heard saying something disparaging. He would.

He lifted the cover of the log and saw the carefully printed signals. Important, possibly vital. There was one other telegraphist, and they worked watch-and-watch, four hours on, four off, hardly meeting except when they changed over. They did not carry visual signalmen, bunting-tossers, among their small complement, so they were always busy either here or up on the bridge.

He frowned, thinking of Ainslie. Easy to converse with, always ready to offer an opinion or ask a question, unlike a lot of officers he could have named. Ainslie was about his own age, and probably came from a similar background. Safe and predictable, until the war.

Weston had volunteered for the navy without waiting to be conscripted. It had been like a door opening, and he had taken to the new life with surprising ease: the drills and the discipline, the camaraderie as well as the hard knocks, even the occasional jibes about his 'posh' accent. He was accepted.

He had served aboard a small sloop on convoy escort duty, as his first ship. When he had been told he had been listed as a candidate for a commission in the R.N.V.R., there had been a lot of handshakes and slaps on the back. *We'll have to salute you next time we meet!* Or, *he's off to join the pigs down aft!*

Ainslie, even Spiers, must have gone through all that.

But for him it had gone no further. Instead, he had been recommended for a telegraphist's course ashore.

His home was in Southampton and he had been given leave to go there following an air raid, in which his father had been injured and the house partially demolished. And his friendly, jovial uncle had been killed.

Uncle Frank. A big, outspoken man who always seemed to put everyone else in the shadows. Like those rare occasions when his nephew had seen him in his black shirt and shining boots, marching down to the docks to sell copies of *Action*, Sir Oswald Moseley's Fascist newssheet.

His mother had sobbed, "Frank was *never* a Nazi! He loved this country! Proud of it!"

His father had had to answer some questions, too, but nothing had been said to his only son in the navy.

Weston had seen his parents become old in so short a time. He could still remember his father's words after the funeral.

"Frank was always pro-British— he fought on the Somme in the last war!" He had added bitterly, "He was anti-Jewish! So what?"

His recommendation for a commission had not been repeated. Nor would it. *So what?*

70

He felt the point of the lead break on the signal pad; he had been pressing it with the force of his anger. Again he thought of Ainslie, and reached for a fresh pencil.

In Coastal Forces, they said it was different. A chance came and you seized it.

A light began to blink across the bench, and he readjusted his headphones immediately.

Aloud he murmured, "Ready when you are, damn you!"

Uncle Frank would have approved of that.

Never give up.

Kearton stood on a grating and shaded his eyes to watch the pilot cutter as she altered course slightly to starboard: it was the same cutter which had greeted them on their arrival here, such a short time ago. He felt as if he had been on his feet for days.

The final approach had been delayed. Orders: no explanation. There had been another air raid, a quick hit-and-run attack, met by heavy anti-aircraft fire. No massive explosions like before, but patches of scarlet against the dark sky, incendiaries scattered at random, keeping the defenders on the move. Not that there could be much left to burn.

They were ordered to take up different moorings this time. Again, no explanation. Hence the pilot boat.

It was a bright morning, the sun hard on the eye but free of smoke, like a welcome.

The new moorings were not at Grand Harbour, but in Marsumascetto Creek, just to the west of it. Fort St Elmo to port this time, imposing as ever, but the bomb scars very visible in the glare. It was early, but there seemed to be plenty of people about, some standing on the spit of land beneath the fort. Children, too, waving and probably cheering, their voices drowned by the throwback from the Chief's engines.

The wheel moved easily in Turnbull's hands, his eyes, like Kearton's, on the pilot boat as she turned toward another creek, a jetty and some floating catwalks. Beyond them was a line of sandstone buildings, some bombed and windowless, but obviously occupied.

Deeper water here, and no wrecks half-submerged to remind them of the siege and the price.

Someone gave a cheer and Kearton saw the other two M.T.B.s for the first time.

He heard Leading Seaman Dawson's thick voice below the bridge.

"Fo'c'sle party, fall in! Jump about! Rest of you, off the deck *now*!"

The pilot was heading back toward open water. A salute this time, but no witty signals. The bundle covered by the flag spoke for them all.

He walked to the rear of the bridge and watched the houses, imagining them clean and mellow in the sunlight. How it must have been, and one day might be again.

He realized that there was a submarine lying alongside one of the long catwalks, her ensign lifting in the warm breeze. Without it, she seemed little different from the photos in the recognition booklets. *Know your enemy* . . .

He looked at the people by the jetty. Uniforms mostly, a working party in overalls. No redcaps this time, but two men in white coats with a trolley. The ambulance would be up there somewhere on the road.

"Port fifteen! Slow astern port, stop starboard."

He watched the jetty, the narrowing strip of water, the first heaving line being thrown and deftly caught.

"Stop engines. Midships." The squeak against the fenders, old motor tyres. And they were alongside.

He saw an officer who seemed vaguely familiar hurrying along the jetty, and he recognized the man who had brought Jethro and his 'specialists' aboard, and then scuttled away as if glad to be rid of them and the lethal tools of their trade.

Spiers was turning from the guardrails to catch his eye and signal. *Alongside and secure.*

In a few minutes the deck would be crowded. Refuel without delay; base engineers to see that the Chief had no defects to report. Instructions concerning the new moorings. He saw the men in white coats coming aboard, Dawson ready to lend a hand.

They could all wait.

He climbed down from the bridge, and knew Turnbull was watching him. He understood: some might not. Even the boat was still.

"Attention on the upper deck! Off caps!"

Ordinary Seaman Irwin was going ashore.

He saluted.

Surprise, or Threat?

A petty officer held the door open and gestured toward some chairs.

"If you wait here, sir, Captain Garrick will be free shortly." He glanced at Kearton, assessing his rank, and perhaps his appearance, without seeming to move his eyes. "He does know you're here."

He strode to a window and attempted to prise it open, but it refused to move. There was tape pasted across the glass as protection against blast, but, less understandably, also a strong smell of fresh paint.

"Shouldn't be much longer, sir."

Kearton waited for the door to close and walked to the window. A courtyard, or perhaps it had once been a private garden. Stone benches, and a circular pond, now empty. And the usual red arrows pointing the way to the nearest shelters. Like the hospital . . .

He did not look at the chairs; if he sat down now it would finish him. The airless room and the smell of paint were bad enough. And someone hammering, deep down, beneath his feet. Part of the cave-like system of tunnels encountered on his previous visit.

He swallowed hard. Anything was better than returning to that. There had been two air raid warnings since they had come alongside, but no untoward activity or gunfire. Or he had been too drained to notice it.

There were voices in the adjoining room, more animated now. Preparing to leave.

The lieutenant, one of Garrick's aides, had finally told them why their mooring had been delayed. A destroyer, H.M.S. *Java*, had been towed from the harbour to be deliberately scuttled, where she could pose no further risk to other traffic. *Java* had been forced to go into dock for urgent repairs after being dive-bombed while escorting supply vessels to Malta. She had been damaged yet again in another air raid while still in dock, irreparably this time, and towed into deeper water to sink. Still dangerous to other ships, she had been raised once more for her final passage. Kearton had heard several similar stories, when there had been no real chance from the moment those bomb-doors had opened.

And *Java*'s captain, if he had lived to see this morning: what must he have been thinking?

He pulled himself together; the voices were louder, more jovial, the door opening. The other door as well, and somehow it reminded him of something his mother used to say when people seemed overeager to be rid of visitors. *All ready with dustpan and brush!*

Two army officers, one a brigadier with a bushy moustache and the loud voice. "We can't let grass grow under our feet, eh?" He shot Kearton a brief look. "Or it'll be growing over our graves!"

He seemed to think it was amusing.

Garrick came to meet him and offered his crushing handshake.

"Thank God that's over! I sometimes wonder . . ." He was leading the way into the other room. "Thought of you sitting out there, probably wondering why you'd bothered to make an appearance!"

75

He waved him to a chair. "We'll leave the door open. Let the air clear." The familiar grin. "In more ways than one!"

The room was full of smoke, and the aroma of a cigar. Here, too, the window was sealed.

Garrick must have seen his eyes. "You know what the old Jacks say about the navy? If it moves, salute it! If it doesn't, paint it!" And he laughed.

He sat down with his back to the window and plucked at his shirt impatiently. "The Chief of Staff is here on a flying visit—only a short one, thank God, but he likes everything pusser, war or no war!"

Kearton had noticed the smart jacket with its gold lace and medal ribbons draped across another chair, unlike Garrick's previous informal rig.

"You did well, Bob. Shan't know the end results for a while, but you almost certainly saved the day." He smiled. "You must be pleased," and barely paused for a reply. "I heard about your casualty. Could have been much worse, but I don't need to tell you that." He reached out for a packet of cigarettes and clicked his lighter. "You could have put the poor chap over the side." He blew out a stream of smoke. "Not much spare burial space at present."

Kearton found that he could relax, unwind for the first time since he had stepped ashore.

It was not an act, a pretence. This was the real Dick Garrick. Testing him. Like that first meeting.

He said, "I'm told that we're on stand-by, sir."

"Yes. Your lads won't like it, but it's what they're here for. We're getting a fourth boat in a day or so— things are moving at last." His back was to the window and against the light it was impossible to see his expression. "There's a canteen of sorts attached to this place. They'll have to make do with that." He picked a shred of tobacco off his lower lip. "Don't want any of them spending their free time in the Gut catching a dose of something unpleasant, when we need them for sea duty!" He laughed shortly. "And yes, there are still one or two brothels open for business, bombing or no bombing!"

He was on his feet suddenly, swinging round toward the filtered sunlight.

"We've got some good men. And given half a chance . . ." He broke off, and snapped, "I told you I was not to be disturbed!"

It was the same petty officer. He stood his ground, perhaps used to Garrick's changes of mood.

"You said I was to remind you, sir."

Garrick looked at his watch. "Bang on time," and he smiled. "Sorry, Yeo. One of those days."

He dragged his jacket from the chair and slipped into it. "I'll contact you tomorrow. I'll bet you need some sleep, otherwise . . ." He was taking his cap from the top of a filing cabinet. "You did damned well. Knew you would. I'll walk with you to the gate and see you over the side."

Just doing his job. Discussions with the loud-voiced brigadier and his companion. Now no doubt another session with the visiting Chief of Staff. The bar would be open.

Garrick nodded to the petty officer.

"A replacement for the dead rating— John Irwin, right? He'll be reporting aboard, forenoon tomorrow."

Easy, almost matter-of-fact. Even remembering the dead seaman's first name. No wonder he always made such a memorable splash in the press whenever he was given the opportunity.

He realized that Garrick had halted on the stairs. *I must be half asleep.*

Garrick said, "What's this? You're a bit off your usual stamping-ground, aren't you?"

A woman's voice. Kearton saw her on the stairway, answering, but looking straight at him. The voice, too, was just as he remembered it.

"I was told it was all right, Captain Garrick. I heard he was here . . ." She paused as Garrick exclaimed, "So much for security!" He grinned. "Didn't realize you knew each other."

She lifted her chin. Like that day near the blitzed cellar, and the Maltese child in tears.

"We've met." She waited for them to join her, and held out a small package to Kearton. "Not perfect, I'm afraid. Best I could do."

His handkerchief. He could still see it, crumpled and bloody in her hand. Her anger and despair, and something stronger.

"Thank you. I never expected . . ."

Someone called from the top of the stairs and Garrick stared up, annoyed at the interruption. "Tell them I've already left!" More voices, and he retorted, "Oh, very well, damn it. But I can only spare a minute!" He ran lightly up the stairs and called back over his shoulder, "We'll talk again, Bob. Very soon." He paused, looking down. "Mrs Howard will take care of you!"

She ignored him, and said to Kearton, "I knew you were back. They said you'd been in action. I wanted to give you this." She shook her head, the dark hair catching the light. Not like that other time, the dust and sand. The anger . . .

She was wearing a plain khaki shirt and matching slacks. No Red Cross or any insignia.

She smiled, for the first time.

"You're staring again," and she held up her hand. "No, *I'm* the one to apologize."

She led the way along a passage, where men were removing old bricks from a demolished wall.

"It's getting like a village around here. Secrecy doesn't mean very much."

He wanted to stop, to look at her. Instead he kept walking, matching his pace to hers.

"Do you work here, at the base?"

She was taller than he remembered; about his own age,

maybe younger . . . The eyes he could recall without effort. Very dark, but without the hostility now.

"Part time." She might have shrugged. "Civil Defense, and helping to rehouse those cast adrift after the raids." Surprisingly, she laughed. "Oh, that's very nautical of me! I've been working with the navy too long."

The gates were in sight, and beyond them the steps down to the pier. She had made her gesture. He had not expected to see her again.

He said, "Where we last met. You live there all the time?"

She stopped and looked out at the first gleam of sunlight on the water.

"Our home is over in Sliema, but there are refugees there, too." She pushed some hair from her forehead. "The bombing never stops."

Perhaps Garrick had been warning him. Or had ideas of his own?

Our home in Sliema. That was plain enough.

He saw a sailor sitting on a low wall above the steps, then he got up, so casually that it was obvious.

Skipper's on his way!

He faced her. "It was good of you to come." He touched his pocket. "To bring this to me. To care."

She looked at him directly. "I owed that to you. It was a bad day, for a lot of people."

They were at the gates. It was over. It had not even begun.

He held out his hand and she took it, probably relieved to be going.

He said, "I hoped we might bump into each other again. When neither of us was on duty."

He felt her hand stiffen.

"Before you leave, you mean? Get sent somewhere else? You must be accustomed to that."

"I didn't mean that."

She removed her hand gently, as if to brush something from her sleeve.

"D'you think that would be wise? I said it was like a village. Remember?" She half turned. More voices. Intruders. "I may be away. But if it helps, you could leave a message."

He reached out and took her hand again, expecting her to pull it away. She stood looking down at it, not at him.

"I'll ask for Mrs Howard, shall I?"

She stepped back, and waved to somebody who was hurrying toward the gates, but her eyes returned to his.

"Glynis. That'll find me."

He watched her cross the road, afraid of losing something. But she did not look back. Perhaps she dared not.

Turnbull seized the back of a chair and nodded to one of the soldiers who had just vacated the table.

"Thanks, chum."

The soldier, a sergeant, grinned.

"Yeah, just like the Ritz!"

Laidlaw joined him and set down his glass between the puddles of spilled beer.

"Give me the NAAFI any day." He looked around. "Never thought I'd ever say that!"

The 'canteen', as it was optimistically labelled, was gaunt and high-ceilinged, with a long counter across one end and barrels mounted on trestles behind, out of reach. It had been a gymnasium at one time: there were parallel bars and a vaulting-horse stacked in a corner, and climbing ropes in a tangled heap nearby. Turnbull lifted his glass and saw a punch-bag too, standing quite alone. Someone had painted a face on it, and what had started off as a name. He noticed that some of the soldiers threw a punch at it when they passed. It was one way of letting off steam.

"Cheers, Jock." It was better than nothing. But not much.

He stared around. If this was reserved for N.C.O.s, what did the rest have to put up with?

But the place was crowded, and nearly all were in khaki. Just a handful of petty officers, H.Q. staff by the look of them, he thought. You could always tell.

Above the din of voices there was music playing, jazz when he could hear a snatch of it, interrupted from time to time by names or units being called over a tannoy.

There were sandbags along one wall, floor to ceiling, and fire extinguishers as well. In case anyone needed reminding.

A group of soldiers were playing cards at one table, oblivious to the noise around them, and the unmoving pall of cigarette smoke. Royal Artillery badges, for the most part: there seemed to be guns everywhere, Turnbull had noticed, even mobile ones just outside these buildings. Not very far from their new moorings. So much for getting any sleep . . .

Laidlaw said, "So we're on stand-by again," and drank. "I've just fuelled up, so we're not going to be dragging our feet for long." He glanced at him. "The Skipper— is he bothered? You know him better than anyone."

Turnbull shifted his glass on the table. The beer was warm. Flat. They should have stayed aboard, down aft in their own mess, had a few hoarded tots and put up with the stench of petrol from the Chief's refilled tanks.

He said slowly, "Out on his feet, I'd think. He's been with the Big White Chief, then he saw the two other skippers. He was even finding time to write to poor Irwin's folks, though God knows when they'll get that." He leaned back. "Rather him than me!"

Laidlaw said, "I'll get a couple more drinks. Then we'd better make our way back for something a wee bit stronger."

Turnbull took out a packet of cigarettes. He was trying to give them up.

He lit one, considering Laidlaw's question. Maybe he was

right about knowing Kearton better than anybody. It happened in this outfit, if you were lucky. But you never knew when *it* could happen. Like Irwin, and all those others.

Like this last time. The sound of engines tearing at your nerves, knowing it was real. It was now.

Is he bothered?

He rubbed his eyes. He had gone ashore this afternoon to collect some information about transport from the Master-at-Arms' lobby by the gates, and he had seen the skipper with the dark-haired woman. Walking and chatting like old friends. But how could that be? And he had seen her hold her left hand to her eyes to shield them from the sun, and thought he caught the glint of gold on her finger. That was trouble in any language.

"Any one sittin' 'ere, mate?"

Turnbull saw Laidlaw returning with two full glasses.

The soldier, a corporal, moved away. "Sorry, mate." Then he saw the packet of cigarettes. "Duty-frees, eh? All right for some!"

Laidlaw put the glasses down and shook some spilled beer from his hand.

"I'll lay odds the Skipper is doing better than this!"

They both laughed, and Turnbull was suddenly glad that what he had seen would remain a secret.

There was probably nothing to it. He reached for his glass. *Bloody good luck to him anyway.*

The glass hit the table, beer slopping against the duty-frees, and the canteen was half empty. The familiar alarm was sounding loud and clear over the music, and this time there seemed to be another, shriller note. A double emergency.

He saw Laidlaw slam down his glass and wipe his mouth with the back of his hand. The glass, like the canteen, was empty.

"Let's move it, Harry! I think we've got visitors!"

Then they were both running.

It was coming to a stark and terrible climax. Worse than before, worse than ever, because of the utter silence. There should be voices, a scream, before the explosion. The mine was still there, closer now, sometimes within reach. He was drowning.

Kearton rolled on to his side and stared into the light, for a few seconds fighting the shadows.

"Sorry, Skipper— it's six o'clock. You told me to call you."

It had been Ainslie's hand which had broken the dream.

The boat was quiet and still, without even the nudge of the moorings or the improvised pier.

He had his feet on the deck, beside the boots which were always close by, ready for any emergency. Three hours since it had ended. It seemed longer. As if he had been in his bunk for days.

Ainslie was saying brightly, "I've got someone busy in the galley. There'll be something to drink in half a mo'." It was a favourite expression of his. "D'you think we'll be on the move again soon, sir?"

Kearton stood up and stretched his arms until his fingers brushed the deckhead, his thoughts falling into order.

"I have to visit Operations at midday. Maybe Captain Garrick will be better informed by then." He was probably still sleeping off the Chief of Staff's visit.

Ainslie snapped his fingers.

"*Sorry*, Skipper, I almost forgot. Ops sent word by messenger. You'll have a driver this time. Make it a little easier, especially after the last raid . . . Just as well we changed our moorings, from the sound of it."

Kearton was halfway to the cupboard where he kept his shaving gear when the casual remark hit him like a fist.

He had been here, in this cabin, when the alarm had sounded. Some of the hands had been ashore in the canteen, and there had been plenty of ripe curses when they had hurriedly and noisily returned aboard, not least from those who had been trying to catch up on their sleep.

There had been the usual *crump, crump, crump* of the heavier anti-aircraft guns, but only a few louder explosions.

"Not even worth uncoverin' guns!" someone had said.

Kearton said, "Go ashore for me, will you? See the Officer of the Day and find out about that raid. Close to our last moorings, you said? Tell him I need to know." He tried to lighten it. "As your senior officer!"

Ainslie was going.

"Right away, Skipper." He grinned. "*Sir!*"

Kearton walked to the side and unclipped one of the deadlights. Grey, but it would be daylight very soon. He thought of the matters demanding his attention. A new hand joining their small company, the replacement for Irwin. The burial arrangements to be confirmed. Garrick had said a fourth boat would be joining their flotilla very shortly. It could take weeks, or it might be today.

He wanted to shake himself. Had that brief action left such a mark on him? Or, like the dream, was it only a reminder of something unresolved?

He recalled his visit to the two other boats, the obvious delight, even envy, at 992's success. And far too many drinks. That was always the excuse.

He had finished shaving by the time Ainslie returned. In the early light, his beard appeared, finally, to have established itself.

He said, "The O.O.D. couldn't tell me much. Or wouldn't. Said it was just a couple of bombs. The others fell in the drink. Best I could do, sir."

Kearton looked into the small mirror. His hand was steady enough; he had not even nicked himself.

"When Number One does his rounds, I'll be going with him." But the door had shut, and he could hear Ainslie's footsteps on the deck overhead.

For their sakes? Or for mine?

He heard a sudden gust of laughter coming from the messdeck, then more, until someone tried to quell it, probably because it was so near this cabin.

He reached for his jacket. It had answered his question.

The car arrived earlier than expected. Whether this was because of the state of the roads, or the vehicle itself, was not explained. An old Wolseley, commandeered at the beginning of the seige, it had seen better days. It looked about the same vintage as Kearton's beloved Triumph.

The driver, a Royal Marine, seemed confident, even suggesting his passenger sit 'up front' for a better view. Which was just as well, as the rear seats were cluttered with a Thompson submachine-gun, several magazines of ammunition, and the marine's steel helmet.

"Just to be on the safe side," he had remarked cheerfully.

It was not far to their original mooring place in Grand Harbour, nothing was far in Malta, but it seemed to take forever. And yet, despite the roughly repaired roads and avenues of bombed or abandoned buildings, there were people everywhere. They had no choice: between raids and warnings of raids, life had to go on.

They passed a group of workmen clearing wreckage, which had half buried a local bus. Two of them waved as they drove by, and the marine responded with a blast of his horn.

"Don't know how they put up with it, poor sods!"

There were several diversions, soldiers putting up new signs, others clearing the way for ambulances.

"Nearly there, sir." The marine braked and changed gear, and swore under his breath as he swerved to avoid a jagged hole in the road.

Kearton leaned forward, steadying himself against the door; he had recognized one of the buildings, or thought he did. It had an elaborate balcony, outwardly unscathed, and he remembered it from that day. The rest was a shambles, gutted houses, their contents piled just clear enough for the car to get through. Brickwork and charred timber, mixed with pathetic pieces of furniture, a doll, a chair with a newspaper wedged against it, as if waiting for someone to return.

More slowly now, crunching over fresh tyre-tracks; more uniforms at a checkpoint. The road was covered with sand, like a beach.

All that remained of the triple-sandbagged entrance.

Like hearing her voice that day. Defiant. *I am home.*

"Far as I can manage, sir."

Kearton stood beside the car. Had something been trying to warn him?

The driver added helpfully, "Bit earlier than I thought. You never know, in this place."

"Thanks." He touched his cap. "Maybe you'll be taking me back."

He did not hear him reply.

He walked past piled debris, his shoe catching on a strand of barbed wire, and more sand.

A direct hit. Even the smell was the same. London, Portsmouth, Valletta.

He saw a low wall, massively built, a gate blasted from its hinges. Part of a building still standing, curtains flapping from windows like torn flags.

"Just a minute! Nobody's allowed in there!"

It was the same lieutenant, Garrick's aide, less smart and composed now, a tear in one sleeve, a strip of plaster across his cheek. But he tried to smile.

"Damn sorry, sir. You took me by surprise." He shrugged, and winced. "Been rather busy around the old place!"

Kearton gripped his hand. It was shaking.

"I'm glad you're OK." He looked at the house; the curtains were suddenly still. "Were there many casualties?"

The lieutenant was staring around, although his eyes were blank.

"Some. I'm not too sure."

He had had enough. Seen enough, done enough. And Kearton still did not know his name.

"Ah, *here* we are, sir!"

Like turning the clock back. The white coat, the patient smile. Why did they all speak like that?

The lieutenant said nothing, and was staring at Kearton now as if he were a stranger. Kearton watched them go, the medic still chattering as they picked their way over the rubble.

Someone else would come looking for him. Nothing had changed. Even if Garrick were to be replaced, or killed, once the wheels were in motion . . .

He pushed open a door. It was partly jammed, but he heard nothing fall. There was damage enough, and a shaft of dusty sunlight through part of a wall, which had been a room. Another door, but it was jammed or locked. Had she been here when it happened?

He heard brakes, another vehicle crunching to a halt. Voices.

He swung round and stared toward the shaft of sunlight.

She was standing with her back to the light, her face in shadow. Quite still, as if holding her breath.

Then she said, "I hoped it was you. Someone said— someone told me as I arrived." She reached up to push some hair from her eyes. "I was afraid you'd hear about it. That you might worry . . ."

He did not know he had moved, but his arms were around here and her face was against his shoulder, and her voice was muffled. "You *are* here. You came."

He felt her shivering. Then she said, "I wasn't here . . ." and looked up at him, her eyes filling her face. "I was visiting one of our typists— the sick quarters. It was her birthday. Otherwise—"

She did not continue.

He looked past her, at the courtyard garden, half buried under debris which he recognized as part of the roof.

"Where will you go? Are you going to be all right?"

His hand was against her belt; he could feel her skin, her breathing.

She said, "It's all arranged. It's not the first time. I was just hoping . . ." She broke off as his hand touched her spine. "*Don't. Please don't. Someone might . . .*" She had stepped back slightly, her arms at her sides. "I have to go now. I— needed to know." And then, desperately, "I'm not making much sense, am I?"

Another voice.

"I think he's in there, sir."

She reached up and touched his face, his mouth. "Thank you . . . Bob."

She kissed him, and turned away in one movement.

"I'll let you know . . ."

She was gone. It seemed as if the car started immediately.

He strode to the door but another vehicle was already pulling up at the barrier.

Another lieutenant was waiting to guide him to the appropriate department, above or below ground, but he walked blindly, clinging to those last few seconds. She would recognize the risk, the danger.

If this meeting had been scheduled to take place at the new moorings, they might never have met again.

He saw the door marked *STAFF OFFICER OPERATIONS*. The rest was a dream.

The meeting was brief and final. Captain Garrick was elsewhere, but had left no room for doubt.

All three M.T.B.s were required for active duty tomorrow, as stated in his orders. Garrick had even left a pencilled apology "for dragging you halfway across Malta" when he had better things to do.

A car was arranged for his return journey.

Afterwards, he wondered why he had not left immediately. She would not have returned to the damaged house so soon. If at all. *I'll let you know.* He could still hear her. Feel her. He wanted to laugh it off, dismiss it. Like a young subbie in the throes of his first affair.

He walked across the scattered sand to the wall, the pots of brilliant geraniums, and tensed as he saw a woman's shadow stooping and crouching, heard her humming to herself in time with the sweep of a broom.

She looked up, and grinned when she saw him.

"I am Maria. Mrs Howard gone away for two or three days." She shook the broom. "I clear up!" She moved toward the other door, which was now open. No apparent damage here, and a bed with a dustsheet draped over it. Her bed.

Maria stopped sweeping long enough to call, "You watch your feet, sir! Broken glass!" She carried on with her work, still humming.

There were fragments of glass neatly piled on a piece of newspaper. Then he saw a picture frame lying in a wastebasket beside a desk, where it might have fallen or been flung by the blast.

More glass. Something made him hesitate, and then lift the frame into the light.

A photograph, taken on their wedding day. She was all in white, a wide-brimmed hat held loosely in one hand. Very young, with a smile he had never seen. Lovely. A domed building in the background, probably here in Malta.

He tilted the frame to look at the man beside her. A soldier, his rank obscured by the angle of the shot, smiling at her, very relaxed. Older than his dark-haired bride, and somehow familiar . . .

The frame fell back into the basket amongst the broken glass. The humming and the broom stopped together, and he called out something he never remembered as he walked toward the door.

He saw the old Wolseley waiting for him, but he knew that if it had not been there he would have kept walking, going nowhere.

How could he be so certain? The smart, confident army officer or the dishevelled, stinking vagrant they had been told to call Jethro . . . One and the same?

To our next rendezvous.

The driver glanced at him incuriously, and let in the clutch with a jerk.

"Sounds as if there's a flap on, sir."

The car edged out into the road where men who had been digging at wreckage were throwing their tools into a dust-caked van. Until the next time.

He turned in his seat to stare back at the house with its demolished roof. The torn curtains had disappeared.

He felt the car gathering speed.

It was not a dream. But it was over.

6

Don't Look Back

Turnbull stood just inside the cabin, his cap pressed under one arm, the usual clipboard in his hand.

"Just wondered if you've any last-minute mail to go ashore, sir?"

He watched Kearton shutting a drawer, then patting his pockets to make sure he had not forgotten anything. Automatic, without thought: he had done the same. Even now, his head was half turned to pick up the familiar sounds and snatches of conversation that merged with the steady vibration of a generator. *His boat.*

Kearton smiled. "By the time any mail scrapes past the censors, the war'll probably be over!"

Feet thudding overhead, the rasp of a mooring-wire. Spiers was making certain there would be no delays when they were ordered to get under way. A hatch slammed and someone laughed. There was no tension; they seemed impatient to cast off. To get away from the raids and the explosions, when they were helpless onlookers.

Turnbull said, "I got the new hand settled in, sir. Seems a steady sort of chap." It sounded like a question.

Kearton nodded. "Good gunnery rate. He'll be with the Oerlikons." Their eyes met. *Dead man's shoes.* Nothing would be said; it never was. But it would take time. "Able Seaman York."

Turnbull grinned.

"*Yorke*, sir." He shook his clipboard. "With an 'e'!"

They both laughed.

Turnbull heard something and said, "I'm wanted, sir." He jammed on his cap. "No peace for the wicked!"

Kearton buttoned his jacket and stared around the cabin, holding on to these last moments of privacy.

It was still bright enough over the moorings, or had been when he was last on deck. But dusk would be early, and they were leaving in one hour's time.

He sat by the little table and tried to see everything at a distance, as if they were all markers on some Admiralty chart. Two destroyers had weighed and left harbour during the forenoon. A routine patrol, and the M.T.B.s would rendezvous with them tomorrow, and if nothing was reported to be on the move they would return to base. He patted his pockets again. It was never that simple.

He had called a hurried meeting with the other commanding officers, Mostyn of 977, and Stirling the Canadian, of 986. The latter had been forthright about it. "They're expecting a convoy from Gib. Stands out a mile. Malta's running out of everything, that's nothing new. But it's getting tough for Rommel too, finally. Supplies are vital."

Stirling had been in the Mediterranean longer than any of them. Greece, Crete, Tobruk. He had added, "Jerry'll be wise to the convoy. He's got a lot of sympathetic eyes watching from Spain— Algeciras. And you can't hide a bloody convoy!"

Kearton opened a scuttle and peered at the sky. No clouds, no smoke. Holding its breath . . .

He closed the scuttle and screwed down the deadlight. In those few seconds he had smelled the extra fuel which had been brought aboard in drums, as it had on his first passage from Gib. But this was different. The Chief would have to top up his tanks at sea, or cast them adrift at the first hint of trouble. One burst of tracer into a deck-cargo of petrol, and the boat would be an inferno.

He felt the deck move, the squeak of the hull against rubber. Restless. Eager to be on the move again.

He got up from the table and hurried to the door. Feet on the ladder, someone almost out of breath. It was Ainslie. He must have run all the way from the pier.

He saw Kearton.

"Fast as I could, Skipper!" He gestured behind him. "Just saw him! Heading right here, *now*!"

Kearton took his arm and shook it gently.

"Take it easy, Pilot. We're all going to need *you* very soon, so just count to ten and tell me."

Ainslie collected himself.

"Captain Garrick, large as life. No aides, no warning—"

Kearton shook his arm again. "Let's go and see what he has to say, shall we?"

He was surprised that he felt nothing, neither anger nor apprehension. If anything, it was relief.

Garrick, with Spiers close on his heels, strode past the W/T office and into the cabin. He tossed his cap on to the table and looked sharply around at the others.

"Just want a brief word with our S.O. Would have come earlier—" He shrugged. "But I'm here now!"

The door closed and Garrick sat abruptly on a chair, as if a wire had snapped. He looked at the door and said, "Good. Don't want half the fleet listening in, do we?" He leaned back and pulled a hip flash from a pocket. "Won't offer you one, Bob, under the circumstances, but I really do need it."

Kearton put a glass quietly on the table, and saw it half filled from the flask. Scotch, by the smell of it, and not the first one.

Garrick saw his eyes and poured another.

"R.H.I.P., Bob!"

Rank Hath Its Privileges. Rarely heard in Coastal Forces, unless used with contempt.

Garrick looked up as something thudded on the deck above him.

"I keep ramming it home. We need more boats like this one, with range and firepower, even if they're not as fast as we'd like." He pushed the empty glass away. "The Chief of Staff was a good listener, I'll give him that. But by the time he's spilled everything to his lord and master, my troubles will have gone to the bottom of the pile!"

Kearton thought of the men on deck, Spiers and Ainslie. They had all seen Garrick come aboard. Laidlaw and his team of mechanics would also know. This was no time for doubt, uncertainty.

"Is it still on, sir?"

Garrick looked at him, perhaps surprised, but concealed it. He leaned on one elbow and grinned.

"I asked for that!" He was fumbling in a breast pocket. "It's still on, very much so."

He had taken out his cigarette lighter, and clicked it deliberately. "The way things are going, I'll be hard put to fill this soon."

"Are we getting more boats, sir?"

Garrick looked away, as though listening to something.

"They're coming, eventually. As I told C.O.S., so is Christmas!"

He smoked in silence for a minute, and when he spoke again his voice was calmer, almost relaxed.

"Convoys are vital, especially here, more especially now. Axis forces in North Africa are on the defensive. In a few months they'll have their backs to the sea, or be trying to cross it. Their supply line is an artery, and Malta, more than ever, is like a poised dagger. Battered, bloody, and defiant— it's a pity some of their lordships can't see that and act on it!" He was on his feet. "I was a lad at Jutland. I hope I learned something from it. I sometimes wonder . . ."

He tugged down the front of his jacket and flicked something from his sleeve.

"I think the enemy will have a plan to stop or divert this convoy. Probably mines. Just the hint of a new minefield is enough to stop things moving. Malta's been through it several times. The mine is cheap, the torpedo is not, and it's a menace long after it's dropped." He looked down at his cap on the table. "The enemy is working on a new type of mine, to be fitted with a cutting device. If it can be perfected, it will sever the sweep as it cuts the mine adrift. One mine, one sweeper: not acceptable odds on any scoreboard." He looked at Kearton keenly. "In Special Operations we've kept our ears and eyes wide open." He half-turned, still listening. "I must be on my way. Would have come earlier, as I tried to explain to your young pilot." He was reaching for the door. "I'll do all I can." He stepped over the coaming and paused when he saw Leading Seaman Dawson.

"They've not enticed you back into the boxing-ring yet, Dawson? Our loss, but their gain if you go." They laughed; Dawson wheezed something in reply, but Garrick had already walked to the ladder. "I'll see myself over the side, Bob."

He paused on the second step and looked down, framed against the dying sunlight.

"It's . . . important."

Kearton went back to the cabin and stood for a few minutes, waiting for the boat to settle down again. No ceremonial, no bullshit. He pulled open the drawer and reached for his repaired pipe. Beside it was the little package, the clean handkerchief.

Not perfect, I'm afraid. Best I could do.

The tannoy squeaked into life.

"All hands! Hands fall in for leaving harbour!"

Just as suddenly, it was quiet again. He picked up his binoculars and slung them around his neck. The generator had stopped. He should be used to this moment, but they would all be watching him, trying to read something in his face, in his manner, that might reassure them.

He hesitated at the door. The desk drawer was still open.

He picked up the little package and folded it before slipping it into his pocket.

Feet skidded to a halt.

"Standing by on deck, sir!"

He closed the drawer, and walked out of the cabin.

"Thanks. Let's go!"

Lieutenant Toby Ainslie pressed his fist against his mouth to smother the yawn. It was infectious: if you gave into it, everybody would be yawning his head off.

The morning watch, but the sky and sea were still like night, although he could dimly see the outline of the helmsman's duffle coat now, and the faint gleam of the compass. Others he recognized only by where they stood or crouched at their lookout stations and guns, or by an occasional voice.

He felt the bridge sway, with the responding creak of equipment and clink of ammunition.

Eleven hours since they had cast off, and wended their way past the harbour defences and out into open water. An empty sea. But in his mind he could see it like a map: they were soon to enter the narrowest part of the Strait between Cape Bon on the North African coastline and the southwestern tip of Sicily. He gripped the handrail beneath the screen and stared into the darkness. About fifty miles abeam from either side. No wonder the convoys had to take such risks to fight their way through to Malta.

He had heard some of the older hands scoffing about it, men who had served in the English Channel, with both coasts rarely out of sight and the enemy often within range. But at least they had had somewhere to run.

He surrendered to the yawn and listened to the engines. Hard to believe by their muted beat that they were the same ones which had roared into monstrous life, as if nothing could control them. And that it was the same two-pounder, clinging to its target, the smoke tinged with red, like blood.

He moved aft and saw the sky, defined by a pale edge for the first time.

He thought of their last-minute discussions, the skipper and the two other commanding officers answering questions, even joking from time to time, apparently at ease. As if they had all known one another for months.

He saw a surge of spray out on the starboard quarter, and knew the other M.T.B. would be keeping station on the opposite bearing. The arrowhead formation gave the widest arc of vision, and was the best for immediate action.

Someone coughed, either to show he was awake or as a warning to others that something was about to happen.

Spiers was talking to one of the gunners, then Ainslie heard him laugh. That was rare enough these days.

Ainslie felt the beard catch against his sweater. He had been tempted to shave it off: that was what everybody seemed to expect. His mind shifted just as quickly. What about Sarah? His girl. *The* girl . . .

She would laugh, tease him. And then . . .

Somebody nudged against him and he saw a mug of something steaming, balanced beside his hand.

"Sorry, no saucer, sir!" The grin showed in the gloom as he groped his way back to the ladder. Ainslie sipped at the enamel mug. It was badly chipped. He felt his mouth crack into a grin. *No saucer.* Better than any salute.

A door or hatch slammed somewhere beneath him, almost lost in the unbroken tremor of engines. The starboard lookout said, "Skipper's comin' up, sir."

"Nothing wrong with *your* ears, Ellis! I'll have to be careful in future!"

He heard him chuckle. *If only you knew.*

He shivered, but it was not from fear. It was like an uncontrollable excitement, the thrill of being part of it. The motion was more pronounced now, and although he knew it was because of the Strait and the nearness of land, it was as if the boat was coming alive, aware of the new day.

Men were going quietly to their stations without any apparent orders or encouragement, some still chewing on the remains of a hasty mouthful snatched before their small galley had been sealed.

Ainslie thought of other ships he had seen, like the smart cruiser at Gibraltar, the shrill of a bosun's call magnified over the speaker system, or the blare of a bugle and stamping feet. Another world.

He leaned against the flag locker and peered aft once more. He could see the side-deck clearly now, a dark stain where a hose had washed away any petrol spilled when the Chief's mechanics had been topping up the tanks from the extra drums. Much of the sea was still in darkness, but it was more lively, throwing up spray from the props and the bow wave's endless crest.

He unfastened his binoculars and trained them toward the M.T.B. on the starboard quarter, her number, 986, clearly visible on the side. The Canadians had painted a large red maple leaf on the low bridge, so there would be no room for doubt.

He turned as more figures appeared on the bridge: relief for the two lookouts, extra hands for the machine-guns, and, of course, the coxswain.

Turnbull took the wheel and murmured something to the helmsman before reporting, "Cox'n on the wheel, sir. Steady on North-forty-West."

He had been right through the boat, above and below deck with Number One, but he was not even out of breath.

Then he said loudly, "Give the compass a wipe, will you?" Someone reached over with a piece of cloth, and Ainslie saw Kearton, with Spiers close behind him, climbing into the bridge.

Kearton walked to the forepart of the bridge and rested both hands on the rail below the screen.

"All being well, we will rendezvous with the destroyers around noon." He paused, listening to the engines. "Fifteen knots, Pilot? Should be near enough." He glanced at the sky, then astern toward their two consorts. Beyond them the horizon was clear, like the edge of a dam. He faced forward again, and his face was in shadow.

He said, "*Minden* is the senior ship, one of the new M-Class destroyers. Well armed, and she can knock up thirty-six knots or more." He paused again and smiled. "Better warn the Chief."

Turnbull eased the wheel slightly, his eyes on the compass.

"I saw her at Portsmouth when she was first commissioned. I think her paint was still wet!"

Spiers lifted his binoculars and focused on a piece of timber drifting between the boats.

"*Minden* will find *us*. She's got the latest radar. Coastal Forces are right at the end of the queue, as usual . . . The Yanks have even got radar in their P.T. boats!"

Kearton watched the other M.T.B.s taking shape in the early sunlight. But he was still hearing Spiers: curt, almost hostile. They could not afford friction in the boat. None of them could.

He felt the wind in his face, and when he looked up he saw the ensign whipping out from its halliard, fabric tattered from constant use. Unlike the new one which had greeted his arrival on board. But instead, he saw the ragged curtains in the empty windows of the bombed house.

"Pass the word. *Uncover guns*. We will test firing directly. I'll call the others on R/T." He looked over at Spiers. "Radar or not, Number One, we'll be ready."

99

Spiers said, "I'll deal with it myself, sir."

Turnbull heard him drop down the ladder, already calling to the nearest gun crew. It was not the time to interfere. *Keep your mouth shut.*

But he said, "I'll warn the engineroom, sir."

Kearton was already there at the voicepipes and handsets, his message to Laidlaw barely finished when the port-side heavy machine-guns opened fire. Sharp and sharp, then silence.

Turnbull said, "Sorry, sir."

"Stand by!"

He braced himself for the next burst of fire, and tried to concentrate on the quivering compass card.

Even that seemed unimportant as he felt Kearton's hand rest on his shoulder.

"No, 'Swain. *I'm* the one to be sorry."

He swore under his breath and reversed the turn of the wheel to satisfy the compass, although neither was at fault. He saw Kearton standing with young Ainslie, watching as the nearest M.T.B. fired a burst of scarlet tracer directly overhead.

"Cease firing! Clean guns!"

But Turnbull ignored it.

He could not even tell Laidlaw about it. It would have to remain another secret.

Suddenly there was a crash, followed by a metallic clatter, then a burst of ironic cheering that broke into laughter. Someone had dropped a sack of expended cartridge cases on deck abaft the bridge. He could hear Leading Seaman Dawson's hoarse voice shouting to restore order, but to no avail.

He looked across at Kearton, and saw his almost imperceptible nod.

Trust, loyalty, or resignation. But they were ready.

The rendezvous with the two destroyers was both impressive and dramatic. From the first moment when they had been sighted, breaking through the misty haze on the horizon and altering course toward the three M.T.B.s, it seemed only minutes before they were in close company. The senior ship, H.M.S. *Minden*, leaned over as her helm swung her in a tight arc to steer parallel with 992, the hard sun lighting up the sleek hull and dazzle-paint. With her impressive armament and a ship's company of nearly two hundred men, she represented a force to be reckoned with. Her consort, *Bristow*, a smaller Hunt Class destroyer, looked almost frail in comparison.

Kearton watched the giant bow wave, like a frothing moustache as it churned away from the stem and rolled toward them.

"Stand by on deck!"

992 swayed as the wash surged beneath the hull, lifting it like a dinghy while *Minden* lay directly abeam, her shadow almost touching them.

Turnbull moved the wheel a few turns to allow for the upheaval and murmured, "Bloody show-offs!"

Spiers stood beside Kearton and heard the squeak of the destroyer's loud-hailer, and saw the huddle of figures on her bridge. One with oak leaves on his cap, whom he had already seen with the binoculars now hidden inside his coat. He almost smiled, cursing himself for caring what some unknown brass-hat would think about being stared at, not without awe, by the lesser fry. But *Minden* was a fine-looking ship. Her main armament was well sited in three twin turrets, with a full span of torpedo tubes and an array of short-range and automatic weapons that would make any gunnery officer a happy man.

The loud-hailer squeaked again. Someone had carried the handset across the bridge, so that the oak leaves would not have to move.

"Good to have you with us! Bang on time, too!"

Spiers relaxed slightly as another voice muttered, "Thanks, Dad!"

"Take station as ordered. Increase to twenty knots!" Another squeak. "Hope you can keep up!"

Kearton waved his hand toward *Minden*'s bridge, and switched off his own handset. He had heard a few comments about *Minden*'s captain, whose humour was best described as one-sided.

He heard Turnbull snap, "What the *hell* do you think you're up to?"

The unknown offender said sheepishly, "It's the Victory Sign, 'Swain! Mr Churchill does it all the time!"

Turnbull turned to the compass again. "Not like that, he bloody doesn't!" But he agreed with the gesture.

Kearton stared astern and watched the other boats lifting, then settling in *Minden*'s wash. Beyond them the sea was empty, metallic in the glare.

Suppose Garrick and his superiors had changed their minds? Or no further news of an enemy operation was forthcoming? Press on to Gibraltar to assist the convoy escorts? He rubbed his chin with the back of his hand. Time and distance were the real enemies.

The last big convoy to Malta was common talk now, especially on the beseiged island. It had happened about six months ago, and had been, at that time, Malta's last hope of survival. The most spectacular convoy of the war, it had been called: fourteen merchant ships including a giant tanker, nothing by Atlantic standards, most would say. But it had been escorted by a fleet, under the flag of a vice-admiral: two battleships, three carriers, one loaded with Spitfires for Malta, seven cruisers and thirty or more destroyers.

They were calling it Operation *Pedestal* now.

And the enemy had known about it, and of its vital importance. Many warships had been sunk or put out of action after endless attacks from the air, and by U-Boats and E-Boats, German and Italian, from Sardinia and Sicily, to the gates of Malta itself.

Only four merchantmen had reached harbour, and then, a day later, burned, bombed and with her decks partially awash, the real prize, the tanker *Ohio*, had struggled through. He had heard that thousands of people had lined the walls to cheer and weep as she had been towed to safety in Grand Harbour. Her cargo of petrol and kerosene had saved Malta.

He thought of Garrick, clicking his gold cigarette lighter and hinting at another convoy, and the measures that might be used to destroy it.

In these same waters. He shaded his eyes again to watch *Minden* picking up speed, taking the lead.

Spiers joined him by the wheel.

"I've warned the Chief, sir." He hesitated. "Something wrong?"

"Just thinking about the last big convoy. You must have heard all about it, at the time."

Spiers said slowly, "We lost a carrier, two cruisers, a destroyer, as well as half the convoy. Touch and go."

Kearton picked up the new R/T speaker. Then he turned and looked astern.

They'll be watching us.

He realized that Ainslie had reappeared on the bridge, notebook in hand, a pencil between his teeth.

He pressed the button, and it made him recall Laidlaw's surprise and obvious delight when he had told him the code name he was adopting for his role as senior officer.

"All units, this is *Growler*. Increase to twenty knots."

He looked over at Spiers.

"There's just us now, OK?"

Spiers tugged at his white scarf.

"OK by me." He smiled. "*Sir.*"

Kearton had been in the chartroom for about half an hour, but it felt like only a few minutes before the bell-mouthed voicepipe took charge.

"Signal from *Minden*, sir. Aircraft at Green one-six-zero. Closing." Calm, unhurried: no mention of radar. They did not need reminding.

"Coming up!" He snatched his cap from the table and folded Ainslie's notebook before thrusting it inside his jacket. Those neat calculations and the familiar schoolboy handwriting must wait.

Aircraft. It had to be an enemy.

He clipped the door behind him and hurried to the bridge, prepared for the sun and the glittering water, harsher than ever after the dimness of the chartroom. The heavy machine-guns in their little turret were already pointing at the sky, and neither gunner nor loader gave him a glance as he paused on the side-deck to stare astern.

On the bridge it seemed very still. Only the occasional sweep of binoculars, or the shift of the wheel, a patter of spray drifting aft from the bows as the hull settled into the extra knots.

Spiers said, "Nothing yet, sir." His eyes looked sore, from the spray, sun or endless use of the heavy binoculars.

Kearton looked toward the other boats, and heard Spiers add, "Both standing by, sir."

He nodded, and raised his own glasses to peer ahead at *Minden*, stern-on, a faint plume of smoke fanning from her sturdy funnel. Her guns were already moving, tracking an invisible target. The other destroyer was keeping station on *Minden*, her silhouette distorted by glare and haze.

He could feel the steady vibration of the four Packards through the deck, and against the side of the bridge. He pictured the engineroom, confined, hot despite the fans, and always noisy. Laidlaw watching his machinery and listening with his mechanics and stokers, among them the round-faced kid called Rathbone. 'Basil'. Who had once worked at Finlay's Garage on the Kingston by-pass.

"Aircraft, bearing Green one-one-zero, angle of sight four-five! Closing!"

Kearton levelled his glasses, up and across the blurred horizon and a long sliver of cloud, balancing himself with the boat's movement. Almost a part of her.

He heard Spiers say, *"Got you!"* Then he saw it himself.

So deceptively slow, turning now, catching the sun like a flashing signal, heading away.

"Staying well out of range!" Spiers sounded impatient, even disappointed.

"He'll be back." Kearton focused his binoculars on *Minden* again. Her guns were unmoving, trained fore-and-aft; her captain would know the aircraft had not appeared by accident. Not out here. A signal would be on its way, if it wasn't already on somebody's desk. Like pieces on a chequerboard, or a chart in Garrick's Operations room. Not flesh and blood.

"From *Minden*, sir. *Maintain course and speed.*"

"Acknowledge."

He looked at the sky. No aircraft.

Spiers said, "The Chief wants permission to top up his tanks, sir."

Ainslie, recovering his notebook, said, "But this time tomorrow . . ." and broke off. "Sorry, Skipper."

Kearton stared across the glittering water toward the M.T.B. on the starboard quarter, her wake streaming astern like a furrow.

"We turn back, or press on to Gib— is that how you see it, Pilot? I think we'll know sooner than that." Then, "Tell the Chief to carry on." And to Spiers, "Fall out action stations, and open the galley."

It was like pulling some lever and bringing them back to life.

Half to himself, he said, "Our Chief must be a mind-reader."

Spiers stopped on the ladder. "I'll get a couple of hands to swab the deck when they've finished topping up." He was already gesturing to someone, but looked up again, and his voice was only loud enough to carry above the engines. "We're going to fight, then?"

He dropped to the deck without waiting for a reply.

Turnbull stepped down from the wheel and waited while the stand-by helmsman repeated the course and speed before handing over.

"Just keep your eyes on *Minden*, my lad. Don't want to blot our copybook with the brass watching us." He tapped his arm. "And for God's sake drop in at the barber's shop when we get back to base, or they'll think we've got Wrens on board!"

The seaman grinned, while swearing under his breath.

Bloody coxswain. Is that all he can think about?

Turnbull made his way aft. He knew exactly what he thought, what they all thought. Expected . . .

He watched the sea, creaming astern and spreading out to the thrust of the screws. There was a breeze now, but not enough to kill the stench of petrol. Two hands were already hosing down the deck. Jimmy the One was detailing some others to collect the empty mugs from the gun mountings, which were still manned and ready for any more snooping aircraft.

He looked at the sea far astern. Like a desert. Not like all those other times. He unclenched his fist. Who would know, out here? Who would care?

Spiers was stooping beside a winch, and he knew why: it was where young Irwin had died. He thought of Kearton again. That was the real difference between the skipper and Jimmy the One. Kearton had raised hell to get the dead sailor properly taken care of, and to ensure that burial arrangements were completed, because 992 would be at sea when it was carried out. He had heard Spiers remark, "It happens. Tears won't bring him back."

106

In many ways Spiers was a good officer, one to serve and to respect. But that was not always enough.

Spiers saw him and said sharply, "Nothing to do, Cox'n? I'll have to change that!"

Turnbull touched his cap and relaxed a little. That was more like it.

"I just want to be sure everyone knows. . . ." Spiers looked past him. "Ah, there you are, Jay. I'll want you with me to check the starboard tube."

"Done it, sir." He was brushing biscuit crumbs off his chin. "But if you'd like to go through it again?"

Chalk and cheese, Turnbull thought. Laurie Jay was their leading torpedoman, and, next to Dawson, the senior hand on 992's messdeck. Thin and loose-limbed, he was reliable and hard-working, both in the running of the daily routine and his prime concern, the 'tin fish'. Like himself, Jay was a regular, and had been a submariner until his boat had been bombed, depth-charged and sunk by German aircraft off the coast of Norway some eighteen months before. He was not an easy man to know. Friendly enough, but very withdrawn. Another survivor.

When a very young seaman had asked him why he had quit the submarine service, Jay had replied, "Too quiet for my taste." They had left it at that.

Jay came originally from Birmingham, 'Brum', as he called it, about as far as you could be from the sea in England. Turnbull sometimes wondered how he had come to put his name down for the Andrew in the first place.

Jay was holding up a pair of pliers now.

"I've got to drop into the W/T office, sir. Something needs fixing." He did not explain. Torpedomen were expected to be able to repair almost anything, from a lethal detonator to a reading-light in the chartroom.

Spiers grunted.

"Report to me when you've finished." He looked at his watch. "And don't make a meal of it!"

He strode away.

Turnbull said, "He's got a lot on his plate at the moment."

Jay smiled coldly. "Tough!"

A figure hurried past an engineroom ventilator, heading for the bridge, and Turnbull was glad of the interruption without knowing why.

"Must be a flap on to make young Sparks shift like that."

Jay clicked the pliers in his hand.

"Looks like the W/T office'll have to wait." He looked over at the nearest M.T.B. "It's why we're all here."

Turnbull recovered his balance as the hull staggered beneath him, and vibrated in protest to a sudden reduction in speed, as if the bows were plunging into a solid wave.

He should have been prepared. *Why we're here.* The stark brevity of the comment made it worse.

The other boats were also reducing speed, their bows dropping in welters of spray. Not an engine failure, so it had to be a signal. He turned quickly, but Jay had disappeared.

"Cox'n to the bridge!"

Turnbull tugged down the peak of his cap and climbed into the bridge. *No looking back.* And here, there was no escape.

7

Flashpoint

Kearton stood on the starboard side of the bridge, his elbow wedged against some voicepipes. Not that he needed any support; apart from a slight swell, the sea was like a millpond. And it was dark, no horizon, the stars faint and scattered. He listened to the engines, throttled down to a steady, regular twelve knots, so that other, insignificant sounds were audible. The creak of the wheel, the rattle of signal halliards from the solitary mast, and always the movement of the bridge machine-guns: to check the sighting, or simply to ease the cramp in a seaman's legs.

It seemed nothing had changed since they had received the signal, and had altered course in response to its command.

He had watched the two destroyers fading into the distance, as if they and not the three M.T.B.s had altered course. At this moment, they were steering almost southeast, retracing those same lines on Ainslie's chart. Back into the Strait. *Just us.*

An enemy transport, a lighter of some kind, had been reported heading south, following the Italian coast. It was carrying a full load of mines. Scattered ahead of the expected convoy, that could mean disaster, not only for the convoy but for Malta.

The lighter, if that was an accurate description, had been lying at Naples, but how good was the information?

Minden had picked up another aircraft on her radar, but none of the lookouts had sighted it. The pilot had either been satisfied with their course and position, or the plan had already been changed.

It reminded Kearton, not for the first time, of something an old hand in Coastal Forces had said, back in those early 'Channel days'. "Decide what the enemy is preparing to do, and plan your attack accordingly. Then you can be sure the enemy will do precisely the opposite!" But it had not saved *him*.

His mind took him around the hull. Gun crews and lookouts, damage-control party, mechanics, telegraphists. Like Weston, who had brought the signal to the bridge. Recommended for a commission but dropped for some reason, although there was nothing shown against him on his papers. Ainslie liked him, and had said as much.

Kearton peered forward at the two-pounder's faint outline, its crew huddled out of sight. A useful gun on a power-operated mounting. And the twin Oerlikons abaft the bridge, which could inflict terrible damage with their six hundred rounds a minute per gun.

He pictured the boats astern, but did not turn to look. Any sign of restlessness could be seen as doubt, or lack of confidence.

He heard footsteps: Spiers coming back after checking the depth-charges. Lighters were usually of shallow draught, and torpedoes, even at a minimum setting, would often run beneath them without exploding. An official warning on the subject had been issued by their lordships: cost versus results. It had provoked some outspoken reactions from Coastal Forces. No doubt the situation looked very different when viewed from across a desk.

"All checked and in order, sir." Spiers stretched both arms and then interlaced his fingers, and cracked the knuckles. "I wonder if it's still on?"

110

"We'll have to stick it out. Otherwise it'll be back to Malta, and try again later."

Spiers rubbed his hand along the screen. "This cloak-and-dagger stuff is reliable up to a point, but I've known it misfire on a couple of occasions." He dropped his voice. "I sometimes think they're still fighting the Battle of Jutland!" Then, surprisingly, his teeth showed in a smile. "But I agree. We should stick it out."

Kearton said, "I'll be in the chartroom. Won't be long. Call me."

It was hard to think of anything but *here* and *now*. But he knew it was the closest they had been since that first day at the Rock.

The light in the chartroom came on as Kearton clipped the door behind him. He could feel the fan on his face, but after the open bridge the air was stale by comparison.

Ainslie straightened up as he rested both hands on the chart.

Kearton stared at the pencilled figures, times and distances, and had to look away. They seemed to blur, like a warning.

He said quietly, "Finished?" and was surprised by its casualness.

Ainslie tapped the chart with his pencil, a habit he no longer noticed.

"Like you said, Skipper. It's today. Has to be. If we believe the signal, it's all a matter of daylight. No captain in his right mind would risk parading a cargo of mines within striking distance of Malta." When Kearton remained silent he tapped the chart again. "Pantelleria. We'll be passing immediately south of the main island in an hour, give or take a few minutes." He attempted to smile, but it eluded him. "I've been over it several times, and even allowing—"

He looked at the pencil. He had broken the point.

Kearton said, "Pantelleria has been a thorn in our sides ever

111

since Mussolini opted into the war." He was thinking aloud, seeing it. "Good harbour. Big enough to transfer the mines to faster, smaller craft." He looked at him steadily. "When it'll be too late to do anything."

Ainslie hesitated. "But if I'm wrong?"

Kearton was at the door.

"And if you're right? We're steering across the bastard's path!" He glanced back. "Keep with me, Pilot. Together, right?"

"But— suppose—"

He waited for the light to die and tugged open the door.

"Sarah will be proud of you!"

He sensed Spiers had been waiting for him as he appeared on the bridge, and Turnbull was turning quickly from the wheel, but his face was in darkness. He groped for the R/T handset, his mind closed to everything else.

"*Growler* to all units." He wanted to shake it; it felt dead in his hand. Hearing another voice, one of the maintenance staff, warning all of them.

This R/T system is entirely new, experimental. Sometimes unreliable.

He repeated, "*Growler* to all units. Stop your engines. Listening Watch." Like hearing a stranger. "Prepare for action!"

"Acknowledged, sir."

He replaced the handset. He felt the engines quiver, then fall silent for the first time.

Turnbull was watching the compass, ticking aimlessly out of control as the hull swayed in the swell. This was not the time for anyone with a weak stomach.

He braced his legs and stared into the darkness, but saw only his reflection in the screen, catching the faint glow from the compass. Now, the waiting game . . .

He thought of Kearton's voice on the R/T intercom. Calm, unhurried, leaving no room for doubt or panic. He had sensed the flash of impatience when the transmission had failed. And why not? It was his decision, right or wrong, and their lives might depend on it.

He steadied himself against the motionless wheel as the hull pitched steeply again, and spray splashed over the screen. Someone was retching. Even the toughest sailor could only take so much.

"Go to him, Ellis. Fetch a bucket." He felt his own stomach contract.

Ainslie called, "Do what you can, but don't be too long about it!"

Turnbull took another deep breath of the salt-laden air. The young lieutenant didn't sound too good himself. *Roll on my twelve* . . .

He heard Spiers ask, "Maybe we should get under way, sir? Do another sweep astern?"

Kearton had moved to the forepart of the bridge, his back toward them.

"Not yet. Too soon." He might have turned, perhaps to look astern for their two consorts. "If we keep together . . ." He broke off as the bucket clattered on the deck. "If you want to do something, Number One . . ." He moved to the compass, and said again, "Too soon."

Right forward from the bridge, Able Seaman Glover twisted round in the two-pounder's turret and grinned at his companion.

"Bloody boat's fallin' apart!" He shook his fist. "If you're goin' to spew up, shift yerself right now, chum, not in 'ere!"

He peered across the gunlayer's sights and saw a solitary star. A touch on the training handle and the power-operated mounting purred into life, the stubby barrel moving instantly. He grinned again. "*Magic!*" But he was alone; he could guess what his Number Two was doing.

He touched the gun again. But not here. *Not bloody likely.*

He stared directly ahead: it was like standing alone in the eyes of the ship. Just the curve of the bows, and then the sea.

Nothing else. It gave the gun a maximum training ability. There was a safety rail between it and the bridge, in case he got carried away and blew it all to blazes, officers and all. He had often entertained himself with the thought.

He leaned his back against the steel, the safest spot in the whole boat.

He had been in the gunnery branch since he had joined, and he had volunteered, if only to avoid conscription into some dreary regiment with a load of squaddies. He had been working at their local grocer's shop at the time, as the errand boy, pedalling up and down those dismal rain-swept streets with a fully loaded carrier, two at weekends, because his boss, Nobby Clark, was too mean to buy a van. He could still see his face that day. *The war'll be over by Christmas.* And, *Don't expect to find this job still waiting for you when you come running home.* Some hopes. He shook his head. *Some job.*

Mister Clark, as he liked to be called, expected hard graft for his money, at all hours. There were a few tips, half a crown for an extra heavy load maybe, and a few pints of mild-and-bitter to lay the dust.

He touched the smooth metal again. The next time he got back to England and up the Smoke, he would show himself at the old shop and tell *Mister* Clark where to stick his job.

He yawned and felt his jaw click. The stars were paler already. It would be dawn soon. He yawned again, then froze. The solitary star was still there. But it was moving.

"Bridge!"

Kearton levelled his binoculars and controlled his breathing to keep them steady. Only seconds since Ainslie had repeated the call from the forward gun. Nobody spoke.

He moved the glasses slightly, his legs ready for any sudden plunge or roll, but there was none. Perhaps it was a false report? Tension, even boredom, often played tricks with a man's vision. He pictured the one in question: Glover. He had seen him often enough, and had heard Turnbull speak well of him.

He eased his shoulders and breathed out slowly. The sea was empty, and if the sky seemed paler it was because he had become part of it.

He had been on so many night watches when strain and tiredness had teased his mind and eyes with illusions.

The binoculars moved again very slowly, then held fast.

"Light, Red four-five." He hardly raised his voice, but it sounded like a shout. He held on to the glimmer of light: in line with the horizon, when there was one. So small, like a tiny star. But strong enough. Now it was gone.

There was no sound on the bridge, and he knew the next seconds were vital.

"Now!" He saw them moving, like parts of a machine. Somehow he had the handset in his free hand, the binoculars dangling heavily around his neck. Maybe the others would not hear him. It was too late now.

"Enemy in sight! Tally-ho!"

The last words were lost in the cough and roar of Laidlaw's engines.

He felt the sharp pressure against his side as the wheel went over, and saw the rising edge of foam creaming away from the stem. The sound of metal. Cocking-levers at the machine-guns, steel helmets being handed around. The battle-bowlers, as the sailors called them, were usually discarded, orders or no orders.

Kearton shouted above the roar of engines, "Twenty-five knots!" and heard Ainslie shout back, echoing Laidlaw's joke.

"With a following wind, Skipper!"

Spiers was waiting.

"Standing by, sir!"

He would be aft with the Oerlikons, clear of the bridge, although nobody ever mentioned the reason. In case the worst happened here. He might survive to command.

He stared toward the horizon again, then astern where other bow waves were suddenly livid against the dark water.

And what if I'm wrong?

The engines answered him.

There was a sharp flash, the sound of a shot, lost in the din of their own approach, and then the glare, like a burning torch in the sea itself.

Kearton held his binoculars as steadily as he could, his muscles raw, expecting the shock of an explosion at any time, or the searing light of a flare.

"Port twenty!" He tore his eyes from the fire, which was already spreading and spitting out columns of sparks. Another vessel, small, and sinking. But enough to trigger off a quick and bloody reprisal.

And enough for us.

"Midships! Steady!" He did not hear Turnbull's response; he was part of it, like the sea, surging away from either bow, and the faint shape against the dying flames. The lighter was turning now, increasing speed.

"Hold your fire!" He saw the first bursts of gunfire, long bright streams of red tracer, rising so deceptively slowly across the sky before curving down and slashing the water like flails.

The M.T.B. on the port quarter had returned fire, and was increasing speed as well as the sea erupted in further bursts of tracer.

His thoughts kept time with the gunfire. The lighter would be well armed with automatic weapons, if it was anything like the ones they had met in the Channel and North Sea . . . He felt the bridge jerk and heard the shots hammer against the hull.

"Open fire!"

He heard the instant response from the twin Oerlikons, trained round to their full extent, so the shells seemed to be ripping past the bridge. The two-pounder was also firing, controlled and steady. He knew without looking that the bridge machine-gunner was framed against the flashes, pounding his fist, and cursing because he was out of range.

He held the picture in his mind, shutting out everything else. There had been more hits, shouts below the bridge, the sharp stench of a fire extinguisher.

They said it was always the same, if you survived. They were wrong. Each time was a new test of calculation and endurance.

"Stand by!" He raised his hand like a signal, although no one was looking. The feel of the hull's trim and stability, the slightly reduced speed to ensure success, all taking second place to the shake and power of the engines.

Turnbull was slightly stooped, behind the wheel. They often joked about it, as if stooping would make any difference. Like the protective steel around the bridge: hammered-out pieces of old biscuit tin, as one coxswain had described it.

He watched the bright tracer, red and green, meeting and ripping in all directions. The smell of cordite and smoke. But nothing but the wheel and compass must matter, and the figure next or beside him.

"Fire!" Both torpedoes together. There was no time left for a second run.

"Hard a-starboard!" Turnbull felt spray on his face and hands as the wheel went over. He thought of Jock Laidlaw, holding on for dear life, machinery flashing and roaring around him, having to guess what was happening above in the real world.

"Both torpedoes running, sir!"

That was Ainslie, distant, almost formal.

"Midships!" Turnbull repeated the order and watched another boat turning steeply in the welter of spray and broken waves from 992's own wake. The attack was over. There was nothing else they could do. The torpedoes had missed their target. Same old problem. Until the next time . . .

The explosion was blinding white, lighting the sea like

daylight, the three M.T.B.s, and even, briefly, the remains of the unknown vessel which had saved them.

The lighter must have been a mile distant, but the shockwave was immediate, as if they had collided with something solid. Even at reduced speed, the engines were deafening in the silence.

Spiers had appeared on the bridge.

"Some damage, port side, nothing serious."

Kearton looked across the water. No wreckage. Not even any smoke.

"I saw someone being carried on deck."

"Overcome by fumes from an extinguisher. He's coming out of it already."

Kearton walked to the opposite side and stared at the Canadians' boat.

"Damage and casualties." He did not look at the empty sea again. All those mines. Now there was nothing.

But for that unknown light, which had looked like a star, those mines would be on their way to join the war.

He said, "Take over, Number One. I must make a signal. We might need some air cover on the run back to base. But we'll have a look at that burned-out vessel, if it's still afloat." He sensed Spiers' doubt, and added sharply, "There's always a chance."

Spiers was tugging at his white scarf, as if to conceal his thoughts.

"Leading Torpedoman Jay deserves a pat on the back, sir. He has the touch."

Kearton looked around the bridge. It was still dark, but the shadows were acquiring features.

"So have you, Number One."

Between decks, evidence of their brief encounter was instantly apparent: splintered planking and the stench of smoke and burned paintwork, which even the fans could not disperse.

But the man who had been half-suffocated by fumes was sitting propped up in a corner, his blackened face lined with runnels as if he had been weeping huge tears.

Leading Seaman Dawson was on his knees beside him, a wet rag in one hand. He twisted round, looking up.

" 'E's OK, sir. I told 'im, never volunteer!" He gestured with the rag. "Couple of 'oles through the messdeck." His own smoke-stained face split into a grin. "But th' bastards missed the galley!"

Someone stopped coughing long enough to call, "We showed 'em, sir!" The coughing began again.

Kearton glanced once at his own cabin. *Just to sit there and be alone. Cut off from everything. Just for a few minutes.*

He pushed into the W/T office and listened. *With men like these . . .*

Weston was there, as if he had never moved. The other telegraphist was with Spiers.

"Noisy down here, was it?"

Weston licked his lips. Then he said, "Once, I thought . . ."

He picked up his pad and held it with both hands. "The signal's ready, sir." He kept his eyes on the pad. "Ready to go."

He did not look up, and Kearton was glad.

Ainslie raised his arm and signalled slowly to the bridge, steadying himself against a stanchion with the other hand. He felt the deck vibrate as the engines responded and went astern, to bring the hull almost to a halt. He had learned the hard way.

He thought it had taken fifteen minutes or less to locate and manoeuvre amongst the spread of half-submerged wreckage and charred fragments. It seemed like an eternity. And all the time the sea and sky were brightening, laying them open as a target. He leaned over the bow, where it was scalloped to allow a free run for the torpedo as it was fired. The tube was now empty. He could see the reflection directly beneath him, ashes

119

clinging and rippling along the waterline. And a corpse, or what was left of it, bobbing past, turning one shoulder as if suddenly awakened.

The vessel must have been carrying fuel, and had been an easy victim. Tracer had done the rest. And now, the waiting and the stillness were taking their toll.

He saw another reflection beside his: Jay, the ex-submariner, who knew more about torpedoes than any of them. How did he feel, now that his part was over? That blinding explosion, a ship blasted to oblivion at the touch of his hand. Two other seamen were with him, hoisting-tackle and canvas slings laid out and ready. Lowering a raft or the dinghy would be too risky. Asking for it . . . He looked away as another corpse dipped beneath the hull, still afloat in its life-jacket.

One of the seamen said, "Too late for you, mate!" Nobody else spoke.

"There's one!" Jay was pointing toward some larger pieces of wreckage, held aloft by trapped air despite the fires and the last explosion.

Ainslie waved to the bridge. The engines stopped.

Jay was saying, "Ready, Ginger?" He was already helping him with one of the canvas slings. "Don't take any bloody arguments!" He patted his shoulder. "There'll be a double tot for you when you've finished!"

Ainslie saw two more hands hurrying to help with the tackle. One was the gunlayer on the two-pounder, who had first raised the alarm.

Ainslie leaned over the side, but heard Jay say, "Leave it to Ginger, sir. He knows his stuff." He twisted round and regarded him steadily. "They know you're here, see?"

The tackle squeaked through a block and someone yelled, "Got 'im!"

"Easy does it!" But there was a scream, sharp, inhuman, and again as the body was hoisted and manhandled on to the deck.

Ainslie was on his knees, although he did not know he had moved, holding one of the hands in his own while he struggled to pillow the head against his legs. Jay was helping him, but the survivor seemed stronger than both of them. Soaked with water and slippery with oil. And blood. Then, as suddenly, he was still. Only his eyes were alive.

Ainslie heard a second body being hauled aboard. Then someone shouting, "Let 'im go! Poor bastard's been through the mincer!" and a splash alongside.

Jay said, "No more, sir. This is the only one."

Ainslie stared at the bridge.

"I'll tell the skipper." He swallowed again, tasting the vomit. *Not now.*

He tried to get to his feet, but one of the hands was gripping his wrist like a vise. He could hear his breathing, short and desperate. The eyes had not moved, fixed on his own.

Jay said, "I'll tell 'im, sir." He was on his feet, a tall, raw-boned figure against the sky. And the sky had gained a hint of colour.

The seaman nicknamed Ginger stooped over them, his body running with water.

He muttered, "No use, sir," and held up his fist. " 'E's got a lump of iron like this in 'is back." He shook his head. "Best leave 'im."

Ainslie felt the grip tighten, as if all his remaining strength was there. And in the eyes.

Jay had already gone, and a few moments later the engines roared into life, and the charred wreckage seemed to move. But it was 992 which was underway, already turning, the first daylight revealing the smoke stains on the two-pounder's barrel, and the darker stains on the deck.

Ainslie murmured, "I'll not leave him."

He watched the shadows sharpen in the strengthening light, moving across the deck as the helm went over and steadied. He

121

could see another boat coming up to take station on the quarter again, her ensign almost silver, her bow wave lifting like a wing. No visible damage. He thought of the jagged scars he had seen when he had leaned over the side. *I was not afraid.*

He felt the grip ease very slightly, and when he looked he saw that the eyes were staring up at him, the mouth alive, as if attempting to speak.

He bent down as far as he could, one hand beneath the tangled hair, feeling the drying salt and the blood.

Close enough to feel the desperation, and that he was losing the battle for his life.

His voice was almost drowned by the returning power of the engines. Italian, maybe Sicilian. As a teacher, languages had never been Ainslie's strong subject.

He was reaching up, as if trying to touch Ainslie's face, but it was too much for him and his hand fell to the deck. The lump of iron had won.

His eyes were still open, his lips forming the last syllables. A name. *Jethro.*

Ainslie struggled to his feet; he had to prise the dead hand from his wrist. Someone reached out to steady him. Jay was back.

"All done, then?" He indicated the water, lifting and surging past the side. "I can tip this one over."

"No!" Then he repeated quietly, "No. Cover him up. They'll need to know . . ."

Jay glanced in the direction of the bridge.

"The C.O.'s waiting."

Ainslie felt the spray against his face, clean and salt. He did not look back, but he knew that the eyes were still watching.

Kearton unfastened the front of his oilskin and made certain his binoculars were still dry. In Malta they said you should never be surprised by the weather: humid and sultry one minute . . . He

122

glanced at the low cloud. Rain the next. It was cold too, and the sea was choppy under a stiff breeze.

He watched the pilot boat, a different one this time, turning now, leaving them to their final approach.

They had passed an outward bound tug, the deck cluttered with tackle and green wreck-marker buoys, and he had seen some of the crew peering at the tracer damage and giving a thumbs-up when they saw 992's small company falling in, caps tilted against the rain.

Their return to Malta had been completely uneventful.

They had been ready, and when aircraft had been sighted skimming at mast-height directly toward them they had expected the worst. Then Kearton had seen a couple of seamen cheering and hugging each other as the two fighters flew as close as they dared, and performed spectacular Victory Rolls more often seen above the cliffs and green fields of England. Spitfires: two of that last convoy of reinforcements, which had been all but destroyed.

Turnbull wiped the spray from his chin with the back of his hand, his eyes never leaving the indicator or compass.

"Somebody loves us," he said.

There were plenty of people about too, rain or no rain, some huddled below the old defences. There were even a few colourful umbrellas, which, like the ancient walls, were shining, and somehow defiant.

Ainslie was beside him, his stubbly beard plastered against cheeks grey with fatigue, and Kearton knew he himself did not look much better.

He thought of the body below the bridge. No flag this time to attract interest or sympathy. Who was he? He had been to see him at first light, but someone else would have to solve the mystery, discover what part, if any, he had played in that sharp and bloody action. But he knew what he had thought before he had uncovered the face.

123

The pilot boat had changed its mind and was turning fussily again. Turnbull muttered something under his breath and said aloud, "All right, Dad!"

Kearton looked across the water, at the buildings and the familiar bomb damage. The dark clouds were so low that he had mistaken them for the smouldering aftermath of yet another raid.

"Port fifteen." There was the old white cone. "Ease to five. Midships." The long mooring pontoons, the wide steps beyond, all slick with rain. He looked at the buildings beyond, and knew he had been holding his breath.

Nothing had changed.

Some figures hurrying to the water's edge: an officer standing apart from the others, watching their approach, two soldiers leaning against an upended stretcher.

Some of them were pointing at the damage, but it did not hold their attention for long.

"Slow astern, starboard." He looked at the steps. "Stop!"

He could imagine them giving a cheer in the engineroom. They must have thought the worst was happening when the mines had exploded.

He watched the lines pulling taut. Most of the onlookers had drifted away.

"Officer comin' aboard, sir."

Spiers was on the bridge.

"All made fast, sir."

"We'll have the dockyard people taking over." Kearton forced a grin. "So screw everything down." He looked astern, and saw the other two M.T.B.s making fast alongside.

Spiers was watching them too, but said, "Does that mean—"

"You'll be in command."

Ainslie called, "Lieutenant-Commander Price from Operations is aboard, sir," and a tired, patient voice interrupted, "*Brice*, if you don't mind."

Kearton shook hands.

"I'd offer you a drink, but . . ."

"Hoped you might." Brice snapped open a briefcase long enough to display a bottle. "Dick Garrick sent this over. Congratulations are in order, I understand." He snapped the briefcase shut. "First things first, I always say!"

Kearton turned to look at the buildings beyond the gates. The rain had stopped. The place was deserted.

They had reached the ladder; Brice seemed to find it steeper than he expected. Not a small-ship man . . .

He stumbled down the last step, then exclaimed, "Oh, almost forgot, what with a corpse to collect and all the usual formalities. Completely went out of my head." He fumbled inside his jacket. "I was asked to give you this." He beamed. "Now, what about that drink?"

Spiers was here, taking over subtly, and together he and Brice made their way to the wardroom, where Brice paused to examine some of the smoke stains.

Kearton turned over the pale blue envelope, recognizing it. There had been some identical to it in her room, lying with the broken glass and discarded wedding photo.

"Coming, old chap? This is the real stuff!"

It was probably just a polite note, warning him off before anything could get out of hand. He put it inside his jacket, and wanted to laugh at himself.

"Coming!"

It was a lifeline.

8

Welcome Back

The office door was already open as Kearton approached, and the same petty officer, a yeoman of signals, was waiting to greet him.

He glanced at the drops of rain on Kearton's uniform.

"I see you dodged the worst of it, sir, but it looks as if we're in for another downpour at any minute. Don't have to keep you waiting this time, either."

Kearton looked around. Exactly as he remembered it: same chairs, and a few magazines, the tape pasted across the windows, even the smell of paint. But the glass was streaked with rain, cutting through the dust, and the sky was grey, more like evening than eight o'clock in the morning.

The base was already wide awake, with men on the march, sloshing through the puddles, and the occasional bugle call, or the impatient rasp of orders or information from a tannoy system.

His own energy surprised him; he should have felt exhausted. A few hours' sleep, encouraged by some of Garrick's fine Scotch, then the inevitable hand on his shoulder, and he was ready to move. He had met the other M.T.B. officers, but only briefly, before making a list of repairs for the maintenance staff to check, and had even managed to swallow some fresh coffee before coming ashore.

He had looked back once in the grey light at the ragged scars along the hull, the splintered mahogany red against the stains. Perhaps it was still not hitting him: his mind had been so geared up for their final run back that what had happened was still being held at bay. Sooner or later, something had to snap.

He realized that the petty officer had halted by the other door.

"Good to have you back, sir." It seemed what he had intended to say from the beginning. "Me and some of the lads went down to see you come alongside yesterday. You did us proud. Not just us." He gestured toward the window. "After all the shit and bombing these people have had to put up with—" He looked away and rapped on the other door.

Lieutenant-Commander Eric Brice crossed the room to meet him. Easily, unhurriedly. As if he were more at home here, bombs or not, than in a small warship that still stank of burning and cordite.

"You're bright and early, Bob!" They shook hands. "The Boss is still away, I'm afraid. But he's bang up to date with everything." He patted Kearton's shoulder as he took the indicated chair. "Sends you his warmest greetings." He smiled, and it made him look younger. "And he meant it, believe me."

He moved to the desk. It was bare but for one slim file. There was no ashtray.

"It's all laid on for the dockyard people to run some repairs. They'll start tomorrow." He was studying the file. "Early. No other damage. Engines, communications—" He tapped the file. "The R/T plays up?" Turning over a sheet. "Well, pretty marvellous, when I consider what you achieved. *Bloody* marvellous, really. Not surprised the Boss is cock-a-hoop about it."

The telephone rang noisily. "Can't very well pretend I'm not here, can I?" He picked it up, said, "Brice, Operations," and seemed to straighten in his chair. "Yes, sir. No, I'd not forgotten, sir. Government House? Of course. Thank you, sir." He put it down. "I sometimes think he actually expects me to bow to him!" And he laughed.

127

In the next breath, he was serious again. "The good news is that you're getting two new boats, not one, as was first reported. Arrival time, a couple of days, unless . . . Well, we won't use that word."

He laced his fingers together and gazed across the desk.

"By the way, Bob, I stood in for you when that young sailor was buried. I thought it was only right."

Kearton guessed he had waited until now, when they were alone: another side to this man who could carry his responsibility with enough gravity to satisfy Garrick, but still keep himself human.

Brice was saying, "There was a naval guard from the base, and a bugler. Not much, but it meant something, I think." He snapped his fingers, different again. "Oh, and the base sent a splendid wreath. A nice gesture. Thought you might have known about it?"

Kearton recalled the letter, which he had reread yet again before stepping ashore. Very short, three lines. That she would be away from Valletta for a few days. That she might be attending Irwin's funeral. Then, underlined, *Do take care of yourself.*

Nothing about herself.

Brice said abruptly, "On the unpleasant subject of death . . . the Intelligence chaps ran the rule over the corpse you brought back with you. No identification— there wouldn't be, of course— but a tattoo, which was recognized. And there was a Mills 36 grenade inside his shirt, primed and ready. For himself or his attackers, we shall never know." He gave a wintry smile. "Luckily the pin held fast when your chaps hauled him out of the drink!"

He stood up and walked to the window.

"Coming down like stair rods." He seemed to recall what he had been saying. "Seems such a tiny gesture in the face of your massive explosion . . ."

Kearton felt his hands tighten around the arms of his chair.

"There must have been even more mines aboard the lighter than we thought." Brice was still watching the rain. "Broke every bloody window for miles. Time they got a taste of their own medicine."

"How did you hear that?"

Brice did not turn. He shrugged, as if it had not occurred to him.

"The Boss kept in close touch at every stage of the operation. It was a great success, but there was always the risk it might go pear-shaped. Only your M.T.B.s were ready and available—smaller boats lack the range and endurance. It was a daring operation, as well you know. Better than anyone."

Kearton said, "Jethro?"

Brice nodded. "It will be forgotten after this."

Kearton released his grip and rubbed the palm of his hand on his knee. Forgotten . . . But what about those who had served and trusted him, and had died because of it?

"Dick Garrick will be back tomorrow, possibly tonight. I'll be the last to know." Brice turned from the window. "I'll lay odds he'll be shouting for you as soon as he hits base, so be prepared!"

They walked to the door, Kearton's wavy stripes, and Brice's straight. They were always having the difference rammed home to them in Coastal Forces. *You're still the amateurs* . . .

Brice said, "See you tomorrow," and paused, looking at him keenly. "You did a fine job, Bob. But watch your step."

The telephone was ringing again. Afterwards, Kearton wondered which one of them it had saved.

The outer office was still empty. Maybe Brice was regarded as second-best while the Boss was unavailable.

He went to the window and looked through the tape at the abandoned garden. Nothing had changed, except the ornamental pond had half-filled with rainwater, and it gave life

129

to the place. He wondered what had happened to the people who had lived or worked here before it had been commandeered by the navy. Like all the other places he had seen, bombed, derelict, abandoned. What had it been like here before the war?

There was no point in thinking about it. That life was gone.

He straightened, unconsciously bracing himself. Back to the jetty: they would all be waiting to hear what he had discovered. That two more boats would be joining them, eventually. That repairs would be given top priority. That, in the meantime, local leave would still be restricted. That would be the worst piece of news. One look at the clouds was enough to tell him he would be drenched by the time he got around to telling them anything.

"Glad I caught you, sir. Thought you might have gone somewhere to celebrate!"

Kearton gathered his thoughts, and smiled.

"What can I do for you, Yeo? Nothing serious, I hope?"

"Well, it's like this, sir." He leaned closer, conspiratorially. "We got a phone call, on our special line. Someone asking to speak to you. Didn't want anybody else. Against all standing orders, sir, but as it was for you . . ." He broke off, staring at the other door. "A lady, sir."

"Thanks, Yeo. Between us, then?"

He followed the petty officer out of the anteroom. Brice was still on the telephone, making sparse comments, obviously speaking to someone very senior. Taking the flak for Garrick.

It was the same staircase. A workman was measuring carpet exactly where he had seen her, looking up at him, past Garrick.

"In the lobby, sir. I wrote down the number, just in case." He glared at the workman. "Waste of time, if you ask me. The whole place is a shambles." Then he grinned. "But it still beats Chatham any day!"

The lobby was more of a box than a room, with a shelf for outgoing signals or messages and a window overlooking the

130

approach road, from which two figures in oilskins were visible, sheltering inside the garishly painted checkpoint.

Kearton sat by a small table and looked at the solitary telephone.

"Here, sir." The petty officer was flattening a piece of crushed paper on the table. "I've told 'em to put you through, no arguments."

The door opened, only halfway, but even so, it almost touched the opposite wall.

"'E's buzzin' for you, Yeo! There's a flap on!"

"I'll leave you to it, sir." He might almost have winked. "Good luck."

"Putting you through."

Kearton stared at the pencilled number. It meant nothing to him. There was no ringing tone, only a few clicks, and the faint sound of someone speaking on another line.

"Still trying."

A mistake, or a change of heart. Like the little note. Polite. Careful.

The table vibrated under his elbow as a large truck ground to a halt near the checkpoint, its bonnet steaming, water splashing down to join the deep puddles on the road.

"Who is that?" As if she were right here, beside him.

"It's me, Bob Kearton." The truck was revving its engine, the driver leaning out to yell at the checkpoint. "I'm sorry. I thought . . ."

He repeated, *"It's me!"* The engine had stopped, and he realized he had been shouting. "Glynis, just got your message. Wonderful to hear your voice. We got in yesterday." The line clicked, like a warning, and he said, "I got your letter, too. It meant such a lot."

"I knew you were here." She hesitated, perhaps expecting the warning click on the line. Careless talk . . . "Are *you* all right? Please tell me."

"I'm fine. I've been thinking about you. Wishing we'd had more time together. I just wanted you to know." He saw the truck beginning to move again. More noise, the table shaking. What was the point? She was married.

"Are you still there?" She sounded tense, and there were voices in the background. She had told him about sharing a new address after the bombing.

"I want to see you again, Glynis. To tell you how I feel—"

The line seemed dead. How could he blame her? If only . . .

"Have you finished?" The metallic, operator's voice again.

But she spoke. "I must go." He could hear her breathing. "If you're sure." Another pause. "Call me."

He waited, knowing that she had gone. More voices in the background, then the tannoy somewhere. *The following ratings report to the Regulating Office.*

He heard none of it, only her last words. *Call me.*

The yeoman of signals returned and peered into the empty lobby.

One of his signalmen said, "Rain's still comin' down in buckets, Yeo. But after all he's been through, I suppose he wouldn't—"

The yeoman of signals shook his head. A good lad, but still too young to understand.

Turnbull stood on the side-deck below the bridge and watched the rain pounding along the jetty and pontoons like a cloudburst. It was cold, too, and yet he had seen some local youngsters running through the puddles as if it were midsummer.

There had been some men in overalls down here an hour or so ago. Notebooks and diagrams; one of them pointing at the tracer damage with a long ruler. He had already passed the word, *don't leave anything lying about*, when the dockyard mateys came aboard. It would soon walk.

He saw Leading Seaman Dawson striding toward him, rain

132

bouncing off his cap, apparently oblivious to the downpour. Nothing ever seemed to bother him for long. Outwardly easygoing, even jovial, but only a fool or a stranger would try and pull a fast one on Pug Dawson.

Turnbull winced as icy rain splashed across his neck.

"All quiet, Hookey?"

Dawson banged his hands together and rasped, "Lot of moanin' goin' on, 'Swain. Nothin's bin said about liberty." He peered through the rain; even his eyelids had been scarred in the ring over the course of many years. "A good run ashore might 'elp."

Turnbull shrugged.

"Skipper's not back yet. He might tell us something once he gets aboard." He thought of the last time. *Not that bloody canteen again.*

He glanced at his companion, surprised that it could still unsettle him. Dawson's eyes were blue, clear and always alert, completely alien to the battered face and veined, broken nose. As if a younger man, a stranger, was looking out from behind a mask.

Dawson thrust out his arm.

"Hell's teeth, a miracle!"

As if a tap had been switched off, the rain had stopped, and where there had been gloom a few seconds ago their shadows stood out starkly against the streaming deck and superstructure. A patch of hard blue had broken through the clouds, and was reflecting in the puddles and the sea alongside.

Dawson grinned.

"Time for some grub. While the galley's still in one piece!"

Turnbull saw the real reason for Dawson's hasty departure, and saluted.

"Anything I can do, sir?"

Spiers removed his cap and shook it over the side. "Rain's stopped, but not for long, I'm thinking." He stared along the

133

deck, at the covered guns and sealed lockers. "Don't want to delay things. Once they begin work, I don't want to give them any excuse for dragging it out. But I don't have to tell you."

Turnbull said, "Some of the hands will have to sling their hammocks ashore. They won't care much for that."

"It's all arranged and in orders. I've left you a copy."

Turnbull gauged the moment. "If the other boats are needed for sea duty during the repair work—"

Spiers interrupted, "They will be, I'm certain of that. Then our C.O., as senior officer, will be going with them. Pilot too, I understand."

Turnbull tried to guess his mood. To be left in charge, in command, should suit Spiers well. On the other hand, he would be high and dry if the other boats were called into action. He felt his stomach muscles tighten. But not like this last time. Not so soon . . .

He said, "Well, Mr Ainslie won't like having to break in another lot of charts!"

Spiers did not respond. Instead, he said, "Who the bloody hell's this? I thought they'd clamped down on wasting petrol!"

A car had pulled up on the road, big enough to be visible beyond the gates. Not camouflaged or painted in drab khaki, but dark blue, and still glittering with rain.

"Must be someone important, sir."

Spiers saw two naval patrolmen emerging from shelter and heading for the steps.

"Well, he won't get far, whoever it is!"

Turnbull rubbed his chin. Jimmy the One was in a bad mood. Again. . . . Someone had walked through the gates, and the two patrolmen were standing fast: the master-at-arms or one of his team must have waved the newcomer through. A civilian, casually dressed, with a bag of some sort slung over his shoulder.

"He's got his eye on us, sir."

"Bloody hell! As if . . ." Spiers looked over the side, and gestured to the gangway sentry who was busy removing his oilskin. Then he said calmly, too calmly for Turnbull's liking, "If it's another bloody expert come to discuss repairs, it begins tomorrow, not *now*. Not after what we've had to cope with!"

"Can I help?" It was Ainslie, looking refreshed, and subtly different.

Spiers swung round but killed whatever had been on his tongue.

He eyed him for a few seconds, then said quietly, "Thank God, you've shaved off that bloody monstrosity." Then he nodded. "Yes, you go and deal with it. Tell him to bugger off—politely, of course."

Turnbull relaxed, muscle by muscle. A close thing, he thought. He should have seen it coming. It was part of a coxswain's job.

Spiers said, "I'll be in the wardroom if you need me. Let me know when the C.O.'s on the horizon."

Too calm. A bad sign. Like the brandy Turnbull could already smell on his breath. A Horse's Neck, and probably more than one. He pictured the little mess down aft. Jock Laidlaw would be there by now . . . And finally it hit him. They were back alongside. No matter where. They were safe.

He realized that Ainslie had returned, almost breathless, as if he had run all the way from the brow. The stranger was still there, now on one of the pontoons, and seemed to be looking at the damage.

Turnbull said, "I'm not too sure that's in order, sir."

Ainslie shook his head excitedly. "No, no, it's all right! Didn't you recognize him?" He reached out impetuously as if to make his point. "It's the man himself. *Hardy*!"

Turnbull was at a loss.

"No relation, I hope, sir?"

Ainslie repeated, "No— no! *Max* Hardy, the photographer.

You must have seen his work in the press— on film? He's famous!"

Turnbull exhaled slowly, and saw his breath clouding like steam.

"Yeah, I remember now. Seen a lot of his stuff, sir. Just caught me off-balance." He peered over the side again: still there. Max Hardy. Of course he knew the name. But here? Now?

Ainslie was grinning like a fool, he thought. Without the beard, he looked even younger than Turnbull remembered from before the stubble.

"Don't worry about security. He's got written authority from the admiral, and from Government House itself!" You could almost see the capitals, Turnbull thought. He was ticking them off on his fingers. "*And* Captain Garrick knows all about it, too!"

The sentry called, "Message from the gate, sir!"

It cleared Turnbull's mind: Kearton was on his way. This was all he needed. *I don't think!*

Ainslie said, "I'll fetch Number One."

Turnbull glanced at the sky. It was clearing; there was even a hint of sunshine.

But first things first. They were safe in harbour. And until the next time . . . He cupped his hands.

"Man the side! Jump to it!"

And he was the Coxswain.

Kearton sat in his cabin and half listened to the sounds around him. The steady murmur of a generator, crockery being stowed in the galley, snatches of music from the messdeck, a ukelele or banjo, switched off abruptly by somebody wanting to sleep. He did not look at his own bunk, nor did he think of the remaining Scotch in his cupboard. Either would finish him.

There was a mug of coffee on the table, ice-cold now. He

could not recall how long it had been there, or even who had brought it.

He stood up and moved to the side. The scuttle was open, and it was dark outside, the air cool against his mouth. He imagined he could smell the land, which seemed unlikely as it was so close. He stretched to ease the knots of tension in his shoulders, but nothing seemed to relieve it, and he thought he knew the reason. It was different here, unlike any warfare he had known. Returning to harbour after a sortie across the Channel, along the enemy-occupied coast, coming back in that hard light of yet another dawn, you usually fell into bed on dry land, and if you were lucky you were none the worse for wear. A shower, a meal provided at the blink of an eye, drinks in the mess later . . . too many, unless you were out again the following night. And the boats would be ready and waiting when the word came.

Here, in these larger boats, you carried your bed with you. And the smells, too. A fresh intake of fuel, men living in one another's pockets. And the reminders: scarred wood and smoke stains, which new paint might disguise once the dockyard workers had departed.

A coat of paint. Was that all it took?

The sort of question Max Hardy might ask, should ask, when he returned to 'see for himself'.

Their first meeting, on Kearton's return from Operations, had been casual, matter-of-fact. Thin, almost hawk-like, Max Hardy was no stranger to the press and documentary world, restless one minute, then stock-still, watching, or lending impact to the next phrase of a sentence. In his thirties, Kearton thought, but he looked older. He had a slight northern accent which came and went, perhaps to suit his mood or his audience.

The hard, bony handshake, and the first words he had spoken, "We've met before, Bob Kearton," had dispensed with unnecessary introductions. "I know something of your background, and why you're here in Malta." The quick grin, almost a grimace, gone before you could measure it. "Or as much as I'm allowed to know. I think people should share some of it, if only to lessen their own burdens." He had punched the air. "Show 'em we're hitting back at the bastards, where it hurts!"

Kearton did not recall having met him before, unless Hardy had been there when he had been given his D.S.C. It had all been too much to remember. There had been several men decorated that day, and he had seen the admiral glancing at his aide's list seconds before to ensure that he had the names right.

He had thought for a long time afterwards of the other names which would never be called, the names of those who had been with him that night, 'when the Channel was set ablaze', as one newspaper had luridly described it.

He found he had his pipe in his fingers; the pouch was already on the table beside the envelope. He had pencilled the telephone number on it, in case he mislaid the yeoman of signals' little note.

Even if he managed to get through to her, what was the point? He had no right, no chance. He looked up; the hull had moved slightly and nudged against the pontoons. Probably the Officer-of-the-Guard doing his rounds, or, more likely, some senior officer going on a social visit somewhere. He put down his pipe carefully. Just for those few seconds, day-dreaming, it had felt like an explosion, like the one which had painted the sky and, reputedly, broken all those windows.

She might still love her husband. Maybe she had never stopped. And even if . . .

"Yes!" A loud rap at the door. Perhaps he had not heard the first one.

It was a young seaman, in uniform, a webbing belt clipped loosely around his waist. One of the duty watch. Kearton was suddenly fully awake: he even remembered the man's name.

"What is it, Lucas?" He could hear voices now.

138

"Saw your light was on, sir." He almost glanced over his shoulder. "But the wardroom . . ."

"Tell me."

"There was a boat, sir. A launch. We thought it was just passing, then it hooked on to the pontoon. We didn't know what to do." He was still staring at Kearton's hand, which was gripping his arm. "Then I saw your cabin light."

Kearton released his grip. *We're all going round the bend.* "You did the right thing." He remembered the sound, the hull moving slightly in the wash. The voices were distinct; he could see the shadows moving in the deckhead light. He did not even know what time it was, but Garrick he would know anywhere. No wonder the handful of men on watch had been taken aback.

He opened the door wide. He could remember Brice's exact words. *I'll lay odds he'll be shouting for you as soon as he hits base.* Had that been only this morning?

Garrick strode to meet him, his cap almost brushing against the light, face in shadow. Behind him followed a much younger officer, a subbie, and for a moment Kearton imagined it had started to rain again; the subbie's cap and shoulders were glistening with droplets of water.

Garrick must have seen his eyes.

"Just been showing him what small-boat handling used to be like, when it counted for bloody something!"

The young officer asked, "Shall I wait alongside, sir?"

Garrick stood in the doorway, one foot resting on the coaming.

"This is more like it!" He peered along the narrow passage. "Well sited, too— between the W/T office and the heads!" He seemed to hear the question and said sharply, "You can carry on, Mister . . ." He snapped his fingers. "I'll call if I need any-one!"

The sub-lieutenant hurried away.

Garrick tossed his cap on to the bunk and sat down beside it.

"Some people!"

Kearton closed the door quietly. The seaman had vanished, and would soon be telling his mates all about the unexpected visitor, and how *he* had handled it.

There was a thin shaft of light from the wardroom, but no sound of life. Garrick was running his fingers through his hair, staring around as if to get his bearings. He had obviously been drinking.

"Sorry to barge in on you at this hour, er, Bob. Lot on my plate at the moment. But I wanted to see *you*, keep the record straight, so to speak."

He coughed and dragged out a handkerchief, and for a minute Kearton thought he was going to throw up.

But he recovered. "Heard you had Max Hardy down here making his number. Good chap in many ways— knows his stuff." He dabbed his mouth with the handkerchief. "Useful, too, if it suits him."

"He knows about the repair work. Seemed interested."

Garrick nodded but was not listening. "Two new boats joining our little group. At long, bloody last, eh?" He was suddenly serious, almost sober. "Both motor gunboats, not M.T.B.s this time." He cocked his head as if to challenge him. "Any objections?"

Kearton leaned back in his chair, trying to relax, anticipating the next tack.

"We can do with the extra firepower." He waited. "Are they arriving soon?"

Garrick unbuttoned his reefer.

"Christ, it's like an oven in here." He seemed to recall the question. "Next convoy. *The* convoy, which thanks to your merry men should arrive unscathed." He swallowed hard. "Well, nearly. I could do with a drink. Bit pushy for a guest, eh?"

Kearton moved to the cupboard. Garrick was tough, a true

professional. He had not come aboard in the middle of the night, or whatever time it was, merely to open the bar.

"I still have some of that Scotch you sent over with Lieutenant-Commander Brice."

Garrick waved his hand. "Good chap, Brice, doing an efficient job in conjunction with our lot . . . Bit of an old woman at times, but knows where to draw the line." He leaned forward. "Good stuff, Bob, malt, from the Isle of Islay. Impossible to lay your hands on it these days." He tapped the side of his nose. "But R.H.I.P.!" And he laughed.

Kearton poured two glasses with care. There was a bottle of soda water left from Brice's visit, but Garrick covered his glass with one hand.

"Don't kill it!"

Then he said, "There's a meeting planned for the day after tomorrow." He raised his wrist and peered at his watch, as if he were unable to focus on it. "*Tomorrow*. Or soon will be. Chiefs of Staff, all the usual suspects." He put down his glass; it was empty. "This time there'll be someone from London. Things are moving at last. Explains why Max Hardy is here. So we must make the most of it."

He watched Kearton refilling his glass and said suddenly, "Your Number One— Spiers, right? A good chap? Due for his own command." He was fumbling for something, perhaps his cigarettes. "All in good time." He looked up as feet padded overhead. "Caught 'em on the hop when I appeared, eh?"

He almost laughed, but checked it.

"I want you with me. Show the flag, make 'em understand what we're trying to do. What we *are* doing." He found the packet, seemed to change his mind, and nodded gently. "But for our handling of the enemy minelaying scheme, the next convoy would be scattered across the bottom of the Med." His face was flushed beneath its tan, but he was still very lucid. "Not just armour and firepower, Bob, not at this stage. It's *people* who

141

will tip the scales. Individuals." He smiled and said, "I think I've gone over the yardarm. Been a long, long day."

He stood up and steadied himself against the side, but the hull was motionless.

"Better go to the heads." He squared his shoulders and pushed open the door.

"Everything all right, sir?" It was Spiers, a duffle coat over his pyjamas. "You should have given me a call!"

Kearton touched his arm.

"Thanks, Peter. Try and get some sleep. Busy day tomorrow." He thought of Garrick, his pride and his pain. "*Today*, as it is now." He heard the sound of flushing.

Spiers heard it too, and said as he moved away, "Extra one for breakfast, then. He can see how the poor live!"

When Kearton returned to his cabin, Garrick was asleep on the bunk. His jacket had been neatly spread across the back of the chair, and the four gold stripes were very impressive in the deckhead light. His fine cap was placed meticulously nearby.

Would Garrick remember anything of what he had said? There must have been a cause, a reason.

He looked at the bottle. It was empty.

Why now, and why here? The Boss, respected, even feared, as head of Special Operations. There were doubtless a lot of people who would like to see him fall.

Kearton pulled a few spare blankets together and sat in a corner of the cabin. In a few hours it would be daybreak, rain or no rain, and Garrick might recall nothing about it.

But Kearton knew he would never forget. Once again, it was a matter of trust.

The master-at-arms stood up smartly, unhurriedly, from his table as Kearton was shown into his office.

"I got your message, sir." His eyes did not seem to move, but they missed nothing: rank, and the blue and white ribbon on Kearton's jacket, even the sawdust on one of his shoes. "I *know*, sir. Dockyard mateys. Few hours' work, and a month of Sundays to clear up the gash they leave behind." He smiled, but it did not reach the cold eyes.

The Jaunty, as he was known, gestured toward the room's other occupant, a rating sitting at a switchboard and wearing headphones.

"He'll make sure you're not disturbed." It sounded like a threat. His hair was cut very short, and was completely grey. A reservist, Kearton thought, or a man who had had his retirement curtailed for the duration. But very much in charge.

He put on his cap and said, "I'll be around, sir." He left the door partly open.

Kearton sat down at the table and looked at the telephone.

He felt like death. Garrick, by contrast, had seemed unaffected by the night's events. He had declined breakfast and gone ashore while most of the hands were still asleep. He had even paused at the brow to return the salutes and called, "I'll walk back to the grindstone— do me good!" Just briefly, the Boss again. "Noon, then. Show our faces!" That was all.

He handed the slip of paper to the man at the switchboard. Although he wore headphones, he had one ear uncovered.

"Won't keep you long, sir. It's rather busy at the moment."

Kearton glanced at the typed and pencilled sheets that seemed to fill most of the table. Working parties, or men listed as sick or unfit for duty. Defaulters, men under punishment. And a few shown as on leave. The Jaunty missed nothing.

He thought of Spiers, dealing with the dockyard workers, who would be in command until the repairs were finished and 992 was ready for sea again, and, if need be, for action. He pushed it from his thoughts.

What am I doing here?

He felt inside his pocket. He had found Garrick's gold cigarette lighter wedged in a corner of the bunk. He really must have been drunk; he was never without it.

There was the meeting with the top brass. Maybe that was why Hardy was here. But Garrick should be used to that . . .

He closed his eyes for a second, fighting the dead weight of fatigue.

I'm not.

"Putting you through now, sir."

Kearton picked up the receiver. She had had time to think about it. To reconsider. Or she might be away somewhere . . .

"Hello— who's that?" A man's voice, curt, impatient. For a second he thought he recognized it, but knew he was mistaken.

"Kearton." He cleared his throat. "Robert Kearton." He thought there were other voices, somebody laughing. A woman.

And then she said, "Hello, it's me. What a surprise! I never expected . . ." A pause, and the other voices were silent; she must have closed a door. When she spoke again, the false brightness was gone; her voice was low, tense, intimate. She might have been beside him.

"So many things I wanted to ask you, and I know I can't. I was worried— so many rumours. You know, the *village* . . .? I suppose you're up to your ears in things again." More voices, and he heard her say as though over her shoulder, "Not now. Can't you see . . .?" Quiet again; she had shut the door.

He said, "I was hoping I could see you. Talk, without having to cut and run like the last time." He could feel the silence, and was painfully aware of his own clumsiness.

"I'm not sure, Bob. You know how things are . . . Actually, you *don't* know—"

He could imagine her shaking her head, her hair across her shoulders, like that day. After the air raid.

"You're not alone, Glynis. I didn't realize. I must have put my foot in it."

144

He heard the man at the switchboard recrossing his legs, waiting to break the connection.

She said, "Just a few people, moving house. I thought I told you." Her voice faded; she must have looked away. "I don't want you to think . . . to believe . . ." Another pause. "Have you got something to write on?" She did not allow him time to answer. "This is the address." She stopped. "If you're— sure."

He heard himself murmur, "It means a lot. To me . . ."

He pressed the telephone hard against his ear, scribbling with a pencil, shutting out everything but her voice.

"Got it."

"Call me first. I don't want anyone to think— to imagine—" She broke off. Someone was tapping at the door. Her door.

He said, "As soon as I can." But the line was dead.

The master-at-arms had reappeared, and looked briefly between him and the operator.

"No trouble getting through, sir? Makes a change."

Kearton guessed his previous call was no secret here.

He held out the piece of paper he had torn from one of the pads on the table.

"I don't know my way around Malta." He heard her voice again. *The village . . .*

The Jaunty peered at the scribbled address.

"Over in Sliema. A posh area, or used to be." He looked up, business-like again. "Quite a step from here. You'll need transport . . ." He seemed to be considering it. "Never straightforward, with all the fuel shortage an' so forth. But when the convoy gets here, things should be a bit easier." He made up his mind. "Leave it to me, sir."

Kearton walked out into the frail sunlight. *The convoy. So much for secrecy.*

He had to find his way to the proposed meeting. It would give him time to think.

But he was no longer tired.

9

And Good-Bye

Lieutenant Peter Spiers closed the cabin door with his foot, without getting up from the table. It was hard to think, and impossible to shut out the noise. And this was only the first day. A handful of dockyard workers and shipwrights, but it felt and sounded like a small army. The wardroom was out of the question: a lot of the side had been cut or hacked away and it now lay open to the waterfront, and anybody who cared to stop and gape at the progress.

Here, at least, he was undisturbed, except by the noise. He wiped dust from the large envelope which contained the duties for the remaining watch on board, and looked around the cabin again. In some ways he knew it better than the wardroom. He had used it when the boat had commissioned, and for their first long passage to Gibraltar. There had been other officers aboard, specialists, in case any faults had gone undiscovered or unreported by the yard where 992 had first tasted salt water. It still looked unlived in, which somehow made it worse: there were no photographs or personal possessions. In the wardroom, Ainslie was always ready to show off his snapshots of his girlfriend, if she was still the same one . . .

Ainslie was in the chartroom right now, as far from the noise as he could get, and although it was noon, he was probably snatching an hour or so of sleep. They split the remaining shipboard duties between them; Ainslie had been quite agreeable. Nothing ever seemed to get on top of him.

Spiers yawned, and felt grit between his teeth. Kearton was ashore at some meeting; Garrick would be there, but others more senior would be running it.

He thought about the action again; it was never far from his mind. Moment by moment, if he allowed it. Trying to recall the timing, the sequences of waiting. And then the brutal reality. Sometimes he saw himself like a spectator, listening to his voice giving commands. Seeing Kearton, as if in the flashes of gun-fire, then that final explosion. Spiers had been in action plenty of times. The memories often overlapped, and only the faces changed. They all went through it, but some you always remembered. He thought of Kearton, in control, even when things had seemed unpredictable. Would you ever really *know* him?

He stood up and stretched. Perhaps they had a tennis court or club in Malta, war or no war. Or was that, too, for senior officers only?

There was a party on tonight aboard 977, Geoff Mostyn's boat, and there would be some hard drinking, unless there was another air raid . . .

He looked at his watch. Kearton would send word when he was free to return. In the meantime, all the non-duty hands were ashore on local leave. Despite all the restrictions, Kearton had managed to find time to fix that. They had been cheering about it, until somebody had quelled the noise with threats.

He glanced around the cabin again, and reached for his cap. Like listening to excuses at the defaulters' table; he had done that often enough.

It was not envy. It was jealousy.

Most of 992's libertymen got no further than the wet canteen which was within sight of the mooring-place. Sailors were like that, believing in *the devil you know*. It was often safer.

147

A few stayed alone. Knowing why, but trying to come to terms with it.

Leading Torpedoman Laurie Jay found himself at the far end of the jetty, beyond the pontoons. Deserted now, or merely avoided because of the din being made by the dockyard workers.

Jay had not intended to come here, just as, in his heart, he had known that he would. From the moment they had been guided to these moorings the first time by the pilot boat, he had accepted the inevitable.

There had been a submarine lying alongside, deserted, resting, only her ensign moving. And deadly.

The berth was empty now. The submarine had probably moved over the water to Manoel Island, north of Valletta, where they had their own workshops and headquarters, or maybe she was at sea again. Cruising at periscope-depth in search of a target, a victim. Or running deep, with all hell breaking loose above and around her.

He walked to the water's edge and looked down at his reflection. Tall and smart in his best tiddley-suit, a pusser's raincoat over his arm.

He could not get used to it. Accept it. It was like being somebody else, an imposter. Even now, if he passed another sailor with the coveted cap tally, *H.M. Submarines*, he somehow expected to know the face, or to be recognized. He was thirty years old, or would be in a few weeks' time, and one of the oldest members of the crew, and in the flotilla. He should be over it, or have cracked up by now.

Everything was completely different. Which was why he had requested the transfer from submarines to Coastal Forces and M.T.B.s. Movement, light, noise. Able to breathe. To escape.

And just occasionally it hit back at you. In Gosport after he had completed his transfer, he had come face to face with a chief petty officer outside H.M.S. *Dolphin*, the submarine base.

An old instructor, or a one-time shipmate. The link was always there.

But the name of his last submarine had been enough. H.M. Submarine *Saturn*. The look of pity, or the look that said, *Why you, and not all those other poor blokes?*

And again, recently, when they had altered course and risked their own safety to pick up the sole survivor from a U-Boat. He had gone below to see the survivor for himself. Wrapped in blankets, shivering uncontrollably as Pug Dawson was trying to pour some rum into him.

It had been like looking at himself.

He had heard that the skipper had been in the drink, and saved by the skin of his teeth. That might explain a lot, and why he had acted without hesitation.

He could remember *Saturn*'s commander quite clearly. Saying good-bye to his young wife within a few weeks of the war, which everybody knew was coming. She had been smiling, but dabbing her eyes at the same time. His son, a small child, laughing and trying to salute everybody.

Again, leading the wild cheering after their torpedoes had sent two freighters to the bottom.

And the last time, at the periscope and shouting, *"Dive! Dive! Dive!"* Like a scream. When it was already too late.

Another world. He could still strip or activate a torpedo in the dark, or with his eyes shut if necessary, but it was all so different.

He thought of one of the doctors at the naval hospital, so young that he must have been a medical student before he had put on a uniform. The red cloth between his two wavy stripes had obviously convinced him he was God.

"You'll have to learn to *adapt*, Jay. Or you'll go under!" He had not even recognized his own stupid joke.

"You're a bit off the beaten track, chum! Nothin' up here but the smell!"

149

Jay turned, caught unawares, but managed to smile. "Just stretching my legs."

It was Glover, a tough, experienced seaman, and the gunlayer on their two-pounder. Nicknamed Cock on the messdeck, probably because he was a Londoner and a true Cockney, or maybe for more personal reasons. From some of the yarns Jay had heard around the messdeck table, Glover always enjoyed a run ashore in the fullest sense.

Cap at a rakish angle, and a bright new gunnery badge on his sleeve, Glover was most people's idea of 'Jack'.

Glover kicked some gravel into the water and grinned. "Thought you was thinkin' of doin' yerself in!"

Jay tensed, and allowed himself to relax.

He said, "Do you fancy a wet?"

Glover looked at him thoughtfully. He half wondered what he was doing here, and why he had caught up with Jay. They lived side by side on the messdeck: in M.T.B.s and most small craft you expected that. Jay was a leading hand, friendly enough when you could drag a few words out of him. But still a stranger.

Jay looked back along the jetty. Men were still working aboard and alongside their boat. Noise, questions that needed answering. The duty hands would deal with those.

He said, "The canteen? I'm not sure. I've heard . . ."

Glover shook his head.

"Nah! Full of bloody pongos and so-called sailors who've never been to sea since they joined!" He shrugged. "You're a regular— you must 'ave bin ashore in Malta in the good old days?"

Jay looked toward the gates and the road.

"I was here a couple of years back. It's all changed since then. The bombing. Shortages." He could feel Glover's eyes on him. Offering something. "If you like, we could take a look. There was one place . . ." He broke off. He was already out of his depth.

150

It made him think of that young doctor again, and he found that he was smiling in earnest.

"Might be lousy."

Glover's grin widened in anticipation.

"A few jars, maybe some music." He gestured rudely with his forearm. "Maybe a bit of the other to round things off!"

They walked toward the gates where a regulating petty officer, one of the Jaunty's little team, was already watching their approach.

Jay said, "We have to be back aboard by twenty-two hundred."

Glover straightened his cap.

"No problem. On an' off like a fly, that's me!"

Jay pulled out his makeshift leave pass, and saw the R.P.O. glance from it to the anchor on his sleeve.

But he could still hear the pompous young doctor.

You'll have to learn to adapt.

He wanted to laugh, for the first time since he could remember. But he knew he would be unable to stop.

The location chosen for the meeting with the V.I.P. from London was not what Kearton had expected. He thought of his father: it was more like one of the building sheds back at the boatyard, long and low, with one end just a few feet from the water.

Captain Garrick returned some salutes, and remarked, "You'd think Churchill himself was coming. Maybe he has!"

There were plenty of vehicles, too. Staff cars, and jeeps, and a larger van with scarlet-painted wings: the bomb-disposal squad. Not much evidence here of a fuel shortage.

Kearton glanced over at Garrick, fresh-faced and smartly turned-out, his fine cap at a slight angle. Alert and apparently untroubled. Only once, when a man in civilian clothes who was standing with two redcaps stepped forward to mutter something

151

about Kearton's identification, did he display any irritation.

"He's with *me*, for God's sake!" The man vanished.

Inside the building, it was already difficult to move. There seemed to be dozens of officers, blue and khaki, and even a sprinkling of R.A.F. types. Some were quite senior, managing to keep a little apart from the rest. Kearton saw the same loud-mouthed brigadier, but he was quiet this time, almost subdued in the presence of his superiors.

Chairs had been arranged in rows, according to rank, or the relevance of this meeting. Most of the chairs were labelled. Garrick's was in the second row, and the one beside it was marked with a number.

Garrick waved casually to a couple of uniforms, and nodded to a few others, then he sat down, tapping the other chair. "Hope this doesn't take all day. The gunners have their mess next door . . . This crowd would drink the place dry in no time!" He laughed and hung his arm over the chairback. Relaxed but in control: how most people saw him, remembered him.

Kearton looked down. There were still flakes of sawdust on his shoes. He wondered how Spiers was coping with the clutter and the noise, all the reminders of that swift, devastating encounter.

Someone cleared his throat noisily, like a signal, and everybody stood.

Sir Piers Lampton was slightly built, and flanked by the Chief of Staff and a major-general he looked almost frail. Very tanned, a neat military-style moustache white against his skin; voice clipped, incisive. He was well known on the wireless in times of crisis or triumph, and seen in the more popular newspapers, often depicted amongst uniforms of all three services, as well as with civilians at war. A rising star in government circles, it was said, especially by the press.

Kearton had already seen Max Hardy in the room, near the front. Security did not apply to him, apparently.

The Chief of Staff murmured a brief introduction and Lampton stood up. He leaned slightly forward, his knuckles touching but not resting on the prepared lectern.

He had come a long way, from London and, someone had mentioned, Cairo, but his well-cut grey suit was not even creased. He might have just stepped out of his office, or a club in Mayfair.

"Gentlemen." He smiled. "You may smoke."

He did not add, *if you must*, although Kearton had heard that on other occasions. Garrick had slipped one hand into his pocket. It stayed there.

Kearton recalled his delight when he had returned the lighter; it had been one of those rare moments.

"God, I thought I'd lost it! She'd never forgive me!"

Who, he wondered? Garrick was not married, although it had been a close thing once or twice, or so he had heard.

The clipped voice was saying, "Here, in the Mediterranean theatre of war, and now, for the first time, we can forget hopes and fears of survival." He had paused, and his eyes, very pale against the tan, seemed to traverse the room. "*Now*, we can plan progression and attack." He tapped the table very lightly with his knuckles. "The road to Europe, and victory!"

There was an outburst of clapping, tentative at first, and then deafening. Kearton heard Garrick murmur, "For Christ's sake get on with it!" although he had seen him initiate the applause.

Lampton continued, and Max Hardy had opened a pad and was scribbling what might have been shorthand.

Lampton touched loosely on the campaign in North Africa, and the vital role of the Eighth Army, holding the Afrika Korps almost at the gates of Cairo before tipping the scales into a retreat. Somehow he managed to include all three services, even the Merchant Navy, when he mentioned the convoys, and Malta's triumph over overwhelming odds. "There was a time when we believed, *feared*—"

Kearton did not hear the rest; Garrick had tapped his arm and was whispering loudly, "They thought Malta had had it, and would have left 'em to it!"

A colonel with red tabs on his tunic twisted round in his chair and glared.

Garrick muttered, "You, too!"

It was soon over, more applause, and the flash of a camera, although not Hardy's. The Chief of Staff waited while a few introductions were made. The names were all on a typed list.

Lampton shook Garrick's hand, looking steadily up at him.

"The First Lord speaks highly of you, Captain Garrick. When I return, I intend to speak with the P.M. at the earliest opportunity . . ." He smiled as the Chief of Staff murmured something. "Would that I had more time, Captain Garrick. However . . ."

Garrick said, "I'd like to introduce one of my team, Sir Piers. Lieutenant-Commander Kearton is very experienced in close action."

Lampton smiled again, dismissing him.

"Another time, perhaps. I am already hard-pressed." He held out his hand. "Remember, *attack*!"

The Chief of Staff said, "This way, Sir Piers. The Admiral, remember?" He looked quickly at Garrick. "I'll see you tomorrow, Dick. Big day."

He turned and steered Lampton past another group of officers.

Garrick picked up his cap angrily.

"Silly bastard! What does he mean, *attack*? What the hell does he imagine we've been doing?" The mood passed, and he was outwardly calm again; like a sudden squall, Kearton thought. "I'll tell Brice to chase up the repair work. In the meantime, you'll be on call for the new arrivals." He looked at him sardonically. "And any sudden flap which may arise to disrupt Sir Piers' *vital* visit!"

A lieutenant who had been hovering on the fringe of the V.I.P.s' reception committee hurried through the departing uniforms.

Garrick recognized him.

"Changed his mind, has he?"

The lieutenant said formally, "The Chief of Staff sends his compliments, sir."

Garrick gave a little, ironic smile.

"And wants me to join him *and* Sir Piers right away?"

He put on his cap, and adjusted it with care.

"One of these days . . ." He nodded to the lieutenant. "Be *honoured*!" And winked. "England expects!"

He was halfway to the door when he turned and looked back.

"Make contact with Brice for me and put him in the picture, will you? Don't want him getting in a sweat. You can use my driver. It'll save time."

Kearton looked at his watch. Most of the others had already gone, glad it was over. Some were still loitering by the main entrance, undecided, or unwilling to return to duty. The senior officer of one of the established M.T.B. flotillas caught his eye and said, "Pity we can't take him out on patrol with *us*. Might buck his ideas up a bit!"

Kearton thought he knew him. Another place, another time.

The driver had seen him coming and seemed unsurprised that he was alone, or by the change of orders. After Brice, what then? He was on stand-by, 'on call', as Garrick had said. The two motor gunboats would soon be here, and so, it seemed, would the convoy.

The car moved out into a street he did not recognize. A few potholes, otherwise it had been repaired very well. Only the buildings and the rubble along one side showed evidence of recent air raids.

He must send her a message, even if he was unable to speak to her.

155

Sliema, or anywhere else outside the base, was impossible. It had been casually said, but 'on call' meant just that.

She might be relieved, anyway. For both their sakes.

The car stopped and he saw the gates, now familiar, and some sailors thumbing a lift from an army truck. Two others, arm in arm, were returning from their run ashore, very much the worse for wear; they would find the steps a real challenge. He saw two naval patrolmen watching them, then purposely looking in the opposite direction. Neither the Jaunty nor his R.P.O.s would be so sympathetic.

The driver got out and studied the buildings as if to reassure himself, and Kearton realized that there had been no air raid sirens all day. But the battery of heavy anti-aircraft guns at the end of the road were fully manned and pointing at the sky, perhaps for Sir Piers Lampton's benefit.

"I'm not sure how long this will take."

The driver, a Royal Marine as usual, almost clicked his heels. "I'll wait, sir!" He seemed surprised that he had been offered an apology.

The same entrance: a few ratings carrying messages, one with a tray of teacups. And the curving staircase he remembered.

The petty officer was a stranger, but he ushered him to the main office without hesitation.

Two other naval officers were already in the adjoining room, but neither of them moved or looked up as he walked past. They were apparently used to waiting.

Lieutenant-Commander Eric Brice looked tired, even rather dishevelled, but was obviously pleased to see him, and the warmth of his handshake was genuine.

"This is just great, Bob! After what you've been through, *and* having the Boss leaning on you, the V.I.P. thing must have just about put the lid on it." He laughed, "But no, you're bright as a button and ready for more!"

He sat back down at the desk. "Been like a bloody madhouse

round here." He ruffled some papers without looking at them. "The repair work should be finished in three days, four at the most. So in the meantime, while you're on stand-by, I could fix you up with a bed over here." He paused. "I wouldn't advise it, though. There's no escape in this place. Believe me, I *know*."

The door opened an inch.

"They've gone, sir. I suggested they try again later."

Brice said, "Good man. Not important, anyway." Then, "Pass the word, Harris. I don't want any incoming calls for ten minutes or so." He looked at Kearton. "Probably all over at the V.I.P.s' party at Government House anyway. There'll be a few sore heads tomorrow, of all days!"

The door closed and he stood up abruptly, as if he were uncertain about something, perhaps the frustrated visitors. "There was a call earlier for you. I wasn't sure if you would be here, or if the Boss had other ideas." He gestured to the telephone. "She called before, I believe."

He was on his way to the door.

"Remember this, Bob. The convoy is due to signal tomorrow." He opened the door. "And it's thanks to you."

Kearton heard him speaking to someone in the other room, then there was silence. There must be over a hundred people working in the building, but even that seemed quiet.

He picked up the telephone, noticing that the ashtray was back in its place.

The operator answered immediately, as if he had been waiting for a call from this office. He did not ask him to repeat the number.

"Putting you through, sir."

No clicks or voices this time. There was nothing.

"I'm sorry, sir. There seems no one . . ."

Then she said, "Hello? Hello, Bob— is that you?"

"Glynis. I just got your message. I wanted to explain." He paused; she sounded out of breath, as if she had been running.

"I thought I'd missed you. That you might ring and wonder what had happened." He heard the quick breathing. "I wanted you to know I was leaving. I was on the road when I heard the phone." She gasped, "Out of condition!"

"Leaving?" Like a door slamming. "Is something wrong?"

"I knew you'd be busy." She halted, but there were no warning clicks; the line remained silent. "I have to move some things from the old address." She paused again, and he heard the breathing. "You know the one. It's not so far . . . and I thought it might be easier for you. I'll have some friends with me. Helping me . . . I'll understand if you can't make it."

He thought he heard a car door, and the sound of an engine.

She had covered the mouthpiece but he heard her call, "I'm just coming!" Then, "Are you still there?"

The folded window blind rattled suddenly; the outer door had just opened.

He said, "Can I come *now*?" She would know exactly where he was.

"If you're sure?" Then, "Yes. I'd like that." Another pause. "A lot."

The line was dead, or she had hung up, perhaps already regretting the impulse.

The outer office was still empty, but not for long. He could hear Brice holding the fort.

He was at the top of the stairs, comparing notes with one of his staff, but he waved a sheaf of papers and called, "All OK?"

Kearton looked down the stairs and saw the driver waiting patiently by the entrance. There were so many things he wanted to know, should have asked, if only to put her mind at rest.

"I hope so. Thanks for your help."

Brice watched him leave.

For your sake, I hope so, too.

He pushed open the door; the telephone was ringing. Ten minutes exactly. Most people in Malta would give anything to be connected to a telephone, even an official line like this one. He thought of the voice, her voice. He had met her several times in one building or another, and had spoken to her once or twice; he had thought her attractive, but wary. She needed to be round here, married or not. He wondered if the Boss knew anything about it. No shred of gossip was likely to slip past Garrick.

Brice stifled a yawn. He felt as if he had not slept properly for weeks, but when Garrick eventually returned from the reception, the booze-up, as he had heard the yeoman of signals crudely call it, he would, as usual, want all the answers.

He reached for the telephone, pausing as he heard the car drive away, and was surprised to find that he cared.

"Operations. Brice here."

"He's on his way." That was all, but it was enough. Garrick was returning earlier than anyone had expected. They could be in for some fireworks.

"Many thanks." He put the phone down gently. It was good to have friends. Especially now.

Kearton climbed out of the car and stood for a few minutes to regain his sense of direction. It was all much as he remembered, but some effort had been made to tidy, if not actually repair, the damage. A few windows were boarded up; others were in use again. One roof was partly covered with a canvas tarpaulin, but the area adjoining it had been left jagged and open to the sky, a grim reminder.

There was fresh white paint around the checkpoint, and an imposing wall of sandbags where he had last seen debris.

Two armed patrolmen were observing from their little hut but made no attempt to question him. It jarred another memory: the car said it all.

There was a small van parked inside the barrier. Nothing else.

He said to the driver, "Can you wait?"

He nodded, surprised. "Forever, if need be, sir," and indicated the checkpoint. "I can have a mug of tea, or somethin'." Then he grinned rather shyly. "Cap'n Garrick said I was to wait, so 'ere I'll be."

"I'll not be long." The driver probably knew that, too.

One of the patrolmen threw up a smart salute as he approached.

"Can you find your way, sir?" He pointed at a pile of rubble. "It's round the other side now, sir. New door since you last came."

Kearton thanked him. The patrolman must have a very sharp memory to recall him, with all the comings and goings he must have to check throughout the course of a watch.

He saw the garden. There was a big crack in the wall, where someone had painted a number, for repair or demolition was anybody's guess. Thousands of houses must have been destroyed or severely damaged during the siege. One more crack would hardly count.

The door opened and she was facing him. Surprised, one hand going to her hair, the other still clutching a sack. "It's *you*! I didn't want you to see me like this!"

He reached out.

"Here, let me. I'm early— I'm sorry."

She held on to the sack. "It's just junk. The last of it, I hope." She threw it on to another pile. "And you're not too early. Far from it."

He took her hands, and held them. "You look wonderful." She did not resist as he pulled her closer, and turned her face so that he could kiss her cheek.

She said, "Not too close. I'm all sweaty after that!" Then she smiled. "You know, you're staring again."

They both laughed and walked together into the house. She was wearing khaki slacks and a pale green shirt, and her eyes and her hair were exactly as he remembered.

"You're worth staring at," he said.

She turned, quite suddenly, serious again.

"Are you really all right, Bob?" There was a slight hesitation, as if hearing his name again, on her own lips, could still surprise her. "We heard so many stories— rumours— one begins to doubt everything."

"I'm fine, Glynis. I had to see you. You see, I was worrying about *you*." He felt her flinch as he held her, without moving, almost touching. She did not look up.

"Remember, I'm all sweaty . . ." He could see her lashes, lowered to shield her eyes. Feel her breathing.

She said quietly, "Please, Bob, I'm only human." Then she lifted her chin, her eyes steady, determined. "And . . . I've got friends here."

There was a thud in the adjoining room, where he had seen the bed, and he heard voices. His hand was still on her waist. She did not attempt to remove it; all he heard was one word, barely audible.

"Please."

She moved away, and he saw the desk behind her. The same basket, empty now.

Then the room seemed crowded, although there were only two of them. Both Maltese, a dark-haired, athletic man with a ready smile which displayed a glinting gold tooth, and a pretty young woman, with the lilting laugh he had heard on the telephone. She wore a gold crucifix hanging between her breasts, and was heavily pregnant. They stood side by side, like children waiting to be introduced.

"Mr and Mrs Falzon." It seemed to break the tension. "Joseph and Stella." She took the man's arm. "Joseph used to work with my father."

He half bowed and displayed his gold tooth again.

"*For* your father, if you please!"

"And this is Lieutenant-Commander Kearton." She smiled, but did not look at him. "Bob Kearton."

Falzon gave a quick salute. "I know." He took Kearton's hand. "Much of my work is at, and for, the docks." He nodded slowly, his eyes serious. "I hear many things which I am not supposed to hear." He released his hand. "I am proud to know you, *the man*." He did not smile now, but repeated, "Proud."

Glynis said, "Sit down, Bob." She had turned, so that her face was hidden from the others. "You must be feeling bushed, if half the rumours are true." She laughed, but kept her eyes on him. "I can't even offer you a proper drink. There's only some sherry." She walked to the desk, her hand resting briefly on his shoulder as she passed. "Just sit there and I'll see what I can find. I'm so sorry— everything's been in turmoil . . ." She broke off as he reached up and covered her hand with his own.

Falzon said, "There is a car outside." His dark brows lifted only slightly. "You are still," he hesitated, "still in demand?"

Kearton grinned.

"I shall have to ask my superiors before I know that!"

They all laughed, but he saw her eyes flicking around the room. Remembering? Regretting?

She said, "Joseph and Stella are sharing rooms with me. So many people have had to be rehoused or evacuated because of the bombing, and the shortages. But I shall still have my office." Her hand moved slightly on the desk, near the telephone in its military-style container. "When *I* am in demand." The others laughed again, but Kearton saw something else. Disappointment, pain? It was neither.

He said, "At least I'll know my way next time."

The girl named Stella had been stooping over a low cupboard, and straightened, gasping, "Almost forgot!" She held out a bottle triumphantly. "The sherry, Glynis! All is not lost!"

Her husband hurried over to steady her, wagging a finger as a warning. But Kearton was looking at Glynis as she whispered, "There will be a next time, Bob? So much I wanted to say. To know . . ."

"I'm the same." She did not hear him.

"Two different lives, different worlds. I don't want you to think I'm one of 'those women'. It's not like that."

He reached out and took her wrist; she did not move or resist.

"I'd kill anyone who suggested it!"

Joseph Falzon was holding the bottle to the light.

"Too late. It has had its day, I fear."

He almost dropped the bottle as someone rapped loudly on the door. Glynis reached it first. It was the Royal Marine.

She looked across the room, eyes in shadow, expression hidden.

"For you, Bob."

The driver peered past her.

"Cap'n Garrick, sir. They say it's important."

Kearton had been expecting it. So had she. It made it no easier.

Important. Like that last time.

He waved to the others and turned away. She walked by his side, her hand through his arm, but hardly touching him.

He could see the two patrolmen by the hut now, and imagined what they were thinking. *Bloody officers. It's all right for some.*

She said, "It's not right. You've only just come back, and now they want you again. You've had no time . . ." She turned her head as the car started and began to manoeuvre away from a pile of debris. "If it hadn't been for me, you wouldn't have come all this way."

They stood by the parked van, and as though it offered some illusion of privacy, he took her hands.

"If it hadn't been for you, I wouldn't have *wanted* to come." The hands tensed. "Next time . . ." He released her. "I'd better go. Promise me you'll take care of yourself."

He turned toward the car, but she said, "*Next time*, Bob Kearton, call me again. Promise *me*." And she was suddenly pressed against him, her words muffled against his shoulder.

"So many things I wanted to say, to explain— and now there's no time!" She pushed some hair from her forehead with the characteristic gesture, and gazed up: he could feel her trembling. "Kiss me."

Not her cheek: her mouth, and then she walked away, toward the house, although she turned back for a moment. She might have waved, or been touching her hair. Or her eyes. Then she was gone.

He was in the car and it was moving before he could pull himself together. The usual barriers and arguments meant nothing. He was *wrong*, no matter what excuses his mind was offering.

He said, "Sorry to keep you hanging about."

The driver shot him a quick glance in the mirror.

"No bother, sir. I know a short cut. If it's still there!"

Kearton looked back, but other buildings had already moved out to hide the road and the checkpoint.

Next time. Like a hand reaching out.

He saw the glint of water, the motionless, moored ships. He could almost hear Garrick's voice. *Important.*

He was ready.

Garrick did not look at his watch.

"You made it, then?"

By the time he had returned Kearton's salute his mood had changed, and the famous grin was on display. "This can't wait. Today, of all days!"

In his best uniform and apparently straight from the V.I.P reception, he was in stark contrast to the clutter of the repair yard and motionless derricks. A few workers in overalls had stopped to stare, and Garrick gave them a wave which was both casual and deliberate. There should have been a camera ready, Kearton thought.

Garrick was saying, "I'd just about had it up to the gills. All that guff about expense and the hard-working souls behind the scenes, for the war effort, and for *us*, for God's sake! As if we were all sitting on our arses doing nothing!"

Kearton waited. He could smell the drink but Garrick was sober, if volatile. Sharp one minute, triumphant, even excited, the next.

"You know, some people, even senior ones, who ought to know better, have absolutely *no* idea what Special Operations can achieve. Have *already* achieved. I sometimes wonder!" He gestured toward a section of armed Royal Marines, and a rope barrier stretched across part of the yard. There was an officer in charge, a young, tough-looking lieutenant who marched toward them and saluted.

Garrick snapped, "He's with me, damn it!" but relented immediately. "Show him your I.D., Bob. He's only carrying out my orders." He nodded to the lieutenant. "Well done."

Kearton saw the smart salute. This was a restricted area; everybody knew that. So why all the extra security?

He realized that Garrick had stopped and was facing him, with his back toward one of the smaller repair basins.

He said, "For months, I've hoped and dreamed of something like this. I've had agents, good men, risking their lives to discover a flaw in the enemy's defences." He was standing on the very edge of the basin, like a showman. "Now, out of the blue, the *Deep Blue*, has come my reward!" He waited while Kearton stepped carefully to the edge. "Ran out of fuel, stopped and helpless, when along comes H.M. Minesweeper *Gabriel*. Now, see for yourself!"

The torpedo boat lay directly below him, held in place by wooden booms, and with mooring ropes and wires reaching out to keep her clear of the rough concrete. As if she were snared in a trap. Italian, about half the size of 992 and the other D-Boats, but with the clean, rakish lines he had never forgotten. Four torpedo tubes; usually able to carry a full cargo of depth-charges to fulfil her other role as an A/S vessel, and equipped with engines which could offer forty knots at the touch of a switch. He could hear them now in his mind. Like the ones they had encountered that night.

He had studied them often enough in the recognition manuals. Fast and deadly: the Italians had, after all, been the pioneers in this class. A crew of eighteen or nineteen. A command anyone would be proud of.

This one had run out of fuel. And out of luck.

"Did they put up a fight?" He could see no damage, or evidence of gunfire.

Garrick was beside him, staring down into the basin.

"*Gabriel*'s skipper fired a warning shot over them. That was enough. The Italian commander had other ideas, and tried to scuttle her." He walked a few paces and gave his theatrical wave to one of the overalled figures who was using a flashlight over the side of a floating pontoon. The man grinned and responded with a thumbs-up.

Garrick exclaimed, "Bloody perfect!" He seemed to recall what he had been saying. "*Gabriel*'s skipper is a bit of a hard case. R.N.R., used to be a trawlerman before the war. He switched on his loud-hailer and told them the nearest land was a hundred miles away. It would be a long swim!"

"And the Italian changed his mind?"

Garrick moved away from the edge. "His crew did it for him!"

Kearton looked again at the dock. "Fuel would always be something of a risk. A range of three hundred miles, sometimes less, at twenty knots?"

Garrick nodded.

"Nothing wrong with your memory, Bob. So we'll not take any chances. We may never get another opportunity like this. I told *Gabriel*'s skipper as much. It's the *catch of the season*!"

He laughed abruptly at his own joke and walked back to the

edge. "Not much time, and we can't afford to waste it." He was thinking aloud. "We'll use one of your boats, to tow this one for part of the distance. Save fuel, and give us time to prepare." He snapped his fingers. "Who d'you suggest?"

"John Stirling, in 986." He felt numb, as if someone else was responding to Garrick's clipped urgency. "He's had a lot of experience in the Med."

For a moment he thought Garrick had not heard him, or had already shifted to another tack. But he said, "The Canadians? If you say so. I'll go along with that."

Then he looked at his watch again. "I'll leave you to deal with, er, Stirling. He's on stand-by, so he *should* be on top line." Then, very quietly, "By the way, the convoy will be arriving in the forenoon, a little later than planned. Had a spot of bother on the last leg, but nothing we can't deal with at this end."

Kearton said, "You'll want the operation to begin before that, sir?"

Garrick smiled.

"I'll have the full details sent to you immediately— or I'll want to know the reason. No time to hang about. We can't keep our 'catch' a secret for long. The prisoners, or someone spilling the beans over a few gins!" He straightened his cap. "Brice knows what to do. He'd better!"

Garrick's new aide was hovering close by now, a wad of papers in his hand; the bomb-happy lieutenant had been replaced. Garrick had seen him, but seemed oddly unwilling to leave.

Then he said, "It'll be your show, Bob. Another rendezvous. Not much warning— there never is. I'm depending on you. So be it!"

Kearton walked toward the barrier, and saw one of the guards waiting to pass him through.

An hour ago? Less? *Next time* . . . Right or wrong, she was with him now.

10

No Guts . . . No Glory

Lieutenant Toby Ainslie sat in a corner of the M.T.B.'s crowded wardroom and wondered why it should feel so different. He knew all but one of the faces here, at least by sight; he had always had a good memory for those. Names were something else. Stirling, the Canadian commanding officer, had made him welcome enough, and had apologized for the lack of hospitality. Time did not allow it.

Like their own boat, this one had been built to exactly the same design, and in the same British yard, and probably launched within a few weeks of 992. All the fittings and armament matched, so there was no chance of losing your sense of direction during the night watches. So where was the difference? Ainslie could not define it, but it was here. The voices, the smells from an identical galley, a couple of framed photographs on the bulkhead, a hockey team on skates, another of a sailing cutter with an iceberg close abeam. But he was still not certain . . .

He could feel the vibrating murmur of generators, hear loose gear being dragged across the deck. *Making ready for sea.* He knew that was the real reason for his anxiety. Maybe if they had been ordered to sail again soon after their last grim assignment, but in their own boat, it might not have been so upsetting. He was not afraid; surely he would know that by now.

There was plenty of coffee, hot and strong. He sipped it gratefully, and saw the first lieutenant, Tom Cusack, watching him. "Too powerful, Toby?" He was smiling, but there was something else, reminiscent of the moment when the Skipper had introduced him as 'Pilot'.

Cusack had been smiling then. "Don't trust us, eh?"

Ainslie listened to the others. Mostyn, the other commanding officer, and his first lieutenant, who would be remaining here on stand-by. And Spiers, holding the fort and keeping an eye on the repairs. It was hard to know how he felt about being left behind.

He darted a quick glance at the other stranger in the wardroom, a Lieutenant Warren: he had not caught his first name. Kearton had met him on the upper deck. It had been quiet, unemotional, and all the more moving for that.

Kearton had gripped Warren by the shoulders and had held him without speaking. Then, "How long? For God's sake, I thought . . ." He had not continued. Warren had nodded, his eyes never leaving Kearton's.

"I thought so too, Bob. Took them six months to put me together again."

Kearton had said to Ainslie, "Eighteen months ago, maybe more. We were based at Dover a while . . ." He had touched Warren's arm again. "It was rough going, at the time."

Warren wore a leather glove on what remained of his right hand. Ainslie had seen it when he had been unfastening a folder of charts: more like a claw than a hand, it was a miracle he could still use it. He had seen Ainslie's expression, and made a joke of it.

"The glove makes it more presentable when I'm saluting my betters!" He had obviously made the remark often, with pain now of a different sort.

Like Kearton, he wore the ribbon of the D.S.C. on his jacket. They were perhaps the same age but Warren, not surprisingly, looked much older. Now he was attached to Special Operations, so he must have volunteered for this latest mission, and was in charge of the captured Italian torpedo boat.

Ainslie had seen some of the Canadian sailors watching him, surprised or pleased when he had thrown them a friendly greeting, and thought of the unknown man who had died, gripping his wrists, his eyes so desperate as he had breathed out the name. *Jethro.* Warren was different. He looked the part, whatever 'the part' was. So why did he and men like him continue to take such risks?

Spiers was glancing at his watch. He had been scheduled to go to a party aboard Geoff Mostyn's boat this evening. That, too, would have to go by the board.

Lieutenant Stirling entered the wardroom, a tall, lean man whose hair seemed almost to touch the deckhead. He had a good reputation, and had already served in the Med before transferring to his own command via England. But Kearton was the S.O. of their little group, and Ainslie wondered if Stirling resented taking second place in this new operation.

He recalled the first lieutenant's wry comment. *Don't trust us, eh?*

Kearton was here now, frowning at something Mostyn was saying to him, then leaning over to flatten a chart on the table.

Ainslie realized that Warren's gloved fist was beside his own on the chart, and he murmured politely, "Sorry, I forgot to ask." He saw the glove tighten, almost imperceptibly. "What's your first name?"

The glove relaxed, and the smile became genuine.

"Another Toby, I'm afraid."

Ainslie stared at the chart.

"I'll call you Mark One, if that's O.K. with you?"

"Very well, Mark Two. That's soon settled!"

He had made a friend. And it mattered.

Kearton said abruptly, "All right, gentlemen. There's no time to rest on our laurels. The convoy is due to arrive in the forenoon, and there may be air attacks." He looked around the wardroom. "So we shall begin Operation *Retriever* at four in the morning. I don't have to remind anyone, this is Top Secret." He looked at Mostyn. "You're on stand-by, Geoff," and smiled. "And it means just that. So be ready."

Ainslie watched him with something like admiration. On the bridge and all hell breaking loose, caring about his crew, and even the man who had died after the explosion . . . then getting them all back to base, only to be ordered to some damned meeting. And now this . . .

The others were standing around the table. They had their written orders, not that those would tell or prepare them for much.

He started as the glove tapped his hand again.

"Operation *Retriever*. That's a dog, isn't it?" He stood up as Kearton beckoned to him, but added softly, "It should be a rat!"

Mostyn and his Number One were leaving, no good-byes, no "good luck". Ainslie wondered if he would ever get used to it: the casualness, the apparent indifference.

Spiers was the last to leave.

"I'll chase up the repairs, sir." He seemed to falter. "This doesn't seem right. I should be here, with you."

Stirling watched him go and waved.

"Don't wait up for us! This one's *ours*!"

Ainslie heard him, and knew it was the worst thing he could have said.

Kearton stood in the forepart of the bridge and watched the sea opening on either bow. A grey, almost colourless morning, with low cloud, and windless, apart from their own progress. The experts had predicted fine weather and no rain.

He had heard Stirling, the C.O., remark, "Don't the lazy buggers ever look out of their windows?"

He did not glance astern. Nothing had changed. The captured Italian boat was still following obediently at the end of the tow, showing her sleek, graceful lines, although regarded and spoken of by Stirling's crew as a bloody menace.

Few of them cared much about the need to conserve her fuel. The tow had reduced their own speed to ten knots. They would be a ready target if anything hostile chose to appear.

Five hours since they had slipped their moorings, and with a dimly lit pilot boat had headed out into open water. That, too, had been strange, almost uncanny. Pitch dark, and so still behind the ancient walls and ramparts it seemed the whole of Malta was asleep.

And yet, when they had left the pilot and steered past the headland, they had been conscious of the silent crowds, dark and unmoving, revealed only by an occasional cigarette, or someone lighting a pipe. So much for secrecy. The convoy was on its way. What had once been the margin between survival and surrender was now a stepping-stone to revenge and, eventually, victory.

Few may have noticed the ill-assorted vessels, leaving nose-to-tail without fuss or ceremony. They might have to depend on that.

Stirling joined him now, one hand resting on the flag locker. He gestured toward the pale shape astern, weaving slightly in response to both rudder and tow-line.

"That guy, Warren— I gather you served with him before? What he's doing now must be a different kettle of fish. Rather him than me."

Kearton knew it was a question.

"I thought he was dead. It was pretty grim in the Channel at the time. Not enough boats, the usual thing . . . He wouldn't be here with us, if he hadn't been vetted for the job."

Stirling looked at the sky, then the horizon, what there was of it.

"So after we break the tow, he heads for the islands, right? Pantelleria— our old stamping ground." He rubbed his chin. "From then it gets a little bit dicey . . . I mean for him and his crew. Can he rely on the rendezvous?"

Kearton tried to relax. It was far better to get it out into the open. And how *did* they know, anyway? It would have begun with a brief message from some agent or collaborator. Then the faces around a table. An improbable plan. A decision.

But instead, he saw Garrick. *I'm depending on you.*

He turned and looked at Stirling, bare-headed against the clouds. Close by he could see one of the lookouts, glasses trained but unmoving, trying to hear what his C.O. was saying.

"The rendezvous is that small island, south-east of the main one. Just a cluster of rocks according to the Pilot's Guide, for what it's worth. Volcanic. God knows how anyone can exist there for long. But that's all we've got." Then he did glance astern. "This unexpected 'gift' was a godsend." He felt his mouth crack into a smile. "Someone would have been sent, anyway. The luck of the game!"

Stirling watched a flash of white on the dull water. A sea bird.

He said, "That gull will sleep ashore, while we're still plodding up and down out here."

Kearton said, "I've been promised air cover for the home run!"

Stirling laughed. He had heard that one before. But the lookout seemed satisfied, and his binoculars began to move again.

There were more voices now; they were checking the tow-line, preparing to cast off. One was the coxswain, a solidly built petty officer who sported a thick black beard with eyebrows to match. He had heard Turnbull speak of him a few times with admiration, if not awe. That in itself was unusual.

His name was Cossette, and he came from St John's. A Newfie, Turnbull had called him. He was standing just below the bridge, the NEWFOUNDLAND flash clearly visible on his shoulder. He saw Kearton looking down and beamed, his teeth bared in a grin. "Ready to go, sur!" Even his accent was different from the others'.

Kearton raised his own binoculars to watch the Italian. A few figures on deck, near one of the empty tubes: volunteers, probably chosen by Warren himself.

He said abruptly, "I'm sending Ainslie. Can we get alongside, or will the dinghy be needed?"

Stirling said only, "Does he know?" Then, "I can go along-side— seems calm enough." He repeated, "Does he know?"

Kearton remembered the moment. Stirling needed his full crew, in case it took longer than planned, or they had to fight; and Stirling was experienced. He knew.

It went deeper than that.

It had been in 986's chartroom an hour ago, when he had been examining the calculations and courses on the charts, the timing and recognition information in the log. And all the while, although it had probably only been minutes, aware of Ainslie's face. Intent. Older in some way.

"Standing by, Skipper. Mark Two to the rescue!"

As if he had known from the beginning.

"Signal, sir! Ready to start up!"

Kearton had seen the brief blink of light from the other boat.

"Cox'n on the wheel, sur!" But the Newfoundlander was reporting to Stirling, not the senior officer. He was only a passenger, until proven otherwise.

The engines coughed twice, three times, and thundered into life, fumes spiralling over the hull until the beat steadied in response to unseen hands below deck.

Someone exclaimed, "Sounds good. Sweet as a nut!" Relieved, like the rest of them.

Stirling said, "Looks about right, sir. Just say the word." He sounded tense, conscious of the moment.

Kearton saw the seamen lowering rope fenders to reduce the impact when the other craft came alongside. No time for mistakes: they were all waiting for his command. No time to show the hesitation that might be mistaken for doubt.

"Cast off."

He climbed down from the bridge and joined Ainslie by the guardrail. It was one thing to face danger or to go into action together, but somehow this was different. He heard a shout, and the squeal of wire as the tow-line was hauled inboard at full speed to avoid fouling the screws. Someone slithering and falling on the wet deck, followed by a few insults and curses. But the job was done, and the Italian was already moving out, foam surging away astern as her own power revealed itself for the first time.

Ainslie stood with the familiar satchel across one shoulder and a carefully wrapped chart shielded against the spray, watching the activity. He seemed very calm, or he was hiding his true feelings well.

Kearton touched his arm and thought he felt it jerk.

"Sorry to do this to you, Pilot." He gripped his elbow. "*Mark Two*. You know what's needed. In and out, no unnecessary risks. We'll be waiting."

The deck quivered as the two hulls lurched together. The Italian boat seemed even smaller alongside. He saw some of the crew, a handful of men, a couple in battledress but without rank or distinction, some in shabby overalls.

He heard one of the Canadians remark, "Which side are they on?" But nobody laughed.

Lieutenant Warren was on the low bridge, the only one in regulation uniform.

Ainslie gripped the rail and watched the hulls slide together again.

"Wish me . . ." He stopped in mid-sentence and jumped down to the Italian's deck, where he was helped by two of the crew.

Kearton waved. He knew what Ainslie had been about to say. He was learning, the hardest way of all.

He murmured, "I do. And I'll be waiting." But it was lost in the roar of engines, the sound trapped between the hulls until they veered apart in a great burst of spray. In a few minutes they were well clear of one another, even as the tow-line was still being stowed away.

Kearton shaded his eyes to watch the other boat turning, showing her narrow stern, already shrouded in foam or surface haze. Only one vivid patch of colour, the red, green and white Italian flag, which had been hoisted to enhance the deception.

Stirling was waiting for him.

"Well, that went smoothly enough!" He seemed glad to be moving again. "I never get used to these hole-in-the-wall jobs." He peered astern, but the sea was already empty. "Rather him than me . . . but I said that, didn't I?"

Kearton said, "I'll be in the chartroom. Any problems, call me."

Stirling watched him climb down the forward ladder directly from the bridge, just a few feet away. He would not get much peace there.

He glanced at the compass, half-listening to the steady revolutions of the engines. Not dragging their heels any more, a target for any unseen enemy. He could feel the coxswain's eyes on him. Wanting some excuse to talk, or swap experiences. He wanted neither right now.

Instead, he thought of the man who had just left him, and was alone now with the consequences of his decisions. And his regrets, if he allowed for such things. Bob Kearton *was* the senior officer.

His mind repeated the same stubborn defence. *Rather him than me.*

Ainslie wedged himself against the table and made another

176

attempt to tighten the deckhead light, and restrict its so far lively response to the thrust of engines and rudder.

It seemed easier, or maybe he was becoming accustomed to the sounds and motion. He glanced around the 'chart space' as Toby Warren had described it, like a large cupboard. The table filled most of it.

He swallowed hard as the hull dipped beneath him again, although he knew the sea was still as calm as when he had climbed, or rather dropped, from the Canadians' bridge. He was *not* going to be sick . . . and he had nothing to throw up anyway. He could not remember when he had last eaten a proper meal.

He rearranged his chart beside those already stowed here, and touched his instruments; they, at least, were familiar. Reassuring.

There was a narrow bunk of sorts across the end of the 'space', like a wire cot. Better than nothing if the going got a bit rough, but a Bren machine-gun and several magazines of ammunition already filled most of it. It made the M.T.B.'s chartroom seem vast by comparison.

He stared at the charts again, his mind clearing. The twist of apprehension he had felt when he had jumped aboard was under control. He was here, like it or not. But he would never belong.

He listened to the powerful Isotta-Franschini engines, recalling Kearton's instant reaction to their distinctive sound before that first deadly encounter. They were doing a steady twenty knots at the moment, but could increase to nearly forty at the turn of a switch. It was hard to believe he could still be excited by the speed and grace of this unfamiliar boat, even in the face of real danger, and the others were the same. He had even heard someone laughing.

He thought of the crew, twelve in number although the original complement would have been eighteen or nineteen. But they were not going to fight. The tubes were empty, and although the depth-charges had been replaced and arranged on their racks, they hardly seemed to fit their new role.

He bent over the chart table again. It was pointless to hope or regret. This was real. *Now.*

He studied the pencilled lines and bearings, the islands, and the smallest one of all, La Roccella del Diavolo, marked with a final cross. Someone, probably Warren, had written the translation starkly and clearly. *Devil's Rock.*

They would make their landfall at dusk. To do so later would be to invite disaster.

And when Operation *Retriever* was over, what then? A fast run back to rejoin Kearton, or would they have to fight their way out?

He recalled Warren's quiet sarcasm, or was it anger? *Operation Rat.* He, better than anyone, knew what they would be up against.

He swore under his breath as the point of his pencil snapped, and looked at the notes and recognition signals clipped beside the charts. Like a giant puzzle waiting to be solved.

He started as a panel slid back at the top of the 'cupboard'. He could smell the sea, feel it on his skin.

Warren was peering down at him, his gloved hand around the panel.

"All done?" He did not wait for a reply. "I'm glad you're aboard, Mark Two. I'm more used to matchbox navigation than your way of doing things!"

Ainslie said, "It's the best I can do," and found he was able to grin back at him. "Devil's Rock— that's all I need!"

Warren called something to the helmsman and turned back, reaching down to grip his shoulder.

"Here we go! As they say in this outfit, *No Guts, No Glory*!"

Ainslie retrieved the broken pencil, remembering one of his old instructors. *Never put it off until tomorrow.* He heard the change of beat as they reduced speed again. To look and to listen . . . It was hard to think of all those other times. When you had been so certain there would *be* a tomorrow . . .

He touched his chin. Maybe he would have another go at growing a 'set'. He had not yet told Sarah about it . . . He could imagine her laughing at him.

He must write to her.

He heard feet moving, forward of the bridge, he thought. He glanced at the Bren gun on the bunk. *Preparing for trouble.* The letter would have to wait. He could still feel the claw-like hand on his shoulder.

Until after tomorrow . . .

The final approach to the island seemed slow beyond measure, and even with the engines throttled down to offer only a few knots the sound mocked all their attempts at caution.

Ainslie stood side by side with Warren in the forepart of the small bridge, conversation at a minimum, hardly daring to use binoculars in case they missed some isolated sign or movement.

Nearer and nearer, the hump-backed island eventually reaching out across either bow, more like a giant shadow than solid rock.

Closer still, and Warren took the wheel himself. He had already mentioned a previous visit to Devil's Rock, in an old fishing boat, on another unspecified mission to land or remove some agents. His description had been terse, almost frag-mented. Rocky bottom. No good for anchoring if a wind got up. Easy to run aground at the southern side of the entrance. An old wreck still there when they found the place. Most skippers kept well clear of it, if they had any sense.

Ainslie saw the forward gun, a slim-barrelled, quick-firing cannon, not unlike an Oerlikon, training around now as if to smell out the first hint of danger.

So slowly now that hardly a crest broke away from the stem, but the echo of their approach stayed with them.

Ainslie saw the faint outline of their Italian flag, lifting and dropping, although he could feel no breeze. He knew that one of the crew was ready with a White Ensign, and had heard another snap, "You'll look great when they wrap you in that!"

No humour that time, only tension, as sharp as a blade.

Ainslie wanted to move, to speak, anything to break the relentless stillness.

No sudden challenge, or cluster of flares like those listed in the captured log book. No burst of gunfire as they headed into a carefully prepared trap . . .

It was clear enough on the chart, an inlet widening into a flask-shaped little bay, the only possible anchorage of this bleak landfall. He heard the wheel move again, Warren's feet shifting as he peered into the shadows. Time had almost run out. They must turn and attempt a different approach, or stand well clear of the island until dawn, despite the vital need to conserve fuel.

Someone shouted and Warren said quietly, "*Got you*, you bastard."

Ainslie saw it, too. A solitary spire of rock that marked one side of the inlet. Whoever had discovered it and marked it on the first chart had left it unnamed. Ainslie took a deep breath and saw Warren waving to one of his crew. The light was going, but he might have been grinning.

The land was already moving out to surround them, quieter than ever . . . but the sky was still clear enough to give shape and substance to the anchorage.

"Stop engines!" Warren turned the wheel and watched the rock spire move steadily across the stern until it, too, was lost from view. "Let go!"

The anchor hit the water and in a few moments the silence was complete.

Warren walked out on to the side-deck and gripped a rail with the claw. Then he looked at Ainslie.

"Made it!"

"Thanks to you."

Warren shook his head. "You got us here. I just have a good memory for the last nasty bit."

Some of his men were checking their weapons. A few had stationed themselves by the small capstan, to pay out more cable, or cut it in an emergency.

Ainslie said, "They all know what to do."

Warren was gesturing to one of them.

"That's why they're still alive." His mood changed. "Now we wait. But we leave at dawn, *no matter what*, see?"

Ainslie stared into the darkness, surprised that he felt no fear or doubt. Because of the man beside him.

"Anything I can do?"

Warren had dragged off his glove and was opening and closing his fingers.

"Nothing much, Mark Two. Me, I'm going to have a drink." He punched his arm lightly. "Don't worry, I'll be all about when *they* get here."

"Do you know any of them?"

Warren looked round instantly as a fish jumped and splashed alongside the hull.

Then he said, "Doubt it. Safer not to, in this game."

They walked a few paces aft and Ainslie saw an open hatch, felt the warm breath of the engineroom. Standing by, ready to move when the call came. He wondered how they felt, with so much depending on them, in a vessel they scarcely knew and might never see again after Operation *Retriever*. He thought of Laidlaw, his own Chief, who somehow managed to make his massive machinery seem almost human. *Old Growler* . . .

He said, "The one they call Jethro. What about him?"

Warren turned toward him. His features were in shadow now.

"Of course, you were with him on that other operation, weren't you? Said to be one of the best. I've worked with him a couple of times . . . I *think*. He gets results." He peered at his watch. "You stick with Bob Kearton while you can. He's special, believe me. They broke the mould after they made him." He sounded as if he might have been smiling. "They tell me you were a schoolmaster in civvy street. Good for you."

Ainslie said, "I'm still learning," and could feel it like a barrier between them. "What about you?"

"I don't see what—" Then his voice softened. "I was a draughtsman, as a matter of fact. Pretty good one too, they told me." He held up the gloved claw and shook it slowly. "But I taught myself to shoot with my left hand, so it's not all a dead loss!"

He patted Ainslie's arm. "They should be making contact in a couple of hours, at the most." He moved to the side and seemed to be staring at the dark water. "Then we'll get out of here, as fast as you like, eh?"

Ainslie could feel the silence, as if he were hesitating, contemplating the consequences of breaking or dishonouring some code.

"As I said, Mark Two, Jethro's one of the best. But don't ever turn your back on him."

Kearton levered his body forward in the canvas chair and sat quite still while his mind came back to awareness. The chartroom was in darkness save for a small light, almost hidden by the charts he had been scanning. How long ago? A few seconds, an hour; nothing seemed clear. But he was instantly awake.

So many watches, all times and in all weathers. The engines, steady, unhurried, the hull lifting and dipping, but no more than might be expected in the open sea.

The usual sounds, or those to which he had become accustomed in an unfamiliar boat. An occasional creak of the wheel, feet, the helmsman's or a lookout, above and behind him.

He found he was gripping one arm of the chair, tensing his entire body as if to withstand something. But there was nothing.

How long? How many miles? He could see the notepad beside the dividers and parallel rulers. He did not need to look at it; the sight of those ordinary instruments was more than enough to remind him of Ainslie and the satchel he always kept close by, a little memento of his last school.

In his mind he could still see the Italian boat heading away, see their faces as he outlined their new assignment, the degree of interest or concern reflecting each man's experience and involvement.

He had thought of little else. Now the worst was over. Either the agents had been recovered, or they had been directed to a different rendezvous. Time or fuel would decide.

If he had been there with them, it might have been different . . .

He stood up slowly, finding his balance, as he had done every day at sea. And he thought of Ainslie, young, light-hearted, embarking on something that was a far cry from the navigation school, or, for that matter, his earlier days in front of a class. He switched off the light and uncovered one of the ports. Darkness: not even a star. He closed it.

He heard someone stamping his feet. It would be cold on watch, even here.

Only half the hands were at their defence stations; John Stirling saw no point in keeping everyone on watch. In the Channel or North Sea, you would expect it. Here . . . in his mind, he pictured the Sicilian coastline and scattered islands. Human endurance took first place.

He heard another sound, like a hatch or door slamming. He knew it was close to midnight: the middle watch was taking over. Perhaps some tea or coffee was on its way.

He raised his hand to stifle the yawn, but found it frozen in mid-air. He was wide awake, and even as he groped for the intercom he heard it come to life.

It was Stirling himself. Unwilling or unable to snatch some rest.

"What is it, John?"

Stirling sounded disconcerted. Because the senior officer was unable to sleep, or because he had been expecting it, despite all the restrictions on unnecessary signals. The enemy had ears too, and used them.

"Urgent, sir." He paused, and in the silence Kearton could hear somebody humming a little tune close by.

"Bring it, will you?" The humming stopped.

He looked at the chair, but remained standing. Stirling was an old hand and knew all the guises. He heard more feet, men going on watch. Everything normal, war or no war.

Stirling came into the chartroom and shut the door behind him. He had spray on his jacket, and probably come along the side-deck to avoid going through the bridge, with its eyes and unspoken questions.

"Priority." He half smiled, but it did not reach his eyes. "Bet that got Cap'n Garrick out of the sack!"

"He never sleeps." Kearton opened the signal and held it to the light. "You've got a good telegraphist on watch, John. Neat and clear, no matter what."

Something to say, to give himself time. When there was no time . . .

"Operation *Retriever* is aborted." He looked at the signal again, the phrases as devoid of emotion as his own voice. It had to be like that, when it should have been written in blood.

Stirling said, "You knew, didn't you? I can't believe . . ." He broke off as Kearton leaned over the table and moved one of the charts.

"They'll be there, on that godforsaken island right now." He looked up. "Waiting for *us*."

184

"Something must have come up . . ." But he knew Kearton did not hear him.

Kearton screwed up the signal flimsy and banged it on the table.

"We can still reach the rendezvous on time." He stared at the door, and sensed someone was standing just outside, listening. It was so quiet; everything was quiet, even the sea and the hull.

He tried to sharpen his mind, outline the next move. Stirling was waiting to carry out the necessary instructions from his senior officer.

He said, "Alter course now, John. *Retriever.*"

Their eyes met.

"And the signal, sir?"

"What signal?"

Stirling breathed out slowly.

"If it's OK with you, sir, I'd like to tell the boys myself." Impetuously, he held out his hand. "They'll want to share it."

Kearton picked up his binoculars.

"I'll be on the bridge."

When he reached the bridge, his eyes slowly became accustomed to the shadows. Most of the watchkeepers had donned oilskins as protection against the cold, and the occasional clouds of drifting spray. He had heard Stirling's voice, unhurried, calm. Like his crew, he was obeying orders. *My orders.* But it would take more than a handshake when the real truth hit them.

A fist came from somewhere with a mug of something hot.

"Best I can do, Skipper." The flash of a grin. "All drinks on the officers when we get back to Base, eh?"

So be it. We're coming.

11

Those in Peril

Ainslie tugged off his cap and pushed his fingers through his hair, if only to break the oppressive stillness. He looked up at the sky, and felt something click in his neck. He had lost all sense of time and thought it was lighter, with a few faint stars showing between the clouds. But he knew it was only in his imagination. In his hopes.

He could have been alone on the little bridge, but he knew someone was crouching by the motionless wheel, and there was another at the machine-gun mounting below the mast.

The hull was barely moving, the water black and silent alongside. He was surprised that he was not tired by the waiting and the tension. He was beyond fatigue: drained would be a fairer description.

He knew Warren was standing on the opposite side of the bridge, although he had hardly spoken, except briefly and softly into a voicepipe. Only once had he revealed any sign of nerves, when one of the crew had complained about the empty torpedo tubes and lack of weapons.

"This is a *bus*, not a bloody battleship! You of all people should know that!"

The shadow had muttered something, but said no more.

Ainslie loosened the watch on his wrist. There was no point in looking at it; there was no luminous dial. He moved it again;

the strap needed tightening. It had been a Christmas present from his parents, the first year of the war.

What would they think if they could see him now?

"I'm going round the boat. Take over, will you?" Warren, beside him, but he had not seen or heard him move.

"D'you think it will be much longer . . ." He got no further.

"How the *hell*—" Warren stopped abruptly. "Sorry, Mark Two. I must be getting past it." He stared outboard, at the dark water or the black edge of land.

He said, "One of my last jobs involved an old fishing boat. I told you. It was all we could do to keep the thing afloat most of the time." He might have shrugged. "Here, we've got W/T we mustn't use, and forty knots at the turn of a switch, and we're still bloody helpless." He turned away. "I'd better show my face and make sure everyone's still awake." He paused, and Ainslie knew he was fastening the glove. Then he said, "Another hour and we get our skates on. Can't risk waiting any longer. No matter what."

Somehow, Ainslie sensed it was a question, and how out of character it was for this strong, driven man.

He answered, "My skipper will be waiting," and tried to find the words. "Maybe there'll be new orders."

"Very likely. Bloody typical." He swung round, even as the sound of a shot echoed in the anchorage.

At sea it would have passed unnoticed, but here and now it was like a clap of thunder.

Ainslie remained motionless, expecting more shots, imagining them hitting the hull and worse. Far worse . . . There was nothing.

Other sounds now, the scrape of a hatch: the engineroom ready to go. A cocking-lever being pulled, then released. The wheel moving only slightly as the shadow nudged against it.

Warren said softly, "Be ready with the flag. Haul the raft alongside."

The raft was a small inflatable affair, which required only one brave man to paddle it ashore.

Someone muttered, "They're comin'. I wonder how many?"

Warren did not turn.

"One less than expected, by the sound of it."

Ainslie was shivering, shocked by the brutal truth.

Warren pushed past him and called to the men on deck, "Stand by, lads! Don't move until I give the signal!"

The raft was already well away from the side, the twin-bladed paddle hardly causing a ripple, and Ainslie sensed that the gun was moving, the slender barrel trained over and beyond it.

Warren said, "Now or never." He could have been remarking on a drill or exercise.

It was all taking too long. Ainslie did not have to look at the sky to sense the closeness of dawn. When it came, it would be sudden. Like the springing of a trap.

"There it is!" A tiny flash, low down. Almost touching the water, unless his eyes were playing tricks.

The man at the wheel said, "What *kept* you, matey?"

Ainslie saw another faceless figure hurry past the bridge, some rope, a heaving-line, looped over his arm and shoulder. And another man lying prone on the deck, a gun already propped and aimed toward the shore. It was the Bren he had seen in the chart space. Now, like parts of a machine, Warren's team was ready for the next move, as if they had been working together aboard this boat for months, not hours.

He heard Warren mutter, "Easy now. Easy," perhaps only to himself. Then he said sharply, "Stand by. Pass the word!" and Ainslie heard the click as he unfastened his holster, and remembered what Warren had said about learning to shoot with his left hand. He was suddenly, nauseatingly alive to the presence of danger. Of death.

He heard the raft before it appeared, almost alongside. Extra paddles this time, and someone half in the water like a corpse, who managed to reach up with one hand as the heaving-line fell across them.

They were being hauled aboard now. Only three of them, one obviously injured or wounded.

A blur of face peered up from the deck.

"That's the lot, sir!"

Warren said curtly, "Hope it was worth it," but again, maybe only to himself.

Then he called, "Get the raft inboard!" He reached out to touch Ainslie's arm without taking his eyes from the activity below the bridge. "Take care of them, Toby. I'll get the show on the road again."

Afterwards, Ainslie was aware of the concern in his voice, and the fact that he had used his name instead of the slightly mocking 'Mark Two'.

As he jumped down to the deck, small things stood out in his mind, and he would never forget them. One of the crew helping the solitary oarsman from the raft. Saying nothing, but hugging him, excluding everybody else. Then one of them gasped, "One more bloody time, eh, Tom?"

And the injured man, who had apparently taken a fall during the final, almost sheer descent to the water's edge, by his accent an Australian, or perhaps a New Zealander: Ainslie could never tell the difference. "It had better be worth it!" Then he had fainted.

Below decks, still unfamiliar and blinding in the sudden glare of lights, Ainslie recognized the third agent, despite the beard and filthy clothing, or maybe because of them. And the pale eyes, keen and clear, as if the rest were merely a mask.

The voice was as he remembered it, clipped and assertive. "We meet again. Makes a change from the blackboard, I imagine?"

Ainslie saw the dark stain across his arm and hip, but when he offered assistance it was declined, almost angrily.

"Not my blood. He tried to change sides, the little bastard. Picked the wrong moment."

And then the engines coughed and roared into life, the hull quivering around and beneath them as if it had been unleashed. Ainslie tasted the fuel, and felt the sudden urgency. After the silence and the strain of waiting, it was almost unnerving.

He said tentatively, "We have some blankets, and hot drinks . . ."

The man he knew only as Jethro was not listening. He was watching his injured colleague being carried past on a makeshift stretcher.

"I shall come on deck in a moment." He turned sharply as another sound cut through the surge of power. The cable had been broken. They were under way.

Ainslie said, "I hope it was all worthwhile."

The eyes flashed with a sudden, cold hostility in the deckhead light.

"Hardly your concern, is it, Lieutenant?" Someone shouted through the hatch and he added, "I think you're wanted." Then he smiled again, disarmingly, and moved aside as Ainslie made for the ladder.

He was grateful for the cool air on his face, the sound of the sea breaking away from the bows, the boat alive again. It would soon be time to alter course and use that pinnacle of rock to guide them through the narrow entrance and out into open sea. He stared at the broken cliffs, still in complete darkness. *Away from this evil place.* No matter what might still be waiting for them.

He thought of the man he had left below. What reaction had he expected? He had been under great strain, and always at risk.

Better to die than to be captured. Like the bloodstains on his clothing . . . It was a different sort of war. The word 'unclean' came to his mind, and he dismissed it hurriedly.

Warren was on the bridge, arms folded, watching the

strengthening light on the water. His part was almost finished, until the next rendezvous. Unless he chose to quit. And somehow, Ainslie knew he would not.

Warren greeted him quite cheerfully.

"Another half hour and we'll be clear of this place. Then you can take over the con, right?" He grinned. "You must open the throttles and see what speed this little box of tricks can do."

He gestured toward the main hatch.

"Now you know what a real-life hero looks like. I'll lay odds he gets another gong after this little lot. Bloody well deserves it, too." Something caught his attention and he moved away, leaving the words hanging in the air.

But Ainslie could not forget the other words, spoken almost as a warning.

Don't ever turn your back on him.

A different war, a covert war, which only those who were directly involved in might understand. Any kind of success must always be measured against the brutal penalities for failure.

He listened to the engines, louder and more compelling as the land moved closer on either beam. He could see it as if it were on the chart, and in his rough sketches. The narrow entrance to this bleak volcanic refuge, which must have claimed so many victims over the years.

"Starboard fifteen. Midships. Steady." Warren seemed calm, absorbed, as if he were responding to the compass and rudder, and not the other way round. Ainslie uncovered his binoculars and lifted them carefully to study the first gleam of water, and the prevailing barriers of land. And there, fine on the port bow, was Warren's pinnacle of rock, like a stark marker, moving away from the headland to be left undisturbed.

He raised the binoculars very slightly, his wrists trembling to the vibration of the engines. The tip of the pinnacle was painted a sudden gold against the sky.

Warren was passing orders to the helmsman, and he wondered what he was thinking. Pride, or relief? He could have been speaking to the vessel beneath his feet.

Ainslie saw the nearest spur of rock sliding abeam, and imagined he could already feel the difference in the motion as they headed into deeper water. He had heard the skipper describe it as 'room to breathe'. He wanted to remark on it to Warren, but for some reason it remained unspoken. Personal.

He peered over the screen and saw the deck, and the arrowhead of the forecastle, the shine of falling spray.

He raised the binoculars and watched the bare hills moving apart, the sky gaining colour and warmth, the first shafts of sunlight. Astern, the sea was still in darkness, as if a curtain remained drawn. *The wine-dark sea* . . . He moved the binoculars again. Operation *Retriever* was almost over. Others would decide . . .

He tensed, unable to move, the binoculars focused, unwavering.

In a patch of clear sky between the hills there was a flaw. An intruder. Tiny and slow-moving, like a moth on a sheet of glass.

He swung round, but someone else had already seen it.

"*Aircraft!* Port bow, moving left to right!"

They were no longer alone, and the buzz of alarms below deck dispelled all doubts.

Warren spoke tersely into a voicepipe. The gun was already training round, seeking the solitary aircraft still invisible to most of the men on deck.

Warren was peering up at the Italian flag, its colours harsh now in the early light.

He allowed his own binoculars to fall to his chest and wiped his eyes with the back of his hand. "Seaplane, probably local patrol. Might give us a miss." He looked at the flag again. "Unless this boat has already been reported captured." He raised the binoculars once more, taking his time. "In which case, old son . . ."

Someone said, "They might not have spotted us."

Ainslie steadied his binoculars again. The aircraft had disappeared, hidden behind the second hill. Beyond it, the light was clearer, like water against a dam. And within minutes, details of the land had emerged. Rough scrub or gorses, gnarled and bleached by wind and sun, where he had thought there was only bare rock. Where a man, and perhaps others, now lay dead.

His fingers, now sweating slightly, tightened their grip on the metal as the aircraft reappeared, apparently on the same course as before, but lower, a wing shining as it tilted in the strengthening light.

Warren said, "He's turning. That might be the limit of his patrol."

Ainslie licked his lips, tasting the salt, and tried to hold the glasses steady, but the motion was more lively now as they drew closer to the entrance, the echo of the engines louder in the throwback from these treacherous rocks, like black teeth laid bare in the new sunlight.

It was a float-plane, the first he had ever seen, except in the recognition manuals, and of pre-war design, slow by today's standards, and lightly armed. But adequate for short, local patrols.

He watched it turning until it seemed to be flying straight toward him. *Enough for today. Please, God . . .*

Warren called, "Stand clear of the gun!" He was watching the aircraft, but his mind was with the boat and his small crew at their various stations. He had donned an oilskin to conceal his uniform if the plane came too close, and Ainslie fumbled at his own jacket. If it was not already too late.

Much closer now. Ainslie could hear it above the mutter of the engines.

Lower too, its shadow flashing across the water as if it were alive.

"Probably from Trapani. I heard there were a few based

there." It was Jethro, one hand resting on the top of the bridge ladder, the other holding an empty mug. The ice-clear eyes rested on Ainslie. "How far do you estimate that is, Pilot?"

Ainslie stared at the plane, surprised that he could come to terms with the question when the grim reality was hurtling over the sea toward them.

"Trapani? A hundred miles, give or take . . ." The rest was drowned by the staccato roar of twin engines, then the shadow was past.

"Thought as much." Jethro put down the mug. "Needed that. Rainwater laced with spoonfuls of brandy is not to be recommended!"

Ainslie watched the plane; it helped to keep his nerves under control. How could the man remain so composed, unmoved by the seaplane's sudden arrival, and what it might mean for all of them? For him?

Warren was at the compass, stooping over it as the land drew away on either quarter. The sea was open. It was theirs.

He said, "Take over, Pilot," and stared at the sky without shading his eyes. "He's coming back for another look." He might have snapped his fingers; the sound was lost in the echo from the engines. "Josh, be ready with the lamp! The signal may have been ditched, but it's all we've got."

Jethro moved across the bridge without hesitation, as if he were used to it. He was watching the sailor by the signal lamp, waiting for the plane to begin another approach. He said almost casually, "If he swallows it, we can head for Base at full speed."

Warren did not turn toward him, or look at him, as if every nerve were focused on this single moment.

But he said deliberately, "You are my responsibility, *sir*, and I am ordered to get you to safety." He broke off to jab the man by the lamp. "Now, Josh!" and continued, "But don't bloody well tell *me* how to do it!"

Ainslie forced himself to concentrate on the *clack— clack—*

clack of the signal, slow and unhurried, as if the man called Josh were totally absorbed by the accuracy and importance of the task, perhaps oblivious to the exchange behind him and the threat it implied. The aircraft was holding its course, the green and red markings on the tail very visible, like the flag flying from their mast.

"Signal's acknowledged, sir." He could not conceal his satisfaction. "Sharp an' clear— not bad for an Eye-Tie!" He was grinning.

Warren crossed the bridge, his binoculars trained to follow the aircraft as it continued into the lingering darkness astern, to Pantelleria, or to Sicily.

He said briskly, "Time to alter course. But we'll remain at half-speed in case that pilot has second thoughts and comes back for another look."

Ainslie listened intently. Warren was very calm again, as if nothing had happened. But what if the recognition signals had been updated, or this boat was known to be missing, and in enemy hands? Signals would already be on their way to the desk of some Italian or German version of Garrick.

He shook himself mentally. The constant strain was having its effect.

He said, "I'll take over, Mark One. South-east, all the way to the rendezvous!"

Warren nodded. "Fingers crossed. Bob Kearton won't let us down. I'm just damned glad to be out of that place." He looked astern, but Jethro was on the ladder, blocking his view.

He stood beneath the flag, one foot poised in the air. No anger; he might even have been smiling, but his face was in shadow.

"I think I smell fresh coffee." Then he looked directly at him. "As you said, *Mister* Warren. It's your decision!"

They watched him leave the bridge and waited until the hatch slammed behind him.

Warren said in an undertone, "One of these days . . ." and did not finish it. Then he said, "I'll be in the chart space." He gave a mock bow. "*Your* domain, I believe. Call me. Anything— call me, right?"

Ainslie watched him go, pausing on his way to speak to some of the men on deck.

He pulled on his jacket and looked at his wrist for the first time since dawn. The memory was like a hand reaching out, and he thought of his girl and the letter he would write.

He gazed at the horizon, shining now in full daylight, showing the way, and he understood. Toby Warren had nobody, and nothing beyond this moment.

He tugged out his rough logbook and strode to the compass.

And the moment was now.

"Ring down, full ahead!"

Kearton heard a sudden click and knew it was the chartroom door. Not loud, but he had been expecting it. And, from the first hint of daylight, dreading it.

Everything was visible now: shadows, gun crews and lookouts had become people again, faces and expressions he recognized.

He stared at the sea in the strengthening light, the swell unbroken, lifting occasionally as if it were breathing.

In a few more hours . . . he stopped the thought. It had been a dangerous risk from the start, from the moment Garrick's signal had been decoded.

He saw the seaman at the wheel, moving occasionally with the spokes, and the bearded coxswain standing nearby, immobile, as he had stood since they had all been called to their action stations. Ready to take over the helm and, if necessary, the bridge. Outwardly watching and listening, but, like the others, hoping, maybe praying, for another chance. They had trusted him. But there had been no choice.

Lieutenant John Stirling was here now, his eyes everywhere, strained but alert. *His boat. His men.*

"Time to alter course, sir. Make another sweep to the nor'west. I was thinking . . ."

Kearton looked at him.

"This is all a waste of time? That we've risked too much already? Is that what you think, John?"

Stirling shook his head. "We both knew the risk— I guess we all did. Choice never came into it." He glanced at the sky. "But time is against us, and we're like sitting ducks out here."

Kearton moved to the opposite side, and knew one of the lookouts had turned. Waiting. They all were.

Stirling joined him and lowered his voice. "Something must have misfired with *Retriever*. A last-minute change in the pick-up, or maybe they had engine trouble— ran out of gas?"

Kearton touched his arm. "Or were captured." But he knew Stirling had already considered the possibilities, and what it was costing him right now. He glanced up at the flag, scarcely moving in the damp air. *Sitting ducks.*

But instead he saw Ainslie's face. Young. Determined. Trusting.

He turned abruptly.

"Make a signal, John. *Returning to base.* Give our approximate position, and estimated time of arrival. And let me know when it's coded up and ready to go."

"I'll deal with it myself." But Stirling did not move. "Nobody will blame us, sir."

Then he walked to the ladder which led directly to the deck. Cusack, his first lieutenant, had already appeared to take his place. Nothing was said, but the whole boat would know by now. There were very few secrets in 'the little ships'.

Stirling was feeling it badly. He had wanted to share all the responsibility from the beginning. But only one could carry it.

Kearton walked to the forepart of the bridge and saw the low bow wave curling away from the stem, the only visible movement. The sea was empty, shining from horizon to horizon, but without warmth.

Or is it me?

He had his hand in his pocket and could feel his pipe there, the one which had been repaired. Not to impress or gain favour. And folded against it, the same handkerchief, still unused since she had returned it.

Small, unimportant things.

And yet . . . Like the moment when Garrick's signal had arrived. Half asleep in the chartroom chair, mind tense but empty. Then suddenly wide awake, as if he were being summoned.

He saw Cusack swing round, and the coxswain pushing himself away from the voicepipes, as if he had shouted at them.

"Call Number One! Belay that signal!"

He heard someone call out from the deck and saw the burly coxswain respond with a thumbs-up.

But nobody spoke. They probably thought their senior officer was having a mental breakdown. Most of them would know of his experience prior to this appointment, and that story would have lost nothing in the telling.

Stirling was here; he must have run all the way from the W/T office.

They faced each other across the bridge.

"Told Sparks to hold fast, sir."

Kearton stood by the compass. How many times? How many miles? Like hearing a strange voice; but it was his own.

"Stop engines!"

He heard the muffled response from the engineroom, and felt the deck shudder as the shafts spun to a halt. The silence was immediate, the hull swaying, slower to respond, gear and fittings clattering as the way fell off completely.

The coxswain cleared his throat. "All stopped, sur."

Kearton stood by the screen and stared through the dried salt stains, toward the bows. Beyond the two-pounder, its crew on their feet, looking aft toward the bridge. At him, and at the horizon line, etched sharply now, tilting from side to side as if in an attempt to dislodge this small, unmoving and solitary vessel.

The silence was complete, closing over him like the sea.

Stirling was waiting. Maybe thankful that it was all over, or soon would be.

He looked at the opposite horizon, still a fraction darker, or some distorted reflection of the island.

"Should I carry on, sir?" Stirling sounded hoarse, as if he had been holding his breath.

They were all waiting. Down in the engineroom the Chief would be itching to throw the switches, sick of the motion. And of the man who was causing it.

He blinked, but there was nothing. He knew Stirling had spoken again, but that, too, was lost.

He had cupped his hands around his ears and heard the sea slopping against the hull. He stood on one of the gratings, as if to gain a few more inches. It was pointless.

"Very well, John—" and froze, unable to move. Like those long-lost nights with his father, waiting, staring at the sky, for the fireworks at a local regatta. *Just be patient, Bobby.*

His feet hit the deck and he almost fell.

"Tell the Chief to give me all he's got!" He saw Stirling swinging round toward him. "*Gunfire!* Stand by to alter course!"

He shouted as the engines roared into life. "Make this signal! *Operation Retriever. Enemy north-west. Am attacking!*"

Stirling had gone, and men were standing or crouching at their stations again, as if suddenly brought back to life.

He wedged his elbows against a rail and tried to hold his binoculars steady against the motion as the boat gathered speed, all else drowned by the roar of her engines.

He saw another flash, on a different bearing as they ploughed across their own wash and picked up the new course. It was hidden immediately by the spray bursting over the bows, and sweeping the bridge like tropical rain.

It was enough. *Am attacking.*

Petty Officer Harry Turnbull reached the top of another flight of stone steps and paused to draw breath. It was not far from the moorings to the various official buildings, but he had lost count of the times he had done it, as if he had been walking for miles. *Out of shape.* Common enough when you served your time in Coastal Forces, where there was not enough space to stretch your legs, or a deck you could call your own. It was an excuse, anyway.

He glanced at the steps, worn down over the years. Centuries of feet. Different voices, strange uniforms. It would be good to get back to sea. *For a bit of peace.*

His mouth lifted at the absurdity of the thought.

He looked at the sky, overcast again. It might invite another sneak raid, but they weren't quite so cheeky now, despite the shortness of the flight from their bases in Sicily. He saw one of the heavily sandbagged pillboxes, guns pointing across the bombed building toward the harbour beyond. There were more fighter planes on the repaired airstrips as well, and he had heard that others had arrived with the convoy.

He loosened his cap. *The convoy.* Like some miracle everyone had been hoping for, but had been afraid to mention. Just in case . . .

He had been on his feet since its arrival, and earlier, when they had watched the Canadian M.T.B. slipping out past the old fortress with the captured Italian in tow. He thought of all those other times. Ships you had known, faces remembered. You tried to keep it all at a distance, if only for your own sanity. But this was different. It was personal.

The work of unloading was in full swing, the harbour alive with lighters and countless local craft, and the repairs to vessels damaged already under way.

The work on 992 was almost finished, although, as with all dockyard mateys, you had to make sure they weren't dragging their feet, war or no war. He saw some men lounging by one of the ancient walls: soldiers, sailors, or civilians, it was often hard to tell in the overalls, boiler suits and odds and ends they wore. Pausing for a cigarette, one already puffing at his pipe, at ease, with nobody yelling orders to shatter the moment.

Turnbull walked past them. The rolled stretchers, still bloody, told the true story.

But now all he had to do was round up the last of their working party, who had been clearing space, not for stores from the convoy, but for beds.

He quickened his pace. A petty officer was standing with some of them, and glanced up from his list.

"All yours, Harry. Time for a tot. At last!"

Turnbull was looking past him. There was a van standing between the open gates, the bonnet still shimmering with heat, and a sentry talking to the driver. It was an ambulance.

The other P.O. said, "Some of our lot. The convoy. One of the escorts caught it."

Turnbull nodded non-committally, ashamed that he felt something like relief.

"Which one, d'you know?"

The ambulance was moving away.

"Destroyer, the *Kinsale*. Tin-fished, then bombed, poor bastards."

Turnbull pushed open the double-doors. The air was cool, even fresh, so the power was operational again. Someone had said it had been knocked out in the last hit-and-run air raid.

It was wrong, but he hated hospitals. Ever since . . . He made himself relax, unwind.

So, back to the boat, maybe a tot with Jock Laidlaw. And try to be patient . . .

Then a woman's voice.

"I'm not a nurse, but I'll stay with him."

Another door swung open and a soldier ran past them. He was wearing a Red Cross armband, and had what appeared to be a loose dressing trailing from his jacket.

Turnbull said, "Here, let me!" His mind was completely clear, conscious of the urgency and of the girl who was crouching beside the only bed that was occupied. She was holding one of the man's hands, the other resting on his hair or forehead.

"Try to lie still. Help is coming." A pause, and she glanced up over her shoulder at Turnbull. "It's going to be all right."

He was young, very young, and his face was the colour of the crumpled sheet. A sailor's blue jersey lay on the floor where it had fallen.

Turnbull said, "I'm here." It was something to say, an offer of reassurance when he knew there was none.

The same dark hair and profile, even the voice he remembered when he had seen her with the Skipper, walking with him on the ramp.

She said, "They're coming now." But she was still looking at Turnbull, and her eyes were pleading.

The young sailor gazed up at her, as if seeing her for the first time.

"Sorry— about— this." He reached out as if to touch her face, but his hand fell against her breast. Then he said, "My first ship," and his hand dropped.

Turnbull put his arm around her and helped her to her feet. There were blood smears on her breast, and she covered them with her hand.

She said, "He's off the *Kinsale*," then she stared at Turnbull with recognition. "I didn't realize. *You're back.*"

There were more voices now, the sound of running feet. He wanted to explain, but all he saw was the old-fashioned clock above the door. *The time* . . . He had thought of little else since the Skipper had left harbour, without him.

"We'll go somewhere. Where we can talk in peace."

She did not protest as he walked beside her, holding her arm, but at the door she stopped, and looked back toward the bed.

He saw that her eyes were wet, but her voice was very calm.

"Safe voyage," she said.

For one of them, it was over.

12

Nowhere to Hide

Lieutenant Warren stood at the rear of the bridge with one arm wrapped around part of the tripod mast in an attempt to train his binoculars. Apart from clambering up to the top, it was the highest point on the boat.

"Same bearing. Port bow. Altered course." He swore under his breath as the hull dipped steeply in the swell, and he almost lost his balance. "We might give it the slip."

Ainslie knew it was pointless to try and use his own binoculars. He watched the compass, and the helmsman's hands easing the wheel this way and that to compensate for speed and rudders.

One of the bridge lookouts had sighted it first, like a tiny flaw in the glare of the horizon. Always a threat here in the Sicilian Channel, hated and feared by the precious Malta-bound convoys at its narrowest part between the enemy coast and Tunisia. The sea bed must be littered with wrecks; so every new sighting was marked down as an enemy until proven otherwise.

At first they had thought the vessel might be a survivor of that last, vital convoy, damaged but trying to finish the last leg of the journey without coming under further attack. Or even an enemy supply ship, attempting to boost stores and morale for the retreating Afrika Korps.

Warren jumped down to the deck.

"Alter course." He leaned over the compass. "Steer South-thirty-East." And to Ainslie, "She's all yours again." He smiled, but his eyes and thoughts were elsewhere. "Lay aft, Jumper, and check the smoke floats. We might need 'em."

"Already done it, sir."

Warren said, so quietly that his voice was almost lost in the sound of engines, *"Do it again."* He joined Ainslie near the compass. "I just hope you're right."

"About the Skipper?"

"About every bloody thing."

The helmsman said, "They won't be able to catch up with *us*!"

Warren shifted his binoculars, but held them very still.

"They won't need to!" He reached out. *"Port twenty!* Pass the word!"

Ainslie saw the spokes spinning, the helmsman's shoulders bent to prepare his body as the deck swayed over.

"Midships!"

Ainslie heard the shot, but his mind refused to identify it. A sharp, abbreviated whistle, and then the roar. As if a shell had exploded alongside, against the hull itself. It was like a body-blow. He stared abeam across the shining water and saw a column of spray falling gently around the site of the explosion. Well clear. And yet . . .

Warren said, "I'll take over until we can lose him." He stepped on to the grating as the helmsman stood aside. "Go and keep an eye on things down aft."

He saw the protest in Ainslie's eyes, but gave it no time for expression.

"You know what they say about keeping all your eggs in one basket."

He blinked, and turned to the wheel again. He must have seen the flash.

Ainslie heard the shot and ducked as the whistle cut through

205

all other sounds. Then the deafening sound, but with hardly any shock against the hull.

He gripped the side of the bridge and saw the spray tumbling down, and spreading across into their wake. Well clear this time, but where they might have been, but for rudder and speed.

It was already far astern, but he could feel it. Taste it.

He grasped the handrail at the bottom of the bridge ladder, and saw the sea surging past and, in places, on to the deck itself. The helm was hard over, and everything was shaking, as if one screw were almost out of the water.

Someone shouted, "Bloody hell, look at that!"

Ainslie twisted round, afraid of what he might see.

He stared up at the bridge, and the small tripod mast where Warren had watched the enemy. For a second his mind did not register its significance, and then he saw the flag lifting and streaming out to the extra speed.

Not the Italian flag, but the White Ensign. It should not have mattered. But it did.

At any moment another shell might find its target: something they all knew, but never accepted. He could see one of the sailors he recognized, recalled the gesture made behind Warren's back after his sharp retort: *This is a bus, not a battleship!* Now he was laughing, shaking his fist.

"Turnin' again, sir!" Somebody slithered past him and called, "Stand by to make smoke!"

Ainslie pulled himself to his feet. The deck was level, the sea dashing past, as if it and not the hull was moving.

"Down!" He felt someone thrust him hard against a winch. "*Get down*, for Christ's sake!"

Like a shadow. And then the explosion.

For a moment longer he lay where he had fallen, his mind reeling from the shock, unable to move. Perhaps it was fear that brought him to his senses, and with it came hearing, and pain.

He rolled over and felt water on his face, then his hands, as he dragged himself against the winch. A direct hit. It was over.

It was like a hand gripping him, shaking him. But there was no one.

He could hear the engines now, and felt the deck quivering as he lurched to his feet. They were still afloat and under way. He held on to the winch and stared toward the bridge. There was some smoke, but the flag was still flying. And the pain in his ribs would be no more than a bruise, caused by the impact when he had been pushed against the winch.

His hearing was returning, and with it came a sense of urgency. Someone had been calling out, screaming, or had that been part of the shock? He stared outboard, at the wave cutting away from the bows, and toward the horizon, but there was too much smoke.

He strode toward the ladder, his mind suddenly clear.

A direct hit would have blown us apart.

Something made him turn, and he saw one of the seamen on his knees, trying to cradle another in his arms as if to shield him from the spray bursting over the side. The boat was turning again. All that mattered.

"Hang on, Steve! We'll get you below. You'll be OK again!"

Ainslie called, "Leave him! Come with me!"

Just a few seconds. All it took. The man's shock, desperation, perhaps hatred as he had stumbled after Ainslie toward the bridge. His friend lay with the spray washing over him, his features like a mask, feeling nothing.

Ainslie gripped the top of the ladder and tried to find the necessary strength. The shell must have exploded in mid-air, the blast hitting the hull like a giant fist. Otherwise the screws would be out of action, and the rest in pieces.

But his mind refused to listen. The bridge was in chaos, made worse by the colourful tangle of bunting that plastered most of it. The flag locker had been blasted from its stand, and the thin steel plating along the side was punctured by splinters, or twisted inboard like wet cardboard where he had been standing only a few minutes ago.

There was blood, too: the man who had been acting as helmsman, before Warren had taken his place. He remembered his warning about 'eggs in one basket'. The helmsman's head had been smashed like one when he had been hurled against the side.

But Warren was alive and at the wheel, leaning over to wipe some torn bunting from the compass, even as he completed another change of course.

He saw Ainslie for the first time and bared his teeth in a hideous grin.

"Come to share the sport?" He stared over his shoulder. "Where's that bloody smoke?" He was wiping his mouth with the back of his hand. "We can still shake this bastard off, if . . ."

Ainslie did not hear the rest. Warren was wearing the same leather glove. Always there, part of him. Of his strength. It was soaked with blood, and had left smears on his face.

He said, "First one's started now." He saw the smoke streaming astern across their curving wake, clinging to it, spreading. Then another. It no longer seemed to matter.

He covered the hand on the wheel with his own. "*Where is it? Let me get a dressing. I'll take over—*"

"Like hell you will!" Warren shook his hand away. "After all the shit I've taken— d'you think I'm going to crack up?" He winced as another explosion shook the hull.

Then he shouted, "Lost the fucking range, have you?" and broke off, coughing, the glove pressed against his mouth.

He said, "Looks like you were wrong, Toby. So was I."

His eyes focused, concentrating, as if he had heard something. "Port engine's missing a few beats. Had about all she can take." He seemed to falter, and took a deep breath. "I must tell 'em . . ."

Ainslie followed his gaze to the voicepipes, one of which was sheared off at deck level, as if by a shell splinter. The mechanics must be wondering what the hell was happening.

He saw the seaman who had been nursing his dead friend standing by one of the machine-guns, watching the smoke drawing a curtain astern, even as two more floats added to the cover.

With men like these . . .

Warren said, "I still think we did the right thing. No matter what . . .'

Ainslie had been pressed beside him, feeling his pain and his anger, but scarcely able to hear his words above the beat of the engines. What now? Surrender, or wait for the inevitable climax when the smoke cleared away? *Just let it be quick.*

And he thought of Sarah, who would be waiting for his letter, and of the first and only time they had made love, when he had received his orders to join the M.T.B. which was now lying at Malta. How it might have been . . .

He flinched as Warren grasped his wrist, and stood swaying with the deck, hardly breathing.

"Look! *Look*, Mark Two, and tell me I'm not round the bend!"

Ainslie turned and stared across the bows toward the horizon. No longer clear, but not with haze. It was smoke. And above it, falling slowly like a vivid green star, was a flare.

"We weren't wrong—" He tried again. "It's the Skipper!"

For a moment longer he was not sure if Warren had heard above the roar of the engines, or if the words had ever left his mouth. Then he felt the grip release his wrist, and Warren dragged himself firmly against the wheel.

He shouted, "*I told you!* They threw away the bloody mould!" There was another explosion, but it was almost lost in the surge of sea and power as the helm went hard over again. "He can't do it on his own!" His teeth were clenched, biting into his lip to control the pain.

Ainslie stared past him, at the changing pattern of clouds.

They were turning completely, on to their original course, toward the Devil's Rock.

He staggered against the violent motion, but managed to join Warren at the wheel.

"Let me . . ." But Warren shouldered him away as he stooped over to apply opposite helm.

"Just this once!" He broke off to rub his face with the glove. When he spoke again, his voice was very calm. "I've worked with Bob Kearton before. A lifetime ago." He peered at the compass and repeated, "Can't do it on his own."

Ainslie saw smoke parting across the bows; the gun appeared to be cutting through and above it.

Then he felt Warren's left hand on his arm, heard the slow determination in his words.

"Tell the others. You know the drill. Life-jackets. While there's still time." He took a deep breath, and regarded him steadily. "Be ready to bale out."

Ainslie wanted to protest, but knew it was pointless. As he moved away from the wheel he saw Warren nod, perhaps twice, and heard him say, "Just do it!" He might have been smiling.

The boat was turning again, another zig-zag, but this time there were no flashes or explosions. He held on to the ladder, looking back at the solitary figure in the black oilskin, framed against the smoke and the scattered, shredded flags. *Just do it.*

He realized that the same man was still crouching behind the bridge machine-gun. That he was gesturing with one arm, shouting, his voice lost in the din.

Then he saw the Canadian M.T.B., a vague outline, a shadow revealed only by the mounting crest of her speed. He could feel it as if he were there, sharing it. *Going in to attack.*

Somehow he reached the hatch, and saw the injured agent, already sitting propped against a locker, managing a thumbs-up despite the motion and the noise, and hung about with life-jackets.

Ainslie dropped on his knees beside him. "We're baling out, OK?" He touched his shoulder. "Don't worry, you'll see Sydney Harbour again before too long."

He nodded, croaking, "Bugger that! I'm from Auckland!"

Someone in overalls had appeared through trapped smoke.

"Ready for the word, sir!" His eyes shifted to the deckhead. "From the bridge!"

Ainslie said sharply, "Be ready to leave! *Now!* That's an order!"

He seized a bracket to steady himself as the helm shifted again.

What was the point? A narrow door had swung open to the sudden lurch, and he saw Jethro standing at the far side of the cabin or storage space. There was light coming from somewhere. Nothing made sense.

It was the shadow etched against a bulkhead that emptied his mind of everything else. Motionless, erect, one hand raised as if in salute.

"What the *hell*!"

Ainslie said, "We're baling out. But we're not alone any more." He was shocked that he could speak so calmly. Hear his own voice, and know each second that passed was like a thread. "Let me take that."

He could hear voices, shouts, tackle being dragged across the deck directly overhead. But if he moved . . .

"Something going right for a change? According to plan?"

The man they knew only as Jethro had turned to stand directly beneath one of the deckhead lights. Amused, sarcastic; there was no time to judge or react.

But one wrong move . . . Ainslie repeated, "Let me have that."

Surprisingly, he laughed and held out the heavy pistol. The same one he had been carrying when they had hauled him from the raft. Not a salute. He had been about to kill himself.

The deck shivered and bucked violently beneath their feet. Lights flickered, and the pace of the screws had slackened.

"You lying bastard! I'll show you . . ."

Ainslie retained his grip on the pistol, the barrel cold in his hand. *If he pulls the trigger now . . .*

He said, "A torpedo." He tensed, the pistol rigid. "One of ours."

He could hear shouting, cheers. Warren would need all the help he could get.

"In that case." The pistol seemed suddenly heavy in his hand. "We'd better get things moving." Irritable, nothing more.

"Ready, sir?" A seaman pushed the door aside, facing Ainslie, but his eyes on the gun in Jethro's hand. "I think you're wanted up top."

He stepped between them, and added, "I can take that, sir."

As Ainslie moved past him he said, "Looks like you won't be needing it."

Ainslie almost laughed, but knew it would finish him.

Even the upper deck seemed different. Useless to look at the clouds now, or attempt to gauge the horizon. There was smoke everywhere, from the floats or the M.T.B. it was impossible to tell. And a thicker, taller column, unmoving. The death of a ship.

He recovered his balance as the deck swayed over again. Altering course, but slower this time to obey the helm. The port engine had stopped altogether. Warren must have known what had to be done, what was coming, and had acted immediately, no matter what he was suffering. He glanced at the dead man by the guardrail, rolling to the motion, as if he had been awakened from a deep sleep.

Ainslie stepped over one outflung arm and ran to the ladder, mind closed to everything else.

"Hold on, he's coming now!"

Warren was still by the wheel, but sitting now on the upended

212

flag locker. He twisted round as Ainslie's shadow fell across his own.

"That showed them, eh?" He began to laugh, but the sound strangled in his throat. "What wouldn't I give for a drink!"

His oilskin was unfastened, and he was tugging at his collar with his free hand.

"Like a bloody oven up here!"

Ainslie saw one of the seamen look across at him and shake his head.

"Let me take over now. I've told the others."

Warren shook his head. "How many?"

The seaman held up three fingers.

"Killed." Warren sighed. "Better that, than . . ." He opened and closed his gloved hand. "Left like a puppet!"

Ainslie saw the blood on the grating, and soaking into the flags beneath his feet.

Warren asked, "What about *him*?"

No name. Ainslie said, "Came through it in one piece."

"He would."

Then he stood up and gestured to the seaman.

"Take the wheel. *Shiner*, that's what they call you?" He nodded. "Thought so. We've not had much time to—" Then he seized Ainslie's arm. "Feast your eyes on *that*! Just like old times!"

He tried to wave, but the pain made him gasp, and he slid his arm around Ainslie's shoulders.

He murmured, "Look at us, like a couple of drunks at closing time."

Ainslie held on to him and watched the Canadian's raked bows carving through the criss-cross of waves as she turned to steer on a parallel course. Like that very first time under training, or when he had been allowed to take over a bridge, and had heard his own voice giving the orders. The hull was shining like glass, her number vivid despite the clinging smoke. The flag, and the Maple Leaf painted on the low bridge. And the empty torpedo tubes. Maybe it was pride; but his eyes betrayed him, and were becoming blurred.

He said, "Let me."

Warren cleared his throat.

"Stop engines! Get ready to help the injured hands across. The others will have to stay aboard." He tightened his hold on Ainslie's shoulders. "*My* job, remember? Can't leave her now."

"I'll be standin' by, sir." It was the seaman who had taken Jethro's pistol.

And now the sound of different engines, the smell of fuel trapped between the two hulls as they drew together.

Ainslie stood at the side of the bridge, watching the narrowing strip of water, the rope fenders and ready hands poised to withstand the first impact.

He saw Kearton directly opposite him, and heard the Canadian C.O. using a megaphone to keep contact with his men on the forecastle. Every man seemed to be waiting, eager to make it as quick and as painless as possible. *Every man.* Even the guns were abandoned.

The hulls lifted and then staggered together, the sea trapped between them and bursting over the decks and bustling sailors like white spectres.

Now there was another officer beside him: the Canadian first lieutenant. At that last meeting, before . . . Ainslie took another grip on himself. When he and Warren had met, and talked together.

Lieutenant Tom Cusack saw the signal from someone on the other deck, and said, "All across. Time to go." He watched the hesitation; had seen it before, too many times. He saw Ainslie's eyes, and one of his own men shaking his head. Eager to leave.

Ainslie barely heard him. He gripped the wheel to steady himself, and knelt down by Warren and one of the Canadians.

"I'm here. We're going to move you."

Warren looked at him steadily. "There's nowhere to hide, is

214

there?" He pushed his hand inside his oilskin, but it fell back limply against Ainslie's arm. He had been trying to say something, but the words had been drowned by the chorus of voices from the boat alongside.

Cusack snapped, "He's dead. We'd better get going, before—"

He did not finish, but stood by the ladder, waiting.

The sailor scrambled to his feet and said to Ainslie, "Did all we could, Lieutenant."

Ainslie lingered, gazing down.

"Did you hear what he was saying?"

The Canadian stared toward his own boat, at the men who were struggling to control the increasing motion between the two hulls. Faces he knew . . . He was getting scared, but something held him here.

He said, "He was talking to you, sir. He called you 'Mark One'."

Ainslie was the last to leave. When he looked back across the widening panorama of broken water, he saw that Warren's flag was still flying.

"Cox'n on the wheel, sur!"

Kearton seized his binoculars to prevent them swinging against the side of the bridge and thrust them inside his coat, surprised that he could still be caught unawares as the hull swayed into another trough and steadied on the new course.

He heard the acknowledgment, and someone shifting his position, as if nothing had happened. Routine taking over. Gun crews and lookouts at their proper stations. How long? Maybe half an hour since they had grappled with the Italian boat, rescuing their own men, and then casting off again. The bearded coxswain from Newfoundland had been down on deck with his men then, guiding the dazed or injured to safety, with an encouraging word or a threatening fist to mark every minute of the struggle.

He stared across the quarter and saw the other vessel lying motionless on the water. Lifeless. There were still a few traces of smoke, but beyond her the sea and the horizon were empty.

And very soon they would be alone. Like that last desperate hour, seeking and then sighting the enemy. Even that was blurred. Maybe you never got used to it. If you did, your own guard would be lowered: as someone had once said, *a victim, not a victor*.

There was always the moment of doubt. A lot of them had known it, but could never describe it.

He stared at the Italian, apparently unchanged, but that too was an illusion. Already lower in the water. She was small, and when she sank it would be suddenly.

Both torpedoes had been fired at the enemy patrol vessel. Only one had scored a hit. Always the possibility of a miss, or of the torpedo running deep, and passing beneath the target without scoring. Like all those times in the Channel and North Sea; the anger and derision which had greeted the Admiralty's words of caution about wasting torpedoes on small targets. Cost, not risk, had been the message.

He dragged out his binoculars, maybe because of the memory. Warren had learned those same hard lessons well. Better than many.

One direct hit would have ended it. *For both of us*.

Warren had known exactly what he was doing, turning as if to retrace his course to the island, into the trap.

The enemy captain had reacted immediately, and had altered course to tighten the noose. In doing so, he had exposed his own broadside. Only a few minutes, and the torpedo had found its mark. There had been an explosion, and a lingering flash, which had shone through the smoke like a torch. Then a second, probably her magazine. Maybe she had been carrying depth-charges.

He looked away and saw that Stirling had joined him. He was

remembering it, too. The enemy's bows appearing through the smoke, as if their attack had failed. Smart, rakish bows . . . just long enough to see that there was nothing else left, before they rolled over and disappeared.

Warren must have seen it also. Shared it.

Stirling said, "Ready, sir." He looked up at the sky. "No time to hang around, I'd say."

"I'll make a signal." Kearton walked to the rear of the bridge and stared astern, at the wake surging toward the horizon.

Ainslie was standing by the twin Oerlikons, with some of Stirling's seamen and a couple of others he did not recognize, watching the Italian's final seconds. But Kearton knew he was completely alone.

Like the moment when he had climbed aboard. His own, "Well done," and Ainslie's, "Perfect rendezvous, Skipper." Not even a handshake. He had had enough. And he was not the only one.

He felt the warning vibration through the bridge as the revolutions increased.

"There she goes!"

He watched the sleek hull settling deeper in the water, exposing one of the motionless screws, and a small raft sliding from the deck and floating free.

Stirling said, "A couple of the depth-charges will explode. At minimum setting, I'm told. The others might blow, too. We've done all we can."

Kearton looked again. She was only a shadow in the water now, and a few pieces of flotsam swirling around, caught in the sudden pressure.

They had the sea to themselves.

Stirling's first lieutenant had joined them on the bridge, wiping his hands with a piece of rag.

"He wasn't married, was he?" No name. They all knew.

"What the *hell* does that have to do with it?"

Kearton waited, counting the seconds. He did not turn. He knew the voice.

The familiar, muffled explosion now, almost subdued, followed a moment later by a bursting pinnacle of water. And another, shaking the hull, then discarding it. It was over.

Kearton saw some of the sailors going back to their stations, but one or two still hesitating, shading their eyes to peer astern, as if they expected the shattered hull to reappear.

"Make the signal, John. *Retriever terminated.*" He could feel Stirling's eyes on him. Perhaps expecting something more dramatic.

He looked across the bridge and saw the other face watching him: Jethro, eyes almost colourless in the glare, with little sign of exhaustion or emotion.

"You should get some rest while you can. It's a straight run now. Grand Harbour. No matter what."

Just words, the first since he had watched him abandon the Italian boat, seen him shake off any assistance almost with contempt. Now it was almost over. A few lines in the log. *Mission completed.* And on to the next operational duty.

"A drink of some kind would go down well." Jethro smiled, but the cold eyes were on the bearded coxswain, who was replacing his cap. He had removed it and wedged it between his knees as the Italian sank, as his own private mark of respect. Without relinquishing control of the wheel, and without taking his eyes from the compass. "Feel better now?"

The Newfoundlander shrugged. "Do *you*, sur?"

Ainslie stepped into the bridge and said, "I'm going to check a few things, Skipper." He nodded toward the chartroom. "I've got to keep my hand in." Then he touched his shoulder unconsciously, and Kearton saw the pain in his eyes. The old satchel he always carried, his navigator's 'tools', was missing. It was still aboard the Italian boat. "I'll manage."

Kearton saw that at no time had he looked at, or spoken to, the man who was standing beside him.

"Aircraft! Green—four-five!"

Kearton did not hear the rest. The guns were already swinging round, men ducking for cover or reaching for ammunition and magazines. A team again, minds slammed shut against memory.

Penalty or reprisal?

Ainslie was halfway to the chartroom, although Kearton had not seen him move.

But he was looking up, his eyes watering as he stared into the sun.

Someone was yelling, cheering, as the wafer-thin shapes turned in a tight formation, three of them, and another flying low, chasing its own shadow across the sea.

Seafires, perhaps from the carrier which had been part of the convoy's powerful escort.

Nothing mattered. They were here now.

Stirling lifted his binoculars to watch the formation begin to turn for another approach.

Then he looked at Kearton. "We made it!"

Kearton tugged out his own binoculars and trained them with care.

The sea was empty, like dark glass.

He knew he was tired, drained. Waiting was the hardest part.

He said quietly, "We had plenty of help."

Maybe, somehow, Lieutenant Toby Warren might know.

13

Victim

Kearton closed the cabin door behind him and pressed his back against it, to give himself time to settle his thoughts. To recover. Everything seemed to have changed during his absence. Like this cabin: the bunk neat and ready, and the brass shell-case emptied. He thought it was from an old destroyer, like his first ship; they were popular and safe places to tap out a pipe or dump the ashes, and could be tipped over the side with all the other gash when nobody was looking. It had been here, tarnished and unused, when he had arrived. Now it was brightly polished.

He pushed himself away from the door and moved to the sloping side, and peered through one of the scuttles. All that was visible was part of the jetty, and a small hut which had not been there when he had left harbour with the Canadians.

He touched his chin, still sore where he had cut himself shaving aboard 986, in John Stirling's cabin. A twin of this one, but completely different.

The sky looked darker. So soon . . . It was difficult to keep things in order, as if the events of the past few days were merely something which had been described to him, instead of having been there every step of the way.

He sat down at the little table, where Spiers had arranged some letters beside his own handwritten log. Three days: less.

It felt like weeks. He looked around the cabin again. Spiers would have sat here, listening to the dockyard men clattering over and throughout the hull. Maybe imagining himself . . .

He stood up, dismissing it impatiently. These same moorings were unchanged, but had been made more crowded by the arrival of the two promised motor gunboats. He tried to bring them into focus. One of the commanding officers he already knew, at least by name, and Spiers had mentioned something about him, but he would meet both of them tomorrow.

He recalled the last minutes as Stirling had conned his command alongside. A thrust astern, then ahead on the other screw while heaving-lines snaked ashore, and then the silence as they came to rest.

The other boats had been fully manned, but their companies had broken ranks and run to cheer and shout, as if they had all been waiting. Familiar faces, and others which were new and unknown. Men peering at the bridge or hull, expecting to see damage or worse.

Otherwise, it had been a quiet return. A few people by the old fortress, and a solitary angler who had pulled in his line as they had passed abeam. He had grinned, and waved at them.

So unlike their departure, that other morning before dawn, when the waterfront had been packed with silent, hopeful crowds. The convoy was still being unloaded, its precious cargo dispersed. The memory of two small vessels, one towing another, would be quickly forgotten.

And he thought of the silence which had fallen when Captain Garrick and some of his staff had appeared at the foot of the steps. Smart, correct, perhaps rehearsed.

Kearton was on his feet again. Restlessly, he made himself look through the pile of letters. Two from his mother: her round handwriting had followed him everywhere. Even to . . . He shut it from his mind. He could still feel the injuries, unless they, too, were only in his memory.

The men from the Italian boat had been met, and guided to waiting vehicles. Some had looked back. Most had not.

And the agent from Auckland, propped in some kind of folding stretcher like a chair, with a man in a white coat looking anxious and irritated as his patient had wriggled round, laughing, when he had seen Kearton on the jetty.

"See you Down Under some day, Skipper!"

The doctor must have given him a jab, but the Kiwi was still grinning when he was lifted into the ambulance.

And another man, one of Warren's crew who had been wounded by a shell splinter, staring up at the sky and the faces around him, then at Garrick as he knelt beside him to shake his hand. But the flashgun and the click of the shutter had told the real story; and the aide had immediately snatched away the cushion on which Garrick had been kneeling.

He felt the cabin shiver slightly as something smaller passed silently abeam. And he thought of Jethro, the face in the discarded photograph, the cold, colourless eyes and the almost casual gesture toward Stirling's men, who were already preparing to top up the fuel tanks. First things first, no matter how weary or elated they might be feeling.

"Something they'll not forget in a hurry!" Then he had looked away, and Kearton thought he had seen Ainslie. "That's what it's all about!"

Garrick had hardly spoken, except to offer a brief handshake and the familiar, photogenic smile.

"Good to see you. We'll talk tomorrow. Brice will put you in the picture."

Then he had walked with Jethro to another car and driven away. He could still see it. Feel it . . . He must be more exhausted than he had realized. Even the name 'Brice' had not registered immediately.

It was over. There would be new orders. Tomorrow . . .

He felt himself flinch at the knock on the door.

It was Turnbull. "Sorry to bust in like this, sir." He did not wait, but went straight to the table. "Me an' the lads thought—" He placed a tray on the table and paused while he removed his cap and wedged it between his knees as he uncovered a jug and a solitary glass. "—you could do with a proper welcome aboard."

Turnbull had been at the brow with Spiers, and his pal the Chief, very smart and official while Garrick had been making his appearance. "Sorry about the stink of paint, sir. But she's all slick an' pusser again now."

Kearton sat down abruptly, with a sensation like a string being cut. The gesture with the cap was another stark reminder: Cossette, the Newfoundlander, removing his cap, his private gesture of respect to a dying ship.

"Join me?"

Turnbull shook his head.

"Busy day tomorrow, sir. I'll flatten anyone who tries to disturb you." He must have seen the question, and said, "Mister Ainslie's flaked out already." He grinned. "These youngsters, eh, sir?"

The door closed again. Kearton tipped half the contents of the jug into the glass and swallowed: some of Garrick's malt whisky, or brandy. It could have been anything. He leaned back, staring around the cabin.

What had he expected? She was married. It would only make things worse for her.

He heard voices, somebody laughing, the sound cut off instantly, as if told to pipe down. *The Skipper's back aboard . . .*

One company again. Another patrol, or one of Garrick's Special Operations: they could be sent anywhere.

We both know that.

He reached for Turnbull's jug, then his hand was suddenly still.

She was alone. And perhaps in danger.

He did not hear the door open, or someone switch off the cabin lights.

There was tomorrow. Like that first flash of gunfire, he was committed.

"Lieutenant-Commander Kearton, sir?" The petty officer's eyes moved to his sleeve and back again. "If you'll wait in here." He held the door half open, as if guarding it. "The meeting will soon be over."

Kearton heard him hurry away. *Over.* What time did they begin here? He himself had been up and about since first light, and had heard Colours being sounded as he had stepped ashore. The pace at headquarters must be hotting up, even more so since his last visit.

He looked around: it was the same room, but he had been brought here through an unfamiliar passageway. And there were different faces, the petty officer's, and a couple at the main entrance. But the sounds were ordinary enough as he had passed various numbered doors: telephones, the clatter of typewriters, a teleprinter, amid the usual peeling notices about careless talk and *Where To Go In An Air Raid.*

He was the first visitor this morning, that was obvious: two of the chairs were still upended against a wall, waiting for the cleaners, and there were some stained cups on a tray beside an English newspaper dated a week ago. CHURCHILL SAYS WELL DONE!

Who to, he wondered?

He stretched his legs to ease the stiffness. He had only been a few days at sea, but it was always the same until the body accepted the reality of solid ground.

He got up sharply and crossed the room, and looked out of one of the windows. Blue sky and sunshine, but the view had changed: he could see the gleam of water now, which had previously been blocked by a building. Now it was only the too

224

familiar pile of rubble. New tape across the glass to hide the cracks. Fewer air raids, someone had said. Too late for those poor devils.

He glanced at the other door: at any minute someone would arrive, and the wheels would begin to turn. He pulled the folded note from his pocket and held it against the window. The master-at-arms at the main gate had handed it to him; he must have seen him walk from the jetty and had been waiting for him.

"Brought by messenger, sir. Can't be too careful around here, with all these comings and goings. Like bloody Piccadilly Circus." He had not winked. There had been no need.

Only a few words, apparently written in haste on a piece of official-looking notepaper. *I saw you. Call me when you find the time. G.*

Little enough, but it was everything. Her safety had been uppermost in his mind, and not merely because of the air raids.

The Jaunty had offered his own telephone without being asked. A woman's voice had answered, with music so loud in the background that she had had to shout, and so had he, until she turned down the sound, or closed another door. No, she did not know when Mrs Howard would be back. Maybe later today. She would take a message. She told him her own name, Maria, and he was there again, in that same apartment, when she had been cheerfully sweeping up the debris and glass from the explosion.

He had left his name. She would know. It would be stupid to make more of it. She was safe . . . He stared through the tape on the glass again, at the distant gleam of water. *I saw you.* She must have been there, watching and waiting when they had finally entered harbour.

He heard the door open with a certain relief, dragging his thoughts back to the present.

It was Brice, frowning, and gesturing to somebody behind him as if to silence another telephone. He looked tired, and very strained, but his smile was immediate and genuine. He took Kearton's hands with both of his own, clasping them warmly, and looked at him without speaking.

Then, "I've counted the hours till this moment, Bob. *Just this moment!*" He released his grip and turned him toward the other door. "Bloody chaos here today!" He laughed, and some of the tension seemed to fall away. "The Boss will be here directly. Nothing seems to shake *him*."

Kearton saw another switchboard in Brice's office. A petty officer sat facing it, a telephone to his ear, one hand poised to disconnect the caller without delay. Not only that, but the room seemed smaller, because of the packing-cases and spare equipment filling much of the space he remembered.

"Moving out?"

Brice grinned and waved him to a chair.

"No such luck. But extra staff have arrived, and the Admiral never asks anyone about accommodation. He just gives the order!"

He sat behind the big desk and stared at an open file of signals. "You must have thought we'd all gone nuts when you got the order to abort *Retriever*. A complete cock-up— conflicting information about enemy intentions. If you hadn't kept your head it would have all gone up in smoke. I don't have all the facts yet . . . but it sounds as if the end result will pay off." He flicked through the signals for a moment. "I never met Lieutenant Warren, but his record reads like *One Man's War*. If I'd had any say in the matter, I'd have pulled him out of the front line. But I suppose he would have refused the offer!"

The switchboard buzzed, and the petty officer said, "For you, sir—"

Brice gave him no time to explain. "I said, no calls! Let some- one else deal with it!"

He had twisted round in his chair and Kearton could see the creases in the back of his jacket, as if he had slept in it. The Boss was a hard man to serve, as Brice had already hinted. This was Garrick's other face.

The P.O. said patiently, "It's the S.O. M/S, sir." He paused. "*Personal*, sir."

Brice glanced at Kearton.

"Oh, well, I just hope—" He picked up the receiver before it could ring. "You're up and about early, Ted— what's new in minesweeping?"

Kearton saw the change, heard it in his voice.

"When was that, Ted? Any survivors?" Silence. "None at all?"

Kearton could not hear what was being said, but he could see it written on Brice's face. In his eyes.

"Yes— old friends. We were at Dartmouth together. Thanks for letting me know." He had already replaced the receiver. The switchboard was buzzing again, but he did not seem to hear it, or the P.O.'s clipped response.

Finally he looked at Kearton.

"Never bloody well ends, does it?" He got to his feet slowly and came around the desk. "Sorry, Bob. This isn't how I meant it to be."

He smiled, but it did not register in his eyes.

"I could have saved you the journey. The Boss rang me just before you got here. He wants to meet you, with the other commanding officers who've joined us— at fourteen hundred hours." He looked at his watch, but Kearton guessed it was merely habit. Perhaps it helped. "Something else came up, apparently. He's with Captain Howard at the moment." He was gazing at the wall-chart. "Or should I say, *Major* Howard— as he soon will be."

Kearton picked up his cap. That last was no accident, or breach of security: Brice was too astute. And he had heard her say Malta was like a village. Nothing remained a secret very long.

Brice had become a friend; and it was a warning.

Turnbull sat with his elbows propped on the mess table, watching his friend, who was facing him. They had become real mates since they had joined 992 together, none closer, and yet Jock Laidlaw could still surprise him. Big, strong hands, scarred from the long watches working with his precious engines, and countless others before these, yet able to carve and fashion small models or toys like this one. Not a ship or an old-fashioned muzzle-loader, which most sailors seemed to prefer, but a miniature church. Complete with opening doors and a perfectly shaped spire and crucifix.

It was for his niece, apparently still back in Dundee. Laidlaw rarely spoke about his family. Of his niece he had said only, tapping the top of the mess table, "She was this high, when I last saw her." His brother was a soldier, and had been serving at Singapore when the Japs marched in. Reported missing, presumed killed, a familiar story at the time, he had turned up later as a prisoner-of-war. In the meantime, his wife had turned to someone else. The young niece was the only link between them.

Turnbull had once asked him, "Do you think you'll be going back there when this lot's over?"

Laidlaw had answered, "Where to, Harry?" That was plain enough.

There was still a smell of rum in the air, and Turnbull could taste it on his lips. He glanced at the door, which was propped open to catch any sound of activity. This was not the time to indulge in an extra tot. With the Skipper ashore at the meeting and Captain Garrick likely to show up in person at any time, it would be asking for real trouble.

Laidlaw bent over his work, touching it with his tiny blade. He must have been thinking the same thing.

"How's Jimmy th' One bearing up? Still like a cat on hot bricks?"

"Got a lot on his plate at the moment."

The lugubrious face cracked in a grin. "Tell me about it."

"Now the two M.G.B.s have joined us, I suppose we'll be on the move again." He peered over at the door again. 992 seemed quiet, and not only because their mess was at the far end of the hull and separated from the rest by engines and fuel. Most of the hands were ashore, making the most of it. Pug Dawson had remained aboard with the duty watch, and would soon warn him if any unexpected trouble showed up at the gangway. If he stayed awake.

Laidlaw had started to wrap his little model in a cloth, but stopped, and was looking at him across the table.

"Tell me, Harry— what's she like?"

Turnbull had told him about the unexpected encounter at the sick quarters. Laidlaw probably knew anyway.

"I think she's smashing. Not like some . . ."

"Her an' the Skipper— d'ye think there's anything in it?"

"Well, it would be a bit tricky, as things stand. She's still married, isn't she? So I don't know how far it's got."

Laidlaw said quietly, "I've seen her two or three times. I wouldn't say no, if it came my way!"

Turnbull recalled her voice, the hand covering her breast to hide the blood of a dying sailor.

"I say bloody good luck to them." He had heard a shout, and running feet on deck. The waiting was over. Soon there would be a face at the door, and he was glad of it without knowing why.

Laidlaw finished folding his package and watched him leave.

He said to himself, "They're going to need it."

It was not what Turnbull had been expecting, but as he strode along the side-deck toward the brow he was careful to reveal nothing. They were waiting for him: Pug Dawson, the gangway sentry, and a soldier. An officer.

He had already seen a redcap standing on the jetty: he was

229

watching two seamen, defaulters, no doubt, busily splicing wire. He was dangling a bunch of keys from his hand, and was obviously their visitor's driver. He could have walked here, Turnbull thought. So much for the fuel shortage.

But instinct told him this was not merely a matter of liberty-men getting drunk, or brawling in the canteen. The neatly pressed battledress and the three pips on his shoulder had Turnbull on full alert, and glad he had refused that extra tot. Apart from the Provost badge and a small flash on his shoulder, the newcomer looked just like any other army captain.

He thought of Cock Glover: *you can always spot a copper, no matter what he's wearing.* He had had a record as long as your arm, until he had wangled himself into Coastal Forces.

The officer returned his salute and glanced at him: only seconds, but it felt like an inspection.

"Can I help, sir?"

Dawson wheezed, "Wants to see the Skip . . ." and cleared his throat, "the commanding officer." But he was looking down at the visitor's heavy boots, scraping his clean deck.

"Lieutenant-Commander Kearton not aboard, then?" Sharp, precise. "I need to see him."

"He's at a meeting right now, sir. Quite an important one, I believe. He's just returned from active duty." It sounded like a defence.

"I know all that." He dragged his cuff away from his watch. "It should be over by now."

Turnbull said, "I can fetch the first lieutenant, sir. He's aboard the M.G.B. astern of us."

He nodded curtly. "The latest arrival. In that case, I shall have to get back to H.Q." He lifted one hand in a signal to his driver. "I'll leave word at the gate."

Turnbull reached out unconsciously, and stopped himself before touching his arm.

"Anything I can do, sir? I'd like to help." He saw the

230

immediate reaction, like a guard dropping into place. It was pointless. But he added quietly, "I owe it to him. He saved my life."

"In that case—"

Dawson called, " 'E's comin' now, 'Swain!" and, ignoring the officer, "I'll 'ave someone mop up this deck."

Kearton walked up the brow, and saluted as he stepped over the side.

"Do you wish to see me? I'm sorry you've been kept waiting."

Turnbull unclenched his fists. So calm . . . like hearing him at the table, dealing with a requestman, or rearranging duties in the flotilla.

"I'm Murray, S.I.B. I'd like you to accompany me ashore, sir." He tapped his breast pocket. "I have the written authority. There's a car."

The gangway sentry muttered, "First lieutenant's arrived."

Turnbull heard himself say, "I'd like to come along too, sir," and sensed the soldier's immediate resentment. "For messages and things." But, surprisingly, he nodded. There was even the hint of a smile.

"I have no objection."

Kearton paused at the brow again. "Won't be long, Number One," and glanced at the officer in khaki. "Right?"

Murray had half turned. "The quicker the better." He watched Kearton salute and the others respond as he stepped on to the jetty, then Kearton stopped and gripped his arm.

"Tell me what this is about."

They fell into step, and only Turnbull sensed the sudden confrontation.

A drill of some kind had been running nearby, repairing something, or clearing away rubble from the last air raid. There was a momentary lull, and the provost captain's voice seemed very loud in the silence.

"There was an incident this morning. Someone was attacked."

Kearton tightened his grip and repeated, "Tell me. Who was she?"

"I didn't say it was a woman." Then, "I think I understand. Do you know someone called Dalli? Maria Dalli? Your name was on a pad by the telephone. An official number. That was how we traced you."

Kearton realized that they had reached the car. A redcap was standing by the door, and two naval patrolmen were waiting to open the gates. Either they knew what was happening, or were speculating wildly. Soon the whole place would hear about it.

He remembered the call, the deafening music, her voice after she had turned it down, or closed the door. Or someone else had closed it. But not Glynis.

"Was it robbery?"

Murray gestured to the rear set, but waited until Turnbull had climbed into the front beside the driver.

"It might have been an intended robbery. Now it's murder."

The car pulled out on to the road and Turnbull saw Lieutenant Toby Ainslie walking toward them, a large folder beneath his arm. He, too, had been at a meeting, with Intelligence, taking him through it all over again, as if he had not suffered enough. He had seen the car and recognized them, and had stopped, staring at them.

But Turnbull was listening intently to Kearton's voice.

"I was ringing Mrs Howard."

"Yes, we know. We had to get hold of her too, of course. She knew the deceased pretty well."

"How is she?"

"I didn't see her. One of my chaps thought she seemed OK, rather shocked. Only natural." He rapped the driver's shoulder. "Here, next turning."

The driver's eyes were reflected in his mirror.

232

"I know, sir."

Kearton saw the same half-demolished building with the ornate balcony; he had barely noticed the journey. Like the meeting: Garrick very much in charge. Shaking hands. Unfamiliar faces. And all the time his mind had remained detached, resisting. Preparing him.

"Where is Mrs Howard, do you know?"

The car was turning again, slowing to lurch across a deep rut.

"She's here now." He winced as the car shook again. "Didn't I say? She found the body."

"I think I knew."

All the car doors were open suddenly. "I shall need a short statement, just a few lines for my report. Shouldn't take long."

Kearton stood on the rough ground and saw the barrier closing behind them. Hurrying figures, a few salutes, someone testing a torch by the checkpoint. Surely it was not that late? But the sky seemed darker, and the air was clammy against his face. Perhaps another one of those brief, fierce storms . . .

He heard Turnbull say, "I'll be standing by, in case." Then he saw her, by the end of the cracked wall, people passing or loitering near other vehicles, and yet quite alone.

She did not move until he reached her, and even then she waited until he had put his arms around her, and her voice was muffled as she rested her forehead against his shoulder.

"You came. They told me, but I wanted to meet you. Just us."

He turned her gently toward the buildings. He could see the same tarpaulin stretched across one of the roofs, the slope leading down to the abandoned garden, an open door, two uniformed figures peering at a map or plan of some sort. Police.

He squeezed her shoulders, but felt no response, and her arms still hung straight at her sides.

"I came as soon as I could, Glynis." He thought he felt her shiver at the sound of her name.

"I knew you'd come. But I was afraid."

"You can come in here now, miss." A pause. "You too, sir."

Again he felt her body stiffen. She said, "I screamed. Couldn't help it. Then everyone was here. I wanted you to know." She broke off. "Poor Maria."

Some of the lamps had been switched off, and he saw two redcaps carrying them toward the parked vehicles.

Captain Murray was standing near the desk, watching one of his men making notes. His cap was on the desk, and without it he looked younger: human, Kearton thought.

Some of the furniture had been moved, and there were chalk marks near the table with its official-looking telephone.

The old armchair was as he remembered it. As if it had been here when the apartment had been part of that other, peacetime Malta. She did not resist when he sat her down in it.

She looked up at him, her eyes filling her face. "I wanted to get here early. I knew you'd call— I hoped you'd come. So I would be waiting to greet you." She rubbed her cheek with the back of her hand, but when he offered his handkerchief she did not seem to see it. "But there was a big hold-up on the road. An accident, or something to do with the convoy . . . nobody said." She looked up at him again. "So I was late. Otherwise . . ." She was staring at the telephone now, and the door beyond it. "Otherwise."

He knelt beside the armchair, and held her tightly against him.

She whispered, "I screamed." Then, "Don't leave me, Bob."

The shadow loomed over them.

"We'll be leaving now, Mrs Howard." An unknown face. "We can run through it again." A pause. "Tomorrow?"

Kearton felt her nod, and said, "She's been through enough."

The voice persisted, "But nothing stolen, you say?"

She shook her head. "There's nothing *worth* stealing." She reached out and took the handkerchief, and looked up at him

234

again, her eyes suddenly alive. "I'll wash this for you. What do sailors call it?"

Kearton smiled. "Dhoby."

Murray had put his cap back on, becoming the policeman again. "I think we've got all we need from you, sir. The wireless was switched on and playing loud music when you called this number. The deceased turned it down while you were speaking." He closed his book, but used it to point at the door. "Or shut that." He pursed his lips. "Quite a stretch, to do that."

A voice called, "Ready, sir?" Car doors slamming.

"Are you staying here, Mrs Howard?"

Kearton said, "I'll be here, until . . ." He looked down; she was grasping his hand. She said, "I have friends coming here shortly." Her chin lifted. "Until then . . ."

Kearton said curtly, "I'll send word to my people," wanting them to leave her alone. But he knew it had only just started.

"One last question, Mrs Howard." Murray was hovering, the humanity gone. "Do you think Miss Dalli knew, or recognized, the intruder?"

She looked directly at Kearton.

"It was why he killed her."

"There'll be an extra patrol in this sector. But if anything occurs to you . . ." He stood by the outer door. "Your petty officer is here."

She stood up, and walked toward him, her hand outstretched.

"Mr Turnbull— Harry. May I?"

Turnbull stared past her at Kearton.

"'Course. As it should be amongst friends— mates—" He took the offered hand. "I'll be back aboard, sir. And put Jimmy— th' first lieutenant in the frame." He seemed to back away. "Sure it's OK, sir?"

"Thanks, 'Swain." Kearton wanted to smile. "*Harry.*"

He closed the door after him, and slid a bolt as an extra precaution.

She had returned to the old chair and tucked her legs up into it. Exhaustion, despair and fear were taking their toll. He covered her with the shawl she had been wearing, touching her hair.

"Do you really have friends coming?"

She moved deeper into the chair. "Stay with me." She was almost asleep, and he thought the police surgeon had given her something.

He took her hand and put it under the shawl, knowing he wanted to touch her, love her. Make her desire him, and no one else. Make her forget . . .

He straightened up and walked to the little desk, and dragged open the top drawer before he knew what he was doing.

The same silver frame: the glass had not been replaced. He closed the drawer again quietly. She was asleep. Beyond fear.

The wedding photograph was still there, but the bride had been slashed repeatedly with a knife or razor, by someone unknown, and still at large with his lust and madness.

And he had been here. Waiting for her. Listening to the music, then opening the door.

And hearing my voice.

"Bob, where are you? Don't go."

He held her, embracing her, before she could move. But her eyes were still closed. Not a nightmare.

"I'm here, Glynis. You're safe."

He had to bend closer to hear her voice, her breathing. A whisper: *"Touch me . . ."*

But she was fast asleep. *Who did she see in her dreams?*

He settled down on the carpet, with his shoulder against the chair.

He was still awake when there was a cloudburst over Grand Harbour, and the telephone began to ring.

When he answered it, the line was dead.

14

A Face on the Shore

"Captain Garrick is in there, sir." The naval patrolman saluted, and added, "Expecting you."

Kearton stared at the wooden hut which seemed to be perched only a few yards from the edge of the jetty, the one he had first noticed on their return from Operation *Retriever*. Hastily bolted together like those used by construction workers, bare and unpainted: hardly what you might expect for a senior officer.

He skirted another large puddle left by the overnight rain and rapped on the door.

Garrick was sitting at a small trestle table, his jacket draped across a chair, his cap beside it. He waved to the only other, very hard chair.

"Good to see you! I want to run over a few things before you start work."

Through another narrow door, Kearton could hear someone flushing water. Garrick shrugged.

"The heads, such as they are. Out of order at the moment, so don't get taken short if you can help it."

There was one telephone, the wire supported on a length of string. Also temporary.

Garrick was watching his expression with what might have been amusement.

"I come here to escape. Brice knows where I am— he can signal me if he's out of his depth."

The door opened and closed again and a figure in overalls, carrying a bucket and brush, squeezed past them.

"All done, sir." He paused. "For now."

Garrick pushed a file of loose papers aside and rested one elbow on the table. "At least we shan't be disturbed here."

Kearton said, "I wanted to see you, sir," and halted as a drill clattered into action. Then it stopped abruptly.

"And I wanted to see *you*." He touched the file. "You've not had a lot of rest since you came to Malta, have you?"

He pulled out a packet of cigarettes and shook it. "I'm up to my ears. You remember Lampton? Sir Piers Lampton? Well, he's still with us, and becoming more involved than I care for. My old father used to say that Guy Fawkes was the only honest man who ever reached Parliament. I suppose I didn't understand what he meant at the time. I do now, by God!"

Just as quickly, the mood passed.

"And I was expecting you to request to see me, despite all you've got on *your* plate. I know all about that unfortunate incident, the death of that poor Maltese woman. I've already had the police clambering all over the place— the usual stable-door tactics." He lit the cigarette, and held the gold lighter quite steady until the flame died. "There are so many people, always on the move. Displaced persons, refugees, to say nothing of our own servicemen, even deserters. I sometimes think that if Hermann Goering himself walked through the gates, he would pass unchallenged." He smiled briefly. "Provided he left his medals back in the Fatherland!" He stubbed out the cigarette, unsmoked. "And yes, of course it worried me. Thought about it quite a lot. Maybe she was having it off with someone from around here and it got out of hand. It happens. Or it was some-one disturbed during a robbery attempt."

He leaned back in the chair, his shirt impeccably white against the drab surroundings.

"All our people are accounted for. Even the unfortunate Lieutenant Warren's crew have been under lock and key, so to speak, since you got them safely back from *Retriever*."

Kearton said, "Mrs Howard is a friend of mine."

"I know that."

"It could have been her."

"I know that, too." He picked up the packet, but it was empty. He said, "No use asking you. A pipe man, right?"

Perhaps it gave him time. "Her husband, or ex-husband, as he will be when the smoke clears, has been with me, or with the Intelligence brass ever since he came ashore. Time he had a break, moved on to something less demanding, if such people ever can." He reached back, into the jacket lying on the chair. "Bad habit. Could do worse." He clicked the lighter again, and watched the smoke drift toward the solitary window, where it remained.

"I see Mrs Howard around the base from time to time. Done a lot of good work with and for our civilian staff. When the bombing was at its height she helped resettle a lot of people needing care or accommodation . . ." The teeth flashed. "Nice-looking, too!"

The solitary telephone jangled.

"Garrick." He blew out a thin stream of smoke. "Ten minutes? Thanks." He put it down slowly. "Well, Brice is awake. I'll have to go."

Kearton waited, knowing there was more. This 'casual' interview had been timed to the minute.

"I read your report, Bob. Proud of you. Hope someone at the Admiralty will eventually take notice of what we're doing out here." He tapped the file, serious again. "I see you've recommended your lieutenant— er, Ainslie?— for some suitable recognition after his general performance throughout *Retriever*. Good of you."

239

Kearton said, "Good of *him*. I dropped him right into it. He deserves something."

"It's not that easy." He frowned. "Some would say that he was only doing his job, which in turn was a reflection of your judgment or choice in the first place." He stood up and slipped on his reefer jacket in two easy movements. "We can talk about it. Maybe a Mention. We'll see." He picked up his cap and blew some dust off its peak. "You'll receive your orders today. A convoy of sorts. Nothing earth-shattering, but I know you'll be wanting to knock your little flotilla into a team without delay." He punched his arm. "But you don't delay much on anything, do you?"

Kearton saw him give the habitual wave to the overalled cleaner with the bucket, and call, "Nice job of work, well done!" And the cleaner staring after him and beaming.

He turned and looked along the moorings. Timed to the minute.

But a man you would never know.

Able Seaman 'Cock' Glover peered around the two-pounder's gunshield, then nudged his companion.

" 'Eads up, Tosh, look busy! Trouble's comin'!"

He dabbed at the training gear with his cloth again, although he could already see his face in it. Not long now, and they could knock off for some grub and a tot. All through the forenoon watch he had seen extra stores coming aboard and being checked under the hard eyes of the Cox'n. He sensed a shadow across the deck. *And* Jimmy the One. Nothing got past him unnoticed.

The Skipper was ashore, so he was in charge. Glover had known and served a lot worse, but Spiers was an officer. *Say no more.* Extra stores meant one thing: they were under sailing orders again. No more runs ashore for a while.

He had spent all of his cash, anyway. The place Laurie Jay

had remembered from his previous service here was a lot of fun, but not cheap. He thought of the girl who had danced for them. There had been other Jacks there, but she had given him the eye. Greek, Maltese, he didn't know, and it didn't matter. But next time . . .

He heard a clatter and saw that his helper had spilled a can of polish on the clean deck. He sighed. A good enough lad, but as thick as two planks.

He snatched up some rags and looked around the mounting, then he exclaimed, "Blimey, Tosh, *that's* a turn-up for the book!"

Spiers had walked right past without giving them a glance.

Glover grinned. "I'll fix it. Cost you sippers at grog-time!"

Spiers had heard the noise, but he was watching the motor gunboat which was moored directly astern. One of the two new arrivals, and to any rookie or landsman no different from 992. She mounted more automatic weapons and would offer a formidable challenge to any would-be enemy, and was a knot or two faster, perhaps, without the extra weight of torpedoes. But the bows were scalloped for them, in case her role might be changed, if so decided.

There were occasional puffs of exhaust as the engines muttered into life, then switched off again. Spiers had noticed some of the base mechanics going aboard, and an electrical officer as well; he had seen the pale sunlight shining on the green cloth between his stripes and recognized him as the same one who had given 992 the OK after her swift overhaul.

So the M.G.B. was ready for sea. *Like us.*

It was not that thought which disquieted him. It was the man he had been talking to, the commanding officer. Like himself, a lieutenant.

'Red' Lyon, as he had become known; and he had revealed the shock of bright ginger hair just now when he had used his cap to emphasize some point. A few who had served with him unkindly suggested the nickname was his own invention.

He was the same age as Spiers, but a year less in seniority, a lifetime, as the old sweats would have it. And it sometimes was.

Now he was here. With his own command.

This time they had met only briefly, when Spiers had been supervising the moorings and Lyon had joined him on the jetty. Cap at a rakish angle, hands in his jacket pockets with the thumbs hooked over the edges, exactly as he remembered him.

"Well, hello!" He had offered his hand. "Spiers, isn't it? You're with Bob Kearton— his Number One, right? I thought you might have jumped up the ladder by now!" And the sharp laugh, which Spiers had not forgotten either. "We might see some action now, so you never know your luck!"

He had turned to speak with some of his men.

Spiers was still angry when he allowed himself to think about it. With Lyon, and with himself for letting it strike home.

See some action. What the hell does he think we've been doing?

He glanced at the M.G.B. again. A command to be proud of. In the right hands . . . He swung away on his heel, but he could still hear the laugh.

There were more tinned stores piled on the jetty, with a petty officer checking his list and licking the point of his pencil.

Spiers called, "You two, give a hand there! They won't carry themselves!"

Glover touched his cap. "Good as done, sir!" and dropped his voice. "That's more like it, Tosh. Bloody officers!"

But his companion was looking astern at the motor gunboat.

"That's 'Red' Lyon down there, Cock."

Glover grinned. "Sounds like a pub. Wish it was."

Tosh did not hear him. "I've read about him. Been in lots of battles."

Glover pretended to yawn. "Tell me about it!"

"He was awarded the Distinguished Service Cross. I saw it in the *Mirror*."

"Yeah? Well, from what *I* 'eard, blokes under 'im end up gettin' wooden ones!" He laughed. "An' don't forget, Tosh, *sippers*!"

Ainslie was sitting in the chartroom and heard the laughter as they passed the door, which was propped open. The door on the opposite side was closed, shutting out the sound of drills and the rattle of anonymous machinery from the waterfront. Although he knew that was not the reason.

Around and beneath him he could hear and sense the usual shipboard sounds and movements: stores being carried or hoisted from the jetty, the trill of a bosun's call, and now, men laughing. All reassuring. Safe.

He stared at the charts he had just finished correcting, bringing them up to date, or as much as anything could be in wartime, with new wrecks constantly in the approaches: always real hazards to navigation, especially to homebound watch-keepers after a rough convoy, when they were thinking only of getting ashore to drown their sorrows. And other, older wrecks, which had been shifted and sunk in deeper waters, or blown up.

He had been working here all morning. In a way, it was an escape. He heard the intermittent bursts of power from another boat close by: under orders, preparing for sea. He tried to ignore it, but the tension remained like a knot in his stomach, and would not be dispelled simply by making pencilled lines and figures on a chart. He stared at the canvas bag he was using to carry and keep his 'tools' in. Weston, the telegraphist, had offered it to him to replace the old satchel. It would never do that, but he had accepted it, touched by Weston's gesture. But it was always there. Another reminder.

Tomorrow, or the next day at the latest. It was an incoming convoy, and they would be there as back-up, and to give them the feel of working together in action. He was able to consider it calmly. *We won't be alone this time.*

He reached up to switch off the chart light and saw his own shadow against the fresh paintwork. Like yesterday: now. The gun raised like a salute, his finger on the trigger.

He had seen him when he had gone ashore, being met by everyone on the base, or so it had seemed. Senior officers, too, and someone taking photographs. He had looked back then at Ainslie, with those cold, pale eyes. They could have been quite alone. But without recognition. Like a challenge.

And nobody else knew. He had not even told the Skipper. He switched off the light, and recalled Kearton's handshake.

Especially not him.

He had heard about the woman being found dead: some attempted robbery inside the restricted area, according to the buzz. There were police and security patrols everywhere when he had been over there being vetted by the Intelligence staff, and he thought it was the last place anyone would attempt to commit a robbery. Now it was murder.

The Skipper had been involved, too, because his friend worked and lived within sight of the harbour. He wondered if there was anything in it. He had seen her a couple of times: she would turn anyone's head, and he had heard somebody say she was married. He hadn't thought the Skipper would get involved with a married woman, so maybe there was more to it than that. Turnbull in particular had spoken for most of them when he'd said, "Bloody good luck to him!"

He thought about Sarah, and the letter which was still unwritten. He had started it and fallen asleep across the wardroom table, and had woken to find someone had taken the pen from his fingers and screwed the cap back on, and left it beside the pad. Number One, perhaps, but it seemed unlikely. Peter Spiers had been almost like a stranger since Operation *Retriever*.

How can that be, in a boat this size?

He glanced at the shutter in the forepart of the chartroom, at his reflection.

Maybe it's me. Have I changed that much? Am I the stranger?

He swung round as the other door suddenly opened, and the outside noises intruded.

"Sorry, old chap, I didn't know anybody was in here." He laughed. "Did I make you jump?"

It was the electrical officer Ainslie had seen earlier, visiting one of the other boats for a final check-up. But in the shadows the green cloth between his two wavy stripes was not apparent. Just his hand around the door, wearing a leather glove.

Now, he knew.

The Chief Yeoman of Signals put the thick envelope on his table and waited as Turnbull signed for it.

"Nothing much you don't already know, Harry. Couple of recognition signals that might come in handy if everything goes according to plan. But your S.O. will expect to be up to date."

Turnbull was listening to the typewriters and the telephones.

"We'll take root if we stay here much longer!"

"That'll be the day!"

"No more runs ashore for a while, anyway."

The Chief Yeoman glanced at one of his young signalmen, who was scrawling something on a blackboard, biting his lower lip in concentration.

"A bit quieter around here now." He lowered his voice. "We've been crawling with cops. Ours, the army, even some civvies, for all the good they've done." He shook his head. "That poor lass. Never stood a chance, to all accounts." He made a chopping motion with his hand. "Rabbit-punch, then strangled, or so I was told."

"They find anything?"

"Couldn't find a bottle in a brewery, that lot!"

Turnbull pointed at the bundle which had just been delivered. "What's that?" and was rewarded with a crooked grin.

"A rowing-machine. The Boss likes to keep in shape. Over here, away from the staff."

Turnbull shrugged. "Maybe he's in love, Yeo."

"He is. Every time he looks in a mirror!" He picked up some papers. "But I've served worse." Then he touched the badges on his own lapels and said quietly, "You've got some service in, Harry." He glanced at the medal ribbon. "Keep your nose clean, an' you should rate promotion yourself." He poked his arm. "Get a nice soft job ashore— like me, I don't think!"

They walked to the door together, the noise left behind them. For once, there was nobody else within earshot.

Turnbull stopped and faced him.

"You know Mrs Howard, don't you?"

"I see her around quite a bit, Harry. Call her 'our Glynis', behind her back of course." He paused. "Not that she's stuck up, like some. But she's got to be careful with all these Jolly Jacks about." He winked. "The wardroom, too." Then, abruptly, "What's on your mind? Have you heard something?"

"I've talked to her. Saw her at the sick quarters with a young chap off the *Kinsale*. He was dying. But there's something . . ." He broke off as a messenger strode past them.

The Chief Yeoman dropped his voice again.

"She was living here in Malta before I was drafted to H.Q. She came out with her father from England just before the balloon went up and the shit began in earnest. Done a lot of good stuff, civilians, welfare." He paused as if listening. "And she got married. Friend of her dad's, to all accounts. A soldier. You know how it is, the war, an' everything."

He paused again. "It was all gossip— but the marriage didn't work out. He was sent away, something happened. Anyway, she wanted to break it off."

A voice shouted, "Call for you, Yeo!"

He sighed. "If I don't see you before you shove off to sea, Harry, I'll keep a noggin waiting for you."

Turnbull nodded. "I'll take you up on that." And then, "There was trouble?"

He waved toward the door, as if undecided.

246

Then he said in an undertone, "She was raped. Hushed up at the time, of course."

"Was it . . ."

"Only two people know that, Harry."

The voice shouted again, "Too late, Yeo! He's rung off!"

He smiled. "I'd better do the same." It was a strong handshake. "Just watch your step, my son."

Turnbull walked across the yard, or whatever it had once been, and looked through a gap in the old stone wall. He could see the water, but the M.T.B. moorings were hidden from view.

He was ready; he had to be. And the rest? *Stay out of it.* His friend had understood, and had warned him.

Others depended on him. He twisted the thick envelope in his hands.

He thought of Jock Laidlaw, and the policeman dressed as an army captain. He had told both of them, *he saved my life.* And the girl with the dark eyes and bloodstains on her breast, who had held his arm and walked beside him.

She probably knew better than anybody: the Skipper was completely alone. He thought of his face, when he had gone to his cabin with his carefully rehearsed welcome. *Me an' the lads* . . . and the jug, which he had found almost untouched when he had gone back to switch off the lights.

They were all going to need him more than ever.

He tugged his cap down over his eyes. *So be it.*

Kearton glanced along the wardroom table and pulled the chart slightly toward him. All the scuttles were open and the deadlights raised. Outside it was still clear with some misty sun, but for security reasons they would soon shut the ports and darken ship; and then, even with the fans at full blast, this place would be like an oven.

"That about sums it up. We slip and proceed at eight tomorrow forenoon. Gentlemen's hours, for a change." There were smiles and a laugh or two. The four commanding officers were here, and Ainslie, squeezed into a corner with his own chart and logbook. Spiers was just outside the wardroom door, listening, but making sure they were not disturbed by unexpected visitors or unimportant signals.

At least the tension had been broken. This was their first meeting en masse: Stirling the Canadian, cheerful, and alert to every snippet of information, showing no sign of strain after their action with the Italian patrol vessel and the recovery of *Retriever*'s survivors. Or maybe experience had taught him to conceal it. And Geoff Mostyn of 977, puffing his pipe and jotting notes on a well-thumbed pad: he had asked a few questions, but seemed otherwise untroubled.

There was Lieutenant Chris Griffin, one of the M.G.B. skippers; it was his first command. Soft-spoken, with a ready smile, he was a West Countryman, maybe Cornish. And Lyon, pointing now at the chart, shaping the convoy's route with his hands.

"Special cargo from Alex, so they've likely been ushered right around the Cape, and up through the Red Sea to Suez. Phew! It would bore the pants off me."

Stirling said, "Hell of a lot safer, though."

Red Lyon nodded. "But if a risk saves time and lives, take it, I say!"

Kearton remembered him, like so many others, from the Channel days. But not so sharply defined then, he thought, and less confident than he seemed now.

He said, "We shall exercise in formation once we're on our own. But meeting the convoy and offering additional escort for its home run will be our main objective." He gauged their expressions. "Four ships— not many, so they must be important. We haven't been told."

Stirling grinned. "Ask me no questions, I'll tell you no lies, eh?"

Kearton looked past him toward Ainslie, ready with his own notes and official navigational details; he had already ticked off a list of final instructions. But Kearton could see the change in him. Feel it. Like someone else standing in for the bright, sometimes shy youngster who had greeted him at Gibraltar. Did any of them remember that?

He saw the new pipe lying across an ashtray near Ainslie's chart. He must have bought it ashore somewhere, or else he had been carrying it around, saving it for some suitable occasion.

It had ended in a bout of coughing.

Mostyn had suggested, "Get some good stuff, Pilot. Pusser's tobacco will kill you!" He had laughed and thumped his own chest. "Don't I know it!"

Red Lyon had said, "Not for boys."

Kearton folded the chart and looked at the open door. Apart from the fans, the boat seemed silent. No libertymen, not even a short run ashore to the wet canteen. *Especially* not to that. Fuel tanks fully topped up. He could picture Laidlaw in his mind, muttering about the extra cans of petrols they had stowed aboard as an extra precaution. As he put it, "an extra bloody risk." Weapons and magazines checked. And the massive torpedoes, oiled and shiny. Always waiting.

He gazed at the bulkhead, as though he could see through and beyond it to their company. A mere handful compared with any major warship, even a destroyer or corvette. But properly handled . . .

"Any mail going ashore? Do it now." He saw Ainslie peer at his own clip of notes, and knew what he was thinking.

The hull tilted slightly as another vessel passed, fairly close. He thought he heard the helmsman being challenged, and the faint response. He watched the flickering reflection on the low deckhead, then it stilled until the next disturbance.

Where was she now? What might she be doing? Working late

in one of the offices, or dealing with a new arrival? Or sitting in the apartment. Listening. Watching the telephone.

He wanted to shake himself. She was safe now. Everybody knew.

"I think that's all, gentlemen," and, forcing himself to smile, "If you'll excuse the formality!"

They all laughed, as he knew they would. It always seemed to help.

Lyon was the last visitor to leave. Somehow Kearton had known that, too.

"Good to be working with you— er, Bob. We can teach them a few new tricks!" He unhooked his thumbs from his pockets and looked around for his cap. "I heard Toby Warren bought it the other day. I served with him for a time."

He shook his head, so that his hair seemed to glow under the deckhead lights. "Too bad— but if your number's on it, that's it." He was looking at Ainslie. "Something I said?"

Ainslie said in a low, cold voice, "I was with him. We were friends." He stood up and gathered his papers. "I must take some mail ashore." He brushed past Spiers in the doorway without looking back. He had left his new pipe behind on the table, and Lyon touched it.

"Too soon. It's a *man's* pipe."

Kearton said quietly, "Cut it out. You know the rule."

He held up both hands. "*Sorree*, sir, I forgot! No names in the mess. *Afterwards*!"

Then he grinned. "He should come over to my command for a spell, and see some *real* officers at work."

Kearton followed him to the ladder and stopped him.

"When you come over to mine again, try and act like one."

He could still hear the laugh when Lyon had reached the upper deck, and knew he had made an enemy.

"Close all watertight doors and scuttles! Down all deadlights!"

Leading Seaman Pug Dawson did not need the tannoy system: his voice reached upper and lower deck without effort, and was usually more reliable. The small galley was shut, the messdeck cleared of everything but essential gear. Anything left lying about would be pounced on by the coxswain, and the owner would have to pay a fine before he could reclaim it.

The few remaining lights dimmed briefly as the engineroom quivered into life. A few of the usual jokes, a grin or two. The waiting was over. It was almost a relief.

Kearton was in his cabin. That, too, looked bare, and more unlived in than ever. He checked his pockets and his notebook; if he had forgotten anything, it was too late anyway.

Always the same . . . He had heard the slam of watertight doors and hatches, the sounds of hurrying feet and muffled voices, and found that he could smile. *It's never the same.*

He pictured the chart again. Going over it with Ainslie, translating the written orders into speed, time, and distance. South-east this time, to meet the small convoy, some of which had pounded all the way around the Cape and up through Suez to avoid the commerce raiders and U-Boat packs. They still had a long way to go to reach Malta once they left Alexandria. He recalled what Spiers had told him about Bomb Alley, but that had been then. Things might have eased off now, with the Afrika Korps at a stalemate.

He thought of Ainslie again, apparently quite at home with his charts while they had been together, but still quieter than usual. Than before . . .

He looked at his watch, and tightened the strap slightly. A bad sign, but it was only in big ships that the meals ran on time.

He stared at the sealed scuttle. Like hearing her voice, her concern.

"You've got to look after yourself, Bob. Promise me?"

At the foot of that same staircase. Yesterday. People hurrying past, tutting if they had to squeeze by, or turning openly to stare. They were alone for only a few minutes.

"I want to be with you, Glynis. There's never a moment."

Someone had called her name then, and held up some letters.

"I must go."

He had already seen Brice hovering, trying not to look impatient.

"I want you to be careful."

She had touched his shoulder, then his face for the first time.

"Oh, Bob, you want a lot!"

"I want you."

But she had pulled away.

He thought he heard someone say, "Nice work, if you can get it!" He had not seen who it was. It was just as well.

He gathered up his pipe and tobacco, recalling the exchange between Ainslie and 'Red' Lyon. That was then. This was now.

Pug Dawson again: "Special Sea Dutymen close up!"

More voices now, less restrained. The usual jokes, silly, necessary. The stand-by helmsman hurried toward the bridge, and a voice called, "Don't forget, Arthur, starboard is on the *right*!"

He replied without stopping, "Is it Red or Green?"

Spiers had appeared outside the door, with the merest hint of a smile.

"Ready, sir. When you are."

"Thanks, Peter." He did not look back.

"D'you hear there? Clear lower deck! Hands fall in for leaving harbour!"

He climbed into the daylight and gazed over toward the jetty and the buildings beyond. Sunshine, but without warmth, and patchy cloud.

The mooring wires were already singled-up and some spare hands, onlookers, were waiting to cast off when the order was given.

The usual clouds of vapour now, the engines muttering in

unison, men lined up fore and aft. There were a few people up on the road, beyond the gates; there might be more closer to the entrance. No secrets here.

He glanced forward and saw a seaman standing up in the bows, ready to lower the Jack when they got under way. Smartly turned out in his best Number Threes, when, within hours, he might be called to action stations.

He shut it from his mind, and climbed up into the bridge.

Ainslie saluted. "Signal to proceed when ready, sir."

So formal. Maybe that, too, was just as well.

He saw Turnbull beside the wheel with his extra helmsman, a lookout, and a telegraphist waiting by the signal lamp. The 'little ships' did not warrant a bunting-tosser.

The machine-guns were still hooded, unmanned.

He lifted his binoculars, but let them fall again.

She might be out there somewhere. Watching . . . It would be asking a lot. *From both of us.*

"Warn the Chief."

"Done, sir."

"All acknowledged, sir!"

He knew Turnbull was watching him, heard him say, "Like old times, sir."

He knew.

He raised his arm and saw Spiers salute.

"Let go, forrard!"

"All gone forrard, sir!"

"Let go, aft!"

He saw the frothing water, suddenly alive, the jetty slowly edging away.

"All gone aft, sir!"

He heard Ainslie call, "All *clear* aft, sir!"

"Slow ahead. Midships."

The land was moving.

The rest was a dream.

253

15

The Hunted

"Port watch at defence stations, sir." Spiers turned away from the voicepipes and glanced across the bridge. He was standing only a few feet away and hardly raised his voice. A formality. Or to make sure that his commanding officer had not fallen asleep.

Kearton pushed himself away from the flag locker, smothering a yawn. Eight o'clock: the first watch. Never popular with sailors, it was neither night nor day.

He leaned against the side and felt the steady, regular motion. A steep swell, but otherwise the same. He had heard the routine reports as the watches changed: four hours on, and four off. Even when you stole an hour or so to sleep, there was always the risk of a sudden alarm. It would be their first night at sea, twelve hours exactly since they had slipped their moorings. After all the noise and bustle it seemed uncanny, the sea empty, disturbed only by their own engines, and the occasional moustache of the bow wave next astern, Geoff Mostyn's 977. In line ahead, playing follow-my-leader, with one M.G.B. keeping well abeam to starboard as an extra precaution.

The nearest land was the Libyan coast, two hundred miles to the south, a place called Sirte, unknown to most sailors but familiar enough to Montgomery's Eighth Army in their bloody fighting up to the turning point, the victory at El Alamein. Only months, and yet it seemed like a page of history.

He looked at the evening sky, still clear from horizon to horizon. No haze, nor any hint of cloud. And tomorrow they would meet the small convoy.

Like hearing Garrick's voice. *Nothing earth-shattering.* But Special Operations would not be involved if it were so simple. Garrick seemed to have a hand in everything.

How much did he really know, or care, about the people who carried out his orders?

He heard Spiers speaking to the helmsman, whose name was Bliss. He had taken more than a few wisecracks because of it since he had joined up 'for the duration'. Turnbull had told him that Bliss had been a greyhound trainer at a dog-racing stadium. He wondered idly what Garrick would make of that.

He looked at the sky again. There would be no moon tonight. Useful for the convoy. *Unless.* "I'll be in the chartroom, Number One. Want to check a couple of things."

It must have sounded like a question.

Spiers said, "I've got the weight, sir," and looked abeam. "And we have 'Red' Lyon on our flank, so we should be safe enough." No sarcasm. He did not need it.

Kearton took the short-cut to the chartroom without leaving the bridge structure. Ainslie was sitting on a stool facing the table, his body swaying from side to side as if he, and not the hull, was moving.

"Just tidying up, sir. No point in turning in." He looked at the cot. "I'll go, then *you* can have a break."

Kearton smiled. "If I fell asleep, I think it might need a depth-charge to wake me up again." He leaned on the table, and then said, "Put it behind you, if you can." He did not look at him. "Easy to say, I know. I've been there myself . . . Most of us have, if we're honest."

Someone laughed, the sound magnified and distorted. The voicepipe had been left uncovered.

"They depend on you, Toby. So do I."

Ainslie remained silent, perhaps surprised by the use of his name.

I was with him. We were friends.

He said, staring at the table, "The agent, Jethro— they're now calling him Captain Howard . . ." He shook his head. "I'm not making sense, am I?"

Kearton waited. "You're doing fine. What about him?"

Ainslie looked up. "He was going to shoot himself, when he thought we'd run into a trap. I knew you'd arrived to get us out of it . . . So I stopped him. Mark One—" He hesitated painfully. "Toby Warren died because of him. I should have let him pull the trigger!"

Kearton held his arm. "But you *didn't*, so it's between us, right? I dropped you in it in the first place. So over to me!"

The voicepipe intruded.

"C.O. on the bridge, please."

Kearton seized his binoculars. "At least he's polite!" The stair-hatch slammed shut behind him.

Ainslie did not move. Not an emergency, but whatever it was, it gave him time.

He said aloud, "You were right. They threw away the mould."

When Kearton reached the bridge it was exactly as he had left it, the lookouts using their binoculars to make regular sweeps of sea and sky, the helmsman relaxed at the wheel, his body moving easily in time with the motion, and someone elevating and depressing the hooded machine-guns as a matter of routine.

And yet he could sense the difference. Expectancy. Something to break the tension and the monotony of watchkeeping.

Spiers said, "Sorry to drag you up here again, sir, but we had a signal from Lieutenant Lyon." He gestured to starboard without turning his head. "He reported sighting some drifting wreckage to the south-east. Requests permission to investigate."

Kearton had already noticed that Weston, one of the

256

telegraphists, was also present, his hands on the signal lamp.

"He didn't use R/T?"

Spiers looked into the distance.

"Thought this was faster, maybe."

Kearton glanced astern and saw the next boat keeping perfect station, and the others following. It would soon be prudent to close up; darkness would be sudden. They could not afford to lose one another at any time from now on.

Spiers knew that, and so did Red Lyon.

He said, "Make, *Affirmative*," and saw the telegraphist's fingers working the trigger of the lamp. Ainslie spoke highly of him, and he had behaved well during his first taste of action, cooped up in his little W/T hutch where every sound and shake must have felt aimed personally at him.

Weston said, "Acknowledged, sir."

One of the lookouts muttered, "Now everyone knows about it!" and his opposite number laughed.

"That's the idea!"

Spiers said nothing.

Tomorrow might be another routine patrol, an exercise to get them all working together. Not the time for settling old scores or feeding new dislikes. He was calm again. *Their senior officer should know that better than anybody.*

"Call me if anything turns up, Number One. Otherwise . . ."

Kearton looked at the sky and toward the horizon.

As he turned his head, he felt his chin rasp against his scarf. Shaving was out of the question. But it reminded him of the moment when she had touched his face. She might not even have noticed, or known what it had meant to him.

That was then . . .

He paused by the dimly-lit compass and knew the helmsman had tensed against the wheel.

"Your greyhounds will be missing you, Bliss," and heard him laugh as though relieved.

"They'll have the hare chasing *them* by the time I get back, sir!"

The ice had been broken. And the need was his own.

Spiers heard the hatch close and used his binoculars again to check the positions of the other M.T.B.s and the remaining motor gunboat. Lyon's boat had long since disappeared, and would be nosing amongst the reported wreckage by now, if any was still there. Lyon was probably using it as an excuse to gain some freedom from their necessarily rigid formation. But he had been careful to tell Kearton first what he was doing. Spiers knew why it was getting him down, but it was no help.

He saw another figure framed against the darkening water and tried physically to make himself relax.

"Can't you sleep, 'Swain? I thought you'd have your head down while it's still quiet."

Turnbull touched his cap. "I heard some excitement just now," and nodded toward the side. "I was on my feet anyway."

Spiers said, "Probably nothing. It'll be lively enough later on, though."

Turnbull said carefully, "Lieutenant Lyon is a bit of a live wire, from what I've heard of him."

"Goes down well in some quarters, I suppose. I can live without it."

Turnbull watched him move restlessly to the opposite side of the bridge. Spiers was usually better at hiding his feelings. As Jimmy the One, he had to be.

The inner voice warned him again. *Stay out of it.* But dawn might bring a new challenge, and they should all be used to that, even the new hands. He, as coxswain, most of all.

He asked quietly, "You mean like the bits that get all the headlines in the popular press?"

For a moment he thought he had overstepped the mark, or that his words had been lost in the steady vibration of Laidlaw's four shafts.

Then Spiers said, "I think it's often overdone. When Operation *Retriever* was over, and the survivors brought back to Malta, I saw a press camera at work, and that Hardy chap doing the rounds with Captain Garrick. And later, when 'Jethro' was being interviewed— I thought that was going too far." He moved to the voicepipes and snapped, *"Yes?"* Then the tension seemed to leave him. "Some fresh ki is on its way."

Turnbull waited. Maybe he had misheard. "I thought Jethro was snatched off to be grilled by the Intelligence people, V.I.P. treatment. He looked pretty well hemmed-in when I saw him." Again, he thought he had gone too far. But it mattered, even more than he had realized. The girl standing in the shadows, and the Skipper holding her. Just holding her, when he had probably wanted to crush her in his arms. And the police; the chalk marks where another woman had been killed . . .

"After that, he was taken out of the base. He must have gathered some useful information for the brass to be so interested!" He touched Turnbull's arm, which was unusual for him. "I shouldn't say this, but I thought our friend Lyon was hoping for a little chat with Max Hardy himself!"

Then he was called to the voicepipes, business-like and very formal, the first lieutenant again.

Turnbull climbed down the short ladder to the deck. He would check around the various watchkeepers and make sure the steady, even motion of the hull was not sending them to sleep.

But all he could think of was Spiers' casual comment. And that last conversation he had had with the Chief Yeoman of Signals. *She was raped.* A tray of thick cocoa, pusser's 'ki', was passing him, but he scarcely noticed it.

He wanted to tell the Skipper. The man most of the others would never really know. *He saved me. I owe him.*

Turnbull did not need to look at the sky; he knew what it was going to be like. Tomorrow, when the sun found them again.

It was never easy. You never took it in your stride. The badges on his sleeve were proof of that.

They would all need the Skipper at his best tomorrow. *It's too damned far to swim.*

The seaman carrying the tray turned to watch Turnbull stride past, and the lookout, who was cradling a mug gratefully between his palms, chuckled.

"Cox'n's goin' aft for somethin' a bit stronger!"

The seaman balanced his tray against the motion.

"Needin' a drop of Dutch courage, eh?"

Throughout his long service, good and bad, Turnbull had retained excellent hearing. He turned and said, "Promise me something, Yorke. When they issue new brains, make sure you're first in the queue, right?"

He continued along the side-deck. Petty and unfair; "pulling rank", they would say on the messdeck.

But soon they were going to need *him*, too.

"Rise an' shine, sir. The birds are all singin' their heads off!"

"Thanks, Ginger. I'm on my way."

The hand on his shoulder, the gleam of a shaded torch, was all it took. Now.

Ainslie swung his legs from the wardroom bunk and reached for his boots, which were directly beside it. Automatic, like his response.

"Mug of char, sir. Just like Mum used to make." He paused by the door, just to be certain he had set the wheels in motion. Ginger was a seaman-gunner, but when he was off watch served as wardroom messman, *officers' lapdog*, as he was known, and could do almost anything in return for a few extra shillings. And he seemed to enjoy it.

Ainslie heard the door close and stood up, adjusting to the motion and listening to the sounds beyond the bulkhead and around him. He was wide awake.

So different from those early days, and nights. Aware of each new noise, afraid to close his eyes in case the alarm bells tore his mind apart. He had even slept fully clothed. It was not so long ago.

He tugged on his boots, so soft and supple now that it was difficult to remember them new. But he could still see the old tailor in his thoughts, standing back to observe as he had put on his first uniform. With satisfaction or amusement, it had been hard to tell. But then he had produced the boots. These boots. "Most of our regular gentlemen prefer these, sir. But in wartime, of course, they're not easy to come by." He had been right, but a handful of notes had secured a sale.

He peered at his watch. Four o'clock, or would be soon after he reached the bridge, and still pitch dark, but not for long. Their tight little world would come alive again. And *all the birds would be singin' their heads off*. But not out here.

He sat down again on the edge of the bunk and went through the usual routine. Notebook and 'tools', life-jacket. He patted his breast pocket. His wallet with Sarah's photograph inside. The photo was looking a little shabby in places, which was not surprising; it was always with him, and he had told her so. She had seemed pleased, and something more. He had thought of asking her for a new one, but had decided against it. It would mean having to get someone to take it. Sharing it . . .

He smiled to himself, sipping the tea, careful not to spill it as the hull leaned over into a trough. He could see the pencilled figures and notes in his mind as if they were on a chart. Fourteen knots. Until . . . He licked his lips. Ginger knew his fondness for sugar: you could stand a spoon in this. He touched his wallet again and thought of Sarah's mother. Difficult to know, and rather severe. It was impossible to see any resemblance between her and her daughter.

He put down the mug, recalling the time she had surprised

261

Sarah putting an extra spoonful of sugar into his cup, on one of his rare, uncomfortable visits to their house.

"Don't forget it's rationed, Sarah. *I* don't have any friends in the black market!"

Perhaps she disapproved of their relationship. Of him. What would she say if she knew what had happened before he had left to join 992? The only time they had ever been alone together . . . It had made him go hot and cold with nerves whenever he had thought about it afterwards. Not any more. He wanted her again, and he wanted her openly, now more than ever.

He thought of Peter Spiers, the faint disapproval whenever he had seen him showing her photograph, or writing to her. Maybe because Spiers never seemed to write any letters of his own, nor did he receive them.

Ainslie stood up again and looked around the small wardroom. Empty now. Private. But he could still see those other occasions, the meetings, the humour, and the doubts. And the last one, before they had quit their moorings, when he had clashed with the obnoxious Red Lyon. And Lyon with the Skipper: chalk and cheese.

At least, out here, they had something special. Like Ginger, who was probably still hovering outside the door listening for signs of life, in case Ainslie had fallen asleep again. And the leading torpedoman, Laurie Jay, who had survived the sinking of his submarine and who, in spirit, had never left that elite service. And the telegraphist Philip Weston, who had been dropped from the list of possible candidates for a commission because someone in his family was, or had been, a dedicated Fascist. He thought of the loud-mouthed gunlayer, Glover. He had heard him speak of Hitler while clearing away some of the damage after the action.

"Pity 'e's not on *our* side, that's what I say!"

He picked up his pipe and tapped it into an ashtray. Both were empty.

He heard a discreet cough.

"All set, sir?"

He put the pipe in his spare pocket. "England expects!"

Ginger was just as quick. "That's why they call it the Mother Country, sir!"

Ainslie punched his arm as he headed for the ladder.

"We don't need Hitler, with you around!"

Ginger was still staring after him as the hatch clicked shut.

It was dark on deck, but his eyes would soon adjust, and by the time he reached the bridge he could see the low crests breaking away from the stem and surging alongside, and even the mast, like a black pointer against the last pale stars. Nothing else in sight, although he knew he would soon be able to see the next astern. Otherwise, Number One would want to know why, and so would the Skipper.

He heard the murmur of voices, a squeak from one of the voicepipes, the helmsman handing over the wheel. *Course to steer, engine revolutions, speed*, and the man relieving him repeating them.

Ainslie listened to the last reports coming to the bridge. He was fully awake now, and refreshed by having had nearly a full watch's sleep below. It had been the Skipper's idea: he and Number One shared the most testing moments, sunset and daybreak. In most boats carrying only two officers, it was normal. God help them if one officer was taken ill. Or killed.

Spiers said, "Not much to report. Some wreckage was sighted. Nothing useful. A couple of corpses." He sounded impatient. "It's all in the log." His face was still hidden by the darkness, but Ainslie could see his scarf. "The Skipper's been up and down a few times . . . I don't know how he does it. I feel shagged out."

It was unusual for him to be so outspoken, as if he needed to talk.

He said suddenly, "We're not meant for this kind of work. I

think some self-important brass-hat sitting on his backside in Whitehall must wake up at his desk and peer at all his plans and clever ideas and say, 'What can I give *them* to do?'" He stared at the sea, but only the scarf moved. "If they ever got up from their desks, they'd trip over the cobwebs!"

Then he said, "Italy will be the stepping-stone back into Europe— Germany's Europe. Anyone should be able to see that. And Malta's the key. Supply and demand . . ." He broke off, and asked, "Can't you sleep either?"

It was Turnbull, clad in a black oilskin, like an additional shadow, as if he was about to take over the wheel.

He said, "I was awake, sir." The oilskin creaked; he must have shrugged. "Just wanted to be on hand."

The helmsman said, "You can take my place anytime, 'Swain!"

Somebody laughed, but Ainslie could feel the tension like something physical.

Spiers moved toward the ladder. "It's a fast convoy, so unless there are any foul-ups, we should make our estimated contact as stated." He swung round. "I'll be in the galley if you need me. I shan't be sorry if . . ."

Ainslie gripped a handrail and watched Spiers' eyes as they lit up like two tiny flares, then he pulled himself around to stare ahead and saw the horizon come alive, a fiery sunset instead of dawn.

A few seconds, but small, trivial items seemed to pre-dominate. Smears of salt spray on the screen like frost; one of the lookouts pointing toward the glow, his mouth a black hole in his face but making no sound. Then the explosion. It was more of a sensation than a sound, a thunder which seemed to reverberate, reaching the hull, holding it like a threat before passing on.

Just as suddenly the fire was gone, snuffed out, so that even the faint compass light seemed to invite retaliation.

"Check with the engineroom. Sound Action Stations."

It was Kearton. Ainslie had not seen or heard him arrive on the bridge.

"Not that anybody will be asleep!"

Somebody even laughed. "Me neither, sir, after that!"

Spiers called, "Engineroom standing by, sir. The Chief is in charge."

Ainslie listened to the brief reports and sensed the urgency. Like the coxswain, the Chief had been on the job. And the Skipper, snatching an hour or two in the chartroom, trying to clear his mind of responsibility and the risks that might lie ahead— how did he stay and sound so calm?

Like now, speaking to Turnbull as if this were part of an exercise, some drill to keep them all on their toes.

"What did you make of it, 'Swain? A tanker?" A pause. "Poor devils!"

"Something heavier, sir. Could have been loaded with ammo, explosives."

Ainslie loosened his grip on the rail. His hand throbbed, as if he had been using all his strength. His nerve.

He heard the click of the R/T handset and tried to imagine the other boats, out there in the darkness. He bunched his aching fingers into a fist again. He could see the next boat astern, pale against the black water, bows thrusting across her own waves, and maybe the one following closely in her wake. It was not so dark any more. . . . In an hour, perhaps less. He tried to shut his mind to it. He was here. He was ready . . . *Brace yourself, Mark One.*

"All acknowledged, sir." Even the man's voice seemed hushed, almost lost in the engines.

"*Growler* to all units. We will increase speed as ordered." Kearton paused, and Ainslie wondered if he would add something, advice or encouragement. Kearton had waited for some static to fade. *"Together!"*

He stepped down from the grating and handed the instrument to another shadow. Except that it now had the outline of a face.

He held up his watch. "Ten minutes, Number One! By the book!"

Then he moved to the forepart of the bridge. He could see the top of the chartroom, a life raft lashed across it, and the twin, power-operated machine-gun turrets on either side. Beyond was the two-pounder mounting, its shield pale against the sea and the horizon. That, too, was visible, the delineation of sea and sky. Most of the stars were gone. And there was a hint of low cloud, or mist.

He readjusted the strap of his binoculars so that they would not bang against the bridge when he moved.

It was neither mist nor cloud. It was smoke.

Like a signal, or as if he had shouted the command himself, the sound and sensation of the engines took on a stronger beat, and he felt the deck lifting in response.

He could see them in his mind's eye. The three M.T.B.s, 992 in the lead, and by now the motor gunboats would have increased speed to take station, one on either beam. Ready to offer extra firepower once action was joined. But when he stared directly ahead he could have been standing quite alone.

He was not. Ahead lay the enemy.

Turnbull stepped clear of the wheel and waited for his helmsman to take over, then rested both hands on the flag locker and began to perform a series of knee-bends. He felt he had been standing so long stooped over the compass that every muscle had seized up.

"Must be getting past it!"

"You know what they say, 'Swain, never volunteer, 'specially in this regiment!" The bridge machine-gunner was looking on, giving a grin, as if daring to relax for the first time.

They had sighted the convoy, "almost to the cross on the

chart", as Turnbull had heard Ainslie describe it. Less one, torpedoed by a U-Boat which had slipped through the escorts, three destroyers and a sloop. The force of the explosion must have taken the U-Boat commander by surprise, and either damaged his boat or made him drop his guard. Depth-charges had blown him and his crew to the same fate as their target.

Signals were exchanged, and the Skipper had received one himself from the Boss; and the little convoy had divided. Two ships had altered course in company with two of the destroyers and the sloop, which had apparently developed engine trouble and might require a tow for the last leg to Malta. Jock Laidlaw knew the sloop in question from his Atlantic days. She was over twenty years old, like so many of the hard-worked escort vessels.

Turnbull stretched again and shaded his eyes to peer at their only guardian. The third destroyer, *Natal*, was big, fast and modern, and no stranger to the Mediterranean. Her captain sounded courteous enough over his loud-hailer, but Turnbull had the impression he harboured doubts about the necessity of the additional protection.

Turnbull had borrowed a lookout's binoculars to see for himself. Oak leaves on his cap, like Captain Garrick, and one of 'those voices'. He smiled to himself. He was being unfair. But he knew.

The real cause of all the excitement was a new, sleekly designed freighter, more like a liner than a vessel for carrying cargo. Swedish-built and probably scarcely painted or equipped when war had been declared, she could boast a speed of twenty-five knots. She was named *Romulus*, and appeared to carry her own anti-aircraft guns and the D.E.M.S. personnel to man them. He had overheard the Skipper saying *Romulus* also had a separate identity and recognition code. So why was she so important?

Even Kearton did not seem to know. "Explosives, something like that," and he had shrugged.

Turnbull looked toward the destroyer again, leading the pack, as Bliss the helmsman might say. She had radar too, an added protection or warning. Number One would have seen that: he was always beating the drum about radar.

He was here now.

Spiers said, "Go around the boat, will you, Cox'n? They're getting too sloppy and idle, now they think it's all going downhill."

He did not raise his voice, he rarely did, but it sounded like a personal admonishment.

Turnbull straightened his back, wincing. "We've been promised air cover for the last bit, sir."

"Just *do* it, right?"

So Spiers was worried, too.

Turnbull climbed down to the deck and made his way forward. He was glad to be moving again; it would get his circulation going. Otherwise, he knew it was a waste of time, an irritation. Nobody would fall asleep, no matter how weary he might be.

He watched the water creaming along the side, spray drifting over the deck and glistening in the sunlight. But no warmth, not yet, and he was thankful for his oilskin.

A few nods, or a hand raised as he checked each position and huddled figure. Little else. They all knew why he was passing. At the two-pounder gun, even Cock Glover had little to say, which was unlike him. Wrapped in a duffle coat with a life-jacket tied loosely around it, he had pointed vaguely in the direction of the *Romulus* and muttered, "I'll bet they're 'avin' bangers an' mash, an' all th' char they want, just by snappin' their fingers!"

Then Turnbull met Laurie Jay, who had been making a few adjustments to one of the torpedo tubes, seemingly oblivious to the spray that burst over the side with each plunge of the stem.

He gave a quick smile as he picked up his little instrument box.

"Twenty knots, they tell me, 'Swain? Suits me!"

Turnbull liked him, although he still barely knew him. Helpful, good at his work; that would suffice. He had seen him go ashore with Glover. A more unlikely pair it was hard to imagine.

"Not long now, d' you reckon?"

Jay glanced at the sea, not the sky, like most sailors.

"A few scares maybe." He nodded. "Sunset. After that, they'll lose the edge."

Turnbull was still thinking about it when he returned to the bridge. Kearton was there, an unlit pipe jammed between his teeth.

"I've had a signal from H.Q. There was another attack on the rest of our convoy. No damage that time. The change of course must have caught them on the hop. Not for long, I'll bet."

Turnbull glanced across the bridge. Spiers was at the voicepipes, gesturing as he spoke to someone, probably the Chief, as if he could see him. Ainslie coming up from the chartroom, yawning hugely as if caught unawares. A youngster again.

Everyone was busy, but the Skipper had still found time to tell him about the W/T signal.

He said, "If we can keep this up, sir . . ."

Kearton shifted the pipe to the other side of his jaw.

"We can. We will." He pulled his cap lower across his eyes and stared astern at the other vessels. Then he said, "Open the galley. Something hot." Their eyes met, and Turnbull sensed that Spiers had looked around from the voicepipes to listen. Maybe to be a part of it.

Kearton had turned away from the sun. *Somewhere else.*

269

Turnbull heard him say as if to himself, "While there's still time."

Kearton felt something brush against him and pushed himself away from the side of the bridge. He was on his feet, fully conscious, but it was as if he had been rudely awakened. It was dark, and the sound of the engines was regular and monotonous, but it seemed louder because of the stillness and the night. He shook himself.

"What is it, Pilot?"

Ainslie said quietly, "It's the Chief, sir."

"Trouble?" He had not heard the voicepipe. And it was about midnight, a warning in itself.

Ainslie must have shaken his head. "No, he just wanted to know if he could ditch some empty fuel cans. Keep his place tidy!"

Kearton reached down to rub his leg, as if the injury was still there.

"No. Tell him . . ." He stared past him at the tiny green light, the emergency buzzer drowned by the Chief's Packards.

The W/T office, next to his own empty cabin.

He pressed the instrument to his ear, one hand covering the other.

"Bridge." He could feel the silence now. "Something for me?"

He heard him clear his throat. "Yes, sir. *Natal*, repeated H.Q." It was the other telegraphist, not Weston; the name escaped him, and nothing else mattered now. He imagined him in his small compartment, the signal pad under the solitary light, very aware of its importance, and his own.

"Maintain course and speed. Two bandits closing from due north." He cleared his throat again. *"I am engaging."* He ended with the time of origin, but Kearton scarcely heard him.

'Bandits': usually fast attackers, probably Italian, but could be E-Boats. The Germans had been moving them down into the Med and the Adriatic. *Natal* had been warned. He thought of Spiers again. Radar . . . She was well armed, with six 4.7s, and a cluster of other short-range weapons, and depth-charges. And two sets of torpedoes, if he could remember clearly.

One of the lookouts broke into his thoughts.

"There goes *Natal*! Boy, she's in a rush all of a sudden!"

Kearton waited. "Thank you. Well done. Acknowledge, will you?"

He straightened up and said aloud, "Unidentified fast craft closing from the north." He saw Spiers' white scarf beside Turnbull's shapeless oilskin. "Pass the word, Number One. The waiting's over." The destroyer, backed up by Red Lyon's M.G.B. on their flank, should be more than a match for the 'bandits'. From Sicily or the Italian mainland; it might take too long to muster an additional attacking force. And at first light there would be air support, if need be from Malta itself.

He rubbed his chin, and only then realized that he still had the pipe jammed between his teeth.

But to be on the safe side . . . He reached over and encountered Ainslie's arm, and felt him jump.

"Chartroom, Pilot. Fix our position as best you can in all this flap, in case we have to lay off another course." He could feel his arm; it was rigid. "A diversion, to keep our prize intact."

Ainslie said, "They left it too late." As if he was telling himself, or searching for some flaw.

Spiers said, "I've spread the word, sir. A few wisecracks, of course, but I've got a good memory for voices." He walked to the side and stared in the direction of *Romulus*. "*They'll* be damned glad, anyway. I can take over while Pilot's doing his stuff." He hesitated, and Kearton could see him, his head cocked on one side. "If you still think—"

He never finished it. There was a thin, high-pitched whistle, which ended abruptly in a scream and a sudden explosion. The night was transformed into searing detail, stark and glacial, all sound quenched by the starshell. The little green light and its attendant buzzer were both trying to raise the alarm, like the starshell, which *Natal* must have fired immediately after her first sighting.

Kearton rubbed his eyes with the back of his hand and fumbled for his binoculars. Everything was unreal: the voicepipe, and a disembodied voice, surely not still asking about used petrol cans? Turnbull struggling out of his oilskin, as if it was trapping him. And something snapping underfoot. He had dropped his pipe on the deck.

The glare was already fading, but the figures around him seemed frozen by it, incapable of movement. And it was still strong enough to see the other vessels astern, dominated by the *Romulus*.

He closed his mind to them. Everything had to be concentrated in the small, silent world of his binoculars.

Surrounded by froth, like some enraged sea monster, saddle-tanks shining glassily on the periphery of the glare, the submarine was alive, and moving.

"Number One!" But Spiers was already running to his station. The ex-submariner, Jay, would be with him, overtaken by events.

Kearton stumbled, but someone grasped his arm. He had the intercom in his hand and waited, counting the seconds.

"Growler to all units! Tally-ho! Attacking!"

"Ready, Skipper!" That was Turnbull, formality forgotten.

"Full ahead! Port twenty!" He felt the deck tilt, and heard the binoculars swing against the bridge armour. *"Midships!"*

He crouched, straining his eyes to hold on to the target, the U-Boat, smaller now without the aid of the powerful lenses.

He saw another M.T.B. sweeping past, shining in the glare, showing her number, 977. It was Geoff Mostyn, known as 'Geordie' to his friends; and he seemed to have plenty of those.

His two-pounder was already hammering out a steady stream of tracer, and another gun of some kind was quick to follow.

Kearton realized that the submarine was fully surfaced, to obtain the best possible speed, and not only that, her deck-gun was manned and had opened fire. Daring, desperation, or cold-blooded courage, she had shown no sign of turning away or attempting to dive. She was still heading straight toward the prime ship of the convoy, *Romulus*.

"Steady! Easy! Steady!" He was telling himself: Turnbull, like Spiers, knew what to do. What to expect.

He felt his mouth go dry as something exploded outside his line of vision. The sound was almost swamped by the rising thunder of engines, but he knew it was a direct hit on Mostyn's boat.

It was now.

"Fire!"

He sensed rather than felt the slight shudder as both torpedoes left their tubes.

"Both running!"

"Hard a-port!" He watched the shadows closing in, like a vast curtain, the sea leaping over the bow as they continued to turn. He had lost count of the seconds, if he had ever begun, but he could still hear them in his brain. Like a giant clock.

"Midships!"

He saw Mostyn's boat, still moving, but very slowly. No more flames, but a lot of smoke. Some shapes below the bridge, others standing by them. The living and the dead.

He pounded his fist below the screen. He could see the *Romulus*, at a different angle now, turning, trying to run, when it was too late. They had completed their alteration of course, so that he saw himself starkly against the screen, silhouetted by a livid, contained explosion. It shook the whole hull, and he thought of the Chief and his little crew in their confined world. It must have felt like hitting a mine.

He shaded his eyes, but the sea was almost in darkness again. Blasted apart by the twin explosions, the remains of the U-Boat were on their last dive, to the bottom.

"Half ahead!" The sky held a hint of colour now. The smoke was clearing away and he saw the *Romulus*, much nearer again; she seemed to tower over them like a cliff. There were people lining the rails, waving, cheers almost drowned out by their combined engines. Cheers . . .

Kearton raised his arm, and thought how heavy it felt.

Ainslie was beside him. "Shall I take over, sir?"

Kearton stared across the water, rising and falling between the various hulls. He could see a tell-tale patch of oil spreading across a few fragments of flotsam. There was never very much after a submarine had been destroyed.

He realized what Ainslie had said.

"We'll go and help Geoff."

Spiers was here, too, and shook his head, only once.

"We'll stand by, anyway. He would expect it." No name. 'Geordie' was dead.

He heard the banshee screech of a siren. *Natal* was returning to take charge. The bandits must have fled, once they knew their ruse had failed.

Spiers said, "I'll go aft and check the towing gear, sir. Just in case."

He must have stopped below the mast and turned, and his voice was pitched a little louder.

"I hope they'll all be bloody pleased to see us when we get back, after this!"

Turnbull kept his eyes on the compass. *I know someone who will.*

They did not need to take the damaged M.T.B. in tow, and, at first light, friendly aircraft flew out to meet them.

Landfall.

16

Commitment

The two officers stood side by side on the edge of the jetty looking down at the smoke-blackened M.T.B. below them. A couple of dockyard officials in stained overalls were beside the bridge, comparing notes and pointing out additional defects; otherwise the boat was deserted, lifeless.

The midday sun was pitiless, but without warmth. Kearton shivered, but the weather was not the reason.

After the urgency and tension of their return, the moorings were deathly quiet and still. Even the usual harbour sounds and movements seemed distant, unobtrusive.

The emergency fire-parties, the pumps, mechanics and men with cutting gear, had long since departed, and so had the medics and stretcher-bearers. Kearton had been here since 977's small company had gone to temporary quarters ashore. It had been hard to gauge their feelings. As someone had remarked, they had been bloody lucky. Kearton had seen one of them giving a grin and a thumbs-up as he marched past, but he had turned to stare back, as if with a true sense of loss. Perhaps it was gratitude.

Apart from Mostyn, who had been killed outright in the first and only direct fire from the U-Boat's deck-gun, there had been two more deaths: the coxswain, who had clung to life just long enough for another helmsman to take his place, and a seaman hit by shell splinters.

Her first lieutenant had not only survived, but had refused the offer of a tow, and had conned the M.T.B. and dealt with minor injuries himself until 977's heaving-lines had been hurled ashore.

He had gone with his men, after a powerful handshake and a smile, and the repetition of his skipper's last words before the action. *"We'll show those bastards!"*

They might never know who he had meant. The U-Boat, or the higher authority which had put him there?

Kearton had gone aboard himself. Reliving it, like all those other times. The smells and the stains, which even the hoses and extinguishers had been unable to disguise. Fuel and ammunition had been spared; even one shell splinter hitting a torpedo would have left nothing but dust on the sea. He had seen where the shell had exploded, in the chartroom directly below the open bridge identical to their own, and the blast had left a jagged hole. *Where I would have been standing.*

"Take more than a month to patch that up." Brice had moved nearer the edge. "When I saw them leading the way, I thought for a moment it was you, Bob." He turned his back on the water, as if he wanted to shut it from his memory.

Kearton fell into step beside him, knowing Brice had not been here waiting since before dawn merely out of friendship or courtesy.

He said, "I told them to lead. They deserved it."

He glanced up toward the gates and the road beyond. Like the jetty, it looked deserted. Everyone would be at Grand Harbour watching the latest arrival, the *Romulus*, and her dashing escort *Natal*, decks lined with men and calls shrilling in salute to her superiors.

He had heard a hooter or tug's horn, and had been surprised at the force of Brice's response.

"One bomb on that little lot and there'd be more than a few cracked windows around here! There would be no cheering then!"

Kearton had seen some fighter planes patrolling in pairs, back and forth across the great anchorage, a rare sight at any time.

He realized Brice had stopped outside the wooden hut, and pulled a bunch of keys from his pocket.

It was locked, and there was no patrolman loitering nearby to ward off unwelcome visitors.

Brice gestured toward the main building above the steps.

"I have to make a phone call, Bob." He pushed open the door. "The Boss has had to abandon this little hideaway, at least for the moment. There's a flap on." He swore under his breath as the solitary telephone began to ring. "For Christ's sake, they know where I am!" He picked it up, and said without inflection, "Brice," and then, "Yes, I *know* that. Twenty minutes." He made a small, impatient gesture. "Fifteen, then." He put the receiver down and stared at it. "You must be dog-tired. I can't imagine what you've been through . . . actually, I *can*." The strain was clear on his own face, and in his eyes.

Kearton said quietly, "The Boss giving you a rough ride?"

Brice did not respond directly. "I saw your friend, Mrs Howard. It was first thing this morning." He shook his head. "No, there's nothing wrong, not like that. She was upset, and I realized why. I wanted to help." He smiled briefly. "Like me, she saw the damaged M.T.B. leading the way, her flag at half-mast. You can guess the rest."

Kearton said, "I didn't think. It's the custom," and felt Brice's hand on his sleeve. "And, thanks. I appreciate that."

Brice said only, "I was glad I was there."

"Where were you?"

"On the old balcony. You walk beneath it on the way to H.Q. I go there sometimes, early, before the balloon goes up every

277

morning. My equivalent of the Boss's little hideaway, I suppose." He sat down abruptly on one of the two chairs. "Why I wanted to be here when you came alongside. I wanted to see you first."

"Trouble?"

Brice shrugged, briefly, like the smile.

"You'll hear it as soon as you make your report anyway. Then you can make up your own mind." He ticked off each item on his fingers. "Operation *Retriever* was not only worthwhile and considered a success, but *our superiors*," he crossed himself with his free hand, "have announced that it offers the perfect key to the next door for Special Operations. The Boss's words, not mine!" He was on his feet again, peering through the smeared window. "You must take the credit for its eventual success." The momentary smile again. "But don't tell *him* that."

The telephone rang, but stopped immediately.

Brice said, "Not fifteen minutes yet. Nowhere near."

Kearton waited, watching him come to a decision.

"There have been a lot of changes around here, Bob, even since we last met. H.Q. is packed to the rafters, or soon will be. We are now known as A.C.H.Q., Area Combined Headquarters. All three services, with ours running things, of course." He regarded him intently. "It will mean flag rank for the man in charge."

"The Boss? I'm not really surprised—" Brice was peering fixedly at his watch.

"A rear-admiral's flag will be hoisted over our heads. I have a contact at the Admiralty," the same quick smile, "my cousin, to be exact, and he tells me another name is on top of the list. One you'll remember, I believe. Captain Ewart Morgan."

The telephone rang and he put his hand on it. "Fifteen minutes exactly." He stood up and reached for his cap. "I'll see you shortly." This time the smile was genuine. "Give her my love!"

278

The door squeaked shut, and Kearton snatched up the telephone.

"Hello?" But at that moment another aircraft flew directly overhead, low enough to shake the entire hut, as if it would fall apart. He waited. "Glynis, darling, it's me."

A few seconds passed, and for a moment he thought Brice had made a mistake. Or the switchboard.

She said, "I'm here, Bob. I heard that, too." She must have turned her head away. There was a catch in her voice. "I can't tell you what it means . . . just to hear you again. I've been hoping, praying . . ." She stopped, and he could hear the aircraft, or a different one, close by. Then she said, "I know you must be busy." Another pause, perhaps choosing her words. Or waiting for the click on the line that would mean someone was listening. *Careless talk.*

He said, "As soon as I can. I'll call you first." It was quiet again; he thought he could hear her breathing. "Are you all right?"

She might have laughed, or cried. "Yes, Bob, *now* I am!"

This time the line was dead.

He waited a few more minutes and then stepped outside into the sunlight; even that seemed warmer. He saluted as two sailors walked past in the opposite direction, and realized that they had either not seen him, or had ignored him.

Brice was waiting at the end of the jetty, shading his eyes.

"Thought I'd lurk here and walk back with you."

Kearton did not reply. One of the drills had started again and would have drowned his voice.

Brice looked back at the little hut and its single telephone wire. That would be taken down; the Boss would not be needing it much longer.

But he had seen Kearton's face, and was pleased by what he had done. For both of them.

*

Captain Dick Garrick was sitting at his desk, a telephone held casually to one ear, but his eyes were on an open file, and a pencil was poised in his free hand. He did not look up as Kearton was ushered into the office, but gestured toward the chair opposite. A petty officer writer was standing beside him, turning the pages of the file slowly and in response to each stab of the pencil. Blackout curtains had been drawn, and there would be shutters in place outside. The room seemed airless, as if the fans were out of action. Again.

Kearton sat down and tried not to lean back. He could already feel his shirt clinging to his spine.

Garrick pressed the receiver against his chest and lowered his voice. "Shan't keep you much longer, old chap." He nodded to the P.O. Writer, who quickly turned another page, as if he had been asleep on his feet.

Kearton looked around the room. A different office, larger, but with all the familiar clutter of maps, charts and statistics. It faced in the opposite direction, toward Grand Harbour itself, where the *Romulus* was still unloading, lighters and barges pressed around her, while guardboats kept all else at a safe distance.

The destroyer *Natal* lay at the far end of the harbour, awnings spread, and most of her men ashore enjoying themselves.

Kearton controlled his resentment. He knew he was being unfair. *Natal* had played her part, before and after the first attack on the fast convoy. Without her radar and the vital firing of the starshell, things would have ended differently. Her captain had apparently told Brice as much.

Brice had remarked, "Know him pretty well. A good captain." And the little smile. "But not renowned for his modesty!"

Kearton looked over at Garrick again, the pencil tapping the file, the eyes elsewhere, impatient now, or on the verge of losing his temper.

Otherwise, he could see no change. Brice had told him the Boss had been at meetings for much of the day, one at Government House with the Chief-of-Staff. Smartly turned out as always, the top button of his reefer unfastened, which seemed to be a habit or an affectation. Hair well-groomed, the same lock loose above one eye, like the photographs. He showed no sign of strain or tiredness.

He thought about Brice's cousin at the Admiralty, and Captain Ewart Morgan, recalling their meeting as if it were yesterday. His steady gaze as he had outlined the new command, and the conditions of promotion. *Acting, of course.* Now it was Morgan's turn, his chance, when all the time he must have thought Garrick would be the next choice for flag rank. They were still rivals; had been, maybe, ever since they were snotties together. A different war. A different world.

Kearton glanced around the room again. The whole place was changing. It was far more crowded; A.C.H.Q. demanded it. Only the old staircase seemed familiar.

Garrick said, "I'm not asking you, old chap. I'm bloody well *telling* you." He put down the telephone and breathed out slowly. "I sometimes wonder!" Then, "Sorry to make you hang around like this. You must be feeling bushed, after the last effort." The barest pause. "Too bad about Lieutenant Mostyn, of course . . . Leaves us one short again."

Kearton found he could accept the casual dismissal; it was the Garrick he had come to know. Up to a point. *No bullshit, except on his own terms.*

Garrick looked over at his assistant.

"You can shove off now." He closed the file with a snap. "But back tomorrow. First thing, eh?"

He watched the door close behind him. "Should have joined the Wrens, that one!" He grinned. "You didn't hear that, Bob."

He leaned back in his chair and studied him across the desk.

"Well, you've been through it again. But it was the right

281

decision. And it paid off." He nodded toward a window, where the curtains had started to quiver. "Fans are running again," and he laughed. "Like the heads at my little refuge— as I thought it was."

The laugh was abrupt and short-lived. "Things are moving fast. Too fast for some around here." He leaned forward, elbows on the file, the lock of hair catching the hard light from overhead. "We may be a boat short, for a few weeks only, but time is getting even shorter in some ways. *Retriever* was a success— I assume Brice told you. A few setbacks, but you must accept that. Win some, lose some— you know how it goes. Otherwise you'd not be here." He laid both hands flat on the file.

"*Romulus* is important, for many reasons, to Special Operations." He brushed the lock of hair aside. "And to you. She carries all manner of explosives, enough to equip an army. And, tucked away in her holds, she brought a separate cargo of torpedoes. The very latest. You'll know all about them. Have read about them, in any case. Homing torpedoes . . . so sensitive they can sniff out a pin on a baby's bum." He laughed abruptly at his own joke. "They can't take prisoners, but they can do just about everything else you might need." The famous smile, as if, Kearton thought, he had just pulled a rabbit out of a hat. "So how about *that*?"

Kearton could hear aircraft again.

"Yes. They were talking about them." He relaxed his right hand, which, unconsciously, had clenched on his knee. "About the time I ended up in the drink."

Garrick stretched his arms. "Well, *they're here now*, ready to do their bit and make life a little easier for us." He looked at the door, although Kearton had heard no sound. "And for *you*!"

The door had opened, and a different petty officer was waiting there.

"Sir?"

282

Garrick got easily to his feet. "Lieutenant-Commander Kearton is leaving." He thrust out his hand. "You've done enough. More than enough. I've laid on a car and driver for you," and as Kearton shook it, "the least I can do." But Garrick did not release his grip, as if to detain him.

"Major Howard did a fine job— I don't suppose even he realizes it yet. The Chief-of-Staff is over the moon— and so will A.B.C. be, when he gets to hear all the details. But knowing him, I expect he has already." He released Kearton's hand abruptly. "I know about your . . . involvement. It is not my concern." His eyes flicked to the file with its red lettering. "*That* is!"

He did not accompany Kearton to the door, and was already using the telephone as it closed.

A man in a white jacket was standing beside a small trolley, the petty officer as well, hiding a yawn as Kearton passed. On the trolley were a bottle of wine in a frosted bucket and a plate of sandwiches.

When did Garrick ever take time off to relax? No wonder some of his staff looked half asleep. Unlike the Boss . . . And his casual use of the C-in-C's popular nickname, 'A.B.C.', made it sound as if Admiral Cunningham was a close friend.

The car was waiting in the same place as before. He did not recognize the driver, another Royal Marine.

The sky was much darker, with a few wisps of cloud but, as yet, no stars.

He gave the driver the address.

"No bother, sir. The road's fully repaired now." He chuckled. "For the moment."

Not much traffic, and all military except for a couple of buses, but it was exactly as he remembered it, had seen it in his mind when he had been trying to sleep in the chartroom, afraid he might not hear the call if he was needed.

Even in the hooded headlights he could see the sandbagged

283

barrier, the white belt and gaiters of the patrolman as he walked toward the car. He could not see his face, but heard him say, "Welcome aboard, sir!" The car was enough. Or had he been there during that last visit?

The Royal Marine was out of the vehicle, holding the door.

"Shall I wait, sir?"

"No, I'll be all right. But thanks."

The marine was gazing at the main building. "Looks pretty quiet, sir. I was told to . . ." He stepped aside as Kearton slid out of the car. "I'm on call 'til midnight, sir."

Kearton could almost feel his eyes on him as he found his way through the other, smaller gate. Only then did he hear him drive away.

The door was open before he could reach it, and he felt her hand guiding him.

She said, "Have to be quick, or they start yelling about the blackout!"

She turned, her hair catching the light from the main room, and he took her by the shoulders gently, feeling her warmth, her stillness, perhaps her disbelief.

"I'm sorry about this. I should have warned you. I could have been anyone."

"They phoned me from the main gate to tell me you'd arrived. Ever since . . ." She reached up to return his embrace. "I *knew* it was you. That you'd come." She led him into the other room, where she faced him again, dark eyes brilliant with emotion.

"So many things I wanted to ask, to know . . ." She was pointing to the chair, and he noticed that it had been moved to the opposite corner; the radio, too, was on another table. He could smell fresh paint, and saw a tin with a brush and some stained gloves on the floor beneath an empty shelf. She laughed.

"Just to *see* you, Bob— I can even read your thoughts.

What's this woman up to now?" Then she came to him and slipped her arms around his neck. "I can't tell you what this means. I've been so worried . . . Then, when I watched you come into harbour—" She leaned back to look up at him. Her mouth was smiling, but her face was wet with tears.

"Let me." She did not move, and he dabbed her skin with his handkerchief. "You see? I'm never without it."

She asked softly, "How long?"

"I'm not sure. Nobody is."

She touched his face, his lips, her eyes never leaving his.

"How long *now*?" She put her hand across his mouth. He could smell the paint. "Don't leave me."

"Unless there's an emergency." Her hand was in his, and he saw her expression as she looked at the paint on her fingers.

"There *will* be, if you see me like this!" She stroked his face, and the scar above his eye. He could not recall tossing his cap aside.

She said, "Kiss me."

She was pressed against him, her breathing faster, like his own. She pulled back slightly. "Again."

How long, he could not imagine. Her lips, her mouth, her tongue were making his mind reel.

He could feel her spine, her skin, where the shirt had worked loose from her belt. He had never forgotten her skin.

Her face was against his shoulder, her voice muffled, unsteady.

"Don't—" And then, "Don't stop."

Then she broke away. "Oh, Bob, I stink of paint! Give me a few minutes!" She was half laughing, still crying.

He said, "I'm sorry, Glynis . . ."

She put one finger to her lips. "You called me 'darling', remember?" She was more composed now, perhaps regretting a momentary impulse.

"I meant it. I know I have no right . . ."

She grasped his wrists, held them briefly, then moved his hands from her waist. "You have *every* right." She stepped a few paces away without turning her back, her face in shadow, her eyes never leaving his. "I want to show you something. Wait a minute, and don't move."

She opened the other door and went in, her shirt still hanging over her slacks. He could hear music, but it was muffled, from the adjoining apartment, which must have been repaired and in use once more.

The door was half-open and she was standing just inside the room, watching him intensely.

"*Well*, what do you think?"

She was wearing a full-length robe that shone in the dim light, dark green; it might have been silk. When she moved closer to the table lamp he could see her feet, small and bare against the floor.

"You look lovely."

"I meant the robe. My mum and dad sent it to me as a present." She shook her hair again. "Took ages to get here. I can't imagine how many clothing coupons it must have needed . . ."

"They're still in England? I didn't realize."

He felt the tension in her body as he put his arm around her and drew her closer. She said, "This is the first time I've worn it," and let her arms fall to her sides, standing very still. "Kiss me, Bob."

He tugged at the sash around her waist and uncovered her shoulder and kissed it, until she struggled to free herself, clinging to the robe, her breasts completely naked.

"No. Not here. Not yet . . ." She was holding him now, taking her mouth from his to whisper, "Every minute . . . every second . . ."

They were in the adjoining room, the only light being that which they had left behind them. The music had stopped. It seemed very quiet.

286

There was a tall mirror on the opposite wall. She was facing it, her back to him, her shoulders bare and burnished by the light.

"I never thought I . . ." She must have moved slightly, and the robe dropped to her ankles. "I can't wait!"

The bed seemed to be the only furniture in the room. But nothing was real except the girl who lay on it, naked now, watching him stripping off his uniform and tossing it to the floor, where it lay with the robe and the tissue wrappings. She said again, "I can't wait," but he felt her body stiffen, her nails pressing into his skin, heard her gasp or sob as she arched her back to resist, and then to receive him.

He heard and saw nothing else. There *was* nothing else.

Eventually they both slept, but awoke together and talked, and rediscovered one another.

It was almost dawn when he opened his eyes and found he was alone.

But she was standing by a window he had not noticed in the night, her body motionless, holding the faint light of dawn like a statue. Then she pulled the curtain and fell beside him again. She pushed the hair from her face and leaned across him.

"I can't believe it. I forgot to clean the paint off my hand!"

He stroked her shoulder and the back of her neck, and they kissed again, deeply and without urgency.

He said, "If . . ." but she covered his lips with her fingers.

"No, darling. *When*." He could taste the tears on her skin.

She showed him where he could wash and helped him collect his scattered uniform; all the time, she barely spoke. The first hint of daylight was touching the sides of the curtains when the telephone rang.

She reached for it, but glanced over her shoulder as if to reassure him.

"It's all right, Bob. They check every call." She said a few words, and then handed it to him. "It's time, darling."

She had put on her robe again, and was looking away. Like the night, it was over.

"Yes? Kearton." He reached out and squeezed her hand, and could see the dried paint on her fingers. He would never forget.

"Mornin', sir. Corporal Marlow." A pause, then, patiently, "Your driver, sir. Standin' by."

"On my way. Thank you."

They walked through the other room, past the desk. The wastepaper basket was empty.

She pulled back a bolt and opened the door a couple of inches. The air seemed cold, and he could smell the salt.

She looked at him without speaking. Holding his hand, then pressing it against her breast.

"The car's here." She dabbed the corner of her eye and held up the handkerchief. "I have this now. It'll be like new when I give it back to you!" The mood could not last, and she held him as if she would never let him go. *"Promise me."* She made another attempt. "I'll be waiting." She kissed him quickly. "Take care." She stepped away. "Darling."

She closed the door behind him, and whispered, *"Don't leave me."*

Some impulse made her reach for the door again, but the driver must have kept his engine running. The car had already gone.

Turnbull walked across the deserted bridge and rested his hand on the wheel. It was still strange to feel it stiff, unmoving. Like the deck under his feet. Today was the third since they had returned to harbour, and it seemed they had never stopped for breath. Cleaning up the hull and taking on stores and ammunition. Topping up the fuel, and having more 'experts' checking for electrical or mechanical faults. There were none; Laidlaw had been outspoken on the matter. It was more than enough without the arrival of the torpedoes, not merely replacements for those fired at the surfaced U-Boat, but of an entirely new design. "You can't miss," as one mechanic had remarked. But he did not have to use them.

He peered at the sky and felt the sun on his face. And it was still early morning. He had heard bugles in the distance: it was Sunday. But not just that. He moved to the side and stared along the jetty. The damaged M.T.B. was gone, in dock somewhere being repaired, or so they said. A good thing. Nobody needed reminding.

He licked his lips but it made no difference; his mouth tasted foul. He had lost count of the mugs of tea or coffee since he had hoisted himself from his bunk. He could only blame himself. And the Chief, although he had managed to stay out of sight, with his engines.

And not only bugles; there had been bagpipes as well. Some Scottish troops must have arrived, or been moved from another part of the island.

Laidlaw had said, "Oh, Christ, a lament. That's all I need!"

He was obviously not as deaf as Turnbull had thought.

977's C.O. was being buried today, or what was left of him. And his coxswain. Turnbull glanced at the wheel again. Nice bloke, he thought; they had met at Chatham a couple of times.

Yes, it had been a long three days. He heard feet on the bridge ladder and frowned.

More than enough, without this.

"You sent for me, 'Swain?" It was Able Seaman Glover.

"I meant *now*, and not when you happen to feel like it!" But he was wasting his time, and they both knew it. "You were brought aboard last night by the shore patrol." Turnbull did not need to pull out his notebook. "Disorderly and insulting behaviour. Cautioned by the patrol, but it seems you persisted. A woman, was it?"

Glover shrugged. "She seemed to think I was made of money. I told 'er straight out, I wanted to rent it, not buy it, th' slag!"

There would always be a Glover in every ship. A good gunlayer, none better, and always ready to lend a hand in his mess. But get him ashore . . . Turnbull said, "First Lieutenant's report. I'd watch my step, if I were you!"

Glover sauntered away, unconcerned. He would never learn.

He saw the gangway sentry leaning out over the guardrail to catch his eye, making a quick gesture with his fist. The first lieutenant was on his way. And from the look of another pile of crates on the jetty, so was more work. Spiers was already in a bad mood. One of the stewards at the base wardroom had told him Red Lyon had been throwing his weight around about the convoy and the U-Boat's sinking. *Our U-Boat*. Or maybe it was because 977's first lieutenant was being given command when the repairs were completed. Spiers was only human, so Glover might not get off so lightly this time.

Turnbull heard another bugle call and looked at his watch. Eleven o'clock. *Up Spirits*. Where had the forenoon gone?

Three days since their return, and all very busy. The Skipper had been with them for much of the time, dealing with their various official or technical visitors, but for that one night ashore. Nobody knew for certain, but Turnbull had no doubts. *Good luck to them.*

But today was different. He had been propped on his elbows at the mess table when he had heard the scuffle of feet, and Lieutenant Ainslie's voice: he, too, had been caught unawares. Not even a bugle from the harbour, but the Skipper was already going ashore. It had to be urgent. They had sent a car for him, and its shielded headlights were still switched on when Turnbull had reached a scuttle to see for himself.

He hurried along the deck and saluted as Spiers stepped off the brow. As usual, his eyes were everywhere as Turnbull made his report.

"Defaulters? Glover?" But he was looking at Pug Dawson, who was busily mustering another working party. And then he said something so uncharacteristic that Turnbull was shocked. "Postpone it, will you? I think we're going to need him. And soon!"

Kearton came out of his cabin and saw Ginger, their acting-messman, standing by the wardroom door, unconcerned, as if he was there by accident. The door was partly open and he could hear their voices, and a short, barking laugh, which he knew was Red Lyon's. He had heard them coming aboard, almost together. As if they had all been poised, waiting.

The rest of the boat seemed unnaturally quiet; most of the hands were ashore for a well-earned break after their extra work. But confined to the base this time, which meant the canteen bar.

He himself had been on his feet since dawn, and some instinct had warned him: he was shaved and half-dressed when the sentry had brought a message from the gate: a car with Garrick's badge on it had arrived to collect him.

Ginger was saying cheerfully, "All present and correct, sir," and trying to keep a straight face. "I told the other gentlemen, try and leave the place like you found it. Clean and tidy!" He did not succeed. He knew more about his own three officers than anybody.

They were all sitting at, or near, the wardroom table, and Kearton waved them down as they attempted a more formal greeting. There was one face missing, and it would be hard to forget him, with that last meeting still so fresh in his mind.

He nodded to Ainslie, who was sitting in a corner against the bulkhead, his chart and sketches and a clip of signals arranged between his hands. He would be remembering it, too, perhaps more than anyone. Geordie's humorous defences against Lyon's sarcasm and hostility, and the new pipe lying on the table . . .

He felt in his own pocket, and stopped himself; his pipe was finally beyond repair.

He said, "We are under orders. Again." He saw Ainslie passing round the typewritten lists; they would not reveal much more than they already knew, or had guessed.

Red Lyon said loudly, "Back to the war again!"

John Stirling did not look up.

"Some of us never left it."

Kearton waited for silence. "Over the next month or so, probably sooner, naval and military reinforcements will begin to arrive here in Malta. Not for survival now, but to attack. We all knew it was coming, once things began to shift in our favour."

He could see Garrick's face, hear his voice. They had been standing on a stone balcony outside his office; it was a miracle that it had survived the bombing, as most of the buildings opposite were in ruins.

Garrick had waved his arm toward the harbour. "Big units will be arriving. Battleships, maybe a carrier or two. This will be so bloody busy you won't be able to pull a dinghy between them!"

"They won't be able to keep that a secret." That was Chris Griffin, the other motor gunboat's commanding officer. And he *was* from Cornwall: Fowey, which Kearton remembered vividly from the one time he had been taken there for a holiday. He had been about eight years old.

He tapped the rough chart.

"You're right, Chris. They won't, and they haven't. The Germans have been moving their own forces. They don't miss much."

Lyon said, "Maybe they don't rely too much on their Italian allies?"

Kearton looked past him: a scuttle was open, and he could see a crane moving slowly up and down, or so it appeared, as another vessel stirred the hull with her wash.

He said quietly, "Well, they should. Some time ago they

began to bring new weapons, overland, or perhaps in so-called neutral ships. That, we don't know." His finger stopped on the chart. "First seen or suspected *here*, at Taranto. Then moved or separated. And now we know they're *here*."

Ainslie saw his eyes, and elaborated. "Sicily, north-east corner, near the Messina Strait." He paused. "A place called Penta. I've marked it. Not much bigger than a parade ground. Used to be popular with yachtsmen, and other small craft."

Griffin said, "Lucky buggers," but he was tracing the coastline with his fingertip. "Small. But too close for comfort, if. . . .' He did not finish.

Kearton glanced along the table. "One-man, explosive motor-boats. We don't know how many, but we do know they are there. Intelligence seems to think their next move will be to Pantelleria." He looked at Griffin. "You're right, Chris. Too close for comfort."

Stirling said as if to himself, "It must have been around two years ago— I'd just arrived in the Med. Things were bad everywhere. Our forces were pulling out of Greece."

Lyon murmured, "In retreat!"

The Canadian ignored him, or perhaps he was somewhere else, in another time.

"The navy was standing by— to check the enemy's progress, they said— and evacuate our troops if it was necessary. And it was. But the Italians had some explosive motor-boats— first we knew of them. One man, one attack. They put the cruiser *York* on the bottom— others too, before anybody knew what was happening. Brave guys, or suicide jockeys—" He slapped his hand on the chart. "But those sons of bitches did the trick. Crete, Suda Bay . . . And I bet *York*'s still lying there."

It was suddenly quiet again. Even the sentry, who had been pacing back and forth above them, had stopped.

Kearton looked at each man's face.

"It's not settled yet. I'll know tomorrow. We're on stand-by. But be ready to slip and proceed at sunset."

Lyon said, "Makes a change from dawn." But there was no laugh.

Kearton stood. "Tomorrow, then." Short notice. But waiting, like doubt, could kill.

He followed them on deck and watched them depart. The sky was still cloudless.

He thought of Garrick. It had already been decided.

We're on our way.

He might have spoken aloud. Telling her.

17

Heroes

Kearton turned his back on the chart table and rubbed his eyes. It was force of habit, but after the open bridge and the surrounding darkness, even the shaded light seemed blinding.

Everything was sealed, so that voices and movements were muffled or lost completely in the regular beat of engines. It was midnight, six hours since they had cleared the harbour limits, and even up to the last moments he knew that a lot of them had expected the latest orders to be cancelled. But almost to the minute, Operation *Vanguard* had been put into motion.

A.C.H.Q. had confirmed that the unknown vessel had indeed departed from the tiny harbour of Penta, and had been reported heading south. How could they be so certain? The harbour and local waters were known to be too shallow for intruders, like submarines. An M.T.B. would be hard put to get near enough without raising the alarm.

Perhaps a small coastal craft had spied out the situation, or one of the Levant schooners which often joined forces with Special Operations.

He turned again and stared at the chart. Pencilled lines and neat crosses. Heading south. By dawn everything might have changed. Been curtailed . . .

Ainslie was standing at the side of the chartroom, one hand on his parallel rulers to prevent them from rattling. There was a steady southerly breeze across the quarter, and the deck was livelier than it had been an hour or so earlier. He had heard the coxswain remark, "That'll keep the hard cases from falling asleep!"

Kearton said, "Unless we hear otherwise, I think our information might be good. It's going to be a long night." He picked up his duffle coat and pulled it over his shoulders. "Do the same, Pilot. It's cold up top."

He leaned over the chart again, but he was thinking of his father. He always had piles of boating and yachting magazines at the yard, often depicting ships and exciting cruises in seas unimaginably far from the Thames. Exotic ports of call, girls in swimsuits and dark glasses, hovering stewards. And everywhere, the sun, especially in advertisements for the Mediterranean. He pulled his coat closer, shivering. His father had always wanted to go on a cruise, but had never been able to afford it. Or maybe it had been a different world in his eyes. A dream . . .

This was the reality.

Ainslie said suddenly, "These explosive motor-boats. Could they really delay an attack on the mainland? I heard about them being used in Crete— we all did— when I was finishing navigational classes." It was too dark to see if he blushed as he amended it after a second. "Well— *starting* them."

Kearton smiled. Sometimes Ainslie made him feel very old.

"It's not a thing we want again right now. A few of those boats could cause havoc if they got amongst the invasion fleet. And no amount of nets, booms or underwater defences could stop determined, dedicated attackers."

He closed his eyes as the light was switched off, then reopened them when the cold air fanned past him.

Ainslie's question had caught him offguard, but he should have been ready for it. They had all heard about the attack at Suda Bay and the loss of the cruiser *York* two years before, as

John Stirling had recalled at that last meeting in the wardroom. And Garrick had displayed a flash of real anger when Kearton had asked him point-blank, "Is Major Howard involved this time?"

"Without him, we'd still be in the dark! Courage, luck, or bloody-mindedness, it's results that matter— to *me*, anyway!"

He had returned to the subject eventually, when Kearton had mentioned Suda Bay.

"Yes, *he* was there at the time. A special army unit. Did sterling work, to all accounts. Was awarded the M.C.— at the Palace, I believe."

Kearton climbed up the sloping ladder and ducked his head automatically as he reached the bridge.

He looked up at the sky, very dark, but with a few thin, luminous clouds moving unhurriedly ahead of the wind.

He clenched his fist inside the duffle coat's big pocket. There was a new moon, sharp as a shark's fin as it cut through the clouds. Only a day or two old.

Like that night when they had suddenly found themselves awake, early or late; neither of them remembered. She had been propped on her elbow, looking down at him, her hair across his shoulder.

"Don't look at it through glass, Bob. It's unlucky. But make a wish."

She had mentioned her marriage that same night.

"Stuart . . ." and he had felt a peculiar shock and surprise when she had used the name, the first time he had heard it. "They called him a hero. I believed it. Until . . ." A few moments later she said, almost inaudibly, "He hurt me. I knew then."

It was enough. They had lain together and waited for the dawn.

He walked over to the compass and peered down at it. North-east by north. He could see the other boats in his mind's eye:

two pairs, M.T.B. and M.G.B. abeam of each other. And the faces of those in command. Trust, loyalty, obedience: it was all and none of them.

Spiers had moved over to join him: another anonymous shape. He must have covered the white scarf with a coat.

"I've sent word for hot soup and sandwiches, sir. After that . . ." He did not finish. There was no need.

Instead he said, "Grand Harbour looked pretty empty when we left. Another convoy went out just before we did. Eastbound, back to Alex— big escort this time, including M.T.B.s, for the first leg of the passage, anyway. I suppose the enemy will know about that, too. They're not stupid."

"You're right, Peter. They're not. And they'll know there's nothing in their way now. Except us."

He thought of her, lying in the dark. *Make a wish.*

The wind was still freshening, and when he looked up he could see the ensign flapping and cracking above the bridge, a pale shadow against the sky. But the moon had disappeared.

Lieutenant Peter Spiers made his way carefully to the forepart of the bridge, wary of anything that might have been moved during his brief absence, or the outthrust leg of one of the lookouts. It was still dark, but he could see the outline of the bridge, and the flag locker like a chequerboard against the dull paint.

He recognized Turnbull's familiar outline by the wheel, the compass light casting only a tiny reflection now against his oilskin. He sensed Spiers' presence and reached out to shake the other helmsman; they had been sharing each watch, an hour on, an hour off. Alertness was everything for the hands on the spokes.

"Wakey, wakey, Bliss! Starter's orders!" He chuckled as the man joined him by the compass. "Nice day for it."

Spiers shivered. Everything was cold and wet: spray carrying on the wind, the deck and gratings slippery underfoot. *Where was the dawn?*

He saw Kearton turn toward him, his face and shoulders framed by a backdrop of whitecaps and broken crests, pursued by the wind from astern. As if they were trying to keep pace with the hull.

"Anything?"

Spiers shook his head.

"W/T office has nothing to report. It's a bit lively down there— Sparks has no horizon to watch to keep his sandwiches under control." He saw him turn again, as if to locate the gunboat which was keeping station abeam. Her bow wave was stark against the dark water. At any moment she would be completely recognizable.

He moved closer and lowered his voice.

"Maybe it's been called off, sir. They might have had second thoughts, or been ordered back to Penta? Our people wouldn't even know."

One of the bridge lookouts was uncovering his binoculars, training them quickly seaward to test them or make certain they were still clean, and, only for a few seconds, Kearton saw the lenses before the lookout completed his sweep. Not black glass any more, but holding light. He looked at the sea. Now there was a horizon. Soon the sun would show itself. And the decision would still be his.

Spiers said, "I'll check with W/T again, sir. Then I can go aft and give the spare hands a couple of jobs that need doing . . ."

"No." Kearton did not raise his voice. "Stay here. With me."

He pulled himself against the screen so he could see the two-pounder's gunshield. That, too, was catching the light, with spray trapped and pooled beneath it, quivering to the beat of the engines.

He could feel the tension around him. Doubt, curiosity,

anxiety. He shut his mind to it. When he reached out the handset was ice-cold in his fingers, and he could hear Ainslie's breathing. Or was it his own?

"You're on, Skipper."

He pressed the switch. "This is *Growler*. To all units. *Listening Watch*." He knew Turnbull had turned his head to hear him. He would know, better than most, what it might mean for them, and for their senior officer. "Stop your engines. Stand by!"

The deck gave a drawn-out shudder, and then submitted to the sea and the swell against the hull.

He said, "Tell the Chief."

"Done, sir." An unfamiliar voice. Were there still some he did not know?

Other sounds, exaggerated by the stillness. Loose tackle on deck, an ammunition belt against the bridge machine-gun, someone coughing or retching, trying not to throw up.

He saw the nearest M.G.B. clearly for the first time. No bow wave, and showing her deck as she idled across the troughs, metal glinting as it caught the light from the horizon.

A voicepipe squeaked, and he heard Turnbull's curt, "Tell him, *wait!*"

Something moved on the foredeck, but it was a shadow cast by the two-pounder.

"Have you got the new course, Pilot?" He felt Ainslie brush against him, fumbling for his notebook.

Bliss broke the silence.

"Gunfire, sir." He was gesturing toward the bows, but staring at Kearton.

Then he heard it. Like those far-off summer days: a woodpecker, unperturbed, searching for food.

"Growler! Take station on me! Attacking!"

He felt Ainslie gasp; he must have gripped his arm like a vise.

"Make the signal!"

The rest was drowned by the sudden roar of engines.

"Rocket, dead ahead!" The lookout repeated it. "Rocket!" Perhaps because of the noise, or to convince himself he had not been mistaken.

Kearton said, "Steady. Hold your course."

Ainslie was saying, "Someone's in trouble—"

Kearton steadied his binoculars. The rocket was already dying, would be only scattered green sparks by the time it hit the sea. They were not intended to last. He exhaled slowly as his mind responded, like a cocking-lever on a weapon. Or the crosswires on a target.

It was easier this time. The deck was steadier, responding to the speed, which was still increasing. Laidlaw was down there, deaf and blind to everything but his gauges and switches.

But there was nothing beyond the tiny image trapped in the lenses, blurred by spray, then sharpening again. Long and low: a lighter of some kind, but with a small box-like bridge and superstructure right aft, like a landing-ship. Shortening now, turning.

"All guns! Stand by!"

He felt Spiers hurry past, but he did not pause or speak. Only the target counted.

He waited for his eyes to clear, but the image remained in his mind. The same vessel which had been described, even sketched, in the reports and in Garrick's red-lettered file.

And there was another ship, at first hidden by the lighter, now moving away and gathering speed. A speed to match their own.

"Starboard twenty!" He tried to keep the binoculars focused on the smaller vessel, following it until it was almost lost in spray, bows on.

"Midships!" He seized a rail as the deck tilted again. Turnbull was turning the wheel, staring at the indicator and compass as if nothing else existed. "Port twenty!"

301

He tried once more, but using one hand and needing the other to keep his balance made each second vital.

The two vessels were farther apart, but the range was closing fast. He sensed the nearest M.G.B. plunging round to hold station abeam. Red Lyon needed no encouragement.

But all he could see was a third vessel, or what remained, left astern and disappearing in the reflected glare. A fishing boat, or one of the schooners which were sometimes used for covert missions.

Garrick might have been about to give him details, but he doubted it.

And she had used his name, only once. *Stuart . . .*

He blinked again to clear his vision. Vivid flashes, and tracer rising and falling slowly, out of range.

He pushed Ainslie away from the side and, as their eyes met, saw him fighting his own private battle, and finally understanding.

Don't keep all your eggs in one basket.

"Ready, 'Swain? Another zig-zag?"

He heard an explosion and felt it pound the side of the hull like something solid.

Turnbull stared at the falling spray and wrinkled his nose at the stench of cordite.

"Say the word, sir!"

He could feel the spokes jerking in his hands. *Full speed.* At this rate . . . But his mind came under control again as the two-pounder opened fire. Cock Glover was doing his stuff.

He repeated the Skipper's order and began to turn the wheel, but the crazy laughter was still hovering. If the Jimmy the One had not postponed Defaulters, Glover might be comfortably ashore right now. Maybe in a cell, but safe.

Another thud, this explosion closer, between 992 and Red Lyon's command.

"Steady!"

"We going in, 'Swain?" That was Bliss, who was crouching, pressed against the voicepipes.

Turnbull concentrated on the compass: nothing else mattered. So many times, and some you wanted to forget. Except one.

"We are, my son. All the bloody way!"

He could hear Kearton's voice, or snatches of it as he ducked his head to speak to the voicepipe, to Spiers and his killick, Laurie Jay.

He flinched as the twin Oerlikons opened fire from aft. They stopped almost immediately. Too quick on the trigger, or merely testing guns?

More tracer now. Low overhead but closer, some ripping across the water as if it was alive.

He thought he heard the buzzer, then the Skipper's voice, clipped, final.

"Fire!" Then, "Hard a-port!"

"Both torpedoes running, sir!"

Kearton strode across the bridge, but had to reach out for support as the hull tilted over in response to full rudder.

"Midships!" They were turning at full speed, the sea surging over the deck, the spray falling like hail. He saw John Stirling's boat, on a different bearing, crossing their wake and heading for the target. The two motor gunboats were exchanging fire with the patrol vessel, but one of them appeared to be slowing down, stopping, feathers of spray bursting along one side. He tried to control his binoculars; the bridge was shuddering as the outer screw rose close to the surface while they settled on their new course. He heard loose gear clattering, someone shouting. Then he saw the supply vessel, full-length this time as she completed a ninety-degree turn. She was a shallow-draught vessel, otherwise she would never have used Penta as a lair. And she was fast. Maybe the new torpedoes were duds. Designed by people who never had to use them . . .

Ellis, their best lookout, was standing beside him. He was shaking his binoculars as if to rid them of spray and saying something, but the words were lost.

Kearton did not hear the explosion. His mind recorded only a blinding flash, and pain, a blow on the head. Then nothing.

Turnbull held on to the wheel and used it to pull himself upright. He stared around the bridge, his brain still shocked and refusing to obey. There was something sodden under his feet, falling apart: it was his personal notebook, his bible. The duties and responsibilities of every man aboard; all the pros and cons. He was never without it. Glover was in it . . . several times . . .

It came back to him slowly. He had been trying to unfasten his oilskin. He had been sweating. And he had felt the notebook fall to the deck. Holding the wheel with one hand, he had stooped to recover it. It had saved his life.

He saw Bliss sitting on the deck with his back against the side of the bridge. His eyes were wide open, unmoving. There was a smear of blood marking his fall, like a brushstroke, and a series of jagged holes, ending in more blood.

He saw Ainslie at the top of the ladder, staring at the bridge as if he were unable to move.

Turnbull shouted at him, "Get someone to relieve me!" He knew the signs. Ainslie had already shown what he could do, but everyone had a limit.

Ainslie said, "Can't Bliss . . .?" and broke off as he saw the dead helmsman, and the other body below the screen. Ellis, the lookout.

Others were coming; he heard Leading Seaman Dawson's thick voice. Turnbull recognized it also, and felt a terrible relief.

"See to the Skipper, will you?"

Ainslie dropped to his knees and used his cap to cushion Kearton's head from the deck.

"Hold on, Skipper. We'll have you fixed up in no time."

He felt Pug Dawson moving past him, two other seamen behind him. One of them took the wheel, and Ainslie heard him calmly repeating Turnbull's instructions.

Ainslie licked his lips, and knew he had come close to vomiting. He felt the sun burning his neck now, and saw that the ensign was scarcely moving.

He heard Pug Dawson say, "Two hits near the waterline, amidships. I got two lads dealin' with 'em. Make do, anyways!" He gave a wheezing chuckle. "Just so long as th' Skipper's OK." And then, "Well, we sank their bloody supply ship— that's somethin' to blow th' cobwebs away! Not that we can tell anyone at th' moment."

Turnbull looked aft along the deck, at the wash stretching away astern.

"I didn't even hear it. Must've been when we were hit—" He recalled what Dawson had said. "Is the W/T knocked out?"

"Direct hit."

Turnbull said, "I'd better get down there."

Dawson patted his arm kindly. "Not unless you got a strong stomach."

Ainslie looked up and said quietly, "Who was it?"

Pug Dawson might have shrugged.

"Weston. Nice kid. I always thought . . ."

Ainslie stared at the flag locker, remembering the last time. The scattered bunting, and death.

He felt a hand resting on his and saw that Kearton's eyes were open, focusing on his face.

"It's over, Skipper. We did it!"

He felt the fingers move tentatively.

"How many, Toby?"

He saw Turnbull hold up one hand.

"Five, sir."

Kearton's fingers were not resting now but gripping, and he

could feel him trying to turn on his side. But it was too much for him, and he let his head fall back on Ainslie's cap.

"Tell our lads— I'm proud of them."

Pug Dawson was kneeling beside them, his square hands fashioning a pillow from some flags.

"Give it a day or two, sir, an' you can tell 'em yerself!"

Kearton lay very still, the sounds and voices merging. Some things were clearer than others: even the explosion, a shell smashing into the deck forward of the bridge. The blow on his head had not been a splinter or a fragment from the blast. He had opened his eyes and found his face almost touching the iron ringbolt which had knocked him unconscious. The impact was already making itself felt. But that would pass.

But when he had tried to move the real pain had prevented him, and he had heard himself cry out before the darkness had closed in again and driven it away.

Another image, like a flashback from some old film. His jacket being unbuttoned, his shirt torn away like paper. Hands: more pain. Darkness.

Another voice: Spiers, very calm, confident. "Cracked a couple of ribs, as far as I can make out. They'll soon put it right."

He must have asked Spiers about the action; he remembered only the curtness of his reply. The anger.

"We did what was expected of us. I only hope they're satisfied!"

He opened his eyes, and knew that Ainslie was shielding his face from the sun with his cap. They must have lifted him on to some sort of support, like a seaman's unrolled hammock.

"I've laid off our course." Ainslie was resting one hand on his shoulder, and it was strangely comforting. "We've had a signal from H.Q." He must have felt Kearton's attempt to move, and the hand gently restrained him. "Our R/T has been knocked out. Lieutenant Stirling's boat came close enough for his loud-hailer— he was full of it. He sank the patrol boat with one torpedo— the other misfired. He wanted you to know. He was actually laughing."

"And what was the signal, Toby? Important?" He was becoming drowsy again. Something Laidlaw had fished out of the engineroom medical cabinet.

Ainslie moved the cap slightly, to conceal his expression.

"Short and sweet. All it said was *Well done!*"

Kearton tried to lie still. Laughing would bring back the pain. Or the tears.

Turnbull was watching Spiers scribbling notes on a signal pad. They were standing near the twin Oerlikons, which still pointed seaward, the barrels and mounting scarred and blackened from a burst of cannon fire. One of the gunners lay nearby, stitched in a length of canvas. It was Ordinary Seaman Yorke. *With an 'e'*, he thought, and wished that he had liked him.

He heard footsteps and saw Glover coming aft with a sack of waste from Dawson's working party. He was grinning.

"You survived then, 'Swain? Tsk, tsk!"

Turnbull ensured Spiers was out of earshot before he snapped, "Don't forget, Glover. You're still up for First Lieutenant's report!"

Glover put down the sack and faced him.

"I've bin goin' over it. An' I ain't so sure." He ticked off the points on his fingers. "Th' Naval Discipline Act. Section Seven, or maybe Eight . . . I think I can appeal!"

Turnbull turned his back on him and watched the Canadian M.T.B., tubes empty like their own, turning now to follow astern.

A near thing, the closest he'd come to buying it since that other time, when Bob Kearton had come back to search for them.

He thought of Ainslie's face as he had reported the signal to the Skipper. *Well done.*

Christ, he thought. Maybe it was just as well their own W/T couldn't reply.

He looked at Glover again.

"When we get alongside and things settle down, you must join me in the canteen, and I'll stand you a tot. Maybe several!"

Spiers was calling him again. There was a lot to do, short-handed or not, before they entered harbour.

But it was worth it, if only to see Glover's face.

Good or bad, they were still one company.

Kearton eased his body over the side of the cot, his feet touching the deck carefully as he tried to prepare himself. It had been a mistake. He should have remained on the bridge, propped up in one corner. What was he trying to prove? It was almost dark in the chartroom, although on deck there was bright sunlight and the sea had seemed almost colourless in the glare.

The final passage had taken longer than he had hoped. The damaged motor gunboat had finally broken down, and had been taken in tow by Red Lyon. Stirling's boat had resumed station directly astern. Their time of arrival at Malta would be mid-morning.

Over the loud-hailer he had told them, "We left together. We enter harbour together."

He moved again and took the weight on his feet, and held his breath as the pain seared his side like hot metal. He clutched his sweater and waited for it to subside. Even the sweater was a mystery, and how they had managed to get him into it without making him pass out.

"Are you sure you should be doing this, sir?"

He sat down again. He had forgotten Ginger, who had been with him since he had struggled down from the bridge. He was standing, legs astride, his back to the chart table, holding an open cutthroat razor, with a towel still draped over his shoulder.

"But if you *insist*." He looked strained and crumpled, but still managed a cheeky grin. "You want to show them your wonderful shave, I expect."

Kearton touched his chin.

"I'm just glad you're on my side!"

"I'll see if it's all clear, sir."

The sliding hatch closed, and Kearton made another attempt. He was ready for the pain, could meet it like an opponent. He took a few steps, not resting against the chart table before he retraced them. He was still trying to recall each moment in order. Sounds, colours, faces.

And the rocket: that was never out of his thoughts. A warning, so that they would not miss the final rendezvous, or a challenge? To show them he was already there, ahead of them. If so, it had cost him his life, and the lives of a lot of others. Only he would have known.

"Ready if you are, Skipper?" It was Ainslie, the sun behind him, his face in shadow.

Kearton picked up his cap but lingered, looking at the table. The charts, rolled or flattened, ready for use. Ainslie's spare pencils rattling together in a little tube, exactly as he remembered them. Waiting for the dawn . . .

"The pilot boat came out earlier. We were hardly near enough to land for me to take a fix . . . He must have been expecting us." He smiled for the first time in many hours, and seemed very young again. "Not soon enough for me!"

Kearton climbed slowly to the bridge. Measuring each step, waiting for and meeting the pain. Ainslie went ahead, and he knew that Ginger was also close by in case he fainted.

The sun dazzled and almost blinded him as he stepped into the open bridge. A quick glance around: faces he knew, some better than others. But other faces were missing, the helmsman and the lookout who had been beside him. The stains were still there.

Turnbull had looked toward him, and he saw the nod. No smile.

Kearton turned to look ahead, almost falling in the process. The pilot was in the lead, exactly as he had imagined it when Ainslie had first brought the news. And not an empty sea ahead, or the merest hint of land, but Malta reaching out on either bow: headland and fortress, and a thousand windows flashing in the sun like private signals.

Spiers tilted his cap over his eyes.

"The harbour seems to have filled up since we left. Glad we've got the pilot to hold our hands!"

Ainslie joined him and said, "D'you want to sit on something, Skipper?"

"No." He reached out immediately, and held his arm. "No, Toby. I'm all right." He stared out at the headland. Crowds of people, someone with a small child on his shoulders; both were waving. He added quietly, "I've got to be. Now."

Turnbull kept his eyes on the pilot, but he had already seen the other ships, some of them huge and impressive. Cruisers. He leaned on the spokes. And a battleship, not one of the 'old faithfuls', but a newcomer commissioned only last year. Somebody meant business this time.

He thought of the moment when the torpedoes had found their target. Like an earth tremor; the flames had still been visible even after the supply ship had been blown apart. And the aftermath, the sea strewn with fragments, the remnants of a midget fleet. He allowed his eyes to leave the pilot and rest briefly on the ships.

We were just in time.

Kearton said, "Glasses, anyone?" and felt the binoculars instantly come within his grasp. "Many thanks." He had spoken almost unconsciously, and did not notice who had offered them.

The pilot was leading them into Grand Harbour itself. *A dockyard job, then . . .*

He touched the thin plating and one of the jagged holes. Close. Too close for some.

He steadied the binoculars with effort. Overlapping rooftops, the crucifix of a church of golden stone almost side by side with the ornate domes of Malta's eastern past; bombed buildings, and repaired ones. People on the waterfront, where he had recently begun to see stalls and barrows displaying fruit, even flowers. And further still, the official building where he had stood on the balcony with Garrick, watching this same great waterway. The other buildings were hidden at this angle, but perhaps she was there. On the old wall where Brice had seen and spoken to her, and done his best to reassure her.

If she was watching now, what might she think? Tracer and shell damage to the hull, but at that distance it might not seem so cruel.

He turned, too quickly, and felt the pain reminding him. It seemed a little less sharp.

"Pilot's altering course, sir!"

Kearton moved the binoculars. The pilot boat would be leading them directly abeam of the battleship. It came to him: he had heard a bugle when he had been trying to find the other building. *Her* roof.

The binoculars were heavier now, and he knew he should take Ainslie's advice, but he braced himself and focused again. A ceremony of some kind seemed about to begin aboard the battleship. Royal Marines, bayonets shining in the glare. He moved the binoculars once more: they felt like lead. Then he held them still. There was a flag flying above the grey super-structure and powerful guns, the flag of a rear-admiral. And they were going to steer straight past, battered and blood-stained, with a ceremony already about to begin.

He gripped the screen.

"Have the hands fall in! Tell Dawson, be ready to pipe!"

Suppose Brice was right? Was it Rear-Admiral Ewart Morgan's flag, and if so . . .

Ainslie saw the battleship's upper bridge rising above him, shutting out the sun like a cliff.

Then he heard another bugle, and saw Kearton's face.

Nothing else seemed to matter. And he was sharing it.

He said, "Not this time, Skipper." There was cheering now. "They're saluting *you*!"

The pilot was sounding his horn. One blast. *Turning to starboard.*

But not before he heard Kearton murmur, *"Us."*